OCEAN OF TEARS

Threads of Fate Book Three

MICHAEL HEAD

PROLOGUE

Agents

An outside observer would think the two people standing at the edge of the hole in space were statues. They looked exactly *like* statues, white marble carved by an artist striving for perfection, but if you were to pay close attention you might notice that every once in a while, the woman would twitch the fingers of her left hand, and the vision of what was shown inside the hole would change.

The man standing next to her—not too close, mind you—would raise an eyebrow in surprise, or the corner of his mouth would turn down in a slight frown. They stood like this for uncountable hours, the passing time not affecting them any more than it would the blocks of marble that they appeared to be.

The other feature that would break the illusion of being statues was their eyes. They didn't have any. The female statue had voids of darkness instead, a black so deep and fathomless that they seemed to be the place where all light in the universe went to die. The male's were a solid blue, as if his eye sockets were instead filled with glowing opaque crystals. The faint light they put off looked cold enough to freeze molten lead into slag in an instant. It might sound impossible for light to *look* cold, but he somehow managed it.

Finally, the woman broke the silence, not bothering to turn to face the man standing next to her as she spoke to him. "It looks bad. I don't see a way for him to get through this without killing himself."

The man, noticing she hadn't looked at him, refused to turn to look at her first. His personal pride wouldn't allow it. He did answer her, just as the vision in the hole changed to an image of a group of five young people huddled around a fire in the middle of a dark forest. "There are enough pieces in motion that even *we* can't predict what will happen. I have tried to shift some of my people into place to help, but they are mortal, and slow. They may not make it in time."

He leaned forward a bit to look closer at the youngest of the people around the fire. "It won't be long until we can speak to him again. If he survives until winter, you can warn him yourself."

"It will be too late for that." The woman shook her head, finally turning to face her compatriot. "I will do what I can through his dreams, but waiting until he reaches his next threshold will end in his death."

The man, secretly relieved that he could finally turn to look at the woman, met her dark eyes with his own cold orbs. "You know, Wrath, if you acted like all the rest of us gods and had some people on the planet to act as agents of your will, you could do more to help him." His words were reprimanding, but his tone was more amused than chastising.

"Pride, whatever in the world made you think I *don't* have my own pawns running around down there?" Her face didn't show it, but she was also amused. Mostly at how easy it was to keep the other gods from knowing her plans.

Not waiting for a reply from the God of Pride, the Goddess of Wrath turned away and faded into the darkness between worlds. Pride stood for a while longer, his eyes on the place she last stood. Before he turned to leave, he waved the hole in space away, returning it to just another blank spot in the fabric of this dimension's reality.

"I feel bad for the poor kid. Any agent of Wrath interfering in your life can't be good." He turned to face the opposite direction Wrath had gone, and stepped through his own fold in space.

CHAPTER ONE

Birthday Celebration

Today was my fourteenth birthday. Okay, so I was only that young in body. In spirit, it was my 654th birthday, and everything was finally going great.

My friends and I had made good time on the road leading to the southern tip of the province. Our goal was a peninsula named 'The Claw.' Once we got there, it would be easy to find passage on a merchant ship traveling to the Western Province at one of the many villages along the coast. We needed to go there so I could convince the king of the Western Province to mobilize his armies to fight the evil dark mana monsters known as *nox*.

It was the mission of the *nox* to convert our world from a place of light and beauty to one of darkness and horror. My mission—handed down by the gods—was to stop the *nox* from doing that. I had to say, the whole thing was turning out to be quite the ordeal. I was lucky enough to find a group of people that were willing to help me along the way, which was why I had been able to get as far as I had.

Four years ago, I had saved the Roh Clan from a bloody

coup attempt and killed my first *nox* while destroying a temple designed to allow even worse creatures into the world. Almost three years later, I fought and killed the man who was second-in-command of the Southern Province. He was possessed by some kind of *nox* royalty or something, so it hadn't been easy. I was arrested for killing him, lost the girl I had feelings for, was almost framed, and then I kicked the ever-loving crap out of the king of the Southern Province. Oh, and I blackmailed him into doing his best to stop the *nox*. It was a whole 'thing.'

Now we were sitting around a crackling fire, enjoying each other's company. We had parked our carriage in a grassy clearing off the main road at a campsite that many people before us had clearly used. There was a ring of long, flat stones spaced out wide enough to allow the carriage to pass through and park along one side. To my left, Jamila and Chu were seated on a stone near the fire while working on a special meal in celebration of the day I was born. On the right, Valerie and Donny were practicing carving designs into some small rocks roughly the size and shape of a copper coin.

My friends had all grown a lot since we left Roh City. Donny was now twenty-two years old, and he had finished filling out his six-foot one-inch frame with hard muscle. His dark hair and brown eyes sometimes gave him a brooding appearance, but his quick smile frequently broke the illusion. Valerie made sure he kept his hair short enough that it didn't cover his features.

Chu had turned nineteen a few weeks ago, and he seemed to have stopped growing at about five feet nine inches. He was muscular enough to make Donny look almost puny, the massive slabs of muscle on his frame making him look almost as wide as he was tall. He also had the traditional Roh Clan dark hair and brown eyes, but his looked almost amber in the sunlight. Thankfully, Chu had agreed to grow his hair out, and it was kept in a ponytail high on the back of his head. His old bowl-cut style had made his head look tiny atop his large frame.

While that had been helpful in picking him out of a crowd, it didn't help him impress his future bride.

The woman Chu intended to marry, Jamila, was now nineteen as well, and she had topped out at a willowy and graceful five feet and five inches of height. Her porcelain skin, long bright red hair, and emerald green eyes made her a beauty that drew the eye of most men we encountered on the road. The heavy calluses on her hands were the only indication of how hard she trained to be as lethal as possible with her two katanas.

Valerie was equally as beautiful, and at five feet six inches she projected a sense of elegance and poise. Her white hair was nearly down to her thin waist, and her pale blue eyes were both fierce and sharp with intelligence. She was now twenty, and almost old enough to marry Donny without worrying about what her family had to say about it.

All five of us were wearing the white linen shirts and brown canvas pants that were self-cleaning and self-repairing that we had gained after placing high enough in the tournament that had been held in the Southern Capital.

Donny and Valerie were trying to duplicate my creation, called a 'popper,' which I was very happy to see. The little buggers took a long time to produce, and they were used up incredibly quickly. Having their help would make the process much shorter. Donny was proving to be particularly adept at working with runes and formations. He already had a substantial pile at his feet.

A popper was an invention I had only come up with fairly recently. Since I was now in a body much weaker than the one I was accustomed to, I had found it necessary to augment my fighting abilities with the creations and inventions my knowledge of runes, formation plates, alchemy, and blacksmithing allowed me to make. The poppers took a relatively small amount of qi to create, and they were nearly impossible to detect. When stepped on, thrown, or otherwise activated, the small stone formed a dense pocket of air about the size of a fist centered around the rock. It would then burst, throwing out a shockwave around five feet in all directions. They made a loud popping sound, hence my ingenious and rather original name, 'poppers.' My friends and I had found them to be an effective, nonlethal tool that had many uses. If you used enough of them at once, they could cause quite the problem for an enemy.

While the others were either cooking or helping to make more poppers, I was working on something a little more lethal. I was making myself a birthday gift. We would be reaching civilization again sometime soon, and I needed to look presentable.

While my physical age was fourteen, my height of nearly six feet made me look closer to seventeen or eighteen. My unruly dark hair, green eyes, and delicate features meant I also caught the eye of a few travelers. Thankfully, due to my personal preferences, most of those were women. As a young man with some wealth built up, I wanted to start looking the part of a person of elevated means. A ragged appearance tended to make people look at you in a negative light before you even said a word to them. Since we wanted favorable treatment on a merchant ship, we would need to look as if we deserved it.

For cultivators, one of the most important items to show wealth was an expensive and powerful weapon. While I had several choices at my disposal, I had decided on wearing my green glass sword. It wasn't really glass, it was malachite, but it looked like clear green glass. Malachite was a very qi-conductive metal, which allowed a high-level blacksmith the ability to impart a complex qi matrix design into any weapon or armor made of the material.

This specific sword had a matrix that allowed it to cut through nearly any material not actively empowered by qi, making it useful and deadly. There was a second—and unfamiliar—matrix embedded in the sword, which supposedly made it possible for me to tame or bond with an animal or beast of some kind. All my experiments with that aspect of the sword had so far met with failure. The most important thing about the sword right now, however, was that it was pretty and thus looked expensive.

The sheath I had previously cobbled together for the sword was little more than a bundle of animal skins tied together and held on my back with a bit of hemp rope. That wouldn't do, not if I wanted to impress the cultivators and merchants that I was about to meet when we returned to civilization.

The one I was currently working on was leather, with a copper throat and clip at the top, and a silver cap at the end. I had embedded a thumbnail-sized emerald in the silver cap to help flaunt my wealth and match the sword's color, and I would tarnish the copper on the throat and clip to make it better match my belt. It had slightly-tarnished copper studs running the length of the beaten leather belt, and no matter what I did to try to improve its appearance, it would not clean up any better than the moment when I first acquired it. Instead of fighting it, I decided to embrace the tarnished look and make it seem intentional. After all, there was no stars-damned way I was going to trade out my magical storage belt, which contained secret internal qi batteries. It had already saved my life more times than I could count.

The work I was doing was actually on the throat of the sheath. I was trying to carve a set of runes that would empower the blade with a sweeping fire attack when I pulled it free, but the narrow opening was making it difficult to carve. I had to adjust the runes to a wind blade that would sweep outwards if I drew the sword quickly, and I finally got it to work. I had just about finished up polishing the sheath when I heard Donny and Valerie start to argue about something.

"…don't think it is funny. That horse has it out for me, I'm telling you!" Donny was looking back at the horses tethered at the edge of the firelight.

"Look, he just likes me. It isn't like Scout is trying to kill you or anything, he just wants me to pay more attention to him, and less attention to you." Valerie was trying not to laugh, but we could all tell she thought the entire situation was hilarious.

Scout was the name Valerie had given her horse. He was a surprisingly intelligent animal that had formed a quick bond with the white-haired woman. She rode him as much as possible when he wasn't pulling our carriage. Scout's enchanted horseshoes and strong constitution meant Valerie could cover a lot of ground when hunting or scouting for bandits along the road. They were quite the pair, and the horse seemed to be smart enough to recognize Donny and Valerie's relationship.

"I just don't think it is natural for a horse to be jealous of a human. I mean, come on, that thing either kicks me or manages to bite me somehow nearly every day!" He eyed the horse some more before continuing. "I still say that time I fell in the river was his fault, too!"

Now everyone was trying not to laugh. That had been pretty funny. A few days ago, while Donny was leading the carriage across a single-wagon bridge straddling a fast-flowing river, he had managed to trip over something and fall over the side. It had taken him almost an hour to make his way back to us, slogging his way along the densely forested riverbank and nearly getting eaten alive by mosquitos. Needless to say, he wasn't in a good mood when he got back.

"Come on, Donny! There is no way someone of your cultivation level could be knocked off the side of the bridge by some horse. You just tripped and fell over the side. Don't blame the horse for you being clumsy." Valerie was practically shaking her finger under his nose, admonishing him for placing the blame on the helpless animal.

The thing was, Donny was completely right. I was the one driving the carriage when it happened. I saw the horse pull back on the rope Donny was holding just as he was about to step over the edge of a raised board. It also happened to be exactly near a gap in the railing, making it the perfect spot on that bridge to trip Donny and send him tumbling over the side. I was also pretty sure I had heard Scout make a chuffing laugh sound when the noise of the splash reached us high over the water. That horse had it out for him.

"Okay guys, food is done!" Chu had laid out enough plates for everyone along one of the long flat stones that made a useful impromptu table. It effectively ended the argument, and I put my new sheath on my belt before getting up. It paired with the belt nicely, and when I slid the sword in, it fit into place as if the sheath had been made for it all along. Which, really, it had been. Donny and Valerie put the poppers they had been making in a sack near the fire. We would divide them up evenly after we ate.

We gathered around to eat, enjoying the nice evening and chatting about what it would be like once we reached the first village along the coast. I wanted to wait until we got farther down the coast before getting on a ship, but everyone else was excited about getting out to sea. None of them had seen the ocean before, and the idea of sailing on a vast expanse of water was exciting to them. They didn't understand how much smoother the journey would be on the larger ships that stayed toward the tip of the peninsula. We still hadn't come to a general consensus when we were interrupted by a voice coming from the darkness.

"Ho the fire! Can we approach?" Whoever it was, they were smart enough to stay outside the ring of my wards. That meant they had to be a somewhat powerful cultivator, since detecting them wasn't exactly easy in the first place.

The five of us just looked at one another before Donny and Chu stepped forward. We had been traveling together for the better part of three years, and fighting as a team for longer than that. It didn't take much for us to fall into positions to support each other effectively. All of us knew what we were capable of accomplishing, so no one was particularly concerned.

"Shouldn't be a problem, stranger, as long as you keep your hands where we can see them." We could hear more than one person shuffle about in the darkness. "And you tell us how many of you there are first." Donny was the oldest and tallest person of the group, so he spoke up first. None of us seemed outwardly tense, but the chuckles from the darkness made us all pull together a little tighter.

"No problem. There are just the ten of us, wanting to

share your fire for a bit." The speaker stepped into the light, his hands tucked into his belt near two sheathed daggers. "There isn't any need for you to worry. We won't hurt you." The grin on his face said otherwise, and the chuckles from the darkness told me that he might not be an entirely honest person. He was dressed in brown leather pants and a worn blue canvas vest, showing off his muscular and heavily-scarred arms. It looked like he had been in plenty of fights with a blade, because the thin lines marking him were layered on top of one another.

We had experienced a few problems with bandits while on the road. Usually, a single display of force had them running faster than the horses, but occasionally there were a few who thought our younger appearance meant we were weak. We usually buried those idiots on the side of the road, if there was enough left of them to warrant the effort. So, considering our recent string of victories, I was feeling pretty confident. Until I heard a twig snap in the forest behind us. Donny lifted a hand to stop him.

"You should probably rethink this, mister. We don't want to hurt you, but we will if you force our hand." He accentuated his point by making his axe appear in his hands. It was a rather nasty piece of work I had put together for him, and it looked deadly enough to make the man approaching us pause.

"Why don't you put that back where you got it? All we want is the carriage." A man shouted something unintelligible from outside the firelight. "Ah, and apparently the horses. The rest of you can keep your things." He pointed back toward the horses and carriage, but none of us bothered to look. It would be stupid to take our eyes off the enemy. He even grinned when no one turned to look where he indicated, as if being caught trying to filch a pie from a windowsill.

"I think you might have us confused with someone else." Valerie had stepped up onto the stone we had been using as a table. "We aren't someone to just lay down our arms and allow you to run off with our things." She pulled out her bow, an arrow seeming to nock itself on the string as if by magic. It wasn't, of course. Valerie was just *that* good.

"Alright. Have it your way. Get 'em, boys, and make sure not to kill the women!" He pulled free his daggers, both of them serrated-edged blades meant to wound and tear flesh as painfully as possible.

None of us moved. I could see the confusion on the man's face as his henchmen ran past him. He stood still as well, waiting to see why we weren't reacting. His answer came when my wards activated.

I hadn't bothered to unleash them manually. I figured I would let these fools hang themselves with their own stupidity. As they crossed the outer layer, a strand of earth qi wrapped around their ankles and dumped them on their faces. Their momentum carried them into the second layer of formation plate defenses, activating a blend of earth and water qi that sucked them into the ground like quicksand. It hardened to stone just as the last traces of the men disappeared under the surface. No one would be able to tell they had ever existed. The only sign anything had even happened was that the dirt had been replaced with a perfect stone circle around the campsite.

The leader looked on with wide eyes. He was clearly in shock at what had just occurred. I didn't blame him. It wasn't every day that you see almost a dozen people die in a split second. Well, they probably weren't dead yet, but not even the emperor was powerful enough to breathe through stone. And none of those idiots were powerful enough to break free of the qi-enforced stone using just their own qi. So, yeah, they were pretty much dead.

"We tried to warn you. But you just don't listen well, do you?" Valerie released her arrow, which struck the man through the base of his throat. He shook his head, as if denying the reality of what had just occurred. We all watched as the man stumbled forward, his daggers falling to the dirt. He dropped to his knees in front of the fire, and it looked like he was trying to speak. Instead, he fell over. Right on top of the bag filled with poppers that Donny and Valerie had been working on before we sat down to eat. Those explosive and highly sensitive poppers that would certainly go off if, say, someone fell on them.

Oops. Stars damn it.

On the bright side, I guess my birthday celebration included fireworks…

CHAPTER TWO

Valerie Goes Missing

The result of nearly one hundred poppers going off at the same time was, well, let's say exciting. We were all blown well outside the stone ring. The horses fared a little better, but the carriage didn't handle it well. None of us had been wearing armor, but I don't think it would have helped. If an explosion was violent enough to break the bones of a cultivator with as much qi reinforcement as we had all used, all it would have done was destroy a perfectly good set of armor.

I'm not sure how long it took Chu to get around to each of us, but he was the guy that brought us all back to our senses. Chu could now use four elements since he was a Meridian cultivator, but wood qi had always been his strong suit. He had been picking up additional training from every healer and soothsayer we came across to augment his abilities, and in most places across the countryside he would certainly be qualified enough to open a healer's shop. His dream was to build a trading empire that spanned the five provinces, but his natural talents meant he would never struggle for a job if his plans didn't work out. I was just glad he was on my team.

After Chu got us up and moving, we made sure the horses

were healed and got the carriage back on four wheels. Which was how we found out the carriage now had only three wheels. Using earth qi, I formed a pillar of stone under the broken wheel to keep it from leaning, but we were apparently going to be stuck here for a day or two to make the necessary repairs. Donny and I were discussing the steps we would need to take as soon as the sun came up when Valerie spoke up.

"I will take Scout in the morning and make sure there aren't any more of them." Donny opened his mouth to say something, but Valerie silenced him with a look. "If we are going to be stuck here for a day or two, we need to know who and what is around us." It took a few heartbeats, but Donny reluctantly nodded.

"You're right." Donny looked at the stone ring that represented the fresh grave of several people. "We might be facing a more cautious enemy if there are more in that group of bandits. Especially after their friends don't return."

Speaking of not returning, we still hadn't found any trace of the body from the guy that set off the bag of poppers. I wasn't even sure if it was possible, but he seemed to have been vaporized. This prompted me to make a new rule. Poppers could only be stored in groups of twenty or less. I would tell everyone about the restriction after we had some breakfast. After sleeping on it, to make sure I didn't want to make it five poppers. Because, well, that was one hell of an explosion.

"I think we should get some rest while we can, then get started with our various tasks after the sun comes up." Everyone agreed with me, so we reset the wards, built a new fire, and went to sleep in our bedrolls with only the stars as our cover.

A few short hours later, Chu was the first person awake. We rose to the smell of fried flat bread and spiced meat, and an oddly quiet forest. Even the small animals hadn't returned to the area after the huge explosion last night. I groaned as I got out of my bedroll. I was still pretty sore from what had happened, so I took a few minutes to pump qi throughout my body to help limber me up.

We sat around the same stone that we had used as a table last night to eat our breakfast. I discussed my new rule to limit the number of poppers in one container or bag, and everyone agreed. What had happened last night was entirely too dangerous to allow a second time, so everyone took a few minutes to repackage their poppers into small pouches of ten. Since we still needed to make more, there were only enough for each of us to have two pouches.

"That isn't nearly enough poppers for a protracted fight, and we are running low on all kinds of other things." Chu was looking over the stacks of formation plates, food, and various other consumable materials. "We have plenty of coin to purchase whatever we might need, but it has been over a week since we last saw a town. We need to resupply, and some of the parts that were broken on the carriage were custom. Jim is going to have to make replacements before we can go anywhere."

"I think this means we need to change plans. Instead of going scouting, I should try to get to the next village on Scout. The rest of you could work on getting the carriage fixed and making more supplies." Valerie was already walking toward the horses. "I will only travel until the sun peaks in the sky, and then turn back. If I see any game along the road, it would go a long way to helping fill the cookpot."

Donny stood up to stop her. "I should go with you. I can ride Cloud, and we can both get supplies." Cloud was the name Chu had given the other horse. Not exactly original, but we didn't keep him around for how well he named animals. "We don't know if there are any more of these bandits running around or not."

"No, that doesn't make sense." Jamila stood and walked over to the two horses to begin saddling them. She was looking at Donny as she spoke. "Jim needs to work his traveling forge, Chu can do the woodworking repairs, and you are the best at making poppers and formation plates. Besides Jim, of course." Donny tried to open his mouth to argue, but she talked over him. "Valerie is the best scout, so she should search the woods around us for more bandits. And hopefully get in some hunting. That leaves me to travel down the road to see if I can find a town or village along the way to get supplies." Now Chu tried to speak up, but Jamila wasn't having it. "Don't you dare say that either Valerie or I shouldn't be traveling alone. We are both perfectly capable of taking care of ourselves." Chu closed his mouth. Probably the best choice.

"Okay then, now that we have a plan, let's get going." I decided to speak up before Donny or Chu managed to say something to make the ladies angry. "Just make sure both of you return before sunset. We *will* come looking for you otherwise."

Both of the girls nodded and jumped on their respective horses. Jamila went toward the road, while Valerie pushed deeper into the forest in the opposite direction. Neither of them looked back. Donny and Chu watched them leave, and they didn't look happy about it.

"Come on guys, we have work to do." They both turned their angry looks on me. "Look, we all know they are just as capable as any of us in a fight. Nothing will happen to them." They didn't look convinced. "Both of them are High Meridian cultivators that could easily defeat any Brain-level cultivator in combat. Unless they run across someone at Saint, they will be fine. And what self-respecting Saint cultivator would stoop to banditry?" That seemed to mollify them some.

We had all grown in power during the second leg of our trip. Donny was now a Middle stage Brain-level cultivator, and Chu was barely above the girls at Peak Meridian. He would probably reach Brain in only a few more months of focused cultivation. I had finally reached the point where my true cultivation level matched my body, if not my ability, at Peak Brain. It was a difficult stage to pass, meaning I would be stuck at this level for a while longer. All five of us were extremely advanced for our ages, and our true combat power was much higher than our cultivation levels when we worked together. We were one hell of a team.

"I guess you're right, Jim." Donny sighed, looking back at where Valerie had disappeared into the trees. "I just don't like it when she goes off by herself so much. You never know what could happen."

"That's not what I was thinking." Chu was packing the supplies back up as he spoke. Donny and I both looked at him questioningly. "Jamila is horrible at bartering! How much gold is she going to waste if she finds a savvy merchant?" We both laughed at him. Chu was Chu.

It didn't take long for the three of us to get started. My traveling forge didn't take up much space when I got it set up, but it put out enough heat that it required me to set up across the campsite from Donny and Chu. Donny had already carved a dozen poppers by the time I even brought hammer to anvil, and Chu was at the edge of the clearing, felling a suitable tree to use for wood.

Normally, you would want to season the wood rather than use it immediately. Chu had enough mastery over wood qi that he could replicate the process in only a short time, making it possible for him to use fresh lumber only a few hours after bringing down a tree. I had only needed to show him how to do it once and he caught on. It had come in handy several times over the past year.

We worked until noon without a break, each of us focused on our tasks. I made us a quick lunch of bread toasted over the fire of my forge that I then smeared with a soft cheese I had saved in the extra dimensional storage of my belt. It tasted of metal. Kinda manly, if I did say so myself.

"This tastes like metal." Chu was munching on the bread as he talked. "And hate. Can I have some more?" Donny was nodding along in agreement, and I burst out laughing. Either I was rubbing off on them, or we were more alike than we would probably want to admit. As I was toasting more bread, Donny started picking over the various carriage parts I had been making.

"It looks like you're almost done, Jim. I'm impressed." He was holding a heavy door hinge I made to replace the one that had been damaged when the carriage fell over. "This part has a bunch of fiddly bits that look difficult to put together. I think your blacksmithing is really starting to improve."

I nodded in agreement. It really had been getting better. "The increases in cultivation levels have made me grow taller and stronger, which means it is easier to work the forge. I didn't realize how my shorter arms had been limiting the power of my hammer swings." I flexed my arms, showing off the corded muscle that bunched up under the fabric of my shirt. "Soon, I should be able to make us all some better armor and weapons. If we want. The tradeoff would be losing the qi-resistance of the scorpion chitin our current armor has." They both thought about it while we finished our second helping of lunch, when Chu broke the silence.

"If you made us some new armor, we could all personalize some runes and formations that would help our individual fighting styles." He unconsciously flexed his own burly arms, sheathing them in a coating of metal qi by reflex. Chu had practiced the move so much that he could perform it without thinking about it. "We could even try to link them in some way, so the more of us there were in the fight, the stronger we would be. Something like a shield that added layers with each person, or maybe a combined attack that built up the longer we fought."

Donny was nodding along, his own imagination going wild. "Why couldn't we still use some of the chitin in a new set of armor? If you were to make everyone a bracer, or maybe a pauldron, that we took from our old armor, we could just turn our shoulder into an enemy qi attack, and it would still do enough to blunt the worst of the damage." Donny shouldered an imaginary enemy as a demonstration. "If we were all standing close together, it would completely dissipate any attack, just like it does already!"

Chu nodded furiously in excited agreement. "Yeah! Jim, you *definitely* need to do this." He snapped his fingers and pointed back and forth at all of us. "And you should make them all different, but the same. You know, the same color and style, so people who see us will know we are all one group. Intimidation and stuff, like Kory used to talk about!"

The excitement died down a little bit at the mention of Kory. He was the missing sixth member of our team. He had been severely injured while saving my life during my last battle with a *nox*. It had been necessary for us to leave him to heal while we continued on our mission to save the world. Despite this, everyone still missed him.

"How about I finish up with the carriage parts first, and then we can all discuss what to do about our armor upgrades?" They both nodded at my idea. "Besides, we would have to draw up some plans before I just jumped straight into making them. Figuring out what runes and formations to use, what their style will be, and even which colors to use will take hours to figure out. And it would be a big mistake to choose any colors without the girls here to tell us what they think."

"That's a good point." Donny had a faraway look in his eyes, like he could see some nightmarish monster the rest of us were too blind to see. "Can you imagine what they would do to us if we picked a color they didn't approve of wearing?" He wasn't the only one to shudder at the idea. *Nox* destroying the world was bad, but that would be *really* bad.

We snapped out of it and got back to work. By the time the sun was getting low in the sky, Donny had over two hundred poppers to divide up, Chu was done with his part of the repairs, and I was hammering in the last few nails necessary to hold everything in place. All we needed was a fresh coat of paint and the carriage would look good as new.

"They should be back by now." Chu had just walked back from the road for the third time in ten minutes. He kept going to the roadside to try to see if he could spot Jamila returning from her trip, but there was a slight curve a few miles farther down that made it impossible to see very far. The surrounding forest was especially dense the closer to the road it got, probably a side effect of the clear cutting done when the road was built. "I have a bad feeling about this."

Donny looked up from his work of separating the poppers into small bags. "Don't worry, Chu. There is still over an hour to full dark. The tall trees just make it seem like it is closer to sunset than it really is." He brushed his hands together as he finished tying off the last pouch. "Come help me separate these into five piles, so everyone can just come and pick up their share without us having to count them out." Chu nodded at Donny and walked over to help.

It was just busywork to keep Chu preoccupied, but I appreciated what Donny was trying to do. For the thousandth time, I was reminded of how lucky I was that the gods had graced me with such awesome people to share my journey with.

I finished my work, putting my traveling forge back in storage, and got a fire started before going over and picking up my pile of popper pouches. I had no idea where Donny had gotten so many little leather bags to put them in, but I wasn't complaining. They looked exactly like a cheap coin purse you could find hanging from the belt of any person you might come across in a small town. It would be easy to keep one ready for use, and no one would ever think it was a weapon. I felt bad for any pickpocket that tried to sneak out a coin or two. They would be in for quite the surprise.

Donny and Chu were using the dim light to draw up plans for our next armor and weapon upgrades. They were mostly arguing about whether a shield design would be better, or some type of group attack formation. I kept my own opinions to myself. They were keeping busy, and I didn't want to distract them. The truth was, I might have been feeling a little worried myself. At the very least, Valerie should have been back by now. She was an experienced enough scout to know that riding a horse through dense forest, in the dark, was a bad idea. It would be too easy for her horse to step into a hole and hurt itself. There was also a sharp increase in the number of creatures that might try to hunt *her* in the dark as well. This close to a heavily-traveled road meant the chances of a large predator were thin, but certainly not nonexistent.

The ringing sound of horseshoes on cobbled road brought us all to our feet. Jamila was making her way up the road with a wide grin on her face. From her posture, and the filled sacks hanging from her saddle, she had clearly been successful in finding a town or village. I heard Chu let out a sigh of relief. Donny, on the other hand, only got more tense.

"Hi boys! Did you miss me?" Jamila hopped down from her saddle and handed me the reins to Cloud. Chu scooped her up in a hug that lifted her feet off the ground. "I'll take that as a yes!" He set her down, and they both quickly unloaded the items she had purchased.

I took Cloud over to the area we had designated as a temporary stable and took off his saddle and tack. As I rubbed him down and filled the small trough with water so he could drink, I saw Donny looking into the trees where Valerie had disappeared. Chu and Jamila were laying out all of her purchases and arguing over how much she had spent. After seeing to the horse, I went to stand next to Donny.

"Clouds are moving in. I think it is going to rain soon." His eyes were looking at the already darkening sky, and I could feel the worry coming off him in waves. "We will have a hard time seeing any tracks in the dark, but if we don't leave before the storm hits, it could wash away any tracks she left behind." I put my hand on his shoulder to show him my support.

"You and I both know Valerie marked the path she took. She is the most experienced scout of the group, so she knows what to do." I had taught her everything I knew about being a scout, and Kory had done the same before we had been separated. She couldn't have been better trained even if she had joined the Imperial Army. "If she doesn't come back soon, we will find her in no time. Don't worry." He nodded, but he didn't come back to the fire with me. Donny stood silent watch over the forest, his eyes watering as he refused to even blink.

"It is getting late. Where is Valerie? Did she already get back?" Jamila and Chu were finally done fighting, and she started to look around for her friend. She was holding a scrap of fabric, probably some kind of gift she had picked up in whatever marketplace she had visited.

I just shook my head, meeting her eyes. Chu quit mumbling to himself about the cost of carrots and looked up from the goods strewn about the stone table, finally sensing the tense atmosphere. Before I could say anything, Donny finally walked over to the fire and pointed back at the forest. We all watched as the last rays of light finally faded away, my stomach sinking in tandem with the sun.

With that simple gesture of his, Valerie was officially missing.

CHAPTER THREE

What the Forest Hides

"We need to split up."

"No, we need to stick together!"

"None of this is helping."

"Let's try sending up some fireballs. If she is lost, she could see them and know where to go!"

"What, and burn down the forest? That's the stupidest idea I've ever heard!"

Everyone was talking over one another, arguing about our next course of action. Kory had been the unofficial leader of our group most of the time, with me stepping in only when it was necessary to do so. When we had continued on without him, our methods had changed a bit. Most of the time we decided everything by committee, with me as the tie breaking vote when needed. Combat plans had still fallen under my purview for the most part, but I was always open to hearing ideas from everyone else. There had been more than once when someone other than myself had come up with the best plan of attack. This was not that time. I needed to take command back, and get moving. We were losing precious time, and my friends were having a rather uncharacteristic freak-out.

"*Enough!*" I manually created the same effect as a popper high enough over everyone's heads that it only caused a loud sound, and didn't blast us with a shockwave. It worked to silence them. "There is only one way to do this that makes any sense. Chu, Jamila, you two stay here in case she comes back to the camp. We can't just walk off and leave our things here unattended anyway, not without knowing what is going on. Valerie could just be running late, or maybe she got cornered in a tree or cave by some monster. If she comes back but needs help, we have to make sure there is someone here to meet her. An empty camp is the last thing she would want to see." Both Chu and Jamila nodded. What I said made perfect sense. "Donny, you and I will go after her. If she *is* cornered by a monster somewhere, I will fight it while you get her out of there. She has her healing medallion on, so unless something happened to it, she should be fine. Make sure you grab Scout as well, if you see him. I know you hate that horse, and I don't blame you, but we need two horses to pull the carriage at full speed. Any questions?" Everyone shook their heads, and we all took a quick moment to get our armor on. Donny pulled out his crossbow as well, taking the time to load it with a heavy bolt.

"Let's move." Donny took the lead, pushing quickly through the brush on the edge of the tree line. I followed close behind, keeping a sharp eye out for any predator tracks—both animal and human. We were able to quickly find her scout markings on some trees that followed a game trail she had taken heading deeper into the forest.

I was able to see in the dark almost as well as in the day now due to my extended use of dark and light qi, but Donny didn't have that advantage. He had mounted a few glow stones on the end of a thick branch, making the forest look washed out in their green glow. I let him push farther away from me, trying to maintain a large enough gap between us that an ambush would only focus on him. He didn't even turn back to acknowledge the tactic, just kept pushing deeper into the forest. I wasn't even sure if he noticed that I wasn't right behind him anymore. It didn't matter. I had his back. Always.

We kept moving late into the night. There wasn't any sign of her running into anything, but I did see several signs of a large predator that had recently taken the trail. Probably a bear of some kind, but from what I could see, it had taken the path at least a day or two before our arrival. The explosion from the poppers was still keeping the majority of the wildlife away, but I saw several smaller creatures watching us as we moved through the trees. The game trail weaved back and forth along the forest floor, meaning we probably traveled twice as far as necessary, but we couldn't afford to simply cut straight through and chance missing where something happened to Valerie.

It was well past midnight when we finally came across the site of a battle. The game trail had intersected with a well-traveled dirt path that ran parallel to a stream. It was clear from the tracks that Valerie had dismounted and allowed Scout to drink. I imagined this was probably where she had planned to turn around, but other events had unfolded.

There was a relatively clear spot where she must have knelt down to get a drink herself. I could even see a knee print in the soft ground near the water's edge. Something must have spooked Scout, because there were horseshoe prints on the other side of the stream, but they were too shallow to indicate a rider was on his back. That meant Valerie had stayed here, standing her ground against the semicircle of footprints that had surrounded her. There were at least ten of them, but when you started getting that high, it was hard to tell exact numbers. A broken arrowhead sticking out of a tree near the center of the circle showed she had put up a fight, but the clear tracks of some kind of cart or wagon showed that she hadn't won. The lack of blood meant that she was either overpowered immediately, or something had kept her from fighting back at her full capabilities. Donny was not happy. Neither was I.

"Her tracks disappear a few yards further down." Donny spoke barely above a whisper. Whether it was from a desire to keep any possible nearby enemies from hearing us, or because he suddenly had a very dry throat, I couldn't tell. "They must have thrown her in the back of whatever left the wheel marks. And they are deep. Whatever they are hauling, it is heavy." I nodded in agreement. Everything I was seeing was very familiar to me from my first life.

"It's slavers. Has to be." I kept my voice down as well. There was no telling how far away they had traveled after snatching up Valerie. "The deep wheel marks are from the heavy iron cage on the back of a wagon. They probably threatened to kill some of their prisoners when she tried to fight back. You and I both know Valerie wouldn't risk someone getting hurt if she could avoid it." Donny nodded and turned to walk farther down the trail. "Donny, hold up. We need to make a plan." He didn't even bother looking back at me as he answered.

"You can make a plan, Jim. I am going to save her." I ran to catch up with him. Before I could grab him and pull him to a stop, he spun around to look at me. "No. I'm not doing this right now. Sometimes, all you can do is smash your enemies. And right now, I am feeling a whole lot like a hammer. You can either be my anvil, or stay here. I don't care. I am saving Valerie." I watched him go. Obviously, I would follow him, but I wanted to give him some space. I didn't want the same thing that happened to Valerie to repeat itself, so I made sure there was enough of a gap between us that any ambushers wouldn't spot both of us. Similar to how we had been traveling in the woods.

The trail we now followed was better maintained than most proper roads found in any hamlet. This was a well-led and well-organized group. They probably sold their slaves to pirates along the coast. We were close enough to the ocean that I suspected we weren't far from whatever they were using as a base of operations. If we found it, I was going to burn it to the ground. I hated slavers. And Donny wasn't the only one who was pissed. Or worried.

It was nearing sunrise when we finally saw an overturned wagon lying on its side near a bend in the road. Both of us rushed forward, our hearts in our throats with fear at what we might find.

There was blood everywhere. Some of the bodies looked like they had practically been ripped apart. Another was trampled into something that I only knew was human because of the presence of a pair of boots. Donny and I split up to search the bodies. I probably should have had him stand off to the side while I did the searching—no one deserved to find the person they loved in this kind of condition—but time was an issue. If she wasn't here, then we needed to hurry. I was already surprised that the local animals hadn't moved in yet, but it wouldn't be long. We were far enough away from the popper explosion that I had no doubt there were plenty of predators in the area.

"She isn't here." Donny had finished searching his half of the battlefield. "I know she is still okay. I would have felt it if something happened to her." He sounded sure of himself. Like he was forcing the need to be correct into his words. "I would *know* it." I finished up my half of the bloody scene, and we both converged on the wagon.

"It looks like you're right, Donny." I held up a broken link of thick chain. "The prisoners escaped. From the tracks, something attacked them from the stream and the captives used the distraction to break free. The tracks are too muddled to see exactly what took place, but I *think* they all kept going down the road. We need to hurry and catch up to them before they run into anything else." Donny didn't even say anything, he just turned and sprinted down the trail. I didn't mean we needed to hurry *that* fast. He was bound and determined to run straight into a stars-damned ambush.

I once again let him get a few hundred feet farther down the trail before I took off after him. We were moving too fast for me to take a close look at the fresh tracks along the road, but it was my impression that at least four or five people were mounted on horses, while another handful were on foot. I had no idea if they were being followed by the people on horseback, or if they were all part of one group. It was hard not to imagine Valerie on foot, injured, and running for her life while mounted slavers mercilessly tracked her down.

We had been running for less than an hour when we finally saw a pillar of smoke rising in the near distance. The smell of burning wood and cooked meat was heavy in the air. My gut instinct told me it wasn't someone preparing a meal. The smell of burnt human was very unmistakable. Pretty sure some people had been burnt up in whatever conflagration was happening around a bend in the road. Donny had stopped in his tracks, waiting for me to approach.

"I don't like this." Donny was staring at the smoke, as if it would reveal all the answers to the questions of the universe. "That smell…"

"I know. Let's cut through the trees instead of taking the road. Keep out of sight the best we can." He nodded in agreement, and we moved off just as the sun rose hazily over the treetops. Donny stayed in the lead, but I moved far to the side so I could flank whoever we came across. What we stumbled upon was completely unexpected. Well, in retrospect, it made sense, but at the time we were very shocked.

A large clearing in the forest was the site of the fire. The road had run straight into a hidden miniature hamlet. I was certain no maps had indicated the presence of any population centers in the region, meaning this place was meant to be a secret. Evenly spaced on either side of the strip of packed dirt were the burnt remains of six wooden buildings. It was hard to see through the smoke, but I knew the lumps on the ground were corpses. And the figures moving through the heavy clouds of soot were responsible for their deaths.

As I was moving to the left of the forest clearing to get in position, I felt a spike of power come from the edge of the clearing. Donny wasn't willing to wait for me. His cultivation level was high enough that he had plenty of elements to choose from when he wanted to attack, but he was strongest in wind qi. Which was what he chose to use when he blasted out a massive wave of energy intended to knock down anyone standing in his way.

It was like a solid wall of air smacked into the indistinct forms, tossing both the living and the dead all over the place. Donny's attack also helped clear away a large portion of the smoke, and even rekindled the fires in one of the burnt buildings. Overall, it was a great distraction, but it didn't manage to actually permanently take down any of the potential enemies. One even stood their ground against the wind, a scrap of cloth covering their features. It was definitely a female, and before I could blink there was an arrow flying straight for Donny just as he emerged from the tree line.

He barely managed to deflect it with his axe, but the sudden move had him off balance. A second arrow blasted into his upper arm, forcing him to drop his weapon. He dove to the ground, managing to dodge the third shaft from the archer before finally tossing a shield formation plate in front of him. I was ready to jump in and help, but there was no fourth attack. Instead, the archer dropped her face covering and put the tip of her bow on the ground before leaning forward and squinting at us. Finally, she spoke.

"Donny? Jim? Where are Jamila and Chu? And what took you so long?" Valerie was bloody, soot-stained, and clearly in a bit of pain. From the look on Donny's face, she was the most beautiful sight he had ever seen. And his tackling hug took her clean off her feet.

I let them have a moment together. Instead of bothering them, I took a quick walk around the miniature hamlet. Which wasn't a hamlet at all. From the sets of iron manacles and the occasional chain, this had been a holding area for the slavers. One of the buildings was still mostly intact, so I went inside to try to see if I could get some idea of what was going on.

This building looked to have been the bunkhouse for the slavers. There were a few bloodstains on the floors, but the absence of cages was a glaring clue. It was just a simple log cabin with three rooms, one a bathing chamber, one a room lined in beds, and finally a kitchen that looked to have doubled as an office. That was where I finally started to understand the scale of what we were dealing with.

Their desk had avoided the fire damage, and it contained an extensive record of just how many people they had kidnapped and enslaved. The dates on the paperwork went back over three years, and the list of names was in the thousands. This was *much* larger than the operation should have been, based on my knowledge of the future. Something had changed, or possibly I had been kept in the dark about the slavers in my first life. There weren't nearly enough bodies lying around to account for an operation of this size and complexity. I scooped up every scrap of paper I could find and put it in my storage belt to look at later. For now, I needed to finish searching the place and find out what had happened with Valerie to land her in this place.

I started looking around for some type of lockbox or storage item they might be using to keep money or valuables in. An extensive search didn't turn up anything. It was probably in a storage ring on one of the bodies. After not finding anything else of note, I decided it was time to go and hear what Valerie had to say.

CHAPTER FOUR

No Need for a Rescue

The air was still filled with smoke when I stepped outside, though the fires looked to have died down for good this time. Donny and Valerie were nowhere to be found, so I headed for a cluster of people huddled at the edge of the hamlet. The group was mostly women, with a few men and children sprinkled in the mix. I didn't bother counting, but there were at least twenty people that must have been recently freed prisoners. Their clothes were ragged and stained, and most of them looked half-starved. As I approached, I pulled out several ration bundles to get some food in their bodies. It was unsurprisingly very well received, even though the people weren't exactly welcoming.

"Thank you, young man." The oldest woman present, probably a grandmother, seemed to have taken charge of the former prisoners. "What brings you to this place? You clearly don't look like any of those slavers, and your gear isn't that of a hunter." I smiled and nodded at her. This woman didn't have a strong cultivation base, but she was certainly perceptive.

"No, ma'am. I am certainly not one of the slavers. Or a hunter, for that matter. I am actually in the same group as the young woman named Valerie. When she went missing, my friend and I left to track her down. Do you happen to know where she is?" Everyone seemed to warm up a bit after that. Apparently, they had a positive view of Valerie.

"Ah, yes, our young savior." Young savior, huh? Valerie must have a great story to tell. The woman pointed toward the opposite end of the hamlet. "Her and the handsome young man she was with went to dispose of the bodies. We all thought it best that was handled out of view of the children." The old woman then looked back at a particularly large man. "They are also dividing up the goods and supplies the slavers left behind." She leaned closer to whisper to me. "Some people tried to take more than their fair share, so Valerie is doing her best to make it even." The scowl on the big guy's face told me he knew we were talking about him. He was taller than Donny, and almost as wide and muscular as Chu. Probably captured to sell as a laborer somewhere. His aura told me he was somewhere close to a weak Meridian cultivator, which made him the strongest person among the former prisoners. I wasn't worried about him as a threat, but I could see how the people here might be intimidated by him.

I thanked the woman for her help, and made my way over to where my friends were toiling away. Donny was stacking the bodies like cordwood, while Valerie sorted through piles of weapons, armor, coins, and various goods. There was quite a bit more there than I expected, given the number of dead slavers.

"Jim! Where did you run off to?" Donny was throwing the last body on the pile. "You aren't going to believe what happened!" He then pulled out a formation plate and threw it on the bodies. A flex of his will, and it made a 'whooshing' sound as it shot flames down into the corpses. Donny would have to continue to power the formation with his qi, but the bodies would be nothing but ash in less than an hour. Not wanting to stand near the stench of the burning hair and crisped flesh, I walked over to Valerie instead.

"So, are you ready to explain what happened?" My question brought a smile to her face, and she nodded toward a clearing off to the side where her horse was munching on the low-cut grass. I hadn't noticed him there earlier, but the red-tinted front hooves and gore encrusted forelegs let me know that the horse had recently seen battle.

"It was Scout. He saved me." She pulled out a set of broken shackles from storage. The red tint to them told me they were some kind of orichalcum alloy, meaning they would keep a cultivator from using qi while they were worn. "I was getting a drink of water from the stream when a bunch of men came out of the woods around me. Scout was spooked, so he took off into the woods across the stream. I managed to shoot at them a few times with my bow when one of them held up a knife to some old woman's throat." She looked over to where the refugees were milling about. "If you could have seen the look in her eyes, you would have surrendered as well. She was so scared, Jim. I couldn't risk her getting harmed." I nodded in agreement. I wasn't there, so it was pointless to try to second-guess her actions. Seeing my nod, she continued. "I gave myself up, and they put these shackles on me."

"That was a brave thing to do, Valerie. Giving yourself up to save a complete stranger isn't a choice many people would make." I moved to pat her on the shoulder, but she handed me the shackles instead.

"It wasn't really that scary, knowing that the rest of you would eventually find me." She motioned to the shackles. "Can you do anything useful with those?"

I looked down at them. "Probably, but that can wait until later. Tell me what happened next." I put the shackles in my storage belt.

"They loaded me in a wagon with a few other female prisoners, along with the old woman. We traveled for a while, and a group of men on horses joined the men on foot farther up the road. The men who captured us kept talking about the things that were going to happen when we got to their camp. It made me angry. Really angry. Almost as if some outside source was fueling my rage." She shuddered at the memory. "It almost felt like someone else took control of me for a moment, and I felt something shift inside me. A power I have never experienced before did something to the lock on the shackles, and all of a sudden, they weren't as tight. That's when Scout made his appearance. He came out of nowhere, and started trampling them. He managed to knock over the wagon, and somehow my shackles came off in the impact. After that, things were kind of a blur. Somehow, between the other prisoners, Scout, and I, we managed to kill all of them. Let's just say after what they were threatening to do, I feel no remorse for their deaths."

Valerie was rubbing her forearm, as if remembering the slap of her bowstring against it as she laid out her captors. "After that, we all decided it was a good idea to go to their base and free any prisoners we could find. There wasn't time to wait for the rest of you to find us. We didn't know if they would notice that their wagon was late, so we just rushed here as fast as we could. The others attacked them head-on, while I stayed back and took them down." She looked over at the pile of burning bodies. "Everything happened so fast, and before I knew it, we had won. Donny and you walked up just as we managed to put out the fires from the battle."

"So, let me get this straight. You willingly surrendered yourself to save a complete stranger. Then, your horse caused a distraction and you broke free. You killed the people that put you in chains, and then led a group of former prisoners to a slaver camp and managed to kill all of them with only the assistance of a handful of women to help?" She nodded. "Valerie, remind me to never get on your bad side." We both chuckled. Her experience with some outside power was concerning, but after a quick scan I didn't sense anything inside her at the moment.

"When you put it like that, I guess it was all a little crazy. It didn't feel like that in the moment, though. We just did what we had to do."

"Spoken like a true hero, Valerie. I couldn't have done it better myself." She blushed at the praise. "Now, how about we get this stuff divided up and get these people on their way? I'm sure they have people out there worried about them." Valerie nodded in agreement, and we got to work.

They had found enough gold to ensure every former prisoner had at least a few coins to help them get home. I supplemented the weapons and armor with some of my own, and set up my traveling forge to make sure everyone had at least a basic set of protection that fit them. As they were taking turns getting their equipment properly fitted, Donny and Valerie flitted about and made sure everyone got their equal share. The only person to complain was the big guy from earlier. Apparently, in his opinion, since he was the largest person present, he deserved a greater portion of food and coin to get him back home. A few harsh words from Valerie shut him up quickly, though, and he left without waiting for me to properly size the iron breastplate he had been handed. So be it. I wasn't going to hold his hand.

It was well past noon when we finally got on our way. The majority of the former prisoners elected to stay at the charred hamlet and spend one more night regaining their strength before heading off to wherever they came from. It wasn't exactly the greatest option, but it was definitely practical. There was no telling the next time they would get a chance to sleep with a roof over their heads, even if it was a little burnt.

The old woman and two young girls chose to return to the main road with us. They would hitch a ride to the next town, and send for their loved ones to come and get them. As we trudged back the way we had come, the old woman decided to walk next to me.

"Your friends seem to be good people, young man." We both watched as Donny put the girls on Scout's back, while Valerie chatted with them. "That young woman was like a ghost, flitting about and taking down those evil men with only one shot. The rest of us were barely more than a distraction."

"I believe it." I watched as Valerie led the way, Scout following close on her heels. Donny was walking alongside them, making sure the girls didn't fall off. "Valerie can be quite dangerous if provoked." The old woman nodded in agreement, and we continued in silence for a while, the two of us bringing up the rear. "I have to ask, did you notice anything odd about her before she broke free of her shackles?"

"I'm not sure what I saw." The old woman looked up at Valerie. "When those men were taunting us, she was practically vibrating with rage. I might have even seen her eyes turn solid black for a moment. But I don't care if she turned into an outright demon, that girl saved us all from a fate far worse than death. And no one will hear anything bad about her from me." I nodded. Black eyes? Rage pouring off of her in waves? This sounded very familiar to me. Almost exactly like a certain goddess I knew. I would have to ask her about it the next time I saw her.

It wasn't much longer until we reached the overturned wagon Donny and I had passed a few hours ago. We had to move closer to the tree line to skirt around the wreckage, Valerie poking around the wagon to see if there was anything we had missed. The girls were chatting excitedly with Donny about it when out of nowhere, a massive tree branch landed right in our path.

I moved in front of the old woman to defend her, and Donny did the same for the girls on Scout. Which left Valerie. She was closest to the fallen branch, and her arrow darted into the trees before anyone else had a chance to react. Out stumbled the big man who had left on his own earlier in the day, an arrow sticking out of his chest where his ill-fitting breastplate didn't cover. Valerie swapped her bow for her cleaver-like short sword and approached our would-be attacker.

"What were you thinking?!" She used her sword to smack the spear the man tried to point at her away. "I save your life, and you turn around and attack me right after? What is wrong with you!"

His only reply was a gurgling roar. The man dropped his spear and tried to wrap her up in a diving tackle. Valerie danced backwards and split his skull for his troubles. Instead of looking victorious, she immediately looked depressed. She turned back to face us with tears in her eyes. Donny was busy trying to calm the girls, so the old woman and I walked over to her. "Why? Why would he do something like this?"

"Child, there are some people that have nothing but venom in their heart." The old woman grabbed her into a hug. "There is no real answer as to why he chose to act how he did. We can't understand it, because he wasn't a rational person. This wasn't your fault." She pulled back to look Valerie in the eyes. "None of this is your fault. You only did what you were forced to do." Silent tears fell, but Valerie nodded anyway. Occasionally, I was reminded how young my companions really were. They might be strong, and exceedingly capable, but they weren't yet numb to the evils of the world. Maybe that was a good thing.

"Valerie." She turned to look at me. "I know it seems hollow now, but you did the right thing." I pointed back to the two young girls on the horse. "He would have hurt them. Hurt us. Don't dwell on this. Let's just keep moving and get back to camp." She nodded, and we continued on our way.

Before we got too far apart, I heard her mumbling to herself. "…stop this. Now I know. From now on, I will do everything I can to make sure good people don't have to worry about losing family members to people like them." I could literally *feel* the determination coming off of her in waves. Valerie had discovered her purpose, and I felt bad for anyone that crossed her.

"One thing is for sure," the old woman said to me as we made our way down the trail, "that girl certainly doesn't need you boys running around trying to save her."

All I could do was silently agree.

CHAPTER FIVE

The Claw

The next few days were relatively uneventful. It took some rearranging, but squeezing everyone inside the carriage was only temporary. The village we dropped them off at was only a little over half a day away, and large enough to have a few places for them to stay. We managed to find a nice inn for the old woman and girls to stay in while they waited for their families to come and get them, and finished restocking on goods.

I went ahead and paid for their lodging so they could save the money we recovered from the slavers. It was the right thing to do. This way, they could use that gold to improve their lives a bit. After the trauma they had endured, I was sure it would go a long way toward moving past things. It was a touching goodbye, and despite—or because of—Valerie's newfound purpose in life, she seemed to be the most affected in saying her farewells.

I knew we were getting close to our destination, because occasionally a strong breeze would bring the smell of the ocean. The carriage was holding together pretty well for the most part, but it had picked up a wobble that was only detectable when we tried to travel at top speed. We tried to fix it, but I didn't have the required knowledge for such fine detail work. Ultimately, I didn't mind. It was a unanimous decision to sell the carriage as soon as we found a vessel to take us to the Western Province. Valerie demanded we find a ship capable of bringing the horses with us, and after Scout had saved her, none of us were willing to argue.

Our slightly reduced speed meant it was almost two weeks after Valerie's fight before we finally reached the first coastal village. The forest road continued its sinuous track right up to the edge of the woods, where it changed into an arrow-straight path headed directly for a sprawling group of buildings. Barely visible due to the slight rise of the land was a single long pier that speared into the clear blue waters of the Ocean of Tears.

The Ocean of Tears was named as such due to the tales of widows crying for their lost sailors at sea. Traveling on the blue waves wasn't a task for the weak. Storms could overtake ships with almost no warning, the violent waves they conjured easily capable of swamping any wooden vessel that dared to risk the deep waters. If that wasn't enough, there were all the monsters.

Flying fish capable of slicing through the hull of a ship like a hot knife through a block of butter, or the terrifying leviathans that could swallow a sailor whole. There were even tales of a shark so big that it could bite entire ships in half, given the slightest of provocation. During my first life, I had only spent a single long voyage aboard a ship of the Empire's Navy, and I counted it among the most terrifying chapters of my entire existence. The necessity of reaching the Western Province before the *nox* could secure a stronghold in the region was the only reason I risked traveling by sea. I would happily take the long way over land if I had the time.

If it weren't for the abilities of cultivators to use air and water qi, humanity would still be confined to land. As it was, every ship that dared to sail out of sight of the shore needed several powerful cultivators that specialized in air qi to fill their sails, and even more cultivators that could use water qi to propel their ships out of the path of the more dangerous creatures of the deep.

It was hard to keep in the shudder of past memories as I recalled the fear that gripped an entire crew of the emperor's finest when a dark shadow larger than any creature had a right to be passed under our ship. The massive five-masted and four-hundred-foot wooden vessel might have served as a nice toothpick for the creature. Absolute silence and the subtle work of dozens of water cultivators was all that saved us that day. That, and an enormous stockpile of luck.

Chu and I were currently riding on the driver's seat of the carriage while the others were lounging inside. I pulled out our map, trying to figure out which coastal village we were looking at. The single pier was an indicator that this place didn't see a lot of shipping traffic, making it an unlikely place for us to find suitable transportation. There weren't any ships docked at the pier currently, but I could see a single set of sails in the distance.

"Anything on the map?" Chu was leaning over my shoulder, trying to see where we were. I shook my head and pointed at where I believed we were on the map.

"I don't see anything here along this part of the coast. Either I am way off on our location, or this village was built after this map was made. Considering how old this map is, I would guess the latter." The map was over a hundred years old, so I felt pretty sure of my guess.

The Claw was either one peninsula that had been split in half lengthwise, or two separate peninsulas that were very close to one another. There were plenty of ancient legends that told of a mighty cultivator that fought against a massive sea monster at the tip of the peninsula when it was still one whole piece, and their battle is what caused the land to split in half. Considering what I had managed when reaching the known heights of cultivation in my first life, I had to wonder if those legends were indeed based on facts.

"Well, I suppose we should go see what we can find out." Chu's voice brought me out of my musings. "And if we're lucky, they might want to buy some of our wares." The need for setting up ocean-faring contracts for his trade empire was a subject Chu had talked about for months. I didn't mind, but I thought it was starting to drive Donny a little crazy. Hopefully Chu could set something up soon, before his ramblings finally tipped poor Donny over the edge.

He snapped the reins and the horses started the carriage moving again. While Chu drove, I thought for a minute about the motivations of my companions. All of them had joined me in my crusade to stop the *nox*, but they had stayed for more than just a single long-term goal. They were here as my friends, among other things. Chu was here to build his trading empire. Jamila had come to get out of the shadow of her father, Elder Tou, and strengthen herself as much as possible. Having Chu along for the ride didn't hurt matters, either.

Donny had come to protect his cousin—meaning me—but I think it was more than that. Valerie had come with us, and he was as smitten as any man I had ever seen. Valerie was here because her best friend had come, and she also wanted to become as strong as she could to impress her family.

After what had happened in the woods, she had refocused on her cultivation with a whole new level of determination. It had bled over into the others, and I had no doubt they would be reaching the next stage of their development soon. Once Chu, Jamila, and Valerie reached the level of a Brain cultivator, everyone in our group would be able to use all six known elements. It would make our already dangerous group even more lethal.

I was still on the fence about showing them the secret to cultivating light and dark qi, but I had plenty of time before it became an issue. Once a cultivator was going from Peak Saint to Low Sage, their body would be completely remade anew with the qi they had stored in their body. That would be the time when I would either have to tell them about the two hidden forms of qi, or let them continue on the traditional path of only the basic elements.

Opening them to dark and light qi would catapult them into the forefront of any clan or sect hierarchy, and I didn't know if they wanted that for themselves. If the emperor ever caught wind of them using two unknown elements, they would be forced to serve him. Their futures would be determined by others, unless they were independently powerful enough to stand against those who would use them for their own gain. That alone was a lot to think about.

The other issue I had was one of trust. Would I be able to trust them with potential power beyond anything that had been seen in our world in who knew how long? I had already been betrayed by someone that I had called brother, and I had known him for a very long time. This group was fast proving themselves worthy of my *total* trust, but I still had a hard time after what Ming had done to me, essentially over nothing but securing his own power. I knew I had trust issues, but if anyone could silently help me work my way through them, it was these four.

We reached the village just as the sun touched the horizon. Even though it would be dark soon, the small village was still lively. They were clearly preparing for the approaching ship that was still at least an hour away. Canvas awnings were being strung between houses, and tables were set up with signs announcing the prices of the goods on display. The whole village was in the process of turning into a giant marketplace. Chu looked like he was about to pass out. This was literally a dream come true for him. We all clustered together near the front of the carriage near the center of the village.

"Okay guys, time to split up. Donny and Valerie can try to find us a place to stay the night. Chu and Jamila should try to sell as much of our excess stuff as possible. Before we get on any ship, each of us should try to store as much fresh water in our rings as possible. Just because we can make fresh water using qi doesn't mean we shouldn't be prepared. You never know what could happen out there." Everyone nodded in agreement. "While you are doing that, I am going to try to find a more updated set of maps. If we are lucky, someone around here might have a map of the Western Province as well. I don't want to show up there blind."

"There doesn't appear to be an inn anywhere in this little village, but we will give it our best shot. My guess is, if there was a place, it would be closer to the pier." Donny and Valerie headed off toward the water.

"I hope they can at least find us a place to take a bath." Chu sniffed himself before making a face. "Just because our clothes can magically stay clean doesn't mean *we* stay clean. Ugh." Jamila nodded vigorously in agreement as the two of them led the horses and carriage off to speak with a cluster of merchants arguing over where to set up their tables to best maximize their sales to the incoming sailors.

I made sure there wasn't anyone paying too much attention to us before I worked my way back the way we had come. There had been a shop of some kind right before the edge of the village that might have what I was looking for. The sign out front was badly faded, but I was pretty sure it showed a pair of crossed feather quills. The crossed quills were the universal sign of the Scholar Sect, a small yet widespread group that were focused entirely on knowledge. Either that, or the sign displayed some form of two-headed bird pecking at the ground. Really, I couldn't lose. Each option was a win in my book.

As I pushed open the door, I heard a bell ring faintly toward the back of the small building. The shop was basically one large room that had been separated into four sections by massive bookshelves. One area was filled with basic seafaring items such as rope, dried rations, and folded sailcloth. The second section was filled with books. Piles and stacks of books, scrolls, and loose sheets of paper that, at first glance, seemed to be centered around teaching cultivation techniques concentrating on water and air elements. Neither were things that I needed.

The final two areas were what I was looking for. One was filled with enchanted items that practically glowed with the power of their internal qi matrixes, and the other was filled with rolled sheets of vellum. Maps.

I was a little surprised to see such a collection of maps in such a small village on the fringes of civilization, but it wasn't too far outside the norm to find at least a few maps in such a place. After all, weren't places just like this one exactly where you would need a map? I wouldn't be shocked if most of them were drawn to show where we had just come from to assist those just arriving in the region, but there were bound to be a few that focused on other areas of the empire.

I quickly made my way over to the enchanted items first. Going through all of the maps without the store clerk to help me would be a headache, but I didn't require much assistance to figure out what most embedded qi matrixes could do. There weren't any notes or plaques to label the various items, so I spun out a few qi threads to inspect the more interesting things on display.

The first item I looked at was a blue marble the size of my fist. It gave off a cool aura, as if it had just been pulled out of a snowdrift in the middle of winter-year. A closer look revealed that if it were fed enough air and water qi, it would create sheets of ice. Very useful for any fishing ship that wanted to preserve its catch for any length of time. I immediately grabbed it for myself. I could make ice on my own, but something like this would make life much easier. Not that I specifically needed large amounts of ice at the moment, but a wise man never turned down a useful tool when given the opportunity.

Next to the blue marble was a series of spirit wood tools intended for specific tasks I couldn't figure out on my own. Probably meant for a ship's carpenter. They were all of a lower quality than the spirit wood ring I already owned, so I moved on to the next row.

I instantly recognized the next three items as devices used for navigation. They were best used as a set, one with a needle that always pointed the same direction, one that helped with knowing your location using the stars, and one that helped detect earth qi. The earth qi detector could let a lost ship know where the nearest shoreline was, or help them avoid underwater hazards when traveling in shallow water. Staying true to my hoarder nature, I grabbed all three bronze and wood creations. These could be useful in any number of situations.

Most of the other magical or enchanted items were either things I could make on my own, or something I already had. The only other item of note I decided to add to my list of purchases was an emergency raft. At first glance, it looked like a plain rectangular block of wood that could fit in the palm of my hand. It had the same qi matrix as my traveling forge, meaning all a cultivator needed to do was activate the runes and it would expand into a full-sized raft in only a few seconds. If the ship we were on happened to sink, this might be the item that meant the difference between life and death. Having another example of a qi matrix that adjusted the size of an object to study would also be a boon. I still hadn't figured out how to get it to work on my own, but this might increase my chances to finally create my own shrinking items.

Not finding anything else of use, I moved over to the map section. Crossing the threshold into the final area of the shop must have been what the shopkeeper was waiting for, because he came out in a flourish. He was an older man, but still showed plenty of vitality. Typical of someone in the Scholar Sect, the shopkeeper wasn't built like a fighter. Instead of calluses on his hands from training with weapons, the tips of his fingers were covered in ink stains. His wiry frame was perfectly erect, telling me that he didn't spend all of his time hunched over books doing research. His long white beard and drooping mustache matched the snow-white topknot of his hair, and the rugged, well-worn boots had seen plenty of miles. All signs pointed to a man that had traveled the world, while the sparkle in his friendly blue eyes told me he enjoyed every minute of it. Definitely an explorer, and most likely a member of the Cartographer's branch of the Scholar's Sect.

"Welcome, young man!" He bowed to me with a flourish, his smooth movements further reinforcing my belief that he was a man of action, if not a man of battle. "Around these parts, I am known as Taft, mapmaker extraordinaire!" I instantly liked the man. He was definitely the kind of cartographer you could trust. Too many mapmakers of the past had used second-hand information or descriptions from others to draw their maps. People like Taft went out and drew the things they saw with their own eyes.

"It is good to meet you, sir." I returned his bow with one that was a little bit deeper than the one he offered me. He was giving off the aura of a Low Saint, making him slightly more powerful than me. However, my advancement level at such a young age put me on equal footing, meaning I didn't have to bow as low as I did. I chose to do so, mostly because he was clearly deserving of my respect. Just because I was over six centuries old didn't mean I was exempt from giving others their due. "I am in search of any maps you might have that show the coastline between here and the Western Province, as well as any recent maps of the Western Province as a whole."

"I have to admit, I am a little surprised at such a young man that is intending to travel so far." He turned to start rummaging through the rolls of vellum behind him. "Searching for your fortune, perhaps? Or just adventuring for the sake of adventure?"

"Neither, sir. My friends and I are on a mission from our clan to expand the reach of our merchants." Not a complete lie, and a feasible reason. "We have already built ties with the Southern Capital, and now we want to expand into the West. Before you know it, our clan will become a major trade partner that spans the empire." The man made a grunt of approval, his attention more on his maps than me.

"Aha!" After a few moments he pulled out a rolled map and set it on the table behind him. "Look that over while I look for some more." I tried to thank him, but his attention had already returned to his stacks of scrolls.

I unrolled the map to look it over. It was a surprisingly detailed image of the western coastline, ranging from where it met the Southern Province boundary at the River of Serpents all the way to the massive mountain range that marked the northern border of the empire.

There were plenty of details about water hazards, as well as several major towns along the coast. A few unmarked dots were probably small villages the cartographer hadn't actually visited, just saw from a distance. Overall, that level of detail and accuracy, based on my memories from my first life, was impeccable.

This man was entirely too good at his job to be located at a tiny no-name village on the edge of the empire. Either he was running from someone, or he had been exiled for some transgression against a powerful clan or sect. It was another example of the systemic problem with our society. A man incredibly skilled at his craft was forced into obscurity because some greater power didn't like him, or his abilities threatened someone with political clout. I had seen it a thousand times, and it still made me angry. Of course, I could have been dead wrong and he was an actual criminal that was running from the law, but I didn't sense any malice from the man.

"These should do the trick." He spun around, his arms overflowing with rolled up maps. "Take a look and let me know if these are enough. I have a few more examples floating around here somewhere…"

Just as he was turning back to look for more materials, his front door was struck by something hard enough that it flew off its hinges and slammed onto the floor. We both spun to see what was happening. In walked a man large enough that he had to turn sideways just to make it through the empty doorframe. I would bet my belt that the stormy look on his brutish face was a permanent feature. The man was shirtless, his bulging muscles covered in scars. The rough spun wool pants he wore had been cut off at the knee, and his bare feet and suntanned skin indicated he could normally be found on the deck of a ship. The bald head and unkempt beard suited his image perfectly. Definitely a nice guy. If you liked them big, mean, and ugly.

He stomped over the broken remnants of the wooden door and moved to the side so a man half his height could enter.

While the newcomer was only half the height, his prodigious gut put him in the same weight class as the bruiser. The ornate robes, heavy gold jewelry, and slicked-back thinning hair screamed scalawag. Maybe scumbag.

"Taft! Those totems you sold me were garbage! They didn't ward off anything! We were less than a week from port when we were struck by a school of Grapplers. I nearly lost my ship because of you!" The repugnant man was shaking his finger at the cartographer, but the look of indignation on Taft's face was pretty telling.

"I told you before you bought them those totems were meant to ward against rodents and pests! At no point did I claim they would fend off anything larger than a rat!" Taft released the hold on his aura, filling the space with an earthy presence. His accusers responded by doing the same, each of them his match in power, but with a definite hint of water.

None of them were skilled enough to balance the qi in their auras, meaning they were like most people in the empire. Pure focus on advancement, no eye to the future. Without a proper balance of the different forms of elemental qi, none of them would ever reach the level of Sage. The shaking finger of the reprobate made me focus on him again.

"You sold me a product advertised to ward my ship from harm. My ship was attacked. To me, that means you owe me the difference in repairs, plus some extra for my troubles." He motioned with his hand, and the bruiser flicked out an elbow that shattered a shelf holding stacks of coiled ropes. "I recommend you hand over the keystone, while you still have a roof over your head."

Taft shook his head at the man. "Is that what this is about? You think a single keystone is enough to open the gate? We are too old, Silas. This shakedown is pointless. Even if you had a dozen keystones, it wouldn't matter. The guardian wouldn't allow you entry into the Inheritance. Besides, it has already moved. According to the schedule, it is somewhere in the Northern Province right now. It would take you *years* to reach the site, and you aren't strong enough to wander those mountains anyway." Taft was looking at the man in pity. "Unless you have a core at the Heavenly level to power a cloud ship, it is useless. And if you had one of those, you wouldn't care about the Inheritance in the first place." The man, apparently named Silas, wasn't happy about what he was hearing. "Just leave me alone, and find your own path to power."

"Fine! If you aren't going to give it to me, I will take it off your corpse! Moose, kill him. And don't leave any witnesses."

Well, I had to say, that wasn't very nice. I decided to let Silas and Moose know how much I didn't appreciate their decision-making process.

I had already spun a few dozen earth qi threads combined with dark qi out from the meridians on the bottoms of my feet and run them underground to surround the two miscreants. The look of shock on their faces when I wrapped them up with razor sharp threads of obsidian-like stone barely larger than my pinky finger was pretty great. Given the fact that they were unable to see or use dark qi, my impromptu prison I created for each of them was basically unbreakable without using an overwhelming amount of their own qi to break free. It also meant their normally impervious skin was vulnerable to injury from them. I made sure the strand I wrapped around their throats was tight enough that they understood any movement I didn't appreciate wouldn't have a happy ending for them, and ensure I could stop them from using their own cores. Taft wasn't overly surprised at my actions. Given the earthy tones of his aura, he must have felt my actions happening underground.

"Gentlemen. Seeing as how you decided to outright kill me without even learning my name, I think it is only proper that I introduce myself." The guy Silas called Moose tried to flex an arm to break free of the strands of stone, but since I was still connected to them, I just tightened them an extra little bit. The shock and fear on his face when they cut into his skin was mildly gratifying. I guess he *could* show more than one emotion. "My name is Jim. Pleasure to make your acquaintance." Silas hadn't noticed that Moose had already tried to break out and failed, which gave him a false sense of superiority.

"I don't care who you are. You just got in my way. Bad luck for you, kid, but it isn't my problem." He tried to turn his head to look at his henchman, so I ran an extra thread over the top of his head to hold it in place. It didn't make him happy. "I don't know what item you have that lets you hold us like this, but it can't keep us contained forever. Moose, take care of this pipsqueak!" Moose, either from habit or a false sense of confidence, tried to follow his order. All he managed to do was cut himself deeper on the sharp obsidian.

I turned to look at Taft. "I hope you don't mind my intervention, but as soon as they threatened me, this became my problem as well." Taft had already retracted his aura, and was looking at me with extreme interest. "Normally, I don't suffer an enemy to live. But since this is your issue, I will let you decide their fate."

He stared at the two hooligans for a bit before answering. "I don't know. I have never been the type of person to kill someone who is at my mercy. However, this attack was completely unprovoked. I knew it was a mistake to tell this toad about the treasures I have found in my travels, but he caught me while I was in my cups."

Silas lunged against the stone threads, cutting himself on their sharp edges. "Call me a toad, will you?!" He was practically frothing at the mouth in anger. The blood dripping down his face was caused by him flailing against the stone arch tight against the top of his head. "You will pay for this! Do you have any idea the power that I wield? People will hound you until the end of your days! When I get out of here, I swear on my life, you will never know a moment of peace! I will—*ahhh!*" He stopped ranting when I tightened the stone threads around his arm. His scream reached an even higher pitch when his severed right hand flopped to the ground. I walked over to him and kicked his appendage away. I had to raise my voice to be heard over his screams.

"Why do I keep running across people like you? You *clearly* don't understand the situation you are in." I glanced at Moose, and the fear on his face said he wasn't as stupid as he looked. At least one of these two jerks was starting to get it. "Now that you have told me what you are going to do to me when I release you, why would I ever let you live?" I turned and looked back at Taft. "This is why I do my best to never allow an enemy to get away. They have a bad habit of turning back up when you least expect it." The pool of blood around Silas had stopped growing. Being a Saint cultivator that focused on water, it meant that he could control his blood flow. It also told me that he had himself under control again. "Now, tell me Silas, after everything you said, why should Taft and I let you leave this place?"

"If you kill me, my people will find out and track you down! They will take revenge on everything you hold dear, and then remove your cursed existence from this world. You don't have any idea how powerful the people I work for are. Any loved ones will be collared as slaves, and work themselves to death in the iron mines of the north!" I cut off his other hand. This time, he screamed even louder. Honestly, I was lucky Taft's neighbors were so far away. If his shop was any closer to the village, I was sure plenty of people would have come to see what all the noise was about.

"So, you openly admit that you consort with slavers. It just so happens that I am on the lookout for people that have more information about a slaver ring my friend ran into not long ago." I tightened the qi strands around Moose a bit more, silently threatening him. Silas was too stupid to realize the predicament he was in, but Moose might still want to live. "Okay, Silas. This is how I see things. First, you come into this establishment and try to kill me. Then, you threaten me and everything I hold dear. And somehow you manage to admit you work for an illegal organization of professional kidnappers that sell their victims to the highest bidder." I looked back at Taft. "This isn't your decision anymore. These two don't walk out of here. Don't worry, I will destroy the bodies." Silas only got angrier, but Moose clearly understood the gravity of the situation. Taft just looked down at his feet.

"If you think that I wil—*urk!*"

I cut him off. Literally. By removing his head.

No sense in stretching things out. I waited for the spray of blood to stop before encasing the entire body in the obsidian-like stone I had conjured. Well, I looted it first. It's good to stay true to your inner self. I even made sure to collect the hands. The use of a few strands of water and fire qi had the store looking spotless. No one would ever be able to tell someone had died here. If anyone were to look for the place a powerful cultivator died, they would usually be hunting for a large battlefield, with massive disruptions in the ambient energy from the fight. There wasn't anything like that here. I walked over to Moose, who had a look of resignation on his face.

"Well, Moose, if that's your real name, it looks like this is the end of your path. No one will ever know what happened to you. You and your boss will just disappear off the face of the continent, no one the wiser." He was doing a good job controlling his fear. Commendable. "Unless, of course, you have some way of convincing me it is worth my time to keep you alive. Something like information about the slavers your boss was working with…" The spark of hope in his eyes was bright enough to light a bonfire.

"I do!" He was actually shaking with the urge to tell me everything he could, managing to cut himself further on the strands of stone wrapped around him. "I can tell you everything! Where they meet, what they pay, how to contact them, everything!" I held up my hands to slow him down. I also loosened up his restraints a bit as a show of good faith.

"Hold on. Let me get something to write on, so I can take notes. Taft, can you pull out some maps, so we can have our new friend indicate the locations of these slavers for us?" Taft gave me a sharp nod, and quickly started shuffling through his stacks of maps. I grabbed a few blank sheets of parchment and a pencil off a nearby shelf. "Okay, Moose, let's start."

He laid out everything. I didn't like how much he knew, especially about how detailed he was on the steps they took to ensure the slaves were mentally broken before being sold. That wasn't all he described, of course. The methods they used to transport slaves, the places they used to hold them, and all kinds of names. Many of them were involved in the government, and more than a few 'upstanding' clans and sects throughout the Empire were actively assisting in the process.

Chief among them was the Flying Sword Sect. The more I learned about the actions of that sect, the more I wanted to burn it down. Definitely something on my to-do list. The systems they had in place were very familiar to the slaver group I had taken down in my first life, leading me to believe this was the same one. Just, you know, a few hundred years before I had discovered it. Either I hadn't taken down the entire ring in my first life, or the group would slowly shrink on its own in the future. Considering how awful the emperor I served—Ming—had been, it was entirely possible he had hidden the full extent of the slavers from me. Bastard.

"So, now you will let me go?" Moose was looking between Taft and I. "I have told you everything I know. Just like you said." For an answer, I shoved a thread of stone through the base of his skull and up into his brain. Probably what I should have done to kill Silas. Much less mess.

"What was that!" Taft was shocked. "You promised to let him live if he told you everything!"

"Did I? Because I was pretty sure I said he had to convince me to let him live. He didn't do a very good job of convincing me." I held up the sheaf of papers and then dropped them on the stack of maps. We had needed a lot of them to organize everything. "He knew too much about their operation to be just a simple henchman. Moose was just as guilty as Silas. There was absolutely no way under the stars that I would have let him walk away." I shuffled around until I found the piece of paper that described what they did to children they kidnapped. "Look at this, Taft, and tell me that hunk of human waste deserved to walk out of this place." He didn't need to look at it. He had been here the whole time. "If anything, I should have taken both of those bastards apart one tiny portion at a time. For a long, *long* time. Killing them quickly was more than they deserved."

Taft couldn't meet my stare for very long. "You are right. I apologize. It isn't like I wanted to let him go in the first place, I suppose I was just shocked you killed him like that." He looked around at his shop, and started picking up the mess.

I took a storage ring from Moose, an almost identical copy of the simple band that Silas had worn, and encased him in stone as well. Cleaning up the small amount of blood that leaked out was only a few seconds of work, and then I put both sarcophagi in my storage belt. I would drop them in the ocean when we finally got on board a ship. When I finished what I was doing, I paid Taft a ridiculous sum of sixty gold for the magic items, maps, and materials I had commandeered during the interrogation. As I went to leave, I saw that he was doing more than just cleaning. He was packing up.

"What are you doing?"

He glanced my direction before turning back around and continued to sweep items into a storage ring. "I'm leaving. Silas will certainly have friends come and look for him, and I don't want to be here when they show up." It looked like he had more than one storage ring, because each hand was making items disappear.

"Aren't you worried that will make you look suspicious? I mean, if I had a friend go missing, and the guy he was visiting ran before I could ask him what happened, that person would move to the top of my list of suspects."

Taft paused for a moment before continuing. "I move around frequently to update my maps." He waved his hand, sweeping his entire map section into a ring. "It would be even more suspicious if I stayed."

"Ah, I see. Where will you go?"

Taft thought for a moment before pulling out a yellow stone, shaped like a brick, that gave off enough power that it had a slight glow. He held it out to me along with a small square of parchment. "I am headed north, to find the Inheritance of the Guide. I want you to take this keystone and map. It is made out of parchment, so you can burn it after memorizing it. If you find yourself in the area, you should give it a try as well."

I took them from him and popped both items in my belt. "I thought you couldn't get inside the Inheritance?"

He chuckled a bit, pulling out a stack of a dozen of the glowing bricks. "Normally, no, but I have collected enough of these things to force my way inside. I won't be able to go to all the areas inside the pocket dimension, but I will be able to get my foot in the door. Someone like you, though, would benefit greatly from entering." While he was talking, Taft had finished storing all the items in the front of the store. "Now, I need to finish packing, and you need to go. There is no telling how long it will take for the people on that ship to figure out their bene-factor is missing. Hopefully, I will meet you again, Jim." He shook my hand, and I left.

My first official day on the coast of The Claw in this life, and I had already killed two people. And maybe made a friend in the process. Life was weird sometimes.

CHAPTER SIX

A Party

I had a keystone to an Inheritance. In my first life, I would have dropped everything and immediately sprinted to the location on the map to find it. This time around, it was merely a distraction to my missions of stopping the *nox* incursion and killing Emperor Ming. Well, Prince Ming, but you get the point.

An Inheritance was a trial made by someone of the Emperor rank—not *the* emperor necessarily—and it was basically a way for a cultivator to find an easy path to the highest levels of strength. When an Emperor-level cultivator was near death, they could use their remaining cultivation potential to make a pocket dimension that held a set of trials and their collected treasures. They would do this in an attempt to find a successor to their abilities.

The vast majority of Inheritances were created from either the founders of the empire during the last Great War, or from before the actual creation of the empire. The entrances to the Inheritances were sometimes static, meaning they never moved, or more frequently, they shifted around in some pattern to allow more people to gain entrance. Many had certain requirements to enter, ranging from cultivation level to specific age limits.

And not all that entered an Inheritance ever made it back out alive.

There were only ten Inheritances that were common knowledge, but I knew of at least thirteen present within the empire. Given the age of the lands, there were likely dozens more that were either closely held clan or sect secrets, or simply hidden and lost to time. Three of the static Inheritances were controlled by the emperor and his Enforcers, which were closely guarded secrets of the empire. All the keystones, or entrance tokens, for the Inheritance of the Shield, Inheritance of the Sword, and Inheritance of Life, were kept in the Imperial City vaults. It ensured the emperor would always control the best defenders, blade masters, and healers.

In my first life, I had entered the Inheritance of the Shield. It wasn't anything like the name implied. For me, anyway. They were often different experiences for different people, as well as odd time gaps for those inside. Instead of learning how to actually use a shield, I had spent over a month of time inside a giant library that was filled with books on tactics, organization, and planning. To the outside world, I had only been inside the Inheritance for three days. That month of learning was what helped me to become an effective strategist, as well as a fantastic spymaster when I had served Ming.

Other Inheritances were based on the elements, like the Inheritance of Storms, or the Inheritance of the Blaze. Those were meant for warriors. The only elemental Inheritance lost to time was the metal element. The Inheritance of Death had moved almost a thousand years ago, and no known sightings had been heard about since.

The most frequently visited Inheritances were crafter-focused. The Inheritance of the Forge, for example, was the ultimate goal for most blacksmiths. Alchemists had the Inheritance of the Vial, and enchanters had the Inheritance of the Runemaster. Only those with ridiculous levels of luck and skill made it into the competitions that controlled those keystones. Although, there were tales of crafters that made a creation so perfect, so *extraordinary*, that the entrance to an Inheritance just showed up at their door. Such tales were often discounted as false, but no one could disprove them either.

The Inheritance of the Guide was based on the belief that you could ascend in cultivation based on the sheer amount of knowledge you could contain. It was a popular belief for those without the skills of a crafter or the heart of a warrior. It wasn't suited to my path, but I wouldn't just toss it aside. You never knew when knowledge could mean the difference between victory and defeat.

After memorizing the map of all the locations the Inheritance of the Guide could be found, I used a wisp of fire qi to burn it to ash. Then I was off to find my friends. It had only been a few hours. I was sure there was no way they could get into trouble in such a short period of time.

I made it the short distance back to the village before I heard the sound of people arguing. Picking up my pace, I managed to find the problem in only a few minutes. Of course, it had to be Chu.

"You made your last mistake today, kid! All I asked for was a discount, and you go and try to rob me like that? I don't think so!" The man yelling was clearly another of the sailors on the ship that had arrived. His clothing was along the same lines as Moose, except he was wearing a faded vest and had more earrings showing than ear. The sailor wasn't nearly as big as Moose, but he was no slouch. A life on the sea had given him plenty of muscle. He also had enough necklaces that their chains would probably work as impromptu armor for his neck and chest. The three men standing behind him were more of the same. All four of them were putting off the auras of Meridian cultivators.

"Rob you? I don't think so! I am already offering Basic and Common-level beast cores at a twenty-five percent discount, and you want more? No! Anything you buy from me will be at full price from now on!" Chu was definitely angry. So angry, in fact, that to most people he probably looked like someone that wasn't paying attention to the other three men slowly surrounding him and our carriage. The fact that he was doing his best to *not* look at them told me he was still in control.

"How about my friends and I just *take* what we want, and you get to live to see another sunset? Does that sound like a good idea?" None of the people watching spoke up against the blatant theft. After all, we were strangers. Why would they bother to stand up for us?

I moved to stand directly behind the leader of the group, so Chu could see me. As soon as he did, he turned his left hand a bit to show me he was holding a formation plate. I nodded and backed off. He could handle this. Chu finally took a hard look at the four people in a semicircle before him prior to answering.

"I don't want to kill you, but I will if you force my hand." All of them laughed at him. Even a few people in the crowd joined in the taunting. Chu just ignored them. "This is your only warning. You will die if you try to hurt me."

Huh. I really was wearing off on him.

The man wearing all the jewelry stopped laughing. He must have finally recognized that Chu wasn't the least bit afraid. Then he noticed that Chu was clearly holding something in his hand. The man took a step back and made a motion with his head to his friends.

"Fine. It wouldn't be polite to the village for us to stain the cobblestones with your blood. Some poor sap would have to clean up the mess. My boys and I will just take our business elsewhere." The four of them turned and walked away, occasionally shooting glances back at Chu that promised retribution. I was honestly surprised at the turn of events. I guess the leader of that little group had some finely-tuned survival instincts.

"Chu, where in the stars is Jamila? She is supposed to be helping to make sure things like this don't happen."

He gave me a chagrined smile. "She really wanted to bathe, so I told her I could handle it. Which I did. It wasn't really a big deal anyway. I could have handled those guys even without a formation plate." I nodded in agreement. He probably could have, given his ability to heal almost any injury at a speed even I found to be extreme, given his level.

"Okay. Let's go. I can tell you what happened to me while we walk." Chu pointed the way to the inn while I steered the horses and carriage, describing what had happened to me along the way. We worked our way through the crowded village and made it to the single-story building serving as the local inn just as I finished explaining the information on the slaver system that was infecting the empire.

"It sounds to me like we should drop off that information to the Elemental Guard." I opened my mouth to argue, but he cut me off. "I know how you feel about the emperor, but that doesn't mean that the entire policing force of the empire is corrupt. If we send out messages using the Auction House, it will ensure it spreads far and wide enough that even the corrupt members can't hide it."

I thought about it for a moment. It was worth trying, even if I didn't like it. I only had one major complaint. "What if, in sending it out to everyone, it somehow tips off their operation and they just go underground? Basically, the same problem we have if we were to just inform the kings about the *nox* using messengers. Without us there to prove the veracity of our claims, and ensure there aren't any possessed people alerted to our messages, they won't ever believe it."

Now it was Chu's turn to think it over. "How about this? We just send the information to the Southern Provincial King, since he already knows about us. He may hate you, but he knows you aren't a liar. If the information comes from him, they might actually do something about it. Speaking of that, do you think he told the other kings about the *nox*?"

I thought for a moment before answering. "He did, but who knows if it worked or not. That is why we have to go in person anyway. I have high hopes about the Northern Province government, but the East and West are more concerned about making deals and gaining power than actually funding excursions for their armies. Our mission is more about making sure they *act* against the dark mana demons. Not just informing them of their existence."

Chu nodded. "Sounds good, Jim." He was about to say something else, but we were interrupted by a stable boy coming out to help with the horses. I jumped down from the seat, and Chu climbed on top of the carriage. "We'll talk more later. You go on inside while I put everything in the carriage into some storage devices. I don't want to leave anything laying around that those sailors we ran into might steal."

I agreed with him before turning and heading inside the unique inn.

It was completely different from the roadside inn where we had fought and killed two cannibalistic humans taken over by *nox*. This one looked like it had started off as a shipwreck, and an enterprising carpenter had reassembled it into a rather impressive hybrid of boat and building. The reason I hadn't noticed it before was because the masts had been cut down and used as support beams to hold it upright, and the upper decks had been cannibalized to make a more even roof. From a distance, it just looked like an oversized single-story building with all the changes. Up close, the whole thing was rather impressive. A massive door had been cut out of the side, and it stood open to allow for patrons to be served at the bevy of outdoor tables and chairs planted in the sand. It made good use of the cool ocean breeze, and the smell of ale and cooked fish wafted out from the opening.

The outdoor tables were filled with sailors. Most of them looked like they were well on their journey to being drunk, which was impressive considering the amount of alcohol it takes to get a cultivator intoxicated. I pushed through the crowded tables and made my way inside to find everyone else.

I saw Donny sitting at a booth in the farthest corner from the door, while Valerie and Jamila were ordering drinks at the bar. Donny was absorbed in carving a design on a blank formation plate, so he didn't see me walk in. The inside was even more crowded than the outside, making it difficult for me to squeeze past. Which was why I wasn't close enough to help the girls when it all went sideways.

Both Valerie and Jamila were very beautiful girls. As such, they frequently got unwanted advances from men. It usually never went past a few words of warning and a growl or two from Donny or Chu. If you throw in a group—consisting mostly of men—that hadn't seen a woman in a while due to their time at sea, then mix in some potent alcohol, it was a recipe for disaster.

I heard the sound of a sailor slapping one of the girls on the butt, and then an outright fountain of blood cascaded over the bar area. Valerie somehow appeared on top of the bar holding her cleaver-like short sword in one hand, and a small bag I recognized as one we had used to store poppers in the other. She looked pissed, and the screams of the man that was now missing a hand seemed to suddenly be the only sounds in the entire place.

"I warned him not to touch me again!" Valerie's expression was colder than a mountain peak in the middle of winter-year. "Would anyone else like to learn the same lesson? Or is this warning enough for the rest of you?" The sailors seemed to be taken aback at first, but then a shout from one of the few female sailors in the group broke the silence.

"You think you can get away with hurting one of our crew?" Why was everyone answering a question with a question? And why was *that* the thing my brain was concerned about? "Let's get her!" With the female sailor's shout, the entire common room of the inn erupted into violence.

Jamila had jumped behind the bar Valerie was standing on, her dual katanas already swinging at the sailors trying to pull Valerie down. Valerie was making short, economical chops into the group suddenly pushing toward her. Each strike dropped someone, whether it was by splitting skulls or severing limbs, I couldn't tell. She was still holding on to the bag of poppers, probably as a last resort if she was about to be overrun.

Meanwhile, Donny was going full rage monster. As soon as

he saw the sailors trying to jump Valerie, he didn't bother to see who was actually involved in rushing the girls or not. He just started swinging around his axe like a tornado of death. A large portion of the sailors turned to face this new threat at their backs, reducing the pressure on Valerie and Jamila.

Since I was stuck by the door, I ended up crushed between the patrons trying to leave and the sailors from outside that were attempting to come to the aid of their friends being slaughtered.

Oddly enough, no one had bothered to use qi constructs to attack one another, yet. Until, that was, a very powerful cultivator that had been sitting at the outdoor tables unleashed a massive wave of wind qi that nearly knocked the entire inn on its side. A large section of the wall around the door was completely blown in, sending wooden splinters as shrapnel through the crowded common room.

I wasn't injured by the blast, as most of the sailors behind me soaked up the impact. Valerie, being on top of the bar, was blown back into the wall of shelves behind her. I was worried about her until I saw both Valerie and Jamila pop back up from behind the bar. Since Valerie was primarily a wind cultivator herself, the air attack didn't manage to affect her much.

The shouts and screams were finally drowned out by the voice of the man that had blown an opening into the side of the inn.

"*Enough!*" The man that stood a full head taller than the crowd was huge. If Moose had a big brother, this was the guy. He was probably close to seven feet tall, yet his giant slabs of muscle made sure he wasn't out of proportion. The bottom half of his face was covered in a massive beard of black hair, which matched the long hair that came out from the bottom of his tricorn hat. His clothes were a deep blue, and he had enough gold trim lining the shoulders and chest of his outfit that I had a hard time even seeing the fabric underneath. I would normally make fun of someone so pompous-looking, but his aura of a Sage-level cultivator made me hold my tongue. "What is going on?!" He pointed at a sailor still standing near the back of the melee. "You! Tell me what caused all of this."

"Cap'n Yon, was them girls over yonder." He pointed toward the bar. "Them's the ones tha' chopped off Smitty's hand, then everythin' wen' to the deeps!" The man, apparently the captain of the sailors that had been causing me problems since they arrived, looked at the girls.

"You are telling me that those two girls assaulted one of my men?"

The sailor furiously nodded up and down. "An' that one over there, Cap'n. He done it too!" He pointed to Donny, who had been backed into the corner by the men facing him. Looking around, it appeared as if Donny had taken out well over half a dozen sailors. In fact, there were less than twenty sailors still standing after the explosion caused by the captain. At least twenty more lay on the floor, groaning in pain or completely still in death. Not a bad showing for one man with an axe and two young women only using short swords.

"The crime for killing a member of my crew is punishable by death. The sentence will be carried out immediately. Men, grab them and take the three to the city square." They shouted in glee and tried to renew the assault on my friends. Since I disagreed with his ruling, I decided it was time to end this.

I had been using my qi extensively the last few hours, so I would have to make this fast. I formed twenty qi threads the thickness of a strand of hair, and used them to pull free the same number of throwing knives on my vest. It held a total of twenty-four knives and two fighting daggers in sheathes that lined the front, back, and sides. I left the four throwing knives that protected my chest, and the daggers that ran vertically along my ribs. The rest were whipped into the bodies of the sailors still on their feet. I had been practicing for a while now, which meant I didn't miss a single throw. Each knife was thrown with enough momentum that they made a sound like a tree limb cracking in two. None of the sailors inside the inn were still on their feet. In fact, the only people still standing were the handful of patrons that weren't sailors, and my friends and I. The loud noise made the captain turn around to see what had happened. I stepped forward to speak to him.

"You aren't on your ship, so your rules are not the law. I recommend you gather what crew you have remaining and return to your vessel, before you don't have enough crew remaining to keep her afloat." Instead of the captain raging in anger like I expected, he simply stared at me and released his hold over his cores. His aura was now attempting to push down on everyone in the area, making those still sitting at the tables outside fall to their knees. I simply sharpened my own aura, causing his to wash around me like a river flowing around a rock. My friends did the same, allowing them to come closer and stand in a line behind me.

Valerie finally broke the silence. "Your sailor tried to assault me, so I merely showed him the error of his ways. The rest of your crew tried to attack me in retribution, and it didn't turn out the way they planned." She waved her hand, indicating the nearly forty men lying on the ground behind her. "I wouldn't recommend making the same mistake they did."

"Mistake?" The captain once again took control of his aura, allowing those around him to finally breathe again. "You are the ones who have made a mistake. I will take my wounded out of here, and gather my crew to set sail. But if we ever see you again…" He left the threat open-ended, the fury in his eyes telling us all we needed to know.

I was already pulling free the twenty throwing knives with my qi strands, getting ready to throw them at the captain as soon as he made his move.

Donny put his hand on my shoulder to stop me. "I know your rule about never letting an enemy live, but it would be best to let him go." He looked back at the destruction caused by the captain's wind qi attack. "This village wouldn't survive the fight between us and his entire crew. We don't even know how many of them there are right now. No sense in making this worse."

I nodded in agreement, and we all stepped aside as the

sailors from outside came in to collect their dead and wounded compatriots. We all watched from the hole in the wall as they left, following their captain down the long pier toward their ship.

"My inn! My poor, poor inn! What have you done?!" We were interrupted by a small man wearing a spotless white apron. "Who is going to pay for this mess?!"

That was when Chu finally showed up. "Wow. What did you guys do?" Chu was looking around at the streaks of blood and shattered wall. "It looks like you had quite the party!"

CHAPTER SEVEN

Catching a Ride

We ended up having to stay at the inn for two days. While we could have just left the mess for the innkeeper to deal with, having some extra time to rest and sell off what goods we could manage was time well spent.

Donny and Valerie focused on fixing the inn, while Chu and Jamila sold everything they could. I used the time to make us each a more subtle set of armor. Our current set used a blood-red leather reinforced with qi-resistant chitin we had harvested from a massive scorpion beast. Everyone was still coming up with designs on a more robust set, so I was doing my best to make something less flashy in the meantime.

Since we would be riding on the ocean, it would need to be something we could take off quickly in case anyone went overboard. Being dragged to the bottom of the ocean because of some heavy pauldrons wasn't a good idea. It would be better if I could make it look like we weren't even wearing armor at all, allowing us to blend in with just about any group we came across. Anyone thinking to fight us would get quite a shock once they realized we were already armored and ready for battle.

To make a set of armor like that, I needed to be able to

cover the armor in cloth. The plates underneath would need to be incredibly thin, meaning I needed to use a type of metal that could easily hold its shape, despite being so limited in thickness. Thankfully, I had just the thing.

A few years back I had destroyed a temple that had been intended to open a doorway between our world and another. The other world was filled with creatures even the *nox* had feared, meaning it was a bad, *bad* place. Blowing it up had literally been a mission from the gods. While carrying out their will, I had found several ingots of an oily metal I had never seen before, but later found out was called adamantine. It was practically indestructible, and no one, to my knowledge, had figured out a way to shape it. Miners considered it junk metal, and threw it away with the other slag during the smelting process. I knew better. The ancient culture that had built the dark temple had figured out a way, given the odd scepter of the metal that I had found, along with the shaped ingots. If they could do it, I could as well.

It had taken me hundreds of experiments—and a few years —to finally figure out how to manipulate it. The secret was light and dark qi. Light qi, when concentrated on the same spot over time, could heat things up even more than the most condensed fire qi could manage. That made the metal so hot that using a simple blacksmith's hammer and anvil was impossible. They would just deform and melt themselves, making it impossible to shape the metal into anything other than a melted blob. Also, fun side-note, it could cause some pretty serious fires if it got away from you. But *I* wouldn't know anything about that…

A few experiments later, I realized that dark qi could hold its form when exposed to the extreme temperatures created by the light qi. Unfortunately, I wasn't able to build a stable structure out of dark qi alone. Which was why I had begun combining it with other elements, such as earth qi. Hence the obsidian-like threads of stone I had used to take care of Silas and Moose.

This would be the culmination of all that work. All I needed to do was make molds of the shapes I wanted, and then drop the superheated metal inside them to cool. Since I only had a short time, I went with a type of armor based on the old brigandine style. Basically, I just needed to make a bunch of small rectangles, and then layer them into the final shape I wanted. Almost like the leather vest reinforced by the throwing knives I already used.

The final product would be a canvas vest that covered the most important parts, and a pair of canvas pants that would require a thick belt to hold them up. It wouldn't be the most fashionable clothing, but it would protect everyone without anyone knowing we were practically invincible. Well, besides the threat of removing our arms and heads. That would still work. Maybe I should make us hats? Or really thin helmets?

While pondering that problem, I made the molds using the earth and dark qi blend. I made sure to set up farther down the beach, just in case things didn't work as I planned. While making them, I decided to include a rune that would leave a faint impression in each piece, as well as a tiny hole in each corner I could run a rivet pin through to hold them together. If I could set the runes in the proper series inside the clothing, it could give me all kinds of interesting combinations. To ensure I had a wide variety of options, I ended up making twenty different molds, each about two inches by three inches. I also made a mold for the pins and backing pieces to hold it all together, in a homemade rivet-style thing. Fiddly-bits were always annoying.

The next step was to shape a bucket that would hold the molten metal I would pour inside the molds. I made sure it was thick enough to handle the extreme heat, and formed a spout and handle to make it easy to pour. The last thing I made was a lid, to help keep the heat even. Looking everything over, I was as ready as I could be.

I dropped in six ingots and started pumping light qi into the bucket. I made sure to use the same meridians that had been manipulating dark qi, in order to keep the wear and tear on my body even. Balance was extremely important, and the gods had warned me that there would be consequences for not using dark and light qi evenly throughout my cultivation system. Ignoring a warning straight from the gods didn't seem like a good idea.

Trial and error had shown me it was best to use a slow trickle of condensed light qi as opposed to a giant wave of energy. That meant it took well over an hour to completely melt the ingots. I used the clawed scepter from the dark temple as a stir stick. For some unknown reason, it didn't react to the heat or light qi in the same way as the metal in ingot form. Probably had something to do with the swirling runes carved in the sides. Or maybe the sacrifices used to make it. My efforts at translation of the strange language were still ongoing. I hadn't given it as much time as I should have, but there were only so many hours in the day.

The heat the bucket was giving off was extreme, making my qi-reinforced skin sweat more than it had in months. It didn't help that the constant use of qi was starting to wear on me. I might have been getting stronger, but I still had my limits. I quickly poured the molten metal in the molds, doing my best to keep it as even as possible. Without light qi being forced into it, the metal hardened almost instantly. I used some qi threads to flip the molds over and pour in the next set. There was enough metal left for nine more sets, giving me an even two hundred rectangles to work with. I made enough rivet pins to hold it all together. Hopefully, it worked like intended. I didn't relish the idea of figuring out a way to stretch wire from the hard-to-work metal.

Not every rectangle was the exact same thickness due to my crude pouring method, but they were all pretty close to one sixteenth of an inch thick. If it were a normal metal, it wouldn't be enough to stop anything more violent than a particularly angry mosquito. Since I was using adamantine, it might as well be inch-thick steel. The only downside was the odd oily feeling the metal had when you touched it. It wasn't actually secreting oil, it just *felt* like it.

Since I was turning this into a cloth-covered armor, it

wouldn't be in direct contact with our skin. Otherwise, no one would be able to stand wearing it for very long. No matter the benefits, a person could only handle the strange feeling for so long before it became incredibly irritating. Definitely a weird metal.

Next, I arranged the armor into the rune patterns I thought would benefit everyone the most. Since the runes weren't actually touching, I couldn't make anything too complicated. For Chu and Donny, our front-line fighters, I arranged the runes to allow force to be evenly distributed across the entire piece of armor. Piercing attacks would be drastically blunted, and blunt attacks would be spread out to reduce their impact. It wouldn't stop an overwhelmingly powerful attack, but my guess was anything less than a direct hit from a High Sage wouldn't penetrate.

For Jamila, I went with a pattern that would direct qi around her body. She would be able to walk right through a qi shield, and a qi construct would lose cohesion as soon as it touched her armor. Things like heat and cold would still affect her, but it wouldn't be concentrated, reducing the damage it could do. It was perfect for her style of ambush fighting.

Valerie was the hardest one to figure out. Given the runes I had chosen, the only pattern that really suited her job as our archer was a slight speed increase. It basically reduced wind resistance, making her a tiny bit faster. It would also make manipulating air qi easier for her, giving her arrows a longer range, along with a boost to her accuracy. I wanted to give her the same benefits as Jamila, but I couldn't manage both. The armor was already tough, so the boost to offense was what I decided to go with.

My armor design was different. Instead of directing qi away from me, I did the reverse. It meant any qi attacks would be drawn toward me, but I could disrupt almost any attack with the precise use of qi threads. The specific benefit I was aiming for was what the armor would do *outside* the battlefield. I could refill my cores at an increased rate, and the pattern I used ensured the focus would be on an even balance of all elements, even dark and light qi. I needed to speed up my cultivation rate to reach Saint, and this was the best way to manage it without using alchemy.

I knew several recipes for alchemy pills that would help, but the ingredients for the formula were found in the mountain ranges far to the north. Not much help to a guy stuck at the farthest southern tip of the Empire.

By now, it was almost lunch. I used the pins to fasten the armor plates together in their proper patterns, and then took a break to eat. Collecting up everything into one of the storage studs on my belt only took a few minutes, and I made it back to the inn before the sun reached its zenith in the sky.

When I arrived, I sat at an outdoor table and finally took a look at what was inside the storage rings I had taken off of Silas and Moose. Moose had stored a massive amount of food in his ring. I guess he wanted to make sure he never went without a meal. Along with a coin purse that was filled with silver, there was an odd assortment of jewelry and other small items of value. None of them would have been able to fit the big man, and it took me a minute to figure out I was holding the items Moose must have taken off of the slaves he had 'broken' for Silas. It made me want to kill the bastard all over again. I emptied the ring into my belt and put it away.

Silas had hoarded gold, not food. Given the size and proportions of the dead man, the irony of Moose being the one with all the meals wasn't lost on me. I shifted all the gold into my designated storage stud that held all my money, and then looked at what was left. A few changes of clothes, an enchanted dagger with a qi matrix that gave it a fire aspect, and several dozen shackles made from red orichalcum. Intended to hold slaves. The last item was a thick ledger. I emptied everything from the ring and put it with the other storage ring in a plain pouch hanging from my belt. I would have to see if my friends wanted them, otherwise I would just give them to Chu to sell for me. I pulled out the ledger to look over as I finished the lunch brought to me by the proprietor.

The ledger was an account of all the people Silas had sold. Most of the names were from small clans I had never heard of, with only the occasional big-name prisoner. The majority of those must have been ransomed, given the amounts written in the ledger next to their names and the blank space left in the purchase column. The prisoners from small clans had mostly been sold to the northern mining sects. I only knew this because of what Moose had told me. Silas had only used initials for the names of the buyers, but most of those lined up with what I knew of the north. For example, the buyer DMS had to be the Deep Mining Sect. Another, HDS, was probably the Hidden Depths Sect. Both were in direct competition with each other, and made up the majority of slave purchases. I wasn't sure how yet, but I was going to absolutely destroy those sects.

The section of the ledger I was having trouble with was the center column. It was marked shipping, but nothing made sense. There were numbers, letters, and even arrows pointing in various directions. It would take some time with the materials I had gathered from Moose to start trying to unfurl the mystery. My to-do list never seemed to get smaller.

A recurring theme that I was able to figure out, however, were the initials at the end of over half of the odd lines of text. CY. That *had* to be Captain Yon. I stupidly let the man slip from my grasp, allowing one of these slavers to continue his nefarious deeds. Next time, he wouldn't be so lucky.

The thing that was bothering me the most was how extensive this ring was. It didn't match with my knowledge of the future whatsoever. There shouldn't be *any* slaver rings this large in the region at this point in time, and I had already run across *two*. I looked back in the ledger, trying to see if there were any clues as to why they were so active. I didn't see anything at first, the only patterns being tied to their ability to ship people to their buyers. Until I looked at the date on the very first page of the ledger. It was only a few days after my birthday, a few years ago. Specifically, it was only a few days after my reincarnation. Meaning this group of slavers was created only *days* after the invasion of the *nox*. A sinking feeling hit me hard.

Pulling out the documents from the first ring of slavers, I looked at the dates of the oldest documents. It was the same thing. The first date written at the top of their books was less than a month from the invasion date. The connection *might* be a coincidence, but it didn't feel like it to me. They were related, which meant there was a ringleader organizing these groups. Finding that person wasn't necessary for my mission of stopping the *nox*. It was most *definitely* necessary for me to find and stop them if I wanted to sleep at night. After discovering this, I couldn't let it go. I would keep my eyes and ears open for opportunities to provide justice to those who had been wronged.

I finished up my lunch and checked up on Donny and Valerie. The repairs were almost complete, and both of them seemed to have made friends with the owner. I left them to their work to see how Chu and Jamila were getting along, which was where I ran into a problem. As soon as I left the inn, I noticed someone was following me.

They were doing a good job of staying out of sight, but their aura control was awful. I was almost to the center of the village before I actually noticed that the same aura kept appearing behind me. It was someone close to the same level as I was, meaning they were either a High or Peak Brain cultivator. Not someone I was particularly worried about, so I decided to lead them on a little adventure.

I skirted the edge of the village square, stopping at a textile shop to buy some silk for the lining of the brigandine armor I was making. If we were going to wear it, I might as well make it comfortable. I also added a thick linen and canvas blend for the outer material, making it durable without being too rough. It wouldn't be self-cleaning like the clothes we were currently wearing, but I would do the best I could.

The longer I was being followed, the more I started to think they weren't actually hostile. I gave them a chance to attack when I swung back through a dark alley, even stopping and bending over to check my boots. They just stayed near the entrance of the alley, giving up a perfect opportunity to strike.

Giving up on figuring it out, I just headed back to the beach to finish the armor. If Chu or Jamila were in trouble, I would just follow the explosions.

The watcher had to stay farther back, since the flat beach didn't give them a place to hide. They were barely at the far limit of my ability to feel their aura, right at the edge of the village. Guessing it to be a spy, I simply dropped a few trap plates around me and got back to work.

Since the adamantine was already hardened, I couldn't shape any of the small plates. It required me to overlap a few sections to get it to fit, but I ended up avoiding any gaps in the armor over the most vital areas. This type of armor obviously required a fair bit of sewing. Luckily, I was able to manage. My time in the Elemental Guard had plenty of rough spots, requiring me to make repairs on my issued uniforms. I was no stranger to needle and thread.

The final products were an ivory-colored vest and a pair of dark green trousers. I had to use my traveling forge to make some belt buckles to go with the thick strips of leather the heavy trousers required. I decided to use four spare storage rings I had, freeing up some space in the pouch hanging from my belt. Riveting them in place inside the leather fold holding the buckle, they would give my friends their own hidden storage spaces. It would be noticed in a thorough inspection, but a cursory one by a regular gate guard or pickpocket might not catch the hidden storage device.

As I finished and put my forge away, I stored everything I had been working on inside one of the belt studs only I could access. Since I was out on the beach, I had already stored most of my everyday items inside my belt. Considering the heat, I even took off my armor vest and stored it with the new armor. Just because it was old didn't mean it wasn't still useful. The only items in the three copper studs others could see were simple camping supplies, along with a small coin purse. The storage ring on my finger opposite my spirit wood ring was mostly filled with feed for the horses, along with a few convenient formation plates.

I didn't know why I was being so cautious. Maybe it was the gods warning me to be careful? In the end, it didn't matter. Some instinct was telling me to keep my items safe, and I wasn't going to ignore it.

As I picked up my trap plates, I realized I could no longer feel the person that had been following me. They must have given up after watching me work on belts for a while. Oh well, so be it. I would just have to pay close attention to my surroundings until I got to the bottom of the mystery.

I made it back to the inn just before sundown, and all five of us sat at the farthest outdoor table from the newly repaired inn as we ate our evening meal. It was another variation of some kind of fish stew, but given the location I wasn't surprised. I *was* surprised the innkeeper sat us so far from the door to the building, but maybe he was just trying to give us some privacy. In fact, this table seemed to be particularly far away. I was about to ask the others if they remembered anyone sitting this far away before the place was wrecked, but Chu interrupted my train of thought.

"The repairs you did look good." Chu was looking at Donny and Valerie. "You wouldn't even be able to tell it had ever been damaged."

Donny finished his mouthful of food before answering. "Yeah, getting the weathered look on the fresh lumber wasn't easy, but Valerie figured out a way to make it look worn." She blushed a bit from the praise, eating more fish stew instead of answering. "We even carved a few wards throughout the place to help protect it from any big storms that might come through. Nothing serious, but it should help hold it together."

"I think this place could use a bunch more runes and formations." Chu was rummaging through his things, trying to find something. "In fact, a group of people came by and bought every single formation plate we had in stock." He finally found what he was looking for, placing a fist-sized garnet on the table in front of everyone. "They even traded us *this* for all the copper plates we normally keep for ourselves! Can you believe it? This thing is probably worth a fortune!"

"That was still stupid, Chu." Jamila was giving Chu the 'I'm-going-to-beat-you-for-not-listening-to-me' look. She was pretty good at it. "Selling our personal defense formations was a bad idea. If they wanted them so bad, you could have just had Jim or Donny make them some of their own. I feel naked without all our tools."

I nodded my head in agreement. So did everyone else.

"She's right, Chu. Some of those designs aren't meant for anyone else to see. Who knows if they could figure out how to replicate some of those traps?" I tapped my ring and pulled out a particularly nasty design that launched some barbed ice spears at waist height against anyone that triggered it. "Something like this could change the way wars are fought."

Chu held up his hands in surrender. "Look, I know which plates are safe to sell. I still have all of the formations we need to keep to ourselves. Most of what I sold were just defensive shields and a few of the nonlethal dome traps. Nothing they could copy would drastically affect the empire."

I let out a sigh of relief. Then I remembered the new belts I had made everyone. I pulled them free and passed them around, along with the new armor.

"That reminds me. Soon we will be going through the more crowded coastal cities. Most of them are filled to the brim with criminals and pickpockets. Right now, our armor marks us as someone worth trying to rob." I held up the cloth armor. "This will help us blend in. And the belts are even better. Everyone try these on first, and then I will show you."

They complied, everyone just putting on the new clothes over the top of our always-clean shirt and pants. The vest looked good with our dark blue shirts on underneath, but the two pairs of pants made them look bulky. Oh well, we could finish changing when we had some privacy. I briefly covered the benefits everyone's specific armor could provide, then leaned forward to whisper the last bit of information. "If you look in the loop holding the buckle on the belt, you will see a hidden storage ring. Everyone, make a blood bond with your new ring and put anything you want safe inside it. Especially any treasures, weapons, armor, and all the rune patterns we want to keep secret. If we do it now, we won't forget about it later."

Everyone was excited about the secret armor, and they surreptitiously transferred their items into their hidden rings. Chu took special pleasure in putting the giant garnet in last. It would probably allow him to buy a palace in any city he wished, so I didn't particularly blame the guy. Just as we were discussing how to practice using the benefits of our new armor, a commotion from the men sitting far out on the end of the pier drew our attention.

Silhouetted by the last rays of light from the setting sun, a ship was just visible in the distance. We quickly finished our meal, none of us wanting to get caught up in another fight with visiting sailors. I was feeling particularly tired, and turning in for the night sounded like a good idea. Just before we got up from the table, the innkeeper came over to see how we were doing.

"How are my favorite customers doing? Ready for another round?" His spotless white apron seemed to match his perfectly white smile. I hadn't noticed before, but it came across as patronizing instead of friendly.

"No, good sir. I think we are all ready to end our evening early." Donny tried to rise, but instead fell face-first into the sand. Valerie got up to check on him, but she ended up just flopping on top of Donny. I looked over to see Chu already passed out with his face in his empty bowl of stew. When did that happen? Jamila was on her feet, reaching for her katanas at her waist. They weren't there, of course. We had just got done hiding all of our things inside our belts. She dropped to one knee, doing her level best to stay upright.

"What have you done?" My words were slurred, and what

came out sounded something like 'Muth ave yu dun?' but he got the point.

"You stupid kids think you can just show up and mess up my place of business? Kill my best customers? I can't wait for Captain Yon to get here. He is going to give you a free ride straight to hell!" He turned to look at Jamila, who had finally fallen to the ground with a thump.

My vision was blurred, and my limbs were heavy. I was still able to angle the hand with my spirit wood ring toward the man who had set us up. When I activated the spear function of the ring, I couldn't reinforce it with any additional qi to extend its length.

It didn't matter. The spear's rapid expansion took him in the temple, dropping the man instantly.

"You can save me a seat in hell, asshole." Well, at least that's what I tried to say. Instead, the motion of the spear springing back into a ring around my finger made me tip backwards off of my stool. I never even felt myself hit the ground.

CHAPTER EIGHT

New Priorities

A boot to the ribs was what eventually woke me up. My eyes snapped open, and instinct helped me catch the next kick aimed at my midsection. I grabbed my attacker behind the ankle and knee, rolling away from them without letting go. They weren't expecting the move, causing them to fall forward halfway on top of me. I struck hard, smashing my elbow into their exposed throat.

The unfamiliar person gagged, the crunching sound of their collapsing windpipe instantly making them panic. Instead of fighting me, they grabbed at their throat. This gave me a great opening for a double eye gouge, so I drove both thumbs through the soft jelly of their eyeballs, popping them like overripe grapes. They tried to scream, but no sound could get past the collapsed airway. I shoved their destroyed face away, forcing them off of me. They fell in a heap, allowing me to jump to my feet, bumping my head on the low ceiling. Without pause, I stomped down as hard as I could on their head, over and over again until I felt the skull weaken and then give way. The smell of voided bowels let me know they were dead. The whole attack only lasted seconds, but the suddenness of it had me breathing hard. Finally, I looked around to try to figure out where I was, and what was going on.

The first things I noticed were the metal chain and shackle wrapped around my left ankle, anchored into a wooden wall. Next was the rolling motion that made me stumble. I was onboard a ship. That was when I remembered what had happened. For some reason, I had terrible luck with innkeepers. I must have been captured, and Captain Yon was taking me somewhere.

My situation wasn't the greatest. I was chained with a shackle of orichalcum, cutting off my ability to use qi. That was probably what gave the man at my feet the courage to kick me. The plate of spilled food at my feet explained his presence. He had come to feed the prisoner. If that was the case, Yon had plans to keep me alive for some reason. Probably to sell me. We would have to see about that.

Taking stock of my items, I realized I was still wearing my clothing that contained the hidden brigandine armor. It had probably saved me from some broken ribs. They had taken my rings and my belt, but my blood connection wasn't broken yet. I could feel they were stationary somewhere above me. I was also very lucky that they hadn't taken off the pants that had my wooden healing talisman which was my homemade substitute for a focusing stone. It was doing its job, already making any pains begin to fade away.

I searched the body at my feet, looking for a key to unlock my shackles. There was a keyring on his belt, but it only had a single key. A key that, of course, didn't fit my shackles. It was probably for the door to the room I was in. The room wasn't square, having a slight curve toward the bottom of the walls, with a ridiculously low ceiling that forced me to hunch over. That meant I was probably on a lower level of the ship. Looking at everything, I noticed that the door was made from narrow slats of wood, as if scraps left over from making the actual ship were just slapped together to create a makeshift barrier. If the rest of the ship was this shoddy, it was a miracle we weren't on the bottom.

My first priority was getting these shackles off. Taking a closer look at it, I let out a sigh of relief. These people were cheap. The small metal lock holding the shackles in place was plain iron. No orichalcum to slow me down.

Second priority was finding my friends. Third would be finding the slaver captain and removing him from the breeding pool. One way or another.

Cracking open the door, I saw a narrow hallway lined with doors. The chain around my ankle wouldn't let me do more than just peek my head out, but it was enough to get a better idea of where I was. I had seen a smuggler's ship before, and that was exactly what this was. The thick ceiling above my head was actually the floor of the ship's hold. The bilge had been expanded and converted into a space for sneaking humans into major ports that used inspection teams. A quick visual inspection revealed a few weak barrier runes, intended to keep the shouts and cries of the prisoners from reaching the ears of those above. What a bunch of human vultures these people were turning out to be.

Not being able to do anything further, I closed the door. Since I didn't have a key, I needed to get my shackle off another way. The *hard* way. Well, I supposed chewing my foot off would be worse, but this was about to hurt just as much.

In my first life, I had served Ming in the Elemental Guard for over fifty years before being promoted to Enforcer. While the Elemental Guard was basically the personal army of the emperor, an Enforcer was an extension of his will. That meant all kinds of things.

Missions could include simply serving as a bodyguard for a favorite concubine, be as difficult as assassinating a threatening rival, as tedious as serving as a judge during trials of law or cultivation competitions, or as complicated as pretending to work as a laborer in a shipping plant in order to secretly gather information. It required Enforcers to be trained to the highest standard possible, in as many areas as deemed necessary. I had served as an Enforcer for many centuries of my life, and a good portion of that time had been focused on training and growing my cultivation base to increase my strength. That was how I had become immune to most poisons, put to use what I had learned in the Inheritance for managing an intelligence-gathering organization, lead troops into battle, and the ability to withstand the most merciless of torture. There was also an incredibly large focus on learning how to escape capture, which included the training I was about to use. Channeling through the restrictions caused by orichalcum.

Before I got started, I moved the body of the jailer to the corner farthest away from me. Dead bodies didn't smell good, and this one was no exception. I tried to angle it so anyone trying to enter the room would have trouble opening the door, but even a weak cultivator would be able to just smash through the flimsy excuse of a wooden panel masquerading as a door. At least it would give me a few moments to react.

I sat down and assumed the lotus position, the shackle forcing me to adjust for a few minutes to get comfortable. It was annoying, and I made a promise to myself to stop getting myself into these situations. And to stop trusting gods-be-damned innkeepers.

The trick to cultivating when orichalcum was touching your skin was to force qi out of your meridians in powerful bursts of energy. Most didn't know this, because no sane person would ever try this method. It put a massive strain on your meridians, risking a rupture of the meridian walls. That was an injury every cultivator knew to avoid at all costs.

The technique also made it impossible to do anything but concentrate on what you were doing. Hence the need to sit and meditate to get it to work. I slowed my breathing, focusing on the qi stored in my lower core. Starting slowly, I began to spin the concentrated liquid energy. To my mind's eye, it was thick and viscous. Like trying to stir a vat of honey. Normally the qi in my core was always in motion, my training making it as involuntary as breathing. It ensured I was prepared to use my qi all the time, no matter what stage of advancement I was in. Since I had been drugged, and then shackled with orichalcum, it was a testament to how far out of normal my body's rhythms had been disrupted.

Once the qi was spinning smoothly, I spun it up into my central core. As soon as the stagnant qi inside my heart core came in contact with the qi from my lower core, it began to copy the spinning motion. After a few minutes it was time to move it into my upper core, the qi inside it reacting faster now that the rest of my cultivation system was coming back to life. Finally, I had my qi circulating throughout my entire body, the energy inside my cores humming with power.

The feeling was like the moment when your sinuses clear after having a stuffed-up nose. I could finally *breathe*, and I couldn't stop the involuntary stretch that helped loosen up the knots in my muscles I didn't even know I had.

Now that things were working normally, I started to focus on the meridian in my left foot. I needed to force out a blade of metal qi that could slice through the lock holding the shackle together. It was a simple qi construct to form, which was important given the circumstances. I didn't want to use the meridians in my hands, because any ruptures there would drastically hinder my normal combat style. That would definitely be a 'Bad Thing,' considering I was currently surrounded by enemies.

I shifted almost a quarter of the qi from my cores into my leg meridians, forcing them to take the strain. It was uncomfortable, like stretching a joint to its limit. Knowing it would only get worse, I then moved the qi from both legs into just the left leg. Now it felt like the proverbial joint had slipped out of socket, and the circulating power was similar to grinding a dislocated limb in massive circles of agony. Breathing through the pain, I was just doing my best to concentrate. On the bright side, my meridian had held together so far. No ruptures yet, which was a good sign.

After arranging the qi into the necessary pattern, I then shoved as hard as I could toward the meridian opening on my foot, aiming at the arching hasp of the small lock. The pressure from the orichalcum contact on my skin was like water pushing up against a dam. Instead of trying to knock the whole dam over, I focused all that pressure into a single point. It worked.

The diminishing effect of the orichalcum meant the metal qi blade was only a fraction of the size it should have been, but it was enough. The impact sliced through the hasp, causing the lock to fall to the wooden floor. I did my best to contain the shout of pain that came with it, but a quiet groan escaped my lips anyway.

Inspecting my meridian, it definitely looked a little frayed at the end. It resembled a piece of worn cloth, showing the simple pattern that held it together. I hadn't blown it out completely, but using it for anything other than drawing in qi was simply not acceptable. One more jolt, and it might break. I needed to be careful.

Freeing myself from the chains, I finally had a chance to move out of my room. It was easy to see in the hallway due to the row of dim glow stones, letting me finally get a better look at the man I had killed. It was hard to tell given how deformed he now looked, but I was pretty sure it was one of the men that had tried to surround Chu back in the market. Not the ringleader, but definitely one of the hangers-on that tried to help.

There were twenty doors lining the narrow hallway, each one with a scrap of parchment nailed to it. I looked at mine, which only read 'mines—20g.' The door across from me said 'fighting pits—35g.' I didn't open the door, deciding to secure the hatch leading down to the area first. If someone was going to come see what was taking the dead guy so long to come back, I wanted to make sure they couldn't just walk in and surprise me. I was at the end of the hall, so I checked the notes on the other doors as I made my way to the ladder at the opposite end.

The next three scraps said the same as mine, with varying amounts for the numbers. I was pretty sure the 'g' at the end meant gold. These bastards already had a price listed for each of us! I was going to enjoy what I was about to do to them.

Moving on, the other doors had various vocations listed. Farmer, servant, and miner were the most common. A few just had a coin amount listed, with only a few gold as the amount shown. The last four doors, the ones closest to the ladder leading up, were the most troubling. One had a messy 'R—5,000g,' and the other three were listed as 'PS—150g.' They were the highest amounts listed, and what I could deduce from their meaning had me spitting mad. Ransom and Pleasure Slave. I was going to feed these bags of human waste their own entrails.

Finally, I reached the ladder leading upwards and saw the hatch at the top. It was solid iron laced with orichalcum, making it the sturdiest thing on this ship I had seen so far. Besides the chains. Obviously, it was intended to keep any possible prison escapes from getting any farther than the hidden compartment. I tried to use the key from the dead slaver to open it, but the key wasn't a match. That was okay. I could work with this.

Since I wanted to be the one controlling who came in and out, I used a thread of fire qi to weld the heavy iron hatch in place. The orichalcum made it almost impossible to affect it with qi, but these pirate slavers were *exceedingly* cheap. They forgot about the hinge pins. I mean, to be fair, the cost of orichalcum hinge pins probably seemed excessive, especially after paying a bunch of gold for the actual hinges. Still, it was a mistake. A few careful adjustments, and they wouldn't be opening this hatch without someone putting in a *lot* of effort. They probably wouldn't even know what had happened for a long time, giving me a chance to organize the other slaves. Potential slaves? Let's go with prisoners. Yeah. We weren't sold yet, after all.

The first door I opened was the one with the 'R' on the

front. Considering the size of the ransom, I was expecting a distinguished member of a powerful clan. Possibly an important member of a sect council, or even the wife of a successful merchant. What I was not expecting was a baby.

Inside the room, a makeshift crib was nailed in place against the far wall. On the floor, a pirate was sitting up from a bare mattress that was laid out in the corner. He was missing his right hand, the stump covered in a dirty bandage. His greasy hair and limp beard matched the description that Valerie had given me of the man that had slapped her on the butt while she stood at the bar. His missing hand confirmed it for me. If I remembered correctly, one of his friends had called him 'Smitty.'

"About time you made it back! I was supposed to be replaced an hour ago. The brat just stopped squalling a few minutes before you got here. I still say we throw the thing overboard. It isn't worth…" His words died off, the confused look on his face meaning he finally realized I wasn't the person he was expecting. "Wait, aren't you one of those kids we went back and snatched? What are you doing out of your cell?!" The qi thread I speared into his guts stopped his questions. He opened his mouth to scream, but a quick step into the room and a swift uppercut stopped that from happening.

"I am so incredibly *happy* to see you, Smitty." I spun a dozen more threads around him, holding the man in place and wrapping one around his throat to keep him from screaming. "I have a few questions for you, and you are going to answer them. The more honest with me you are, the less this has to hurt." I twirled the thread in his guts in a circle, and his muffled screams woke the baby. It started crying, so I went over to pick the child up. It quieted down almost immediately, my past experience with my own children coming in handy. "You woke the child. That wasn't nice. I would recommend you try to keep it down. Like I said, the harder you make this, the longer the process takes." I rolled the qi thread in his belly the other direction, but this time he only whimpered. "Good. I'm glad you understand." I rocked the child to sleep and placed it back inside the crib. This time, I dragged the man out into the hallway before continuing. "Now, where were we? Ah! I remember…"

The questioning took longer than I expected. Smitty had a lot to tell me, and some new information he provided had me questioning my plans. Chief among those issues was how I would handle the situation we were in.

I hadn't been knocked out for a few hours. I had been unconscious for a *week*. My friends had all awakened days ago, but for some reason the poison they had used worked exceptionally well on me. Considering the amateurish vibe I was getting from these people, it might just be a miracle I was still alive. A miracle, or a small wooden talisman that constantly sent a trickle of life qi into me. Didn't matter which.

The week of time that had passed by meant we were farther out to sea than I had expected. My long life had given me many skills, but sailing was not one of them. I had no idea how to get us back to land, or how to manage the crew for months at a time. Don't get me wrong, I could lead people. But I had enough experience to know that operating something as complicated as a sailing vessel was not the same as holding a village against a beast wave. That was like comparing apples to anvils. One mistake out at sea, and no one would survive the aftermath.

Another important issue was the baby. The scraps of flesh at my feet formerly known as the 'handsy slaver' had told me the child belonged to a powerful woman in the Feng Clan. The same clan that were the founders and controlling members of the Auction House. I had a complicated relationship with them, mostly due to my lack of understanding as to my position as a 'Friend to the House.' I was pretty sure it was a good thing, but the bond that tied me to their organization had been forced upon me. Either way, I now had a responsibility to get the child to the nearest branch of the Auction House. I wasn't the type of person to ignore a kidnapped child, even if I still didn't trust the family they came from.

So, now I had a different set of tasks, and time was running out. It wouldn't be long until someone noticed the two people I had already killed had gone missing. If there wasn't a member of the prisoners that knew how to sail a ship, we were in serious trouble. I needed to find out who I was dealing with down here, and then it would be time to make a plan.

CHAPTER NINE

A Distasteful Deal

I walked down the hall, opening doors as I went. I only spared the people inside a quick glance before moving on, focusing primarily on finding my friends. I eventually found them back near the end, close to where I had been held. Donny had been in the room marked as a fighter, while the rest of us were marked as miners. I couldn't help but wonder why Valerie and Jamila hadn't been marked with the 'PS,' considering their looks. Maybe it was their cultivation level?

Our reunion was unfortunately interrupted. After unshackling my friends, the rest were clamoring for release. If it weren't for the runes carved on the ceiling, I had no doubt the racket would have alerted the entire ship to our activities. It made it almost impossible to speak to one another, so we just split up and began freeing everyone. We would talk after things calmed down.

I made my way with Valerie back to the area with the hatch, leading her straight into the room with the baby. The noise had caused it to start crying again, but Valerie immediately jumped to the challenge. I left her there, and went to free the people marked as pleasure slaves. Which was where I got the answer to my earlier question.

It wasn't necessarily that Jamila and Valerie were too strong. The problem was, they were too old.

All three of the people in the 'PS' cages were around my age, fourteen. Two girls and a boy, all of which were surprisingly afraid of me. It wasn't until I got back out into the hallway after freeing all three of them that I realized I was absolutely *drenched* in blood. I had gotten used to my clothes always cleaning themselves, so I hadn't noticed that the outer layer of clothing I had on was literally dripping with blood and viscera. The interrogation had been pretty messy, after all. Not because he had tried to hold back information. No, it had been messy because he was a slaver that wanted to throw a defenseless baby overboard because it was an inconvenience to him. I had made his ending as painful as I could.

My only regret was that his friends hadn't seen it happen. That was the only way to stop people like that. Make them so afraid of the consequences of the crime that they never commit it in the first place. Word of what transpired would have drastically cut down on new recruits, and maybe even made a few of the vultures decide to retire early. Oh well. I guess I would just have to do it again, and keep on doing it until they got the message. That thought put a smile on my face. Sometimes, doing the right thing could get messy. And I didn't mind getting messy in the least...

Eventually, we had everyone free of their shackles. Most of the people present appeared to be middle-aged, near forty, and all but a few of them were rugged and strong. Good for slave labor. Nearly everyone was a Brain cultivator, meaning their true age was probably somewhere around a hundred years old. I looked like a child to them, but hopefully they would see age didn't matter in this situation. Before anyone could do something crazy—like blow a hole through the side of the ship and sink us—I climbed halfway up the ladder and shouted for their attention.

"Attention everyone! Can I please have your attention for a moment?!" That didn't work. I should have known. It never works. Luckily, none of my friends had their belts taken from them. Now that they could access their qi, they could tap into the storage rings hidden inside them. Donny passed me a small pouch of poppers, so I pulled one out and threw it against the nearest door. Which, in retrospect, was a bad idea. I should have realized the shoddy things couldn't have taken the impact. The wood shrapnel that blasted out from the impact caught everyone by surprise. There were a few screams, mixed with some panic. The tight quarters didn't make it any better. A few people closest to the door were bleeding from some light wounds, and several people were looking at me in a very unhappy manner.

That was when things started spiraling out of control.

"Enough! Somebody get that guy down from there. After that, the strongest of us need to band together and try to take the ship! There can't be more than thirty of them, and if we hit fast, we can kill them all before they know it!" The speaker, which happened to be the guy behind the door marked as 'farmer,' got plenty of support. I needed to stop them, before this went any further.

"Wait! Don't do this. We are in the middle of the ocean, and without a crew that knows how to sail, killing everyone would doom us all!" That caused a few people to back down.

Until the farmer spoke up again.

"Are you a coward, boy? How hard can it be to steer a boat? Just because you are afraid to fight doesn't mean the rest of us are! Come on, boys! We can do this! Anyone who isn't a coward, follow me!" The farmer then threw a qi construct, after shouting the stupid moniker 'Dragon Thrust Board Basher' at the ceiling over his head. Something annoying like that, anyway. I wasn't really listening. It did, however, blow a hole in the ceiling, allowing him to jump through. He was followed by ten others, leaving me with just my friends, the three teenagers, and a baby. Not the start I had envisioned.

In less than a minute, we could hear the sounds of fighting going on above us through the hole. The element of surprise hadn't lasted very long.

"That isn't going to end well…" Chu was standing at the opening, looking up at the hold. "What are we going to do?"

Donny shook his head in reply. "Before that, I want to know what happened to Jim. What took you so long?" Valerie moved the baby to one arm so she could punch him in the shoulder. "Ow! Okay, okay, that came out wrong. I mean, thanks for getting us out of there, but where have you been all week? Were you hurt?"

Jamila stepped forward before I could answer. "Not now. We need to get up there and see what we are dealing with. There might be a way we can salvage something from this." She walked to the hole and jumped up, Chu following close behind. Jamila was right. We needed to get in front of this.

"Donny, Valerie, you stay here and protect the kids. I will try to get my belt back, and then secure the hold if I can. At least that will give us some room to maneuver." They both nodded, Donny pulling out a tower shield that almost completely filled the width of the hallway.

"They won't get past me." I felt a flex of power come from him, and the runes carved on the front of the shield glowed with energy. "*Nothing* will hurt them. Now go, before we run out of time." I nodded at him and used a bit of qi to help strengthen the muscles of my legs so I could leap into the ship's hold above me.

The hold gave me a better idea of the size of the ship we were in. It was narrower than most ships with three masts, but at almost three hundred feet long, it still managed to have plenty of storage space in its massive hold. Instead of having walls or bins to break up the space, the whole thing was one giant cavern. The only thing keeping it from being a wide-open room were the three wooden pillars that had to be the base for the masts, and a single row of stalls at the rear. Which was when I noticed our horses had somehow made the trip with us. I guessed the pirates decided the pure white horses were worth enough gold to bring with them. Valerie would be happy. Donny, on the other hand, not so much.

The low ceiling meant the crew quarters were directly overhead, instead of in cabins to the front and rear of the ship. All of this added up to a vessel that would ride low in the water, had a narrow breadth of water resistance, and plenty of sheets aloft to catch the wind. Whoever designed this ship wanted it to be fast, without sacrificing cargo space. Basically, the perfect pirate ship.

The hold itself was practically empty, meaning the captain and crew were planning to 'find' their cargo on the open ocean. The only way to do that, of course, was by stealing it. I hadn't seen the sun yet, but according to the man I had vigorously interrogated, we were currently headed toward the western shipping lanes.

Their goal would be to catch fat merchant ships working their way from the west, around the Claw as they traveled to the Eastern Province on the other side. Once the pirates had their fill, they would sail for the pirate enclaves dotted along the coast of the Western Province, eventually making it to the northern edge of the empire where they could sell any slaves they hadn't managed to offload by that point. It was a good plan, if a little ignorant of how markets worked. They would be bringing back the same items produced by the west, into the western marketplaces. I guess when you didn't pay for the goods in the first place, you didn't care about maximizing profits.

What appeared to be faint daylight was coming in from a door at the top of a short flight of stairs on the far side of the hold. I started toward it when I felt the tingle from my blood connection with my belt get stronger. It was somewhere toward the back of the hold, near a small pile of crates that were strapped down to the floor with strips of thick leather. After a few minutes of shuffling items around, I eventually found a sealed crate with several enchanted items inside.

My belt was rolled up and off to one side, so it took me a

few seconds to find it. Once it was on, I finally let out a sigh of relief. I hadn't realized how connected to it I was. It really wasn't a good thing to be so attached to an item. If I lost it for good, I would be in a very precarious position. I would have to work on a solution to my dependency on an item sometime, but now I needed to get a move on. Before leaving, I made sure to grab my spirit wood ring as well, slipping it onto the middle finger of my left hand. Everything else I left where it was. I didn't know if it was safe to store them in my belt, and I didn't want anyone with a blood connection to any of the items to be able to track me.

There was a loud crash from somewhere above me, and the ship shuddered as if it had been struck by something. I sprinted for the door, determined to do my best to keep the ship in one piece.

The next floor was the crew quarters and galley. The only people there were the dead. I saw one of the prisoners near the stove, a cleaver wedged in his skull. The rest of the bodies belonged to the crew.

Considering I didn't know how many people were actually on board, this might be a majority of the crew, or just a small portion waiting on a meal during a break. I wasn't sure which option to hope for.

I moved toward the next set of stairs, finally seeing daylight. There were shouts, and then a loud cracking sound. I rushed to see what had happened.

The midday sun made me squint against the reflection of the bright light coming off the water around us. There wasn't a speck of land in sight, and only a few clouds marred the blue sky. If it weren't for all the pandemonium, blood, and violence, it would be a beautiful day. Which, when I thought about it, was pretty much the story of my life.

It was pretty obvious the loud cracking sound came from the small raised forecastle at the front of the ship, where a former prisoner had been embedded in the wood. He didn't look like he was having a good day. The man who had put him there was standing with his back to the mainmast in the center of the deck. Captain Yon.

"Surround him! He can't take all of us!" The remaining former prisoners were standing with the farmer, doing their best to bring the man down. Chu and Jamila were at the rear of the ship, where half a dozen members of the surviving crew were trying to hold them off. Considering who the slavers were facing, I gave them less than two minutes to keep breathing. When I turned back to see how the others were doing, however, things had quickly turned against the former prisoners.

And by that, I meant they were all missing their heads.

In the two seconds it had taken me to look back at my friends, the captain had pulled out a curved scimitar and swung about himself in a devastating move. The inexperienced people facing him hadn't stood a chance. The captain looked like he was about to jump in to help his crew, so I knew I needed to stop him. I didn't want to risk Yon hurting my friends.

"Stop!" The use of the qi construct trick that made my voice boom like a clap of thunder helped get their attention. I had learned my lesson. No poppers this time. Plus, I didn't need to use some stupid moniker. "If we kill each other right now, we all die anyway!" That brought everyone to a halt. From the look on Yon's face, he knew exactly what I was getting at. Even if he managed to kill my friends and I, there wouldn't be enough cultivators left alive to fight off even a weak sea monster. Piloting the ship might be just as impossible, but I didn't know how bad that situation might be. Jamila and Chu separated themselves from the people they were fighting, and Yon lowered his sword.

"You recognize the problem now as well, I take it?" The haughty tone of Yon's voice led me to believe he thought I was stopping the fight because I was afraid I was going to lose. If this rotten piece of garbage only knew the truth, he would be thanking the gods I was thinking about survival more than revenge. That could come when land was in sight.

"I realize that we are already too few to win a fight against a leviathan. If this goes any further, even the winners will ultimately lose before this ship can make it back to shore." I made a motion for my friends to join me by the door leading back to the lower decks. "I propose we make a deal." He raised an eyebrow at my statement.

"What kind of deal, kid? You want me to promise to let all of you go?" His smirk told me all I needed to know about that idea.

"No, you giant bag of excrement. I am not stupid enough to trust you. What I *do* trust is your survival instinct. And your greed." He definitely didn't like it when I called him names, but he smiled when he saw I had his priorities figured out.

"If you are smart enough to figure out what is important to me, you are smart enough to know that any deal we make goes overboard as soon as we make it to port." He sheathed his weapon before crossing his arms.

"More like as soon as we see land. But this is how I see things. We need you and whatever sailors are left to sail the ship." He nodded. "You need us to help fight if any monsters show up." He nodded again. "Your *real* cargo is the baby. That kid is worth enough for you to retire on. Or whatever it is you want to do." I pointed at Jamila, Chu, and myself. "We want the kid to survive as well." Yon opened his mouth, but I cut him off. "Not because we know the baby, but because it is a *baby*. Any sane and decent person would save a baby if they could."

The idea seemed to confuse the man. *Stars*, I wanted to kill this guy.

"So, what is your proposal? You keep the kid or something?"

I shook my head in the negative. "No, my proposal is simple. I know you need to get to the Western Province to ransom the kid. That is the only thing that makes sense for you to go that direction, given the flow of the shipping traffic in the region." He seemed surprised that I had figured that part out. It had been little more than an educated guess, but I must have been spot-on. "That is where we were headed anyway. The only thing that makes sense, as I see it, is for my group to stay below in the hold, while you and your men get us to the Western Province as fast as possible. We will take care of the kid, and any time you need us to help fight off a creature of some kind, we come and help." If that idea didn't work, I was willing to allow him to keep the hold and we would go back to the smuggler's space. Thankfully, he didn't try to argue.

"You can keep the hold, but I better not see you trying to sneak out. No poisoning our food. I will provide a single meal a day, two for the kid. That's all. And if I yell for help, you all come running. No trying to get out of fighting." He was trying to limit our food to weaken us. Too bad we had plenty of food stored in our devices. That would be a fun surprise for later. "Agreed?" Yon held his hand out to shake. I didn't take his hand.

"Agreed. But know this, Yon. As soon as we make it to shore, we finish this fight. Only one group will walk away from this mess."

He gave me a confident smile. "I wouldn't have it any other way, kid. Now get below so we can clean this up. It is only a matter of time before something smells all this blood. None of us wants that."

The three of us headed below decks. It left a bad taste in my mouth to let them live, but for now I had no other choice.

CHAPTER TEN

Fish

The next three months were torture. Not literally, but riding on a ship with a baby was the opposite of fun. The three teens weren't much better. If I heard, 'Are we there yet?' one more time…

A positive note was the focus we could all give on our cultivation. The Ocean of Tears was dense with ambient qi, allowing my friends and I to advance at twice the speed we could on land. Since the density of plant life and animals on the surface was almost nonexistent, that meant there were less things fighting for the energy to advance. I also noticed both of the horses were staying perfectly healthy and happy, despite the lack of exercise and fresh air. It might have been the enchantments, or it could have just been all the attention they were getting from everyone. After all, we were pretty short on entertainment, and the horses did make a nice distraction. Especially when Scout would find a way to kick Donny halfway across the hold.

I did my best to get the teens to meditate and cultivate with us, but none of the three seemed to have the drive and focus for self-improvement that my friends and I had. It wasn't surprising, considering the greater majority of the population was the same way. It was why only a small percentage of cultivators ever made it past the level of a Brain cultivator. About one in ten citizens of the Empire would ever make it that far, and most of them would only reach it in their dotage. It was closer to one percent of the population that ever saw Saint, and only about *half* of that one percent were young enough to still fight when they did so. Sage, Duke, and King were even more rare. The teens not having the grit and determination to advance was definitely no surprise.

The boy, Connor, was from a small clan that ran a large vineyard on the banks of the Great River. The two girls, Fatima and Karima, were from a small nomadic clan that traveled along the coast of the Claw. They were all wood cultivators, which was probably why they were attractive enough to be singled out by the slavers. Wood cultivators didn't have many scars, and tended to have clear and beautiful skin.

All three were typical of the victims of slaver rings. I was mildly disappointed in their inability to rise above their upbringing and expand their views of the world, but it seemed to be beyond them. They were obsessed with a cultivator's age and level, instead of ability. Which was what had gotten the other prisoners killed. Some people couldn't learn from others' mistakes. They were doomed to repeat them.

In fact, after they had overheard that I was the same age as they were, none of them wanted to have anything to do with me. To the point of actively avoiding me. I had no idea why. All five of us had taken turns trying to teach the teenagers how to fight, but none of them took that seriously either. Especially when it was me trying to do the training.

They at least knew enough not to stab themselves in a fight while using a spear, and I had even given Connor a set of armor he could fit into. It was just a simple steel breastplate with a leather helmet, greaves, and bracers, but he had pranced around in it for almost a week when I first gave it to him. I think he was trying to show off in front of the other two teenage girls. The only positive thing I could say about all three of them was their willingness to take turns watching the baby.

And oh, the baby. It was a little boy, who by this point was finally able to start crawling. Since we didn't know his real name, we all just called him Every. Because he was good at getting into *everything*. He also hated sleep, and at less than a year old, was already taking poops the size of a full-grown man. Oh, and every time he ate beans, I was pretty sure we could have classified his farts as some type of toxic swamp gas. I wasn't sure if I should be impressed, or just disgusted. Of course, the crew served beans frequently, and the little stinker *loved* any meal with beans, meaning we were frequently subjected to the toxic fumes in the enclosed space of the ship's hold.

Let's just say it had been a long three months.

We had been stuck in the hold the whole time, only heading out on deck to grab our daily allotment of food from the crew. It was long enough to confirm we were at least traveling in the right direction, and the earth qi detector I had bought from Taft would let us know if we were getting close to land. Otherwise, we might wake up to Captain Yon and his crew ready to kill us instead of giving us food, considering our deal to finish the fight.

I had just sat down to practice some alchemy when I heard shouting up on deck. It wasn't the usual kind of shouting, which was basically just Yon yelling at his people every time they so much as sneezed without his permission. This was the shouting of people organizing for a fight.

"Alright guys, it's time!" I jumped to my feet, quickly storing the alchemy items I had laid out around me. Everyone else seemed excited. I didn't blame them. If anything, at least this would stop the monotony of the past three months. Chu was the first one on his feet, but everyone else wasn't far behind.

"Yeah! Finally!" Chu pumped his fist, his other hand already holding a long spear he was having trouble getting through the door. "Something to do!" Yep, definitely excited for a fight.

"You three know what to do." I turned to speak to the teenagers. One of the girls, Fatima, had the baby in her lap already, while Connor was struggling to get his breastplate on. Karima took pity on the boy and came to help him out. "We will be right back. And if anyone besides us tries to come through the door, just use one of those copper disks we gave you." They all nodded, and I ran to join my friends on the deck.

As I came out the door, I noticed the evening sunlight made the white sails look as if they were sheets of flame. We were moving at a very high speed, the sails straining against their ropes. On the poop deck, at the rear of the ship, the captain had one of his sailors at the wheel while he stood next to them, blasting a concentrated cone of wind qi at the sails to eke out every bit of speed he could manage. The rest of the crew, along with my friends, were all leaning against the railings on the left, or port side of the ship. I looked out past them, and finally saw the problem. It was fish. Not just any fish, but stars-be-damned flying fish.

Flying fish were normally a nuisance that was manageable closer to shore. Here in the deep water, the schools of fish could get *huge*. Like the one headed straight for us. It was like a blanket covering the ocean. There had to be hundreds of thousands. Maybe millions. I could see the edge, far in the distance. Based on our current speed, we wouldn't make it in time.

The danger came from their wing-like fins. They could slice through a wooden hull with little effort. Human flesh wasn't even an obstacle they would notice. There were enough flying fish out there that the only thing remaining after they passed would be a field of splinters. We were in trouble. I was not willing to go into the afterlife to tell the gods I had failed my mission because a bunch of *fish* killed me.

We needed to go faster, and we needed more time. I had something that might help one of those two, and Valerie could help with the other. I ran over to the group, grabbing Valerie and Donny from the crowd.

"Valerie, you need to get over to the mainmast, and concentrate as much wind as you can on the foremast at the front of the ship. Donny, set up some formation plates around her that gather qi so she can refill her cores as fast as possible. We need to speed this thing up!" They both nodded and took off. Next, I grabbed Chu and Jamila. "I will need you to help me position the ice. Once a sheet is formed, you two will need to figure out how to layer it on the ship for protection."

They both looked confused until I pulled out the large blue marble I had grabbed from Taft. The one that could almost instantly form thick sheets of ice. While it might have been intended for fishing boats to preserve their catch, I was going to repurpose it to add a thick layer of armor over the hull. It would slow us down, but we might actually survive.

I moved over to the railing and started dumping qi into the marble. I hadn't used it yet, so I was surprised when a square of ice started forming *around* it instead of *under* it. This was going to be harder than I thought. I turned back to look for Jamila. Instead of standing close to me, she was trying to get the rest of the crew to stop just staring at the glimmering wave of metal fins coming toward us and convince them to come help. They were frozen with fear, unable to do anything but watch their death approach.

"Jamila! Ignore them. They are all slavers, and cowards at heart. We won't be getting any assistance from that lot." She nodded and ran over to me. I held up the ice block to show her the issue. "I need you to slice these cubes in half when they are fully formed, then pull out the marble so I can make another one!" The sound of the approaching wave of metal-finned fish was like the loudest and largest set of windchimes ever made. The sharp blades rang against one another as they jumped in and out of the water. They were getting close enough that I needed to shout to be heard over them, though far enough away that we still had time to act. I looked to Chu, who was still by my side. "That means you will have to hang them from the ship yourself! Once you get the side covered, try to save as much of the masts as you can!"

He shouted something in reply, but it was getting too loud to hear anything.

I started expanding the block of ice, and I didn't stop until it was about ten feet square. That was the size I started to feel resistance from the marble, so I decided not to force it any farther. Jamila was waiting for the moment it stopped growing, and a blade of fire qi sliced through the block of ice in agonizingly slow motion. It gave me a chance to gather more qi into my cores. The usual pace of refilling my energy stores was still suffering from the damage to the meridian in my left foot. I still had twelve of my thirteen meridians to draw from, which was the number for most cultivators, but their narrower size made it harder for me to keep pace. At least the ocean provided plenty of qi to draw from.

The moment the two halves separated, Jamila tossed me the marble to start on another one. The whole process had taken less than three minutes, and we had two usable pieces of 'armor' for the ship. I did some mental math, and came to a simple conclusion. We weren't going to make it in time.

Instead of dwelling on it, I got back to work. Chu had already wrestled one of the halves to the front of the ship, using his mastery over wood qi to form brackets on the side of the ship. He used the brackets to hold the ice in place near the surface of the water. At least the front ten feet of the ship would make it.

By the time he had the second ten-foot square in position, we had two more ready for him to drop into place. That would give us the front forty feet of the ship covered. Only two hundred and sixty feet to go. Not to mention the masts, forecastle, castle, and rudder. We were doomed. Which was when Donny came running over. He tried shouting at us, but we couldn't hear a thing.

After a few seconds he came up and cupped his hand over

my ear and shouted. "What are you doing?!" Now it was my turn to look confused. "You don't have time to armor up like a turtle! You need to charge in like a bull!" It was like getting struck by lightning. Of course! If a strong defense couldn't save you, the only choice was to go on the offensive!

I grabbed his shoulder and nodded to show I understood. He went over and grabbed a square ice sheet from Chu, and headed to the starboard side of the ship. Donny wasn't as strong in wood qi as Chu was, but he was good enough to copy the wooden brackets and drop the sheet of ice in place. As soon as he did, Jamila and Chu seemed to instantly realize what we were doing. Once again, I had to congratulate myself for finding such an amazing group of people to partner with. Teaming up with them might have been the best decision of my entire six hundred and fifty-four years of life.

Valerie noticed what we were up to, and she started directing her blasts of wind qi to slowly turn the ship into the oncoming wave. We didn't have enough time to armor the whole ship, but we had *plenty* of time to armor the front. We could drive straight into them like a battering ram and cut through to the other side. It was our only chance.

Our actions weren't in keeping with the self-preservation instincts of the crew, unfortunately. Without any prompting from their captain, two of the twelve remaining sailors came rushing at Valerie's back, their sabers raised to strike her head from her shoulders. Since I was busy expanding the next block of ice, Jamila handled them for me. Her shuriken sunk into the base of their skulls before they even made it two-thirds of the way to Valerie. As for the rest of us, we didn't even turn around. We weren't afraid of these idiots in the least, and ten sailors were almost as good as twelve. The captain would just have to make do with the personnel reduction.

By the time Valerie had the ship turned in a long curve to face the flying fish head-on, we had positioned enough ice to form a giant 'V' shape on the front, with sixty feet of vertical ice protecting the bottom portion of the first two masts. It was only a little more than half, but the hope was none of the fish would reach that high. We didn't have time to do anything more, even if we wanted to.

Captain Yon had fought against Valerie at first, directing his wind qi to counterbalance her actions. After seeing what we intended, the man finally started to help. Once he threw his weight behind Valerie's, our speed started increasing at an incredible rate. He might have been no better than a fermented butt-nugget, but I couldn't fault his mastery over wind qi.

Heh. Butt-nugget. I needed to remember that one.

As we closed with the fish, the chiming noise of their wings brushing against one another was overtaken by the sound of their metal wings slicing through the air. It was as if a thousand swords were being swung through the air all at once, creating a roar of sound that seemed to grow more and more furious the closer we got.

The ship reached the maximum speed possible with all the extra wind resistance the ice was causing, but it was still fast enough to practically skip over the waves. There were a few ominous groans from the ship, causing more than a few people to look at the masts nervously. The shoddy vessel held together, thankfully, and we hit the front edge of the fish just as Chu dropped a final block of ice along the front of the castle, angling it to protect the man steering.

Hitting the wave of flying fish was akin to slamming into a sandbar. We shuddered to a halt; the only thing keeping us facing forward was the constant pressure from Valerie and Captain Yon. Everyone not prepared for the impact was thrown forward off their feet. I hoped the baby, teens, and horses were okay. None of us had time to warn them in all the rush.

I could faintly hear the sound of cracking ice as the fish skipped off the barrier, or slammed into it head first, hopefully killing themselves on impact. The vast majority of the monsters passed us by, like a glittering wave split by the prow of the ship. If it weren't for the incredible risk of dying, I would recommend trying it sometime. The sight was breathtakingly beautiful.

After almost a full minute of being held to a standstill, the wave of fish started to taper off enough that we started moving again. We were still moving sluggishly, but everyone managed to let out a sigh of relief. It seemed like we were going to make it. Unfortunately, the foremast and mainmast hadn't fared as well as I would have liked. Their sails were shredded by the fish that skipped upwards off of our icy prow, and the mizzenmast at the rear was somehow missing a hefty chunk out of it at the halfway point. It wouldn't be doing much for a while.

Seeing that everything was in hand, I took the opportunity to check on the kids below. As I reached the doorway, the smell of blood wafted out. I rushed down the stairs, yelling for Chu. I didn't know if he could hear me over the sound of the fish or not, but I didn't have time to wait.

CHAPTER ELEVEN

As the Tide Turns

Despite the shoddy craftsmanship, the thick wood of the ship meant the hold was much quieter than it was on deck. My eyes adjusted quickly to the dark interior, which was when I saw Connor standing over Karima with a spear through her chest. She wasn't moving.

Fatima was holding the baby, huddled in the corner near the horses. I approached Connor slowly, seeing tears trickling down his face. It was obvious that whatever happened was an accident. I didn't even need to ask, because as soon as he saw me, Connor jumped away from Karima and started hollering.

"I didn't mean to! We were just talking, and then the ship jerked forward, and I fell, and she was standing in front of me, and..." He choked up, unable to continue. Behind him, Fatima had finally stood up, shouting and angry.

"You idiot! What have you done!" Every started crying, the commotion too much for his sensibilities. "You killed her! I can't believe this, after everything she did for you!" She was at least aware enough to set Every down in the crib Donny had fastened to the wall near the stables.

Instead of dealing with that drama, I knelt to check on

Karima. A quick inspection with some wood qi revealed what I had already suspected. She had died almost instantly. The spear had penetrated directly into her heart, and without having a body strengthened by an unlocked heart core, she didn't have a chance. Even a healer standing right next to her when it had happened wouldn't have mattered. Suddenly, I heard the clatter of a formation plate hitting the ground. Crap.

I spun around just in time to see one of the trap plates we had given the teens hit the ground in front of Connor. I tried spinning up the qi in my brain core to slow time, but the heavy use of my qi to build all the ice made me slow. I managed to speed up my perceptions just as the trap went off. It was one of my simpler designs, a basic set of vertical wind blades that travel six feet from the plate in all directions. Clearly, Fatima hadn't been listening to me when I had described what it did, because she was still standing within range of the disk she had used to try to kill Connor. Karma didn't wait to pass judgement.

Both of them were bisected, Connor perfectly, and Fatima just a few inches off center. Their bodies hit the ground in slow motion, neither of them having the necessary natural resistance to wind qi that would have potentially saved their lives. All I could do was form a dome of water qi to keep their blood from running all over the floor. The loss of life sickened me. One stupid mistake led to another, and three teenagers, kids, scared and far from home, all ended up dead.

It was Every that snapped me out of it. I don't know how long I stood there, watching as the two bodies fell to the floor in slow motion, but it was long enough for the blood to stop pumping from their corpses. Must have been a while.

The sound of Every's cries eventually reached my ears, and I allowed my perception of time to return to normal. I couldn't remember a time when I had felt this tired. Not in this life, at least.

I stored all three bodies in my belt before going to pick up the baby. As I comforted him, I used a few strands of water qi to clean up the blood. I also made sure to pick up the formation plate, and put the spear back in the storage stud I used as an armory. I didn't bother to save the armor Connor was wearing.

As I laid Every down for a nap, I realized I was angry. Not at Conner, and not at Fatima. They were both just kids in a bad situation, and neither handled themselves well. They were *put* in that bad situation by Captain Yon and his ilk. I was going to make him pay.

Leaving Every alone wasn't ideal, but I needed to go back on deck to see what was happening. And to figure out why everyone hadn't come back down to the hold yet. I dropped a shield formation plate at the foot of the crib, and poured a small vial of liquid qi onto it to activate the invisible barrier. It would run out in about twenty minutes on its own, or less if something tried to break through. Either way, it should be enough time to gather my friends and get back down here. The sounds of the flying fish had faded, meaning we had survived our confrontation with them and made it out the other side. It was time to regroup. And time to mourn.

When I started back topside, I started to make out yelling, and then I saw what was taking my friends so long. All four had their backs to the railing, about fifty feet from the doorway I was standing in. They were surrounded in a half-circle by the sailors, with Yon standing behind his men. He was shouting over their heads at my friends, while pointing back at the bodies of the two sailors Jamila had killed when they tried to attack Valerie. My anger at the slaving bastards was reaching a boiling point.

"…killed them for no reason! They weren't even close to her yet! You took two of mine, so I demand two in return!" His gaze was lingering on Valerie and Jamila, his purpose for this as transparent as his character. Yon's eyes flickered over to me, dismissing me as a threat.

That was when I realized the man had never seen me fight. He had seen Donny, Jamila, and Valerie throw down against his men, but Chu and I were a mystery to him. While I seemed to be close in age to my four friends, a closer inspection would reveal the youthfulness of my appearance. He must have noticed I was the youngest of the group, and therefore decided I was the least threatening. Time to fix that.

"I don't think so." My voice wasn't loud, but it was firm enough that it carried over the sound of the ocean and creaking of the ship. "In fact, *you* owe *us*, Yon. And I am collecting that debt today. Right now, in fact." Something in my tone must have warned him, because he finally turned to face me. So did most of his crew.

"What are you talking about, kid? I didn't kill any of you." Yon cracked his knuckles. "Not yet, anyway."

I pulled the body of Karima out and used a strand of qi to throw it at him. I felt bad, using her body like that, but she had already left this plane of existence. The only thing left was a meat bag.

"You brought those kids onto this ship against their will. That makes their deaths your responsibility." He didn't have any reaction to my statement, and he didn't flinch when her corpse slid across the deck to stop at his feet. "Would you like to see the other two as well? Their ending wasn't as neat, so the cleanup would be more work."

"The way I see it, those three aren't worth the value of two trained seamen." He still hadn't even looked at the body. "We still aren't even."

Okay. He was just asking for it now.

"You are right, Yon. We aren't even." I threw the remains of Connor and Fatima at his men, spraying them with gore. "Your men threatened us." I spun out a whip of fire qi from my left hand. "Assaulted us." I spun out a whip of metal qi from my right hand. "Kidnapped us." I used the meridian in my lower back to form four invisible strands of air qi, then used them to lift myself a few inches off of the wooden deck. "Planned to *sell* us." My last step was to use the meridian at the base of my neck to form a shield of water qi that wrapped around my torso, arms, and legs. The strain of the day, mixed with the show of force, made it harder than it should have been. But I didn't let them see that. "And now, after we *save* your *useless life*, you threaten us?!" I lashed my whips, splintering wood with the metal whip and burning a large swath of decking with the strand of fire. "We *definitely* aren't *even*. Those kids were worth a hundred of you stars-be-damned motherless dogs!"

They were all backing away from me now, and Yon finally seemed to realize I wasn't just some pushover scared kid, like he was used to dealing with. I snapped my whips at their faces, backing them up even further. My friends finally took the opportunity to break free of their encirclement, rushing to stand behind me.

"Fine! Fine, kid. Just stop, before you burn the ship down!" Yon and his men had backed up all the way to the opposite railing. "Please! You'll kill us all!" I paused, allowing the whips to fall to the deck. As much as I wanted to finish this and end all of their miserable, pointless lives, I pushed down my anger and reabsorbed the qi I was using to power my constructs.

"Don't worry, Yon. We will balance the scales soon enough." I turned my back on him, showing the Sage cultivator I didn't see him as a threat. My friends and I walked single-file through the door leading back into the hold.

Silence was the only answer from Yon and his men.

CHAPTER TWELVE

Healing Pills and Fighting Thrills

The next week was a hard one. Even though I pushed down the anger I was feeling, it didn't go away. Everyone else was feeling the same. The loss of the three teens hit us hard, but Every was feeling it the most. We all took turns trying to cheer him up, but the boy still missed them terribly. I think he could also sense our sadness. It was a time of quiet contemplation for all of us.

Yon and his men had stopped feeding us altogether. The day after the confrontation, when I went to get our allotment of food, the only man on deck was the man at the wheel. He had looked at me nervously, afraid I would lash out and kill him. I thought about doing it just to spite Yon, but I just turned around and went back inside without saying anything.

They were obviously trying to weaken us even more, considering the upcoming confrontation was bound to happen soon. Considering we had been at sea for over three months, we certainly had to be getting close to the shores of the Western Province. It was still several more months of travel to reach the Western Province capital, but our deal was just to reach the province itself, not the capital.

I had used the quiet time to work on some alchemy. My

damaged meridian would heal slowly on its own, but a few Meridian Cleansing Pills would turn long months of painful healing into just weeks. The last three months I had worked on improving my skill whenever I could. I had the ingredients and the knowledge, just not the actual body skills, if you will. Just as I found out with my blacksmithing skills, it was one thing to *know* something; it was another to be able to do it well. If I messed these pills up, it could cause more damage than the original problem. The ingredients to the pills weren't hard to come by, but the process of creating them was a difficult one.

First, I had to mash up Green Willow Sprouts into a paste, then let it soak in a bowl of liquid qi. The liquid qi would eventually evaporate back into the environment, but it would leave behind a fine powder that was the base for the pill. Next, I boiled some Fire Flower with Trauma Root, turning the red flowers and black roots into a purple paste that I had to bake until it turned into *another* batch of powder.

Finally, the last ingredient came from the dangerous Sap Sac. They would sometimes explode when you tried to harvest them, making it the most expensive item of the mixture. Luckily, I hadn't paid for any of these ingredients. I had 'procured' them from my uncle, after his last attempt at killing me. A tiny puncture in the side of the sap pouch allowed me to drain the viscous honey-colored liquid inside, and I drained it directly into my cauldron.

Applying even heat to the bottom of the cauldron, I had to wait a while for it to come to a boil. I then had to add the purple powder, stirring it until all of the mixture was a smooth consistency, similar to cake batter. I then had to add the Green Willow Sprout powder one spoonful at a time. Too much at once wouldn't allow the qi built up inside the magical herbs to mix properly, so it was an agonizingly slow process that strained my meridians for most of the afternoon.

I was using the meridians in my elbows instead of my hands to cast my fire qi threads, since I needed my hands to actually spoon in the materials. They weren't as used to the extended usage as my hand meridians were, making them ache like a pulled muscle. That was something I would need to correct. All my meridians should be able to function just as well as the ones in my hands and feet. I made a mental note to train using a more even mix of my body's cultivation system. After all, that was something I already knew how to practice. Trying to remember everything I needed to do after being reincarnated was a pain, sometimes.

Eventually, I had everything mixed together properly. Once the thick paste was bubbling in the cauldron, I added six large vials of liquid qi, filling the cauldron to the brim. It thinned out, turning the concoction into something a passerby could easily mistake for a brown beef broth. The fragrant herbal smell might confuse them, but that would be an understandable mistake. Alchemy looked a lot like cooking to the unaware.

I placed the lid on the cauldron and turned up the heat. I needed the liquid qi to evaporate quickly. Some alchemists used plain water when they made these pills, but by adding the liquid qi, it increased the potency. It would make the pills unusable to anyone below the Meridian level, due to the concentrated energy. Since I wasn't planning to sell these, it didn't matter. My friends and I would all be able to safely take the pills, and hopefully they would provide the impetus we all needed to advance another stage in our cultivation.

Forcing the mixture to boil off the moisture faster required me to check it frequently. After only a few minutes, it was ready for the final step. I cut off the heat, and used a braided thread of wood and earth qi to start stirring my concoction. The trick was to evenly condense the ingredients, while simultaneously forcing them into dozens of pill shapes no larger than the nail on my smallest finger. Only long practice allowed me to do this without wasting a large portion of the mixture. Holding the shapes in place with the forced pressure eventually formed the pills I wanted.

Dumping the contents of the cauldron into a canvas sack, I finally got a look at my finished product. There were exactly one hundred pills, each exactly the same. They were an earthy brown color, with flecks of purple and green that sparkled in the dim light of the hold. They would easily receive a grade of Expert from an Alchemy Tester, perhaps bordering on Master. My former instructors at the Enforcer Academy would be proud.

Sorting the pills into five equal pouches, I immediately took one to begin the healing process. It dissolved quickly in my mouth, and it tingled as I swallowed. The influx of energy almost doubled me over, and I had to actually strain to control it. After a few minutes, I was able to direct the fluctuating qi toward the damaged meridian in my leg. It seemed to sense the damage, and latched on to the area without further prompting.

I instantly felt an itching sensation, letting me know the pill was working. It wouldn't heal the frayed meridian completely with just one pill, but it would certainly help it along. I estimated it would basically be one month's worth of healing time, meaning I should be back to normal after three or four more pills.

I took the time to scrub the cauldron clean. I didn't want the remnants of the herbs used to interact with whatever I made next. There was no telling what kind of reaction it might cause. After putting everything away, I went around and passed out the pills to all my friends. I described, in detail, how best to concentrate the energy they provided after taking them. This wasn't the first set of pills I had provided them, so there weren't many questions.

We were just sitting down to eat our evening meal when the ship sharply changed direction. All of us looked at one another. This wasn't good. We hadn't changed our heading since the flying fish, which meant the crew was up to something. Valerie went to grab Every from his crib, and Donny moved to cover the door. Jamila and Chu ran to inspect the earth qi detector and directional needle to see if we were nearing land. I put away our food, sealing the stew pot and cooling down the heating stone so I could store them inside my belt. We didn't want to leave anything out that could go flying around. Everyone reconvened next to Donny.

"There isn't any land in range of the detector." Jamila was fiddling with her katanas as she spoke, trying to get them arranged just where she liked. "And we shifted farther northwest, away from the empire. I have no idea what they could be up to, unless they saw something topside."

Chu was getting his brigandine armor in place, but he stopped to answer her. "I agree, however I don't think it is a monster this time. They might hate us, and be afraid of Jim, but they have to know they need us to help them fight."

Donny shook his head. "They wouldn't call for us if they thought there was enough time to get around the monster." He was already in his armored clothing, and I could feel the fluctuations of his cores as he readied himself for combat. "It could be something else. Something they don't want us knowing about."

Valerie shifted Every in her arms, his bright blue eyes wide as he looked around. Even the baby knew something was up. "I will stay with the baby. I can cover the door with my bow, and I will be ready to release the horses if we need to escape." She looked back at Scout. "I know it wouldn't do much, but I won't let them drown inside this dark ship."

I nodded. "If we have to, we'll just follow the plan." I held up the rectangle of wood and blue marble I got from Taft. "I will activate the emergency raft, and then start making ice blocks. They float, and we can use them to salvage as much of the ship as we can. The only way we are leaving this thing is if it sinks. And all of the crew is dead."

I received sharp nods of agreement. All of us were on the same page. None of the slavers would make it off this ship.

"Jim, let me take point." Donny was still holding onto his shield, foregoing his usual combination of axe and dagger. He held a spear in his off-hand, probably so he could maintain some distance from the people he intended to fight. "You hang back and handle Captain Yon. The three of us can take the rest of them."

I fell back, willing to go along with his plan. I took a moment to mount the green glass sword with my improved sheath on my belt, right next to a pouch that held the ten poppers. We didn't want a repeat of the forest clearing.

Just as we were about to rush up the stairs and out the door, the situation changed again. We all felt as two cultivators somewhere far in front of the ship unleashed their auras, unveiling the power of their cores. They were easily at High Saint, maybe even Peak Saint. In reply, Captain Yon unveiled his own core, and a Low Sage aura pushed down on us from where he was standing on deck. I could tell he must have been standing on the castle, near the wheel at the rear of the ship. Every started to cry, the pressure hurting his small body.

"I've got him, you guys go!" Valerie was already setting up a shield plate near the stall doors, so she could protect the horses and Every at the same time. "Stop him from doing whatever it is they are planning!"

We took off, sprinting to the deck to see what was going on.

What was Yon planning to do? Act like the pirate he was, was what he had planned. In front of the ship, and a bit to starboard, a two-masted schooner seemed to be trying to run from us. It was rigged in the square topsail manner, giving it a good balance of speed and stability. I estimated it to be around one hundred and twenty feet long, making it less than half of the size of the ship we were on currently. Normally, it would be able to easily outrun a three-masted ship that could only utilize about half of its sails. It looked like they wouldn't be able to manage it this time.

It was clear the schooner had recently suffered from a fire. The actual ship seemed to be mostly damage-free, but their sails had more holes than my cheap Uncle Hu's underwear. At least they were cleaner. They were doing their best to outdistance us, but Yon was giving it his all. The blasts of wind qi he was sending into our sails had us humming through the water, and there was absolutely no way we wouldn't catch them at this point. In fact, our current momentum alone would allow us to pull alongside them in only a few minutes.

Yon noticed this as well, so he stopped pushing out wind qi and started absorbing as much ambient qi as possible to refill his cores. I could feel the suction of his meridians from halfway across the ship, drawing in an incredible amount of power. He wasn't just a Low Sage. He was a Low Sage ready to move into Middle Sage. The two Saint cultivators onboard the schooner didn't have a chance.

As we got closer, I finally got a look at the flag the other ship was flying. It was an Imperial Navy flag, marking it as property of the emperor. From what I knew of the Navy, most schooners were used for two purposes. Long distance messenger ships, and pirate hunters. If it was a messenger ship, it would have a crew of six or eight. If it was a pirate hunter, it would range from somewhere between ten to fifteen fighters with another five or six sailors.

The irony of a ship designed to hunt down pirate ships, about to be pillaged by a pirate ship, wasn't lost on me. Considering my hatred for all things emperor, I even thought for a second about just going back down into the hold and allowing Yon and his men to sink the wayward vessel. My conscience won out in the end. The crew of the schooner were most likely just innocent men and women trying to make a living for their families. Allowing Yon and his crew to murder them wasn't something I was willing to countenance.

"What are you doing up here? Get below where you belong!" Yon had finally noticed us, as he had lashed the wheel in place so he could walk away from it. He was wearing a full suit of hardened leather armor, including a thick set of leather gloves with the knuckles lined in razored steel. A brawler's weapon. It clashed with his normal use of the scimitar riding on his belt, but I wasn't surprised by his choice. His size would make it hard to beat him if we were just using fists. He lifted his chin as he met my eyes. "This has nothing to do with you."

"Planning on adding more innocent lives to your tally, Yon?" I moved to approach him, allowing my friends to head toward his crew that were already lined up along the railing. "Do you honestly expect me to allow you to get away with something like that?" He smirked at me, confident in his own power. Enough time had passed since our confrontation, allowing his mind the opportunity to downplay his earlier fears.

"Allow me? I don't expect you to *allow* me to do anything!" Yon pulled his scimitar free of its sheath. "What I expect you to do is go back into your hole, like the good little rabbit you are!"

Had this dung beetle just called me a rabbit? He had this whole situation all kinds of wrong. First off, I was most definitely *not* a vegetarian. And second, I was going to beat him so bloody his own mother wouldn't recognize him. I put my hand on my own sword, ready to draw it and launch a wind blade at his face.

"This ends today, Yon. I should have just killed you the first day, and taken my chances with the ocean monsters. At least they are only following their natural instincts. You have no such excuse."

His smirk fell into a frown, and he opened his mouth to say something. Which was precisely when our ship struck the schooner with a lurching crunch that threw us all sideways.

I managed to stay on my feet, but Yon and I ended up on separate ends of the ship. He had headed toward the forecastle, trying to position himself to jump onto the schooner. I had stumbled to the rear, the short wall of the castle stopping me from going any further backwards.

The rest of Yon's crew had been split. Five were fighting Donny, Chu, and Jamila, while five were on the forecastle with Yon, preparing to jump onto the smaller ship. It was a drop of almost twenty feet, so they were waiting for the schooner to stop rocking from the impact before jumping down. No sense getting wet if you didn't have to.

Seeing that my friends had the five sailors—who weren't

even wearing armor—easily in hand, I sprinted for Yon. If he made it across, the other crew didn't stand a chance.

I pulled my sword free of its sheath as I jumped up onto the forecastle, sending the wide blade of wind it released into the backs of the sailors' legs. Three of them tumbled overboard, hopefully to be crushed to death between the hulls of the two ships. Yon and the two standing closest to him were protected by a thin air shield that flared to life the moment before impact. He flicked his hand in my direction, silently ordering his two crewmen to handle me while he went to the other ship.

Not today, asshole.

I spun out a whip of metal qi from my left hand while using my right to wield my sword. The two sailors ran at me, sabers raised to hack me down. I used my oversized brain core to speed up my perception of time, making it seem as if everything else had slowed. Suddenly, it was like everyone else was moving underwater. I jumped forward, straight at them.

I floated between the two sailors, using a smooth circular swing of my sword arm to avoid pulling a muscle or damaging connective tissue while moving at such a high speed. The green malachite sword, glittering like glass in the sun, was quickly coated in red.

To my eyes, the hands holding their weapons seemed to float free of their wrists, propelled by the blood shooting out of their newly created stumps. Their faces twisted in pain and disbelief, and my backswing sliced through their calf muscles as I flew between them. They didn't deserve to die quickly. I would come back to finish the job, nice and slow, as karma demanded.

Yon had already cleared the railing, and I watched as his body slid over the side in slow motion. His disgusting face was twisted with glee, the thought of murdering innocent people bringing him true joy. This guy needed to die.

I swung my metal whip forward, snapping it as hard as I dared. It wasn't going to be long enough, so I extended it by forcing out more qi. There was just enough time to catch him under the nose, the whip wrapping around his head and jerking him to a stop. His weight jerked me forward, and I returned time to normal.

The railing stopped me from going overboard, and I braced both legs against it to keep from sliding farther. Yon was flopping around like a fish on the end of a fishing pole. Apparently, getting whipped in the face and dangling by your head wasn't the most enjoyable experience, no matter your cultivation level.

I had to quickly sheathe my sword again so I could use both hands on the whip. As I started to pull his heavy weight back onto the ship, I could see the crew of the schooner staring at me with wide eyes and open-mouthed wonder. I supposed seeing a Peak Brain willingly take on a Sage cultivator wasn't exactly a common sight.

There were only a few more seconds of struggling with the weight before Yon wised up and started fighting back. I couldn't actually see him due to the curve of the hull, but I could feel as he shifted on the other end of the whip.

That was when I went airborne.

It turned out I had drastically underestimated his physical strength. As I flipped through the air, I managed to slightly slow down time again. I could see where he had simply punched through the thick wood of the ship for a handhold, and grabbed the whip with his other hand. Considering my trajectory, he must have pulled down hard enough to gain some slack, and then snapped my whip like *he* was the one wielding it. Considering it actually originated from my left-hand meridian, I had gone flying when the impetus of the whip finally reached me at the other end. The sharp pain in my wrist confirmed the theory. It had snapped like a dry twig, my bones not willing to continue the wave energy imparted by the whip, and his strength.

I severed my connection with the metal qi just as I hit the water. I went down like a stone, my cloth-covered brigandine armor dragging me under faster than I expected. A quick use of my storage belt had it off of me, and I started floating back to the surface. I used the time to set the bones of my wrist, my adrenaline making the pain nothing more than a mild nuisance.

The wooden healing token hidden in my waistband was already doing its work, but I sent a swirl of life energy into the bones to help the process along.

My head broke the surface just in time to see the two Saint cultivators on the schooner get smashed back into the deck of their ship. They must have used my distraction to launch their own attacks against Yon, but he was already standing back up on top of the forecastle of his own ship, ready to strike them down as soon as they tried to come back. At least he wasn't on their ship yet. It would only take him a few seconds to kill the weaker members of their crew.

Not trusting the bones of my left arm to take my weight yet, I used my right hand to form a strand of metal qi. One quick flick of the wrist, and I managed to secure it on the railing across from Yon. I reeled myself up by drawing the metal qi back into my cores. I flopped onto the deck, taking a deep breath to center myself before getting back on my feet.

It was time to finish this.

CHAPTER THIRTEEN

Tips and Tricks

Yon still hadn't noticed me. His focus was on the two Saint cultivators, who were doing a decent job of keeping him busy. He was laughing as he batted away their attacks, occasionally launching his own blasts of wind qi against their ship below.

I checked on my friends, but they were all doing okay. They were down to fighting one person each, the bodies of two sailors splayed out on the deck proving the effectiveness of their team-work. The two men I had hamstrung earlier were trying to crawl their way belowdecks. Valerie would enjoy that.

My attention went back to Yon when I felt a massive buildup of qi coming from his direction. When I looked over at him, he was standing with his feet spread wide, arms raised above his head. Between his hands, a ball of roiling energy was slowly growing larger. It looked like he was intending to just blast a hole through the schooner, or possibly annihilate one of the Saint cultivators entirely. It was the perfect time to strike.

Once again, I unsheathed my sword, launching a wind blade at the back of his head. He was so wrapped up in his utter domination of the schooner's crew that he never even noticed my attack until it smacked into his skull hard enough to double him over and slam his face off the railing. His own qi construct lost cohesion, causing a backlash that sent Yon flying into the foremast when it exploded. I couldn't help but chuckle. My attack might not have been strong enough to split his skull, but I didn't want that anyway. I wanted this guy to *suffer*.

"Oh, I apologize. Was I interrupting something, Captain?"

His only reply was a growl. That was okay. This wasn't the part where he needed to talk anyway.

He kicked off the foremast, launching himself at me with both of his massive arms outstretched to catch me up in a crushing hug. Unfortunately for Yon, I wasn't much of a cuddler.

I ran straight at him, then dropped to my knees to slide underneath him as he sailed over my head. I dragged my sword cross-wise across his chest, slicing through his armor and deep into his pectoral muscles. His dive ended in a roll, and he managed to pop back to his feet. Blood trickled down his armor, coating his leather-clad torso in a sheen of red. I planted a knee and spun around to face him, set in a similar position to a sprinter's crouch. He grimaced, touching a hand to the slice in his armor.

"That is quite the sword, kid." Yon pulled his own scimitar free of his belt, spinning it around his body in a dazzling display of swordsmanship. "I will enjoy adding it to my collection."

"Funny, I was thinking along the same lines. Only I want to make a goblet from your skull, and drink to my victories in battle from it." I brought my hand to my chin, thinking for a moment. "No, that would mean you were one of my greatest enemies. That glorifies you entirely too much. After all, you were little more than a bump in the road for me. An annoying bump, but mostly inconsequential nonetheless."

He growled again, this time following it up with a blast of wind qi from the hand not holding his sword. Oh, he wanted to fight with qi? That was my favorite!

I sheathed my sword again so I could spin out a net of wind qi threads, throwing it at him. His attack was broken up by the multiple points of intersection with my attack, and both fizzled out. Next, he tried a spear of blue flames that I simply shifted to the side with two strands of earth qi, sending it over the side where it was extinguished by the ocean. That was followed by a dozen balls of spiky ice, propelled at me with eye-blurring speed. They shattered against a row of metal qi threads, only managing to cool me down a few degrees. Finally, Yon decided to try something more on the scale of a Sage.

"That's it, kid! I didn't want to do this, but you leave me no choice!" Yon thrust both hands above his head, and a giant spike of power came from him. *"Lightning Leviathan of the Abyss!"*

What the what? Who came up with the names for these attacks? I mean, leviathans have nothing to do with lightning, and 'the abyss' is supposed to be a dark place. The opposite of something bright. Like, maybe, lightning? Ugh, so dumb.

Since the dingleberry was kind enough to tell me the nature of his attack by literally shouting it at me, I just formed a net of earth and metal qi threads around me and fastened their ends into the deck of the ship. When the furious assault of a tentacle-shaped lightning construct smashed into me, the lightning just grounded out into the ship. I was completely unharmed.

"Nice try, Yon. Is it my turn yet?" He seemed torn between confusion and anger. I must have been the first person weaker than him that had no problem standing up to him in a fight. "This isn't even hard for me. With every attack, you waste massive amounts of qi, while I only need to use a miniscule amount to make a few *tiny* little strands of qi to beat you. At this rate, your cores will be empty before I even have to dip below half. You are so outclassed by me, Yon, that it's pathetic."

"Pathetic?! I'll show you who's pathetic!" He pulled a pouch off his belt, loosening the ties holding it closed. "Your puny body won't stand a chance against mine!" He threw the pouch at me, a red powder trailing behind it.

Expecting some kind of poison, I unsheathed my sword again, using the wind blade attack provided by the sheath to slice into the bag. It exploded on impact, sending a cloud of the red dust flying everywhere. I did my best not to breathe it in, holding my shirt sleeve over my nose. The powdery substance coated everything in sight, but I didn't feel any adverse effects. Yon just started laughing. I didn't understand why until I tried to send out a blast of wind qi to blow the powder away. The qi seemed to melt away as soon as it touched the fine dust, only managing to stir it slightly.

Yon used my distraction to his advantage, throwing himself at me in a blur of leather and steel. I barely managed to get my sword up in time to block his scimitar, but his razor-coated fist came in from my left and blasted me off my feet. It was my turn to bounce off the foremast, the impact knocking the air from my lungs. Instead of taking advantage of my weakness, the idiot decided to taunt me.

"You see now, don't you? There isn't any way for you to beat me!" He waved his hand around us, indicating the red powder coating the area. "No matter how good you might be as a cultivator, it means nothing when surrounded by orichalcum. Now, you have to face me without the help of qi. Just your might, against mine!" His monologuing gave me the chance to catch my breath, and inspect the cuts to my face his razored gauntlet had given me.

All my hard work strengthening my body with qi had certainly paid off. The two hidden forms of qi—light and dark —I incorporated into my skin, organs, and bones made them even stronger than they would have been with just the known six forms of qi. While it hadn't saved me from a broken wrist earlier, it had kept me from shattering my whole arm. Just like now, with the gashes to my cheek and chin. They were deep cuts that reached bone, but nothing was broken. I could still function.

"A simple fight, your skills against mine? That's what you

were looking for, Yon? All you had to do was ask." I activated my spirit wood ring, ordering it to deploy into a shield. My left wrist wouldn't be able to take a direct hit, but it could at least deflect a blow or two. The orichalcum couldn't stop the qi already stored in the ring, but I couldn't refill it as time went on. I probably had five minutes until it went back into a ring. "This suits me just fine." Seeing that I wasn't cowed by his size, he roared in anger and rushed to meet me in the center of the ship.

Yon led with a horizontal swing of his scimitar, trying to cut me in half at the waist. I didn't even bother deflecting it, just took a half-step back to avoid his swing. He followed up with a jab from his left fist. I spun sideways, sword leading the way. I managed to hit him in the forearm, causing him to jerk away in pain. My green sword had caught the armor near the edge of his gauntlet, giving it the ability to slice through and into the meat of his arm. It wasn't a deep slice, but it did set the tone for what was about to happen.

He spun away from me, twirling his blade to force me back. I didn't let him break away, instead using my shield to knock his scimitar over my head. Seeing an opportunity, I used the last of the energy stored in the ring to morph the shield into a spear. It hit in the gap left in his armor where his leather backplate didn't quite reach his sword belt on his waistline. The spear only punctured his skin a few inches, but his hiss of pain told me it hurt. Likely it had been some time since he experienced this form of sensory input. I was happy to remind him.

The spear snapped back into a ring, creating a spurt of blood that trailed down the back of his leg as he finished turning to face me. Now I was missing a shield, but he was having trouble standing up straight. The downside to his orichalcum trick was the drastic reduction in healing speed. I don't think that realization hit him until right now.

His next series of attacks were all lightning-quick slashes combined with sneaky follow-ups from his fists. I had to admit, the guy knew how to fight. I managed to deflect or dodge all but a backhand from the hand wielding his scimitar. I traded the blow for a stab at his face. I had been aiming for his eyes, but he managed to turn his head enough that I only managed what had to be a painful slice through his right ear. Its lower half was dangling from his head, and I could tell it bothered him. Especially when he shook his head and he could feel it flopping around. He had only managed to hit me in the same place as before, adding to the wounds I already had in the area. Just like before, it didn't slow me down.

It was on our fourth exchange of blades that I started to notice he always lifted his trailing foot when he punched straight forward. It made him overextend himself just a little, which gave me an opening I could exploit. I grabbed the pouch containing the ten poppers off my belt, snapping the leather cord that held them in place. As long as none of the orichalcum powder got inside the container, they would still be able to go off. My only choice was to throw the whole bag to ensure the powder didn't come into contact with them as they impacted the deck, meaning I only had one chance for this trick to work.

My moment came when he tried the backhand move again. He swung backwards, and followed up with a straight left jab that I had to roll backwards to avoid. I tossed the bag slightly behind him as I dove away, hoping that it actually worked.

It did. The ten poppers weren't anything like the explosion in the forest clearing, but they certainly got the job done. It might have been because the pouch helped to contain the detonation for a split second, or it could have just been I had an exceptionally good popper or two in the bag, but it managed to create quite an effect.

The decking splintered, shooting spears of wood outward in a giant circle. I unfortunately caught one in the left wrist, breaking the already weakened bone a second time. Yon caught it a little bit worse.

My intent had been to knock him off balance, and have a chance at getting another good hit in. The hunk of wood that protruded through his left shoulder did me one better. So did the knife-sized splinter sticking out of his left elbow.

I didn't give him a chance to pull them free, instantly jumping to my feet and renewing our fight. He was no longer able to follow up his wild scimitar swings with his heavy punches. It let me keep him on his back foot, always backing away from my precise thrusts aimed at his face and quick slashes targeting his legs. It was only a matter of time until I cut him down, and he knew it too.

On my next flurry of sword swings, I managed to knock his scimitar far enough to the side that he was forced into a back-wards roll to avoid a slash aimed at his neck. The maneuver drove the wooden spike in his shoulder deeper, renewing his loss of blood and forcing him to stagger. Seeing my chance, I darted toward him. Which was what he was waiting for.

Just as I closed the distance, he threw his scimitar at my face. I ducked, but he had used the distraction to get close enough to tackle me to the ground. He managed to get a hand around the wrist holding my sword, and started crushing it with his monstrous grip. I felt my bones snap, and my sword fell from my limp fingers. Even weakened by blood loss and an inability to use qi, Yon was still ridiculously strong.

Considering his size advantage, I was having some real trouble. He tried to position himself on top of me, but I managed to roll on my side and push away from his inner thigh using my free hand and arm as a brace, even though it hurt like hell because of my broken wrist. It caused him to fall forward on top of me, where he just started hammering his good arm into my ribs. I got a leg between us and pushed him away, wrapping my legs above his hip bones and locking my ankles together behind his back. I tried to roll our combined body weight so I could get on top and start raining down elbows into his face, but I couldn't get enough leverage with two broken wrists.

He finally managed to wriggle himself around so he was facing me again, but I still had my legs wrapped around his abdomen, keeping him from crushing me again. All he could do was start to drop his right elbow into my thigh in an attempt to force me to let him go. Which, believe me, didn't feel very good.

Looking around, I came to the realization that I only had one possible option to me at the moment. I lifted my left arm, where the wooden splinter as big around as my thumb pierced my wrist. This was going to suck.

I drove the wooden spike into Yon's bicep, using his forward momentum from an elbow strike to help me drive it in deeper. I twisted my wrist down, trapping the wooden spike between my bones so I could pull it free of his arm without losing it. Which might have hurt me more than it hurt him, considering how he basically ignored it.

My next swing caught him high in his unarmored armpit. That got his attention. He couldn't hold back the flinch the stab caused, so I used him pulling away from me to finally unlock my ankles and reposition my legs so I could kick him in the face with my right heel. Yon only leaned back about six inches, but it was enough space for me to wrap my legs around his neck. I flexed hard, squeezing as much as possible. He tried grabbing at my legs with his right arm, but the damage I had done to it had weakened his grip. It was only a few moments longer before his eyes rolled back in his head, the lack of air forcing him to pass out.

I held on a full minute longer, doing my best to make sure he wasn't faking it. His dead weight was trying to fall on top of me, so I shoved him to the side. I let out a sigh of relief. This had been a much harder fight than I thought it was going to be.

"Stars, Jim! What happened to you?!" I turned back to look at Chu, who was running up to check on me. I held up my broken arms to stop him.

"No! Don't come any closer." I looked around at the red dust still coating the area. "That's orichalcum dust. If you get any on you, it will take some time before you can cultivate again."

"That explains why you had such a hard time." Chu shouted over his shoulder at Donny. "Get Valerie! We need her expertise to blow all this stuff overboard." He looked over at Yon. "Did you kill him?"

I shook my head. "I don't know. He might just be knocked out. We need to get some of those slaver chains wrapped around him before he wakes up." Having said my piece, I sat with my back to the foremast to rest and wait for Valerie.

CHAPTER FOURTEEN

Dealing with Officers

Once she made it up on deck, it only took her a few minutes to direct enough wind to blow the majority of the dust overboard. I was still coated in the stuff, so Donny pulled out one of the waterskins that worked like a storage ring, allowing it to hold several hundred gallons of water. Or wine, if you were so inclined.

He seemed to thoroughly enjoy spraying me with water, which felt like it was only a few degrees above freezing. I did *not* thoroughly enjoy it, which is why he was probably having such a good time. After getting cleaned up, I was able to start healing myself right away. Even though the fight had been a hard one, I still had plenty of energy left in my cores.

Yon was still alive. Chu had wrapped him up from neck to ankles in orichalcum chains, then secured him to the mainmast with several loops of rope. He wasn't going anywhere for a while.

I was put on Every detail while Donny and Chu started gathering up the bodies of the sailors. Valerie had finished off the two that tried to sneak away, and the other three had managed to kill the remaining sailors. Slavers. Slaving sailors. Whatever.

Jamila and Valerie were searching the ship, and bringing everything that might be of value up on deck so I could store it in my belt. The horses were exceptionally happy to be out in the fresh air, and Every was amazed at the sails flapping in the wind. It was his first time outside in months, and the boy seemed to love it.

Right as we were about to toss the dead bodies of the sailors over the side, four people from the other ship jumped onto the deck. They were all ready to attack, in full plate armor with shields and spears positioned for a fight. I couldn't help but laugh. They were clearly not versed with combat on the open ocean, meaning their schooner was certainly a messenger ship. Their armor would certainly lead to their death the moment they fell overboard, unless they could put it in a storage device like I had done with my own. Don't get me wrong, I was still pretty new at fighting over water, but these guys must have been even more inexperienced. If they didn't have storage rings, they would find out really quickly just how deep the ocean was here.

"By the power of his Imperial Majesty, the Emperor, you are all under arrest for the assault of his representatives during the execution of their appointed duties! Submit yourselves immediately, or face the consequences!" The man who was shouting was the only person with gold filigree on his armor, marking him as either a lieutenant in the Imperial Army, or a captain in the Elemental Guard. He wasn't wearing the cape that distinguished which service he was a member of, leading me to believe he was of the former. An Elemental Guard would never be caught out of uniform, especially when given the time and opportunity to fully prepare.

Considering it had been well over thirty minutes since the two ships collided, I was pretty sure he had plenty of time to put on his full uniform while working up the nerve to board our ship. I wasn't able to see their appearance due to their helmets covering their heads and round shields held up to protect their faces, but most of them appeared to be rather young and inexperienced. This was most evident when they didn't know what to do after being ignored by my friends and I. "Hey! I said to submit yourselves, you, um… pirates!"

"Hold on, would you?" Chu stood up from his task of dragging bodies to the edge of the ship. "There are plenty of creatures out here in the deep ocean, and you don't want these rotting bodies to attract their attention. It's best to get them overboard as soon as possible, so they don't have to go hunting for their meat."

That made the lieutenant lower his shield a bit, letting me better see his wide eyes. That must have been new information for him. Poor guy was greener than most grass.

"Creatures? What kind of creatures? How far away are they?" Thankfully, the man standing next to him planted the butt of his spear on the deck and laid a reassuring hand on his shoulder.

"Don't worry, sir. While there might certainly be sea monsters in the area, those bodies will distract them long enough for us to leave." The speaker was shorter than the officer by a good six inches, but he exuded a presence of firm authority. His battered armor showed signs it had seen heavy use, and the silver filigree marked him as a high-ranking sergeant. Probably at least a platoon sergeant, but he could be an even higher rank, given the type of ship they were on. The two of them were the Saint-level cultivators that had briefly fought against Yon, meaning the captain of their ship was only a Brain cultivator. He must be either a talented sailor, or related to someone important. I was sure I would see which soon enough.

"Very good, Sergeant." The lieutenant straightened up a bit. "Men, arrest these pirates, then finish throwing those bodies over the side. And be quick about it." The other two soldiers stepped forward, ready to do their officer's bidding. I stood wearily to my feet, still holding the baby.

"Look, Lieutenant. I think we got off on the wrong foot

here." I pointed to Yon. "That is the pirate over there. Him and his men kidnapped us, and were in the process of transporting us to the Western Province to sell us as slaves. If you follow me, I can show you where—"

"Silence! Your mutiny against your captain is of no matter. You were still a member of the crew that attacked a messenger of the emperor, and as such, the penalty is death by hanging. Sentence will be carried out upon arrival at the nearest town with a regulation gallows, and a magistrate in attendance to confirm the verdict. Now, put down the child, and submit!"

I could finally see his face, and he looked barely old enough to be allowed into the service, and shaving wasn't a daily chore for him yet. If he was a day over nineteen, I would eat my belt. He was definitely a cultivation prodigy, but that didn't make him any less of a total asshat. I sighed, then placed Every on the deck behind me. Donny and Chu had already started to come closer, but I waved them away. I could handle this.

"I understand you are new at this, Lieutenant." I pulled out two trap plates, holding one in each hand. "But you need to stop and think for a moment. If this was a mutiny of the crew against their captain, wouldn't it make more sense for us to fight him *after* he wore himself down fighting you? And shouldn't you at least take a look at the evidence we are attempting to show you before condemning us all to death? Most importantly, isn't it a good idea—"

"Your words mean nothing to me, pirate!" He flared his cores to emphasize his shout. "You are on board a pirate ship, not currently in chains, even though you claim to be a prisoner, and you—" I threw the two trap plates at the men, each of them designed to hit those in its radius with a blast of earth qi that increased the gravity they experienced by four times the norm. The ship decking groaned in protest, but it just barely managed to hold. The soldiers might have been able to withstand the attack had they been expecting it, but the suddenness of the assault had caught them off guard.

"I let it go the first time, Lieutenant, but I do not appreciate being interrupted." I walked to the edge of the gravity field so I could look down on him and his men. The sergeant had managed to only drop to one knee, but he still hadn't managed to ramp up the qi in his cores to strengthen himself enough to stand. "What I was trying to say—before being rudely interrupted—is something I think you should take to heart. Most importantly, isn't it a good idea to not anger the person that managed to take down a Sage-level cultivator by himself?" I stepped into the gravity field that was holding them all down, my qi-reinforced body allowing me to walk with little difficulty.

"*Don't...do...this...*" The sergeant was struggling to talk while fighting to stand, his attachment to breathing keeping him from using his qi.

It was a problem many cultivators had. Most clans and sects taught their young children to control their lower cores with their breathing. Its location near the diaphragm made it an easy mental connection for them to make, and it had to be trained out of cultivators once they reached adulthood. Many didn't bother with the difficult process. I knelt in front of him, looking him straight in the eye. The lieutenant lying next to him could only wheeze. The other two soldiers were already unconscious.

"Don't do what, Sergeant?" I looked down at the officer. "Kill you all? Or just kill this stupid lieutenant for threatening my friends and I? By his logic, even the baby should be put to death! It is technically a member of the 'crew,' and therefore subject to the same ridiculous laws as the rest of us." I pulled a plain stiletto knife from my storage, holding it above the officer's face. "All I have to do is let go, and this pompous *idiot* won't trouble you any longer. I am sure his stupidity has caused you no end of trouble."

I met the eyes of the sergeant, and he slowly gave a shake of his head.

"*No...is...good...kid...just...new...to...this...*" I put the knife away. Then I bent low so the lieutenant could see how serious I was.

"I need you to remember this, Lieutenant. I could have

killed you all, and no one would have been the wiser. Instead, I am going to deactivate the formations holding you down. You will join me in an inspection of this ship, and we will document everything we can about the methods used to kidnap and smuggle prisoners. We will interrogate the pirate captain, and you will record the proceedings to ensure all the details of the illegal slave trade he is a part of are passed on to your superiors. Then, you and your men are going to help us move our things, including our horses, onto your ship. We will be joining you on your journey. Considering the direction of travel, I assume you are headed to the Western Provincial Capital. Is this true?" He couldn't answer, but the sergeant made a grunting sound I took to be an affirmative. "Good. Then let us be on our way. No one wants to remain on this ship any longer than they have to be."

I deactivated the formation plates, and the sergeant was on his feet immediately. I halfway expected him to try something, but instead he bent down to help the lieutenant up. Instead of being angry and shouting for my head, the officer was quiet. The sergeant pulled him off to the side, where they talked in hushed whispers for several minutes. While they were talking, the other two soldiers finally woke up. They were smart enough to read the situation, and walked over to join in the conversation. After what appeared to be a general consensus, they turned to face me. We all stood there for a moment, none of us speaking.

The lieutenant finally broke the silence. "I, um… I apologize." He said it in a rush, as if he was unused to apologizing for anything. "Perhaps I was too quick to judge the situation. I would be happy to take a look at the evidence you are willing to provide, and I would be happy to assist in the interrogation of the prisoner."

"Good. Follow me." I turned to head down into the hold, but looked back over my shoulder to speak to them first. "And just to make things clear. If you just made plans to double-cross my friends and I, you should make new ones." They stiffened, confirming my suspicions. "Don't make the mistake of confusing kindness for weakness. I won't spare you a second time." The four of them turned back to whisper to one another once again.

You couldn't trust anyone these days.

CHAPTER FIFTEEN

New Ship, New Problems

The process of documenting everything was actually the work of several hours. Yon's personal quarters were a treasure-trove of information. There were enough maps, charts, timetables, dates, lists, and contact information to fill a dozen notebooks. I made sure to make copies of everything, my ability to slow time by speeding up my perception of it gave me the opportunity to finish while the lieutenant took his own notes.

We then walked them all through the hidden slave quarters under the hold, and showed them the chains used to keep the prisoners subdued. Valerie did a good job of telling them about what happened when we were kidnapped, and explaining how we had been living in the hold the last few months. By the time we were finished, I didn't think there was any way they could still think we were a part of the pirate crew. The two soldiers and sergeant surely believed, it was only the young officer I was concerned about. Finally, it was time to interrogate Yon.

"I think it is only proper that Sergeant Ward and I question the prisoner. We are properly trained by the empire on the techniques that best work to gain knowledge from prisoners."

I just looked at the officer with a dead-faced stare. Hadn't I proven myself capable to him yet? "Fine." The lieutenant stood up straight with my acceptance, happy to be in charge again. Time to stop that before he got a big head. "But he isn't your prisoner. He is mine. I will be present during your questioning, and if you fail, I get to try."

He deflated a bit. After trading glances with his sergeant, he nodded. "That is acceptable. While we question him, your people and my men can shift everything over to our ship." He turned to look at Scout and Cloud. Both horses were standing near the rear of the deck where Valerie had set up a drinking trough for them. "It will take some work to find a place for everyone."

I agreed, and we went to where Yon was tied up. As we approached, I saw that he was finally awake. Given his wounds, I was wondering if he would just quietly bleed to death. Apparently, his Sage constitution kept that from happening.

"I was beginning to think you had forgotten about me." He was grinning, trying to show he wasn't worried about us. The blood still dripping from his ear ruined the image he was going for. "I can already tell you, it isn't necessary to interrogate me. I will happily give you any information you are looking for."

This, of course, made the lieutenant extremely happy. "Excellent. Let's start with the slave markets." He pulled out a fresh notebook and started jotting down everything Yon was saying. It matched what we had found in his cabin, meaning the man was actually telling us everything. It was infuriating.

I had been looking forward to working him over ever since I met the guy. He knew it, too. I must have let my disappointment show on my face, because he kept smirking at me as he answered questions. I occasionally cut in to ask a few of my own, and he even answered those honestly. The bastard.

We finished up with the questions just as they managed to get the horses transferred to the schooner. It had survived the impact with Yon's ship relatively unscathed, helping the process along. They had rigged up a makeshift crane to lower them down somehow. I was just glad I didn't have to be a part of it.

I now had a good overall picture of the slaver operation, and could easily stop it with a few words in the correct ears. When we got back to the empire, I was going to do my best to shut them down with a vengeance. I also wanted to have words with the ringleader, a man Yon called Lord Heian. He was somewhere in the Northern Province, and that was where I was headed after I was done in the west. Some further investigation would be necessary.

"What now? Are you going to arrest me and take me back for questioning? I don't mind being a witness for the magistrates." Yon was talking to the lieutenant, but looking at me. His smug face said it all. He knew the officer would love the accolades bringing in a pirate captain and slaver would bring him, and it would give him plenty of opportunities to escape custody. It was incredibly difficult to keep a Sage cultivator locked up for any lengthy period of time. That was why most were just forced to serve a term as a soldier on the northern border and released after a few years. Or executed, if the crime was bad enough.

The lieutenant didn't even look at me before finally answering Yon. "That would probably be for the best. I will lock you in the hold, where you will remain until we reach the Western Capital." The lieutenant was looking around for his men so he could have them move him. "There you will answer for your crimes, and most certainly be executed upon the completion of the investigation into the illegal activities you and your friends have been up to." Not seeing his soldiers, he turned and started to walk towards the railing to yell over the side. I took two steps forward and grabbed him by the shoulder.

"No, Lieutenant. I don't think so." He tried to pull free of my grip, but I didn't let him move away. "That is my prisoner, and this is currently my ship by right of conquest. My ship, my prisoner, my rules."

"I understand your frustration at the situation, but surely you understand the need to bring this man back to the empire. Why, the information on the whereabouts of the people he has already sold could mean the difference between a poor soul finding freedom, or remaining a slave for the rest of their life!" He was looking down his nose at me, secure in the validity of his argument.

I pointed at his storage ring. "You mean the information already documented and contained inside your ring? I was there when you found it, remember? No, you won't be getting a medal out of this one." He opened his mouth to argue, so I pulled out a familiar-looking formation plate. The lieutenant visibly flinched, the memory of what I had done earlier still fresh in his mind. "You have two minutes until I send this ship to the bottom of the ocean. I recommend you use them well." He turned and sprinted for his ship, shouting something to his men. I wasn't worried. My friends were already on board, and they would make sure the schooner wouldn't leave without me on it.

I walked back to the middle of the ship, in full view of Yon. I placed a bucket from my storage belt on the deck and pulled out a large vial of liquid qi. I poured the whole thing inside, filling it over halfway. Then I made a few adjustments to the runes on the formation plate, increasing the yield from four times normal gravity to twenty. It should be enough to get the job done. I dropped it in the bucket, but I didn't activate it yet. Yon had been watching me the whole time, his face slowly becoming more concerned with my actions. Due to his position, he hadn't seen the lieutenant run for his ship.

"What are you doing? What is that? Where did the other guy go?" His voice was still steady, but my lack of answers made him even more nervous. Instead of answering, I moved the bucket closer to him. It needed to be in the proper position. Finally, I had everything where I wanted.

"It's simple, Yon. I told you before I would balance the scales." I pointed at the bucket near his feet. "That device helps weigh your sins. For every wrongdoing you have committed, it gets just a little bit heavier. Too much weight, and it will drive you and the mast you are tied to straight through the bottom of the ship, all the way to the ocean floor." He wasn't sure if he should believe me or not, but I didn't care. It would give him something to think about while his soul waited for judgement in the dark expanse between worlds. I pulled out the lid to the bucket and sealed the container. I didn't want the ocean to wash away the liquid qi powering the plate too soon. "Goodbye, Yon. I hope you suffer and burn for countless eons before being reincarnated into the body of a disease-riddled squirrel. Who later dies in a fire."

"Wait!" He shouted after me as I walked away. "We can talk about this! Don't do this! I can give you the numbers to my accounts wi—*urk*!" His voice was cut off when I activated the formation plate with a flex of my will. He was slammed into the deck, which only held for a few seconds before a circle twenty feet in diameter dropped into the hold below. The mast went with him.

The entire ship dipped low enough in the water that I had to reach *up* to grab the railing of the schooner. I grabbed it just in time, as the hull of the ship finally gave way and Yon was sent plummeting into the dark waters. The sudden lack of weight allowed the buoyancy of the ship to almost throw it up and out of the water. The schooner was rocked sideways, and the waves pushed it away from the doomed vessel. It was already starting to sink, the massive hole right in the center allowing the disturbed water to rush inside the spacious hold. The entire crew watched in silence as the ship slipped under the waves.

"How did you…? What did you…? What *was* that?" The lieutenant was standing near my elbow, both hands on the railing and wide eyes staring at the place the slaver's ship used to be moments before. I looked around the new ship, seeing a place on the deck roped off for our people—and horses—with a canvas stretched out to provide some shade. I headed that direction. "I asked you a question! Now you are on *my* ship, and you have to answer me when I say!" I noticed all four of the soldiers were still in full armor, and they just so happened to be positioned so I was encircled by them.

"What happened, you asked? I already told you the answer, Lieutenant. It is a mistake to confuse kindness for weakness. Sometimes, a *fatal* mistake. If you do, bad things can happen." I saw out of the corner of my eye when Sergeant Ward motioned for the soldier next to him to put away the set of shackles he was hiding behind his back. I raised the corner of my mouth in a smile, letting him know I had seen it. "Are there any other questions, Lieutenant?"

"No, um, not at this time." He seemed confused as to why I wasn't being arrested right now, but he wasn't willing to say anything with me standing there. "Now that you are on board, those that cannot pay for passage are required to work the ship. Given that you were kidnapped, I feel free to assume you do not have the necessary coin to pay for your journey. You will be expected to report to the ship's captain immediately for your assignment." He then turned abruptly and walked away, headed for the hatch at the rear of the ship.

What an idiot. I literally *just* plundered a pirate ship! Of *course* I had the gold to pay for our trip. I mean, I probably had enough gold and cores on me before we were even kidnapped that I could have bought two or three of these schooners outright, but that wasn't the point. This guy was plain stupid. I looked pointedly at the sergeant and he just shrugged his shoulders, as if to say he hoped the lieutenant would learn, someday.

Oh well. I actually didn't mind helping to work the ship. It would give me an opportunity to learn how to actually sail and pilot a ship. The next time we were stranded on a boat out at sea, we wouldn't be dependent on others to sail the ship for us. I guessed it was time to find the captain of this tub and see what kind of man he was like.

CHAPTER SIXTEEN

Rough Seas

As it turned out, the captain wasn't much of a man at all. Luckily, *she* turned out to be pretty great. Captain Hail was happy to have the extra hands we provided. Apparently, her orders were to leave their last port of call with all haste, meaning she hadn't gotten the time to collect a full complement of sailors before leaving. The lieutenant had refused to allow his men to assist her crew with ship operations, citing some regulation about soldiers and sailors not being allowed to mix unless during combat.

What an absolute blacksmithing implement.

"Good! Now tie that down, and make sure you secure it!" I was up in the rigging, listening to her shouted instructions and trying to help replace the last of the damaged sails. "That should be the last of them! Jim, get in the crow's nest, and keep a sharp eye! This isn't a pleasure cruise!"

I waved in agreement and worked my way to the rope ladder on the foremast to climb my way to the top.

We had only been on the ship for two days, but all of us were already in a much better mood. The ability to stay outside had been incredible, and the ship's crew instantly fell in love with Every. After we explained his situation, all of the four-person sail team, the cook, and captain herself had instantly volunteered to help watch the baby. Which was good, considering the munchkin's ability to find himself in precarious positions after only a few moments of being without a dedicated individual to watch him.

Once I reached the crow's nest, I looked back down at the ship to see how everyone was doing. Every was below decks at the moment with the cook, and two of the regular crew were sleeping the day away in preparation for their turn at night. A ship at sea required constant shifts, and our presence allowed them to gain the rest they had been missing out on.

Captain Hail had done an excellent job keeping her ship in the best shape possible considering the circumstances. The lack of sleep and need to let small issues wait until later had piled up over time, however, which was why we had come upon a damaged ship in the first place. According to her, a single fire wisp lamp had somehow broken during the morning shift change, and it had managed to burn through a good portion of their sails in less than a minute before they could recapture it. I hadn't known a fire wisp lamp was even allowed on a ship until then, but I supposed it did make sense. When properly contained, the tiny creatures were a great early warning system for monster attacks. However, their rarity made it uncommon for their use in such a mundane manner.

The captain had only been using what she had at hand. The fire wisp had allowed her to keep only one person on night watch, allowing them to at least rotate through the responsibility. Now that we had arrived, they could finally catch up on lost sleep.

As I had surmised earlier, the captain was only at the Brain level of cultivation. The reason why she had been elevated to captain was due to her qi control, making her a rare gem in the Empire's Navy. In fact, I suspected she was the closest person I had ever met to my own skill level since reincarnating. She could only manage such fine qi control when using wind and water qi, but that was still more than most would ever do.

The climb to the crow's nest had been somewhat harrowing. I hadn't realized how much the tiniest of ocean swells could translate to such drastic swaying motions at the tip of the masts. It gave me a new appreciation for the people that chose this job as a profession. They had nerves of steel.

Once I got comfortable, I took a long look at the ocean around us. It was nothing but dark water for miles in all directions, with a slight breeze from the south giving the sea a light chop on the surface. Far in the distance there was a dark cloud bank, but it was too far away to be of concern yet. We were headed directly away from it, so hopefully the ship would outrun the storm.

Looking back at the people running around below, I contemplated what our next steps should be. I needed to speak to the Western King, but I didn't have a letter of introduction from the Southern King that would grant me an audience. I would have to figure something else out. In my first life, the Western King allowed a small gathering of townsfolk to speak with him once a month. That person wouldn't be the king for at least another century or two, and I didn't know what the current ruler was like. I would have to see what the situation looked like when I got there.

The most pressing issue was Every. I needed to get the boy to the nearest Auction House possible, and ensure he was returned to his parents. They were probably worried sick about him. That would be my first stop when we reached land. That would allow me to hopefully reunite him with his family.

After dropping off Every and seeing the king, it would be time to head to the Northern Province. We were already partially into the fall-year, meaning we were looking at traveling northward during the winter-year. It got so cold in those mountains that even Sage cultivators ran the risk of freezing to death without the proper precautions. My little warming sticks I had used to keep us going last winter-year wouldn't be enough to save us, so we would need to purchase the proper clothing and heaters before heading out.

I was still lost in thought when our ship was rocked hard enough to throw me out of the crow's nest. I caught myself on the rigging just below the platform I had been standing on, the rope burning my hands before I could stop myself from falling. Scrambling back up into the nest, I frantically looked around to see what had happened. The dark waters didn't show me anything, and the ship stopped rocking from side to side after a few bursts of air qi from the captain. Whatever had just hit us, she was doing her best to get us out of the area as quickly as possible. I could hear the creak of the timbers from the masts and the humming groan of ropes pulled as taut as possible. For a ship the size of a schooner, the trick to staying alive was speed. And they were certainly built for it.

From my place high up above the ship, I couldn't see any damage beyond a few casks rolling around on deck. They must have broken loose from the impact. It was hard to tell, but I think it was Donny who had already chased one down, and was positioned to stop the other. There was plenty of shouting coming up from below, but I couldn't make out what they were saying.

While I was watching, I saw the captain form a tube of air qi that slowly stretched up toward my location at the top of the foremast. When it finally reached me, she was able to speak as if we were standing right next to one another.

"Jim, did you see what hit us?" I was impressed at the clarity of her voice given the distance and wind resistance her communication construct was dealing with. "Because whatever smashed us, it was *big*."

I shook my head, and then felt stupid because she obviously couldn't see me.

"No, Captain Hail. I didn't see anything. The waters are so dark that I can't make out anything below the surface." I looked around again as I spoke, wishing that I had better news.

"Is there anything at all that you can see? Another ship in

the distance, a wake from anything besides us underwater, something?!"

"No, nothing. There is just that storm behind us, but it is far enough away that we shouldn't need to—" I was cut off by the captain.

"A storm? How big is it? You know what, never mind. I will be up in a bit. I shouldn't have expected you to know what to look for after only two days on the crew. My mistake. Make some room up there for me, Jim. I will show you what kind of storm to look out for." She dissipated the construct and I saw her pass the wheel off to Valerie, who took over duties as the wind provider for the sails. She was able to reach the crow's nest in about a quarter of the time it had taken me to climb up, her long experience allowing her to use the sway of the ship to her advantage instead of fighting it like I had.

"Welcome to the top, Captain." I shifted to one side, reaching down to give her a hand for the last few feet. She was surprisingly heavy, given her short stature. Hail was only a few inches over five feet tall, and more wiry than thin. Her dark tan skin, brown eyes, and black hair indicated she was from the island chains off the Eastern Province coast. The seashells braided into her hair were all a solid white color, denoting that she was one of the clanless from the region. I only knew that due to my first life, when I had spent some time among the islands trying to track down a fugitive while I was an Enforcer. It had been one of the better pursuits of my life, with days spent in the jungles and nights on the sandy beaches. Maybe I would visit after the *nox* were dealt with. Her sharp eyes noticed my wandering attention, and she slapped me in the back of the head to bring me back to the moment. I could have dodged, but I let it happen. I deserved it for letting my focus wander.

"Pay attention!" She shook her finger in my face, close enough that I was risking an eye gouge. "That is the first and most important rule of the crow's nest!" Having put me in my place, she took a few seconds to look around. "Do you see how those clouds in the distance seem to look more like a black wall than normal gray storm clouds?" I nodded my head, agreeing with her assessment. "That means it is a natural phenomenon known as a 'qi storm,' and it means trouble. They can last for weeks at a time, and there isn't anything we can do to stop them."

I raised my eyebrows in surprise. I knew about qi storms, but they were incredibly rare, and normally formed during winter-year. Having one this far out of season seemed strange. I said as much to the captain.

"Isn't it the wrong time frame for a qi storm? And why can't we just outrun it?"

She shook her head, no longer even looking at me. Instead, she was paying close attention to the waters around the ship. "Sure, on *land*, qi storms usually come around during winter-year, but out here, in the deep ocean, they can happen any time." She pointed off into the distance. "But that is the real threat." It took me a few seconds to see what she was talking about, but then I finally noticed the frothing waves headed in our direction. "Ah, you finally see it. We can probably outrun the storm, but we aren't the only things running from it. Any qi-sensitive creatures out there are trying to stay in front of the storm as well. Meaning they are being driven straight for us. And that means we have a few rough days ahead."

I grimaced, realizing exactly what she was talking about. We were in for a fight if some of the more rambunctious monsters running around decided they were hungry for a snack.

"What should we do then, Captain?"

She didn't answer at first, still staring at the frothing waters in the distance. "We have two choices. Try to make a run for it, or swing around and head straight into the storm." I looked at the cloudbank, then looked at the size of the ship. While not a tiny vessel, it wouldn't fare well in the massive sea swells that were bound to be inside such a tempest.

"I think I like the first option better. Trying our luck inside the storm seems foolhardy."

She nodded in agreement. "Yes, as long as we can fight off

the sea monsters, we should be okay. Otherwise, we will have to risk the storm to avoid whatever it is that is churning up the waters like that." I looked again, this time forming a small lens of water qi intended to enhance my vision. I might have been imagining it, but I thought I saw a tentacle the size of our mainmast swinging around a shark like it was Every playing with a toy. It must be my imagination playing tricks on me.

"What next? Is there some way to make the ship go faster?"

She nodded, pointing to the deck below. "Don't worry, I can handle that part. You just stay up here and keep a sharp eye out for monsters, or other ships." I voiced my agreement, and she started the climb back to the deck. "Oh, and Jim?" I looked down at her. "I will let Lieutenant Smythe know about the incoming monsters, but you might want to get some of those formation plates everyone keeps talking about ready. You never know what we could run into out here." With that final warning, she left.

I had a bad feeling it was about to be a long couple days.

CHAPTER SEVENTEEN

Leviathan

It turned out to be a long *week*. We all spent time rotating through shifts as the person providing strong winds, keeping watch in the crow's nest, or tending the sails. We were managing to stay in front of the storm, but it was taking all of us to manage it. There were also several fights with sea monsters, which the soldiers mostly took care of. My friends and I could have handled them, except the genius Lieutenant Smythe informed us it was not our place. So, we stood back and let them have their fun. Well, it was fun to watch. I didn't think they were enjoying it nearly as much.

"Sir, next time we have to fight a bunch of slime eels, can you wait until we are clear before slicing them into pieces?" Sergeant Ward and his two soldiers were completely covered in a sticky green slime after an overzealous Lieutenant Smythe went a little crazy with his qi construct. "It is going to take us several hours to get our armor clean. Sir." His words might have been respectful, but his tone certainly wasn't.

"Battle is messy sometimes, Sergeant. I would think someone with your experience would have already learned this lesson." Smythe seemed not to notice his disrespectful tone. Or just didn't care.

I had learned over the past week that he was from a branch family of the Xing clan, meaning he was a distant cousin to the emperor. The Xing clan had been in power since the founding of the empire, and had such a monopoly on cultivation aids and techniques that they should continue to remain in power for generations to come. Case in point, the lovely Lieutenant Smythe. He was actually in his early thirties, but had been extensively sheltered his entire life due to his speed of climbing the cultivation ranks. Reaching the level of Saint at such a young age truly was remarkable. It was just too bad he turned out to be such an asshat.

I had seen it hundreds of times before. A clan or sect gets their hands on a gifted child, pumps them so full of cultivation pills and elixirs that they practically choke on them, and tells them the whole time that they are the greatest gift to the empire since the emperor himself. In all my years, I had *never* seen that end well. They universally turned out as terrible people, and my fellow Enforcers and I had frequently needed to put them down like the rabid dogs they became. Or, in the case of Ming, I worked for one. I would be putting *that* dog down as soon as I was given the opportunity, rest assured.

"Here comes some more!" Valerie shouted down from her place in the crow's nest. "You might want to get ready!" She had ended up spending most of her time up top, occasionally using her bow to discourage the rampant sea monsters from approaching the ship. Until today, when Smythe had told her to stop. He was of the belief that he and his men were solely responsible for the ship's defense, and her actions were hindering their efforts. So, to say that Valerie sounded happy about announcing another wave of eels would be an understatement. She was *loving* it.

"Ready-up, men! Quit fooling about and prepare for the next wave!" Smythe, who was spotlessly clean due to his position at the rear, received more than one negative glance from his men.

I turned back to my own task, spinning out another thread of wind qi and pushing it into the mainsails. The slight lurch from us picking up speed caused Sergeant Ward to slip on the goo covering the rear of the ship, almost sending him over-board. I could barely contain the chuckle that tried to sneak out. The whole thing really was hilarious.

My boost to our speed gave the men a little extra time to get ready, and they were somewhat prepared when the eels caught us. The fight was going well, right up until the time that they suddenly broke off the attack and swam away as fast as their squirmy bodies could manage.

"Great job, men! You have them on the run!" Smythe approached his soldiers and looked like he was about to pat them on their backs. After seeing globs of goo roll down their armor and splat onto the deck, he changed his mind. "Um, ah, yes. Well, mission complete. Let's head below, and give the crew a chance to clean the deck, shall we?" There was grumbling from everyone, and not just the soldiers.

"Wait. Hold on. They just gave up and swam away?" Just then, Valerie shouted a warning, pointing behind the ship. The man standing at the wheel glanced back, seeing the bed of eels disappear into the dark ocean waters. His face went as white as snow, and he jerked the wheel towards port, throwing the ship sideways. "*Captain*! Captain, we have a problem!" He was shouting at the top of his lungs, and motioned for me to put on more speed. "Captain! Trouble on deck!"

"What is it?" Hail came out from her cabin, tucking her shirt in as she rushed towards the wheel. The sleep lines on her face meant either the sudden direction change or loud shouting had woken her from a nap. "What did you see?"

"It's nothing, Captain Hail. I don't know what your people are shouting about, but the danger is now gone." Smythe was standing with his hands on his hips, like a hero out of some story. "My men and I drove off the attacking creatures, and we are free to continue."

"Captain, they didn't scare those slime eels off. They were *running*, and it wasn't from us." The ship's pilot looked about, still pale with worry. "I don't see it yet, but it must be out there."

"Really, must you go on?" The officer seemed upset that the sailor was ruining his chance to show off. "I already told you, they were running from—"

"Oh, just shut up, would you?" Hail wasn't even looking at Smythe. "Anyone with half a brain could figure out that an ocean predator only runs from one thing." She shouted up to Valerie. "Val, what did you see?!"

"Tell us then, Captain." Smythe was really upset he had been cut off. Funny, considering how much he liked to do it to other people. "What do ocean predators run from?"

Hail finally looked back at Smythe after getting the all-clear signal from Valerie that whatever it had been was no longer there. "Simple." Her voice dropped an octave. "An even bigger predator." Which—since it was how the world loved to work— was when a tentacle nearly as large as the ship rose out of the water less than a hundred yards off the starboard bow.

"To arms! All hands, to arms! *Leviathan!*" Valerie was shouting as loud as she could, and had already sent two arrows toward the massive creature headed our direction.

"Lieutenant, you and your men need to strap yourselves down. This could get rough." Hail put action to her words, shooting a blast of wind qi at the sails hard enough to make the ship dip low into the water, before skipping up and onto the waves with a jolting slam. "Jim, you focus on getting as much wind on the foremast as you can. I will handle the mainmast."

"Yes ma'am, will do." I ran to the center of the deck, dodging the sailors running around as they made sure every-thing was tied down properly and the sails were fastened so as to give us every inch of available sheet. It was a tight operation, everyone doing their best to help get the best speed possible out of the little ship. Out of the corner of my eye, I saw Jamila running below with Every held in her arms. Good. We hadn't been concerned with the eels since all of us were around, but this was entirely different.

Just as I was reaching for a rope to tie myself to the main-mast, so I could start giving us a further boost of speed, the ship was struck from below with such force that we came completely out of the water. I went flying. When we came back down, I felt an ominous shudder pass through the wooden hull. It wouldn't survive another blow like that.

When we were sent airborne, I had almost been thrown overboard. I managed to catch myself as I flew past a rope that held the yardarm of the foremast in place. The extra height the position gave allowed me to catch a glimpse of exactly what we were facing.

Yon's ship was almost twice the size of the schooner. The monster now attacking us would easily be considered twice the size of Yon's ship. To put it mildly, we were screwed. To add insult to injury, the hit from the leviathan had slowed our speed considerably.

Both Donny and Chu were tossing formation plates over the side by the handful, their various attacks doing little more than annoying the giant creature. One of our more powerful plates, an ice blade attack meant to cut a high-ranking cultivator in half, only managed to scratch a single tentacle. This was bad.

Dropping back to the deck, I ran to Hail. She had stopped providing wind for the sails and was instead having an argu-ment with Smythe.

"…wouldn't matter in the least! They don't weigh enough to make a difference, and I refuse to throw innocent men, women, and *children* over the side, just to give us a little extra speed!" Hail was in his face, her hands both balled into fists.

"It isn't your call, *Captain!*" Smythe was clearly afraid, his focus more on the leviathan than the argument he was having with Hail. "My mission to deliver this message takes priority over a bunch of civilians! The blood oath you swore to the emperor requires you to prioritize your mission above all else!

Besides, they might provide us with the distraction we need to get away!"

Well, all it took was a little fear, and the true nature of a person was revealed.

"I have an idea, *Lieutenant*." My voice cut through the tension like a knife. "Why don't we throw you overboard in chunks? You know, like chum. All the blood will certainly distract the leviathan for at least a few minutes."

He didn't even have the decency to look ashamed. "Threaten me all you like, but it doesn't change her oath. Or anyone's oath. They are sworn to obey my orders when the mission is threatened, and their cultivation bases will force them to do what I say, whether they want to or not." He wasn't wrong. When a cultivator swore an oath, especially a blood oath, it was magically tied to their cores. If they broke that oath, they would break their cores, effectively killing themselves.

"Well, that means I only have one option." I sighed, a defeated look on my face. Smythe opened his mouth, probably to give the order to throw my friends and I overboard. I shoved my hand in his mouth, balling it into a fist so he couldn't bite down or pull away. "I guess I have to kill you before you can give that order." I jerked him closer to me, so I could whisper in his ear. Sergeant Ward was sprinting to save him, but he was too far away to reach me in time. "You forgot who the biggest monster is. It isn't the leviathan. It's *me*." His eyes widened in fear, and he tried to say something. I didn't give him the chance.

I spun out a thread of dark qi, melting his throat from the inside out. His body fell away from me, his severed head still on my fist. Sergeant Ward finally made it over, but he stopped when he saw there was nothing he could do.

Hail just looked relieved. "You killed him. Thank the stars." The captain looked back at the leviathan, where most of the crew were either casting qi constructs or using spears to keep its questing tentacles from finding purchase on the ship. "Now that he is out of the way, what ideas do you have? At this point, I am open to suggestions."

"By the power vested in me by the emperor, I am placing you under arrest for the murder of Lieutenant Smythe Xing." Sergeant Ward was fumbling with some shackles, the rocking of the ship making it difficult for him to get them open.

"Sergeant Ward, if you attempt to arrest me right now, I will cut your arms off and use them to beat you to death." Since I needed to use some light qi to balance my hand meridian back out, I released a beam of concentrated light that instantly turned the head still on my hand into ash. The 'flashy' display proved my point better than any further threats could have. "The idiot was going to throw my friends and I overboard—including the baby—in an attempt to distract the leviathan long enough to get away." He had taken a step back when I destroyed the head, but that comment stopped him. "I could argue in any court that what I did was self-defense. I might even win. After all, as soon as it came out that a military officer was willing to sacrifice a baby to save his own life, they would shut down any investigation rather quickly. We can't have officers look like cowards to the people, can we?"

Sergeant Ward put the shackles away. "No. That is clearly conduct unbecoming of an officer, and any magistrate will judge it as such." He bent down and took two rings and a scroll case from the corpse. "But the Xing clan will not see it that way. No matter what I say or do, they will want revenge for killing one of their up-and-coming stars." His eyes met mine. "Expect more than one poisoned drink, or knife from the shadows. Their reputation can't risk you telling that story."

I nodded, showing that I understood. "Can we *please* deal with the giant squid monster trying to eat us all now?" Hail was moving the ship in a slow circle, leading the leviathan on a chase that benefited us. Like all squid, it could dart forward in a straight line very quickly. It could not, however, make sharp turns nearly as fast.

Checking the approaching wall of dark clouds, I made some quick calculations in my head. Looking back at the leviathan, I could only see one way we made it out of this. Luckily, I had the items we needed to get it done.

"Captain!" She cut off the conversation she was having with Ward to look at me. "How much longer do you think the storm will last?"

"It has already been at least a week. I figure it will start to die off in another day or two. Why? Are you thinking we make a run for the storm to throw it off our trail?" She looked doubtful. She had already come to the same conclusion I had. It would catch us the moment we straightened out our direction and rip us to pieces.

"Yes, but not without doing something to slow it down first." I pulled out the two stone sarcophaguses from my storage belt. I had been meaning to get rid of Silas and Moose for a while now, but I hadn't gotten around to doing it yet. Good thing, too. Now was my chance. "I was serious about the chum idea. It might just work."

I cracked open the stone holding Moose and Silas. Normally, a storage device slowed or stopped the decay of an item, allowing them to be stored indefinitely. Since the bodies had been sealed in an airtight container, the natural process of decomposition had only been slowed down instead of stopped. Let's just say, the smell wasn't the greatest. To make it worse, I used some threads of metal qi to dice up their bodies into chunks. I had a strong stomach, but that just about made me lose my lunch.

"Gah! What in the stars is that!" Sergeant Ward was backing away, an errant gust of wind blowing the smell straight into his face.

"That, my dear Sergeant, is the smell of our salvation!" Hail had a grin on her face. She was well aware of the fact that the smellier the chum, the better it worked. This would work great.

I shoved what was left of Moose overboard first. The leviathan responded instantly, and I got my first look at its snapping beak. The mouth was surprisingly small for such a large creature. Which, naturally, gave me another idea.

"Hail, when I tell you, I need you to go straight. I need to be able to see the leviathan up close for my plan to work."

She only nodded in response, apparently trusting me enough to risk a few moments of danger to give me an opportunity to buy us some time.

Sergeant Ward didn't feel the same. "Plan? *What* plan?! You just want to be able to watch as it rips us apart?!" He was clearly losing it. Considering the circumstances, I guess I could cut him some slack.

"Why would I do that?" I dragged the body of Smythe over to the railing, stuffing a block of wood down his shirt. "I'm on the ship too, remember? Now stop arguing, and help me. We need to shove the chum and the body over at the same time. Got it?" He nodded, and pushed the stone coffin to the edge of the railing. "Okay, Hail. Now!"

She straightened the ship out just as the stone and body of Smythe splashed into the ocean. The coffin sank, but the chum floated on the surface. It wasn't until I didn't see the body of the lieutenant bob to the surface that I realized I had forgotten to remove his armor. It was sinking. Butt-nuggets.

Just as I was about to yell at Hail to turn again, I saw a flash of light gleam off of one of the leviathan's longer tentacles. It had caught him! All that chum must have had the creature flailing about for anything large enough to grab ahold of. I watched as the massive tentacle brought the body to its beak and crunch into the armored hunk of meat. Perfect.

With a flex of my will, I activated the emergency raft the leviathan had just shoved in its mouth. It expanded to full size almost instantly, forcing the beak open wider than it was ever meant to go. The sound of its beak cracking and surrounding soft tissue tearing apart was audible over all the shouts, screams, splashes, and other ambient noise. The sound the creature made afterward was loud enough to shake the boat.

It wasn't quite a scream, as it was beyond the ability for our human ears to hear. Scout and Cloud, on the other hand, could hear it just fine. The normally stoic animals absolutely freaked out, nearly ripping apart the makeshift pen that held them on deck.

The sound actually caused the entire ship to vibrate hard enough that the topmost yardarm on the foremast came untied and crashed to the deck, narrowly missing the sailor trying to calm the horses. As it was only one of the smaller topsails, any loss of speed wouldn't be immediately noticeable.

Captain Hail was the first to act, sending a fresh burst of wind qi into the sails to increase our speed. The leviathan didn't seem to notice, writhing in pain and trying to pluck out the raft still lodged in its mouth.

As we gained in distance, the crew began to cheer. I was almost bowled over from all the backslapping I received. Even Sergeant Ward shook my hand, giving me a long and contemplative look. Valerie, who had been in the crow's nest this whole time, dropped down to more easily speak with us.

"Um, guys, why is everyone so happy?" We all looked at her, confused as to why she would be asking, considering what had just happened. "You do realize we are headed straight into the qi storm, right?"

That sobered us all up quickly.

I turned to speak to Captain Hail. "Do we even need to go into the storm? We dealt with the leviathan. It should be okay to continue as we were, right?"

She shook her head no. "We only hurt it. That thing is still back there, and it is probably even angrier. The storm is still our only chance." Everyone looked back at the writhing monster in the distance, its full bulk rising in and out of the water for the first time. I was wrong. It was more like *ten* times the size of the schooner.

"Yeah, definitely the storm." Chu had come up behind the group without me noticing. "I vote the storm. Anyone else? Better yet, is anyone *against* the storm at this point?" No one said anything. "Okay then, storm it is! Captain, if you would, please?"

She put action to words, and we took off for the roiling mass of clouds. I couldn't help but think of something my father used to say, a long time ago, back in my first life, right before I had been kicked out of the Roh clan. I said it quietly, so no one would hear me.

"Well, out of the cookpot, and into the campfire. Good luck." I felt like we might need it.

CHAPTER EIGHTEEN

With the Bad, Comes the Good

The storm wasn't as bad as we had feared. It was worse. The real problem didn't come from strong winds or big waves, which were insane enough by themselves. No, the worst part of a qi storm was the qi. There were wild fluctuations in ambient qi levels, enough to threaten any cultivator with a sudden influx of qi that could easily overwhelm and rupture meridian or core walls. And the occasional dead spot, where there wasn't any qi beyond that contained in the water itself, which made a cultivator incredibly tired after only a few minutes of work.

The one to handle it the best was Every. Since he didn't have any open meridians, and his cores hadn't even fully formed yet, the storm didn't affect him in the least. The soldiers and ship's crew just did their best to avoid hurting themselves. For my friends and I, it was a great training exercise in qi management and control.

In fact, it allowed Chu, Jamila, and Valerie to all break through to the Brain level. If we hadn't been in such dire straits, the entire crew would have celebrated their advancement. Chu, of course, was beside himself with envy. Both Valerie and Jamila had caught up to him. The massive qi influxes, combined with the pills I had given everyone, allowed them to skip past Peak Meridian in only a day, while it had taken him a lot longer to reach that stage. It was practically unheard of, even for me.

Donny and I had also managed some increases, but our higher levels meant we required more time to compact our qi into the necessary crystal-like density to advance. He did manage to catch up to me at Peak Brain, but he was just starting the conversion. I had almost completely converted my qi to the proper density, and I only needed a few days of uninterrupted peace and quiet to finally advance to Saint. That wasn't happening anytime soon.

While those advancements were great and all, we still had to deal with three major problems. The complete loss of direction and location, the constant need to tend the sails during the massive wind gusts, and all the leaks. Yes, leaks. Again.

The fight with the leviathan had damaged the schooner more than we first realized. There were seams along the hull that were allowing water to leak through, and the bilge was constantly in need of pumping to keep the deck high enough above the waves to be safe and avoid being swamped. Whether it was the drop from the initial hit, or the vibrations from the screams, the ship was in bad shape. Several times we had been forced to risk blowing out our cores from qi fluctuations just to push the water out of the ship. And no matter what we did, every time we tried to seal the leaks more would just form.

As for being lost, my directional needle and earth qi detector devices were the only items that could tell us where we were, and even those were spotty. Sometimes the needle would just spin in circles, and other times it would jump around in random directions. And the earth qi detector kept getting thrown off when we hit a qi dead spot. I had no idea if either of them were working at all. I guessed, on a positive note, at least we were making *great* time.

All of the crew continuously commented on how fast we were going. The ship spent most of its time skipping off of the waves like a smooth stone on a calm lake. Except the water was anything but calm, and the smooth stone was a wooden ship over a hundred feet long. With leaks. I was just surprised at the comparatively gentle ride this produced. There were only light bounces over the water, and none of the jarring hits I expected from such a wild speed.

We were constantly soaked from the lashing rain, and none of us had seen the sun or stars for over a week. In fact, the storm didn't seem to be weakening at all. It had stayed at the same intensity for almost a month, if you counted the time we were running from it. I couldn't help but wonder if it was another side-effect of the *nox* incursion into our world throwing the balance of qi into disarray. The effect was like traveling in a pocket of darkness, surrounded by an even darker field of nothingness. None of it felt natural.

While I was contemplating the issue, I could feel Sergeant Ward come up behind me. He just squinted into the storm, both of us flexing our knees with the slight bounce of the ship off of the waves as we held onto the railing. I spared a glance back at Scout and Cloud, who were both asleep in the leather slings he had managed to make for them. It had probably saved them both from a broken leg, as they hadn't been handling the ride very well. Horses had to lock their legs when they fell asleep standing up, and neither had been willing to lie down on the wet deck to sleep. The slings had given them a long-needed nap.

"Thank you." He gave me a confused look. "For helping the horses. It was a good idea." He nodded, his face still obscured by the faceplate on his helmet. Even after I had killed Smythe, they still wore it all over the place. I had no idea why.

"I thought you should know, I used my reporting talisman to update my commander."

I looked back out at the waves. "I felt you send it yesterday." He seemed surprised. "Something like that requires a lot of power to use. I could sense it leave the ship while I was cultivating."

He nodded. "Yes, it does. It took most of my qi to manage

it." Ward pulled out a silver pendant shaped like a teardrop. "In the report, I only said Lieutenant Smythe died during the leviathan attack. I didn't mention your name, or the names of your friends." Now it was my turn to look surprised. "I won't be able to leave it out of the full report, but at least this way you can have a head start. The full report won't reach the Xing clan for at least a few weeks once we reach shore. Maybe longer, if I don't see a superior officer to debrief me when we reach the capital."

"Thank you. You didn't have to do that." He didn't say anything for a while, instead using the time to draw in some of the currently abundant qi in the area. It made sense. He had needed to use most of his qi to send the message.

"Lieutenant Smythe was a terrible officer. A bad leader, a poor decision-maker, and an even worse person. I hated him, and I couldn't wait to be transferred once we delivered his message to the garrison commander." He took a deep breath, and let it out slowly. "But he was still an officer in the Imperial Army. All I have done is given you more time to contemplate your end. You can't hide from the Xing clan. You can only run. And like a fox chased by hounds, eventually you will be caught. And killed." He turned to face me, his cold blue eyes the only thing visible. "What I did was no mercy. It only prolongs your torture."

I couldn't help it. I laughed. "Oh, Sergeant Ward, how little you understand." He only seemed to get angrier, so I held up a hand to stop him from butting in. "Prince Ming, soon to be Crown Prince Ming, is a man I have had *extensive* dealings with. You might even say that there isn't a single trick his men could try that I don't know about. Or helped invent, for that matter." Ward didn't exactly take a step back, but he was definitely leaning away from me. He probably couldn't decide if I was telling the truth, and therefore far more important than he had believed, or if I was just bug-nuts crazy. "Trust me. The Xing clan can send who they want. I am not worried."

"If what you are saying is true, why didn't you announce

yourself as an agent of the royal family when we first met? It would have changed how many things turned out." Instead of sounding angry, he seemed subdued. Sad.

"Should it have, Ward? Should a citizen of the empire, when illegally captured and enslaved, who breaks free from their bondage just to save members of the Imperial Army, then find it necessary to mention their political connections to get proper treatment and consideration from those same members of the military?" Like Ward, I was more sad than angry. "Well, Ward? Or should we have just been treated fairly and with respect from the beginning?" He didn't answer. Instead, he turned to leave. "Oh, and Ward?" He paused. "I never said I was an agent *for* the royal family. I am an agent only for the empire. And what is best for the empire is not always best for the royal family."

With that, he left. Which was when it finally got through my thick, stupid skull.

I ran to catch up to him, and he reacted by pulling a spear from storage and leveling it in my direction. The slick deck meant I couldn't stop in time, so I had to use a quick deflection of wind qi from my left hand to help sweep the spear sideways so I would miss it. Ward tried to follow up by sweeping my legs with the butt of his spear, but I managed to hop-step over it and collide with him, knocking us both into the railing.

"Stop, Ward! Stars, I'm not attacking you!" He wasn't listening to me, his body already going through the motions long trained into muscle memory. If I hadn't had the same training centuries ago, it would have been difficult to stop the series of sweeping blows and swift stabs aimed at my torso and legs. Ward was entirely too textbook, his attacks not deviating from the same drills taught to every recruit from day one in the military. It spoke of a lack of experience fighting trained opponents, which I used to my benefit. As soon as he made a low sweep intended to smash my knees, I took a diving leap straight for his face. He tried to bring the spearhead back up to stop me, but I was already too close.

His armor protected him from any real injury, but when we slammed to the deck with me on top of him, I heard the whoosh of expelled breath leaving his body. Getting the wind knocked out of you hurt *every* time, no matter how tough you were.

"Ward! Knock it off! I just want to talk!" He was still struggling beneath me, his eyes wild. "Your talisman! Ward, you said it worked with only one use of your core's capacity. Where is it tied? Where you came from, or where you are going?"

He tried to headbutt me off of him. Fine. Want to fight dirty? Two could play at that game.

I shifted around enough to access my belt, and grabbed a familiar blue marble from storage. Placing it on the center of his breastplate, I pumped enough qi into it that he was instantly covered in about two feet of ice from head to toe. That should cool him down. What had made him go so crazy in the first place? After waiting almost a full minute, I used a strand of fire qi to melt the section of ice around his head. He took a gasp of air the second his mouth was free, choking on the meltwater. Served the jerk right.

"Ready to talk now, butt-nugget?" Ha! I remembered! "Or do you want me to just freeze your head and get this over with?"

"You'll never get me to talk! I know what you are now, you admitted it yourself!" He was still a little out of it.

"Ward, what in the hell are you talking about? All I wanted to do was ask you a question before you went back to your cabin, and you attacked me with no provocation!" I was shouting into his face, trying to get through whatever was going on.

"My oath demands your death, assassin! There is no other way this ends!" Ah, crap. Some kind of oath, coupled with his sudden and erroneous belief that I was a hired killer, had sent him into crazy town.

"Stars, you idiot! I am not an assassin!" He was still struggling to break free of the ice encasing his body. "Never once did I say I was a killer for hire. You just assumed that, and your oath triggered a reaction. Now stop it, Ward! Think! If I was an assassin, you would already be dead the moment you outed me." That finally got through to him.

"You swear, on your cores, that you aren't an assassin?" Well. That was a tightrope question if I had ever heard one. As an Enforcer, I had certainly assassinated a few people. But I had a workaround.

"I swear, on my cores, that I am not a dark assassin serving an evil master." After I didn't double over in pain, Ward finally started to calm down.

"I might have overreacted a little bit." I snorted in disbelief. A little bit? "I apologize. Now, will you please free me from this block of ice? It is starting to get cold."

"Fine. But if you go crazy again, I am totally throwing you overboard." Melting the ice enough to pull him free only took a few seconds of work, and I put the blue marble back in my belt before he could see what I had used to capture him like that. Let it be a mystery for him. "Now that all of the crazy is over, can we talk?"

"Once again, I'm sorry. We were just briefed before leaving on this mission that there has been a resurgence of the dark sects, and most especially the assassin clans. There were even confirmed sightings in the Southern Capital during a tournament held last spring-year."

Oh Ward, if you only knew.

Instead of bringing up the past, I focused on the present. "Yes, the dark sect hiding inside the Flying Sword Sect. I know. That isn't what is important right now. What *is* important right now is the transmission you made." The rapid change in subject just about made his head pop, if the wide eyes were any indication of his internal thought process. "You said it only took you emptying your cores *one time* to send the message, right?" He nodded in agreement. "Then I need to know two things. Is that a standard issue communication device, and where is it tethered?"

"Oh, that's easy. Yes, it is a standard messenger issue, and it is tethered to the garrison of our destination. Why?" I practically jumped for joy.

"A Saint cultivator of your power level should have to empty their cores at least two or three times to reach the Western Capital. Unless, of course, we were closer to the garrison than we thought!" It took a minute, but the implications finally clicked.

"We're close!" He did jump for joy. "Do you know what this means? How much distance we have traveled?" I nodded, just as excited as he was. "We must be moving close to the same speed as a cloud ship!"

"I know! Quick, run and tell the captain! I will try my direction equipment to get a better read!" He nodded, running off to find Hail. I moved up to the crow's nest, doing my best to get a reading from the earth qi detector. I couldn't be sure, but it seemed to be picking up more than it was yesterday. And the needle seemed to point off to starboard more often than any other direction. The storm must have been pushing us parallel to the coast, instead of farther out to sea. It was an incredible stroke of luck. I climbed back down in a rush.

"Jim! What's this about figuring out where we are? Did you finally figure something out with those pieces of junk you love to play with?" Hail was already at the wheel, Ward practically bouncing from foot to foot. The loss of direction had been wearing on all of us more than we were willing to admit.

It took some time to explain everything to her, but eventually Hail seemed to finally realize what we had already figured out. She turned the wheel, and we slowly turned to the right. We were almost to our destination, and we were more than two months ahead of schedule. Maybe the storm wasn't all that bad after all.

CHAPTER NINETEEN

Burning Ruins

We cleared the qi storm two days later. It was night when we emerged from the clouds, but the stars seemed so bright to our light-deprived eyes that we all needed to squint. If we had broken through during the day, more than one person would have needed healing to be able to see properly.

As soon as we could look at the stars without tearing up, Captain Hail was able to pinpoint our location. Somehow, we had managed to travel all the way around the southern edge of the empire and were already over three-fourths of the way to the Western Provincial Capital. What should have taken almost a year of travel had been done in less than half the time. Not nearly as fast as a cloud ship, but certainly better than what should have been possible.

Discussing it as a group, we all agreed that the best course of action was to head toward the coast and follow it farther inland. It would slow us down for the final leg of the journey, but no one wanted to be out of sight of land again after the adventures we had already been through. That, and the leaks were getting worse.

So, we headed towards land at full speed. Not the wave-skipping full speed of the qi storm, of course, but the normal full speed of a messenger schooner. Which was pretty fast, compared to most sailing ships.

It was another two weeks before we reached the sight of land, but the only thing that greeted us were empty beaches and thick forests. It wasn't much of a surprise. The empire was mind-bogglingly huge, and there were only so many people. The amount of developed land next to the Ocean of Tears was less than a tenth of one percent of all the available coastline, and most of that was along the land owned by the Southern Province. It should be some time before reaching a village or city.

The change in weather was great for Every. The boy was up and running around after some heavy coaching from the cook. Not a single person on the ship appreciated him for it. Every somehow managed to get in the way of everyone, and somehow disrupt any work going on, all at the same time. I was beginning to think the kid had a gift.

Scout and Cloud also appreciated the clear skies and warm sun. They were so happy, in fact, that Scout didn't try to kill Donny for three straight days. It was practically a miracle.

I ended up taking over the majority of the shifts in the crow's nest. Valerie's bow wasn't as necessary as her abilities with wind qi, and the shallower water meant we had more warning when creatures approached. Which was why it was me that spotted the smoke early one morning, just as the sun crested the horizon.

"Smoke! Someone get the Captain! And Sergeant Ward!" The scrambling figures far below told me they had heard my shouts. Soon enough, both Hail and Ward were sharing the small crow's nest with me.

"It looks like a forest fire to me." Ward had his hand over his eyes, trying to shade them from the bright sun. "I don't think it's something we need to worry about."

"Not according to my maps." Captain Hail wasn't bothering to shade her eyes, her long experience at sea apparently making her immune to the glare coming off the ocean waves. "There is supposed to be a small unnamed village around here somewhere. That's probably it." A spur of land was between us and the origin of the smoke, requiring us to sail around it to see what was burning. Whatever was on fire, there was a *lot* of it.

"How old are your maps, Captain?" I shifted to give her a better view. "Because that is a lot more smoke than some small, unnamed village should be giving off." She didn't reply, just calmly returned to the rope ladder and started making her way down. I had been around her enough to know she was taking her time so she could give herself a few moments to think before making a decision. Ward was right behind her, trying to do the same thing. Figure out what to do. Finally, Hail made a decision.

"Arms! All hands, to arms!" She left off the usual statement at the end, telling everyone why they were scrambling to get in position to fight. Hail just went to the wheel and took over, using a burst of wind qi to help us navigate around the tiny peninsula blocking our view a little faster. As we edged our way around it, we all finally saw what we were dealing with.

It was a massacre. The small village had been burned to the ground, with most of it still smoldering. Even from almost a thousand yards away I could still make out the splashes of red in the sand next to what looked like bundles of cloth. Blood. And bodies.

Without me having to say anything, the captain had already slowed the ship for an approach. The burned remnants of a pier indicated where it was deep enough for us to safely coast to a stop. We got as close as we could before someone lowered the small jollyboat over the side. It was little more than a rowboat, but it was big enough for Ward and his men to all go ashore in one trip. I volunteered to man the oars.

No one was speaking as I rowed us onto the beach. We didn't need to. All of us could see that some of those bodies were too small to be adults.

Ward and his men split into two groups, him by himself and

the other two staying together. They were headed to opposite ends of the village so they could perform a sweep and look for any survivors. Barring that, hopefully they could at least find a clue as to who or what managed to do this. And then I would kill whatever, or whoever, did this.

I didn't know these people. None of them were my responsibility. But I couldn't just stand aside while innocents were killed. It wasn't in my nature. If I had learned anything in my long life, it was to embrace the things I was good at, and not ignore the little voice inside my head that told me what I should or should not do. The last time I had ignored that little voice, I had ended up dead, and cracking open a gateway to the *nox*. If that wasn't the biggest 'lesson learned' moment in the history of learning your lessons, I didn't know what was.

While they did their search, I walked the beach, trying to recreate in my mind the events that must have transpired. The natural flow of qi in the area was still disrupted, meaning this had happened within the last day or two. The heavy smoke still rising from some of the charred remains of the buildings made it more likely the mass killing had been carried out less than twelve hours ago.

Considering the silence from the soldiers, they hadn't come across any survivors. The only sounds I could hear were their occasional coughs from the smoke, and the constant crashing of waves onto the shore. Even the animals had been slaughtered.

I approached the body of a man that had died trying to shield his wife and child. There were slashes through his back, bisecting his spine. The four neat lines were evenly spaced, like the claws of a monster. I knelt down, peeling aside his torn clothing to get a closer look. It was too clean to be from the ragged claws of a monster. This was the work of humans.

It could have been pirates, or maybe raiders. If it had been pirates, the bodies would have been searched for valuables. Raiders wouldn't have killed all the animals. They would have taken them back to their base of operations, or at least harvested the meat. No, it was something else at work here.

Sometimes, like when a virulent disease infects an entire community, an overzealous king might send his soldiers to quarantine the village. If anyone tried to leave, they would be killed. An entire community being wiped out all at once was practically unheard of, but not exactly nonexistent. Especially if it benefitted the leader ordering the quarantine. There was only one problem with that assumption. The bodies would have been burned. Their attempts to make it look like an animal attack might fool a casual inspection, but I had seen this before. This wasn't a massacre. It was an extermination.

Looking around for tracks, I only found a few sets of boot prints that might or might not belong. The lack of a trail leading into the village from the surrounding forest meant the attackers had arrived and left by ship. It was an educated guess, given the lack of evidence, but I felt secure in my assumption. Someone had ordered this small village to be wiped off the map, and for no reason that I could discern. It disgusted me. This was proof there were far more dangerous monsters out there than just the *nox*.

While I was still poking around where the beach met the forest, there were suddenly shouts and screams from the opposite side of the village from where I was standing. The soldiers were under attack.

Thinking they might have found a member of the group that had killed all of these people, I ran to see what I could do to help. As I rounded the edge of the burned buildings closest to the border with the forest, I realized I was wrong. The smell of blood and stinking bodies had already begun to permeate the area. Which attracted the animals hoping for a quick and easy meal, leading them straight to Sergeant Ward and his two men.

All three had their shields and spears at the ready, and at first it looked as if they didn't need my help, so I began to slow down. The five creatures they were facing happened to be a rare species of giant lizards called Earthen Reptar. Reptar were characterized by scales formed of thick sandstone-like material, making them immune to most piercing attacks. To take one down, you first had to shatter the scales to reach the vulnerable flesh beneath, making any fight a long and dangerous one. Their jagged teeth were coated in a paralyzing venom meant to make prey easier to consume, and quick straight-line motions strengthened by their powerful clawed legs ensured running away from them was never an easy option. Almost the size of a horse, they were commonly found in more tropical locations. Finding them here seemed very out of place. Ward and his men were doing a good job of facing the uncommon beasts, taking their time to gauge the speed and reach of their attacks. Then the *nox* walked out of the forest.

It had been a while since I had actually faced a *nox*, especially one fused with something besides a human. I had faced one that bonded with an animal before, turning a Spotted Snow Leopard into a monstrously huge creature with dark mana-infused tentacles and a penchant for destruction. This one went a different direction.

The Earthen Reptar had shrunk into something that looked more like a large dog than a lizard the size of a horse. The thing that gave it away as a *nox* was its obsidian scales. It was reminiscent of the dark qi and stone qi combination I had used on Silas and Moose, but the Reptar had taken it to the next level. Black caustic smoke seemed to waft off the creature, coming from the gaps between scales. It sizzled against the foliage it drifted across, melting the grass and leaves at its feet as if they were coated in acid. This was not a creature you allowed to get close.

"Back! Fall back! Don't let it touch you!" I shouted as I started running toward them again, pulling out a pair of shielding plates as I tried to flank the monsters. Ward either didn't hear me, or chose to ignore what I was saying. I was still over a hundred yards away when the *nox* attacked.

Ward, being a Saint cultivator, was managing to hold off three of the original Reptar by himself. His two soldiers had each been fighting just one. When the smaller *nox* had approached, the two soldiers moved closer to one another so they could better provide mutual support and protection. Not seeing it as a threat, neither cultivator paid it any extra attention.

Which was why they were both killed almost instantly.

The *nox* Reptar, or *nox*-tar—yep, that's what I was going with—spit a glob of venom at the shield of the soldier closest to it, causing the round hunk of wood and steel to melt like a piece of ice thrown into a blacksmith's forge. The soldier just managed to throw it down before it could reach his skin, but it was already too late.

What actually killed the two soldiers were the fumes the melted shield put off. The moment they breathed in the corrosive fumes, their faces started blistering as if they had been roasted over a fire. Their screams didn't last long. Whatever happened to their lungs must have been almost instant for them to drop so quickly. In fact, they died so fast that Ward hadn't even realized there was no one standing to his left side yet.

I had halved the distance to the fight, which meant I was finally in range to throw the shield disks accurately. Managing to land one right behind Ward, I activated the dome shield just as the *nox*-tar spat another glob of deadly venom at his back. Since the shield was designed to block all incoming and outgoing physical attacks, it managed to even keep out the dense fumes that were beginning to suffuse the immediate area. I had thrown the second dome shield a little farther than I intended, so when I activated it, all it managed to do was separate the two groups of monsters. All of which were completely unimpeded from running straight at *me*.

I turned right back around and ran, all six of them following close behind. I dropped one of my formation plate traps designed to turn the ground into quicksand for a few moments before reverting to solid stone, in the hopes of catching at least one or two of the Reptar. I needed to reduce the numbers following me if I was going to have a chance of winning.

Instead of running down the beach out in the open, I angled for the still-smoldering remains of the village. It was the only place I could think of that would allow me to split them up. The forest wasn't dense enough this close to the village, and I wanted them on unfamiliar territory.

I felt the ground shake as one of the Reptar slammed into the edge of the quicksand pit my trap had created. I looked back in time to see it manage to climb out and continue its attempt to run me down. The lizard that was trailing behind the pack wasn't as nimble. It only managed to get one limb free before the quicksand reverted to solid gray rock. The other four avoided the trap entirely, just running around the edges of the circle without even slowing down.

The *nox*-tar was gaining on me, and I could hear as it took a deep breath in preparation of launching another of its venom attacks at my back. I pulled out the silver bow that allowed me to infuse arrows with elemental qi and nocked an arrow as I took a hard turn towards what had been the main street of the village. I started pouring as much wind qi into the bow as the simple wooden arrow could hold, doing my best to gauge the distance from me to the *nox*-tar.

The creature managed to show signs of a cunning intellect, spitting its glob of venom in an arc intended to intercept my path, instead of just lobbing it straight at my back. I didn't have time to aim, just pulling back the string and letting loose the arrow by instinct. Luck was on my side, and the arrow hit the glob dead center.

Being nothing more than a small steel broadhead, wooden shaft, and goose feather fletching, the arrow was dissolved on contact. Which, considering how things worked out, was definitely a good thing for me.

The moment the arrow was destroyed, the wind qi contained inside it burst apart. It shot the acidic venom straight back into the faces of the Reptar following me in a concentrated cone of burning fury.

While the *nox*-tar was unaffected by its own toxin, the other four creatures were definitely *not* immune. By the time it actually made contact with them, it was more of a heavy mist. The monsters' stone scales were thick enough to protect them from the worst of the damage, but their eyes were vulnerable to the unnatural melting effects of the acidic material. Their roars of pain were music to my ears.

The blinded Reptar lashed out at one another, their instincts driving them to attack anything that came close. Both the *nox*-tar and I watched as they literally tore each other limb from limb in an orgy of blood and violence. The *nox*-tar seemed more than intelligent enough to realize it was now in danger, and slowly started backing away from me with a hiss.

I was not willing to let it get away, but I knew the strength of the obsidian-like scales it was covered with, having used similar materials in the forging of the brigandine armor I was currently wearing. Fire, air, earth, metal, dark, and light qi were all useless against it, and water qi was only good for containing it, or wearing it down over time. I had no real way of truly damaging the *nox*-tar without getting extremely close to it so I could shatter the scales with a blunt weapon of some kind. Which was also not my normal fighting style, and the acidic vapor bleeding through the gaps in its scales were a key indicator that getting close to it was a really bad idea.

I decided to try to lock it down. Using the meridians in my knees, I spun out some thick threads of earth qi. I launched them underground, trying to surprise it. As they shot out, the *nox*-tar showed off some impressive speed. It did a tumble, dodging the strands as they slammed into the ground. I tried running it down, but the toxic mist hovering around it made getting close impossible.

A quick darting motion brought it closer to the village, so I pulled another formation plate to keep it from getting away. If it were to make it amongst the buildings, it would make it easier for it to escape. The formation plate shot up a field of whipping metal qi strands, driving it closer to the earth strands again. The trap was a short-lived one, but it lasted long enough to get the job done. I managed to wrap one strand around the tail, and another around its midsection. It was locked down tight. Then its stupid tail popped off. Stars-dammit.

The tail coming free released more of the dangerous fumes, forcing me to back up. It managed to wriggle free before I could launch a blast of wind qi to clear away the poison. Since the creature was free, I allowed the earth qi strands to dissipate. Holding it down wasn't going to work.

The *nox*-tar had been slowly backing away from me while I was trying to come up with some way to kill it. Just as I was about to give up and try trapping the creature inside a dome shield similar to the one Ward was still stuck inside, I saw the monster skitter sideways, moving away from the beach and putting its back to the forest. Since it was backing away, that meant it wanted to escape back into the woods. Why would it avoid the beach?

Wow. Sometimes I was a complete idiot. What happened when you threw a rock into a pond? And what would happen if I threw a rock-covered creature that still needed to breathe into the ocean? It would sink. And it would die.

I tossed out a handful of poppers around the *nox*-tar, the small explosions making a nice distraction. It also stirred up the qi in the area enough that the monster didn't notice as two strands of water and earth qi ran underground and sprang up behind it. All I had to do was grab it by a leg, give it a spin for some momentum, and fling the stars-damned thing into the sea.

As I had theorized, it couldn't swim. No amount of acid would save the dark mana demon now. I would be sure to swim down and collect the body before we left. I hadn't been able to study the Spotted Snow Leopard after killing it, as the method I used managed to leave nothing behind. This time I would get the opportunity to try to see what changes a *nox* had on the internal structures of a beast. You never knew when information like that could prove vital to winning a fight.

After all, knowing is half the battle.

CHAPTER TWENTY

Dealing with Loss

I had to use some wind qi to clear away the deadly vapor from the shield protecting Ward. He was clearly not happy at being trapped inside the dome shield, but I couldn't hear what he was shouting at me through the barrier. The shouting died down a bit once he saw what the vapors did to the trees I blew it toward. I could see the realization wash over him that the only thing keeping him from sharing the same fate as his soldiers was the shield I had thrown.

While waiting for the plates to deactivate, I went to check on the creature still trapped in the stone quicksand circle. It had given up trying to get free, and watched me as I approached. It seemed subdued, as if resigned to its fate. Seeing it in such a state made it hard to just kill it outright. Earthen Reptar were a rare animal to find, making me question whether I should kill it or not. I suspected their presence in this region was due to the *nox* leading them here, and not because it wanted to on its own.

Why the dark mana demon led them to this tiny village, and if it had anything to do with the massacre of the villagers from an outside element, were still a mystery. Deciding to let it go, I used a strand of earth qi to smash up the stone around it. The beast looked at me for a moment before running off. I knew it was impossible, but it felt like the monster had said a silent thank you. The trap plate took a few more minutes to find, but I made sure to put it back in storage.

Next, I collected the beast cores from the dead Reptar, finding them all to be at the Common level. Many recipes used powdered cores in both alchemy and blacksmithing. Even weaker cores were worth my time to gather, and these earth qi aspect cores could be combined with a few steel ingots to make an otherwise heavy plate of armor lighter than normal smithing would produce.

Finally, as I was finishing up with the bodies of the monsters, Sergeant Ward was freed from the shield. He silently walked over to the bodies of his slain soldiers. I decided to give him some space, gathering up the shield plates and moving farther down the beach towards the burnt village. I still needed to search it for clues, and confirm if this truly was an extermination instead of something else. Finding the *nox* made me feel the need to double-check.

I was poking through a pile of ash near the center of the village when Ward trudged up to talk. He was definitely mourning the loss of his soldiers, and I didn't blame him. It was never easy when you lost the people under your command. No matter if it was your fault or not, you still end up feeling like a failure.

"I don't think those creatures did this." He was looking around, using his spear to poke at the burnt timbers of what looked to be the remains of a vendor's cart. "They would have eaten the bodies. And these buildings would be melted, not burned."

I wasn't sure what to say to him. He was clearly stating the obvious just to break the silence. It would be weird for him to receive advice about how to deal with losing troops from a teenager. Although, that same teen had just saved his life. I decided to go along with it, and let him work through things on his own.

"I agree. This wasn't done by beasts or monsters at all." I held up the stub of a torch I had found. "It was an attack carried out by humans." I kicked over a pile of charred wood, exposing the burnt remains of a small child. It looked like they were trying to hide, their tiny frame curled up in the fetal position. "I said that wrong. It *was* monsters that did this."

"Do you think it was raiders? Perhaps there was a passing pirate ship that saw them as an easy target?" His voice was quiet, like he already knew what he was saying didn't fit the evidence. I turned to look at him, and he couldn't meet my eyes. Either he knew this was a purposeful extermination, or he was having trouble facing me after I had saved him. Probably a mixture of both.

"This was meant to look like a beast attack, but it was poorly carried out. The extermination squad someone sent here was lazy. They probably didn't expect anyone to make it here so quickly, but their amateur work would still be visible even a few days from now." I pointed to the burnt vendor cart that he was standing beside. "That was probably a produce cart, or maybe a tinker's station. The cart is too far from any of the buildings to have caught fire from them burning down. That means it was lit on fire on purpose, which disproves a beast attack. And even if beasts somehow managed to kill every single man, woman, and child, not every untended cookfire would have resulted in *every* building being burnt to the ground." I waved my hand as if to say, 'look at all of this!' and pointed back towards the beach. "And the most obvious problem is the pier. What monster takes the time to douse a wooden pier in an accelerant, then burn it to ash?"

Ward looked around, taking in the destruction. "I see what you are saying, but why would anyone in a powerful position order an extermination squad to attack a sleepy seaside village like this one?" He finally looked up at me. "Those are supposed to only be used in the event of a plague, or if the security and safety of the entire empire is put at risk. There are too many unburnt bodies for it to be a plague extermination, and I can't fathom a security risk from an out-of-the-way place like this!"

"Exactly, Ward." I started to walk towards the beach, headed to where the body of the *nox* was most likely to be. I needed to collect it so we could leave. "That is *exactly* the problem."

"Where are you going? Don't you think we should bury the dead before we leave?" He was quick stepping to keep up with me. "It doesn't feel right to leave them like this."

"If we bury the bodies, we will only be hiding the evidence others might discover. There will eventually be more people nearby that saw the smoke, and they will come to investigate." I pulled out a matched set of stone formation plates and handed them to Ward. "My hope is they are intelligent enough to come to the same conclusion we have. That is how rumors spread, and how those responsible for this will be forced to explain their decisions. Otherwise, these people will never see justice."

"That is a really good point." He seemed to genuinely be upset by the extermination, and the thought of those respon- sible facing justice seemed to perk him up a bit. "But, what are these things for?" He held up the stone disks, the carved runes covering both sides.

"That is a perimeter barrier." I spun my hands in a circle motion and nodded back at the village. "While I swim out and get the body of that creature, you are going to set those up all around the village. Make sure you space them evenly apart, so when we leave, I can activate them and protect the evidence for as long as possible. It will keep any more scavengers away for at least a few days, hopefully long enough for someone else to make it here. If it is a human cultivator, all they would need to do to get inside would be to move the stones farther apart. An animal won't know to do that."

He nodded and ran off after agreeing to do the job.

I managed to track down the body of the *nox*, but I quickly ran into a problem. It was rolling in the surf not far from where I had thrown it in, meaning the thing had been trying to run its way back to the surface before finally drowning. As it was exposed to sunlight by the receding waters, it was like the creature was decaying before my eyes. Something about the dark mana used to change the Reptar into an obsidian death-monster made it fall apart quickly after death.

Instead of being able to leave right away, I was forced to do an inspection of the corpse right there on the beach. The hard scales of black glass-like rock protecting its skin were flaking off like old bark on a dead tree. I could break them off with my bare hands, and the flesh underneath was already smelling strongly of rot. Rolling it over onto its back wasn't hard because it was too heavy, rather it was because it was falling apart every time I tried to push. Eventually, I used a few strands of earth qi to help, and its belly was exposed. I had the creature splayed open so I could get a look at its insides after a couple quick slices with a dagger. Oof. And I thought this thing smelled bad on the outside!

A quick inspection revealed the muscles, bones, and organs to all be incredibly dense. It was as if the *nox* bonding with the creature somehow caused it to double—and then some—in durability, but upon death the artificial evolution of the Reptar caused the unnatural flesh to break down at a highly accelerated rate. The *nox* was strengthening these beasts, but it seemed to be burning them up.

I wasn't sure if a host could reject their possessing *nox* if they wanted to at some point, either human or beast. If they did, it looked like they wouldn't survive the experience. The only thing holding them together after being changed by the *nox* was the *nox* itself. So, new note to self. Do *not* get infected or possessed by a *nox*.

The core of the beast ended up being tiny, no bigger than the first digit of my smallest finger. For comparison, the cores inside the other Earthen Reptar were about the size of an apple. I was disappointed with it, until I took a closer look at the small crystal. It was dark qi aspect. I might be holding the very first harvested dark qi core on the entire planet. Even better, it wasn't Common-level like the others. This core was at *least* at the density and purity of a Sky-level beast. Maybe even Heaven! I had no experience with a dark qi core before, so I couldn't be sure. Most Sky and Heaven cores were also about the size of cantaloupes, so figuring out what this little core should actually be considered was a bit beyond my expertise. I would have to look at it some more later. I stored it in the same stud as I did my most valuable items, where it wouldn't be detected or accessible by anyone else.

Not willing to risk the bones, fangs, and claws quickly decaying like the rest of the beast, I didn't bother to gather them up. They were incredibly dense, and might be useful in alchemy, enchanting, or blacksmithing, but this wasn't the time. Sergeant Ward was already waiting for me near the jollyboat, and the sun was approaching its peak in the sky. We needed to go, before the tides turned against us.

I made sure to activate the wards before we shoved off. For some reason, I noticed that Sergeant Ward had collected the bodies of not just his soldiers, but the remains of the Reptar as well. It seemed odd to me, so I asked him about it as I rowed us back to the schooner.

"I noticed that you collected up the bodies of the beasts." He was staring off into space, and the sound of my voice made him jump. I kept talking, pretending I hadn't noticed. "Why did you bother?"

Ward looked back at the village before answering. "You and I were able to figure out what happened to those people very quickly, but others might just see the torn-up bodies of those big lizards and think they were responsible for everything." He turned around to face me again. "People like the easy, obvious answers. They don't want to be bothered to look at the hard truth. I didn't want to give them the easy answer." He was quiet for a bit longer. "I was furious with you. When that shield dropped, I wanted to kill you. I should have died fighting beside my soldiers. Or you should have saved them, and not me. But the hard truth is, I know you did what you could." He looked down at a storage ring he was holding in his hand. Probably where he had stored his soldiers' dead bodies. "I was doing everything I could to hold back those beasts. They were doing a good job wearing down the other two. Then, that dark one showed up and they were dead before they even knew what was going on."

I let out a sigh. At least he was working through his grief and rage quicker than most. I just wish I knew what to say. I had a lot of experience with loss, but no matter how many years I persisted, I still hadn't learned the secrets to handling the anguish he was going through.

I was going to say something, but he interrupted me. "The only thing I could have done better was take the search more seriously. We didn't know if it was clear of enemies or not, but we acted like it was."

"Ward, it isn't a good idea for you to agonize over this." I looked back at the ship, making sure I was still rowing us in the right direction. "There was no planning for that creature." I thought about explaining the *nox* to him, but now wasn't the time. "I have never seen a beast have such fast-acting deadly venom in my life. There are plenty out there that are corrosive like that, or beasts with venom guaranteed to kill you if it touches your skin in any way. But to have the ability to melt metal on contact, and then the *fumes* be instantly deadly? No one in their right mind would ever imagine such a thing existed." We both fell silent at that.

Everyone onboard the ship was subdued when we returned. The obvious absence of the soldiers, coupled with the abject sadness of Sergeant Ward, told the crew everything they needed to know.

The sense of loss permeated the ship over the next two weeks of travel. I was able to finally finish healing the damaged meridian in my foot during that time, and my friends had all grown subtly stronger over the same stretch of time. I hadn't thought of it at the time, but the pills I had made and distributed to all of them helped strengthen their bodies and cultivation more than it should have. The reason? I had included dark and light qi when making the pills. Even though they didn't know to distribute it in their bodies, since they couldn't sense its presence, I had no doubt they had absorbed it in some way. All four of them just seemed more *solid* than they used to be.

We were rounding a curve in the coastline late in the afternoon when we saw another pillar of smoke in the distance. I thought I could also see the faint blip of a blue sail from a ship just on the horizon, but I was staring into the sun. Even when enhancing my vision, I couldn't be sure. If so, that meant an Imperial Navy frigate was running around out there. And if that was the case, it should have been sailing *towards* a burning village. Not away from one. The choppy waves had nothing to do with the sinking feeling in my stomach.

This time, we went to shore to inspect the burning village in a much larger group. Donny, Valerie, Chu, Jamila, Sergeant Ward, Captain Hail, and a sailor—who was wearing a red shirt and inexplicably mumbling about unfair situations—took two trips to get ashore. The cook was watching Every for us. Somehow, I still ended up being wrangled into doing all the rowing.

We searched the area thoroughly, which took us late into the night. This was more like the size of a town, and we were doing our best to check every inch for survivors. Once again, it only took us a few minutes to realize this was executed by an extermination squad that only nominally attempted to hide the truth. They might have been sloppy when it came to hiding their actions, but they were certainly efficient in killing. There were no survivors.

As we were headed back to the ship, everyone seemed to be angry more than any other emotion. Except for the guy in the red shirt. He seemed to just be happy to make it back to the ship.

Which was when his legs got ripped off.

CHAPTER TWENTY-ONE

Swimming is Good Exercise

None of us saw it coming. I had picked him, Captain Hail, and Sergeant Ward up last. They were all taking turns climbing the rope ladder to get back on the schooner when a creature that looked like a praying mantis mixed with a hammerhead shark came out of the water and scuttled up the side of the ship. Ward barely had time to let out a shout of warning before red shirt was yanked off of the ladder and fell into the ocean with the creature hanging onto his legs with its crooked arms.

"What in the *stars* was *that*!" Captain Hail was looking around wide-eyed, trying to see where they had gone. Sergeant Ward tossed a fire construct into the air to provide more light, and I copied him and formed another on the other side of the jollyboat. Hail finally acted, sending a ball of compressed wind qi into the area near where they disappeared. "I haven't seen *anything* like that in all my years on the sea!" The ball of compressed air disappeared under the schooner, and only a moment later the red-shirted sailor sprang out of the depths only a few feet from where he had gone under.

He popped back up to the surface in a froth of blood and screams. The Captain and Sergeant managed to drag him into the boat before he could be sucked back down. I tried my best to see where the horror had gone, but it was too dark to see anything.

My friends, who I had already brought back to the ship on my first trip, started casting more balls of fire at the water in an attempt to try to discourage it from coming back up. It didn't work as planned, but it did let us find the creature.

Since there was light and fire all around the ship, the thing must have thought the only 'safe' place for it was directly under the jollyboat. Which it had no problem suddenly turning into a bunch of toothpicks.

I was sent flying, somehow managing to get hit in the face and groin at the same time by two entirely separate oars. What can I say? Even *I* had some ungraceful moments. Since all I could see was oar, I had no idea where everyone else ended up when the jollyboat stopped being so 'jolly.' And stopped being so 'boat,' I guessed.

As I hit the surprisingly cold and dark water, I was once again reminded of the fact that wearing armor while on a ship could be a bad idea. My brigandine was dragging me down quickly, so I had to pop it into storage once again. As soon as I did, I started to float right back up to the surface. I made sure to not struggle and flail about. There was already blood in the water, and predators loved a meal that wiggled. No sense in giving them what they wanted.

My head crested the surface just in time for me to catch a fireball to the face. This was *seriously* not my night. Luckily, it was a weak one, primarily intended to illuminate the area and not actually burn something. I was already wet, so it only managed to singe me a bit. That didn't make it fun to get hit in the face with a fireball by any means, but I was aware it could have been worse. I might have needed to shave my head. Or worse, I could have lost my eyebrows! Chu would have never let me live it down.

At first, I just floated where I surfaced. I was trying to gauge the situation, but it seemed as if everything had gone crazy. The red-shirted sailor that lost his legs was screaming his head off still, making it hard to hear what everyone else was shouting. That is, until he was suddenly cut off with a gurgle and splash.

Whelp, now I knew where that horrifying creature was, I needed to move.

I used an influx of qi into my muscles to help power me along. It was only a few seconds of hard swimming to the dangling rope ladder, but just as I was getting close, I sensed a flash of dark qi behind me. I spun up the qi in my brain core to speed up my perception of time, and used it to evaluate what was going on. Turning very gently so as to avoid injuring myself, I caught a glimpse of the creature coming up behind me.

It was another stars-damned *nox*! I knew when I sensed the dark qi that was what it had to be, but I wanted to visually confirm it first. That first glimpse on the side of the ship made me think this was a possibility, but when I saw the sharp black ridges that formed the praying mantis limbs, I had no doubt. I was only guessing, considering the complete lack of information, however it seemed as if some species of shark bonded with a *nox* and it gave it limbs of some kind. It didn't make any sense to me, but I wasn't a dark mana demon from another dimension. I suppose it didn't need to make sense.

Seeing as how the *nox* was almost within striking range of me, I spun out a braided thread of qi in the shape of a noose with a rigid portion I held onto, similar to a catch-pole. All I had to do was put the circle of qi in front of the shark-thing and it ran right through it, catching it above the shoulders, where the neck would be if it had one. It had a lot more momentum than I was expecting, forcing me to angle my body sideways to avoid impacting straight-on with the ship behind me. I was knocked farther down the side, nowhere near a convenient place to get back onto the schooner. The creature, seeing me knocked away from my escape, only pushed toward me even harder. Which, of course, sent me on a fun little journey through the water.

And by fun, I mean the opposite of fun.

I was shoved against the hull of the ship, forcing me to release my ability to slow time so I didn't injure myself. Then I was dragged along the full length of the ship, bumping along like an angry bumblebee trying to get nectar from a flower. It was a miracle that I wasn't covered in splinters by the time I cleared the rear of the schooner. I did manage to clear off some barnacles, which I suppose was a positive. Cutting myself on them wasn't nearly as positive.

The *nox* kept pushing, and the noose and pole worked like a fulcrum, spinning me around in the water so I was suddenly behind it. Which made the shark *nox* very upset. It began swimming in a circle, trying to get to me. We were spinning fast enough that it was hard to keep my head above water. It was like trying to ride a tornado. A shark-nado.

No, that's too stupid of a name, even for me.

Taking the offensive would have been great, but I was having a hard time even holding on to the stupid monster. After a few minutes of spinning us in circles, it finally figured out this wasn't working for it. Instead, it took off in a straight line, headed deeper into the ocean.

Since it stopped the crazy thrashing circles, I was able to actually do something. Concentrating on the loop of qi, I began to tighten the noose slowly but steadily. I was almost a quarter of a mile from the ship when it finally slowed down. By then, the noose had already caused a deep divot in the creature's thick hide. There was no getting loose now.

I kept up the pressure, tightening it until the thin braid of qi managed to break through its thick hide and draw blood. Realizing now that the loop of qi was actually a danger, the *nox* decided to dive straight down. Stars damn it.

I managed to take a deep breath before going down, but I didn't have enough time to form a bubble of air qi around my head. Which was something I should have done earlier, but didn't think about until just now. Figured.

Knowing that I couldn't risk going nearly as deep as the *nox*, I forced the noose to tighten as hard as I could. It was a fight between my willpower and the strength of the *nox*. It took far longer than it should have, but eventually the monster slowed its descent.

The weak thrashing of the shark finally stopped, and even underwater I heard the cracking sound of something important in its neck area breaking. I was running out of air, and the bleeding cuts along my back and shoulders from the barnacles slicing into me were aching like a sore tooth. My wooden healing talisman was having a hard time, since there was only water qi all around it. Time to go.

I definitely wasn't willing to just leave the *nox*, so I dissipated the qi strand wrapped around its neck so I could get close enough to put its body in my storage belt. Which was dumb. I blame the whole 'holding my breath and can't breathe right now' thing for the mistake. Because as soon as that qi strand came undone, the monster was on me in a flash.

Of *course* it was smart enough to play dead. Ugh.

The cracking sound from its neck must have been something important, if not exactly lethal, because its entire right side wasn't moving. Just the left side was almost enough to kill me anyway. I managed to activate the shield of my spirit wood ring just in time to fend off the dark qi chitin arm growth, the sound of it scraping across like two pieces of steel shrieking against one another. I guided the mantis-like blade away from me, the motion spinning the creature in the water far enough that I got enough separation between the two of us to cast out another loop of braided qi. This time, it only caught on one of the broad protruding arch sections of the 'hammer' on the hammerhead shark. I tightened down anyway, and used the length of the qi strand to keep it at bay.

Air was really becoming an issue now. I started swimming upwards, dragging the crippled creature with me. It would have been much faster to leave it behind, but in the dark waters I would never find it again. There was no way I could just let a *nox* escape like that. After all, according to the gods there were only two hundred or so that came into our world. I had killed eight already. This would be number nine.

It fought me the entire way, and I might have even blacked out for a moment, only moving on instinct, but I made it to the surface. I floated on my back so I could take in great gasps of air, and the amount of time for the spots in my vision to go away was certainly concerning. The entire time I was struggling to return to normal, I was being jerked around by the stupid *nox*. It was having problems adapting to having one side paralyzed. I had the distinct impression that this *nox* wasn't as intelligent as some of the others I had dealt with. Maybe it was due to the creature it bonded with? Or perhaps there was something more to that hierarchy the Chancellor had mentioned than I realized. Was a higher-ranked *nox* smarter than a regular one?

The long struggle had started to wear me down. It wasn't as hard of a fight as some others, but getting beaten up and then dragged through the ocean was far from fun. I concentrated on the braided thread of qi wrapped around the head of the shark, and frayed it out a little so each individual element was tight against its hide. I wanted to see if the nox had any specific weaknesses to one type of qi over another. According to the gods, every *nox* was weak to at least one element. I hadn't really gotten a chance to test it like this before, so I decided to take advantage.

I tightened down on the threads once again, this time paying close attention to see if any of them managed to break through the tough skin of the deformed shark. It was barely noticeable, but I thought the metal qi and earth qi strands seemed to be able to tighten deeper into the *nox* than the other elements. Just to be sure, I formed a small blade construct of each element and blasted them, one at a time, into the exposed sections of the floating shark.

My test confirmed it. This *nox* was barely scratched by the other elements, even light and dark qi, but metal and earth definitely made it bleed. It was too dark to see how deep each gash went, but I didn't want to light up my location for any regular sea creatures running around out here. A shark didn't have to be a *nox* shark to register as a threat.

Okay. Enough playing around. It was time to get back to the ship. I thrust a thin blade construct of metal qi through its brain, finally putting an end to the exhausting battle. It went directly into my belt, before it could start to decay like the last one. I could see the ship off in the distance, the sails seeming to glow from the reflected lights of the torches on deck. This was going to be a long swim.

CHAPTER TWENTY-TWO

Patterns of Destruction

I wasn't sure how long it took me to make it back to the ship, but I knew how long it *felt*. Which made it a surprise when I finally flopped back on deck and the sun wasn't peeking over the horizon yet. How long could one night be?

"What took you so long?" Chu was standing over me, hands on his hips like he was scolding a truant child showing up late for dinner. "We have been waiting here for over an hour!" That's it? Just one hour? I sighed. This really was the night that never ends. "You are lucky we didn't have anything else going on, or we would have left you!" Chu's tone wasn't serious, letting me know he was actually just relieved to see me.

"You know, Chu, I would have been here faster if someone would have been *helping me*." I sat up, the cuts on my back and shoulder still leaking blood. "But instead, everyone decided to just let the stars-damned sea monster drag me halfway back to The Claw!" The crew and my friends appreciated the sarcasm, and couldn't help a few chuckles from escaping.

Captain Hail came up from below to see what the commotion was about, and came over to check on me. "Are your injuries from that creature? Did you see where it went?" She was leaning over me, trying to inspect my wounds. They were already visibly starting to close now that I was out of the water and my wood qi healing talisman had more varied forms of energy around it to absorb. Instead of answering her, I stood up and took a few steps away from everyone so I could pull out the dead *nox* and show it to them. Which was definitely a mistake.

"Here you go. This was the creature, and it—gah! Ugh, pffft, ugh, ah stars, the smell! It got in my mouth!" When the damaged body of the *nox* dropped onto the deck, it was like dropping an overripe melon onto a cobblestone road. The wet, smelly, slippery, decaying flesh splattered everywhere. The smell was a mixture of spoiled milk, rotten fish, and an outhouse all rolled into one. It was so bad, I swear I saw a sailor standing close to a particularly large piece of meat choose to jump over-board rather than stay near it.

"Why?! Why would you do this to me?!" Chu had gotten the worst of the splatter, a veritable wave of stinking blood and guts washing over his feet up to his thighs. "I am going to have to *burn* these clothes!"

"Oh, it smells so bad it makes my ears hurt!" Jamila, who had been standing not far from Chu, actually had her hands clamped on her ears. That was definitely a weird reaction.

"That's it!" Captain Hail waved both hands in a sweeping motion, knocking the corpse and most of the bits of flesh and guts over the side using wind qi, then repeated the motion and washed the worst of the ooze and blood through the gaps in the railing. "Don't ever bring something like that on my ship again!"

While I didn't blame Hail for her actions, it was still frustrating. I hadn't gotten the chance to look for another dark qi core inside the monster. Knowing how important it was to have more than one crystal core so I could compare the two to each other, I knew what I needed to do. Jump back in the ocean and get the stupid thing before it sank to the bottom.

On the bright side, jumping back into the ocean at least washed off most of the stink. The cold wasn't fun though. Neither was swimming after the sinking upper half of a quickly-disintegrating creature in the rapidly-declining light. At least I remembered to form a bubble of air qi around my head this time.

I resorted to using some threads of water qi to form a net and capture the falling creature. It was only a few moments later that I had another small dark qi core, and a disgusting cloud of rotten flesh I was floating in. Which, considering the day I was having, was when a flash of fins and teeth shot through the murky water less than a foot away from me.

Whelp, time to go then.

Luckily, I was able to quickly get away without incident. This time, it was just regular sharks attracted by all the gunk created by the decaying *nox*. As I swam back to the ship, which had drifted farther away from me, I thought about how crazy that had been.

Storing the body of the shark *nox* in my belt should have at least slowed the decay rate, if not outright stopped it from happening altogether. It had also decayed much faster than the lizard *nox* had broken down, which led me to believe that the more changes to the original form of the creature the *nox* went through, the faster it would turn into mush after death. And nothing, not even storing it in an extradimensional space, would stop it from happening.

I felt like I was on to something important, some key bit of information, but it eluded me. So be it. It would come to me eventually. I finally made it back to the ship, vowing to put swimming lengthy distances near the top of the list of things I hated, right next to pointlessly long staircases and Imperial Royals.

And cannibals. Couldn't forget the cannibals.

After flopping back up onto the deck a second time, I was surprised to see it was just my friends and I left on deck. All of the sailors must have gone below, and even Sergeant Ward was missing. A quick look up into the crow's nest answered that question, but brought up another. I had never seen Ward take a shift up top, just like my friends and I had never been allowed to be alone on deck. Captain Hail had made sure we were always supervised by at least one experienced sailor at all times. It wasn't a matter of trust, but more of a failsafe in case of emergency. I would have done the same in her shoes.

Also, the stink of the dead *nox* was gone. Except for the lingering scent on my clothes, which I vowed to burn. Thankfully, they weren't enchanted in any way, and I had long ago stored the cloth-covered brigandine that just *looked* like clothes. Burning them wouldn't be any real loss.

"Jim! Glad you're back." This time Donny was the closest person to me when I got to my feet. At his greeting, the rest of my team stopped whatever they had been doing to come over and talk. "Are you going to tell us why you jumped in after that stinking carcass?"

"Everyone come closer, so I can show you." They complied, crowding around me as we formed a tight circle near the rear of the ship. "Where is everyone? Normally we aren't left alone."

The first to answer was Valerie. "The crew is all below, having a wake for the sailor that died." She looked down at the deck between her feet, as if trying to see them all toasting to the memory of their dead friend. "There aren't enough of them left now to always have someone up with us, anyway."

I sighed. There hadn't been many people on the ship in the first place. "Well, it works out for us." They all watched as I pulled out the two dark qi cores, holding them up in the starlight for them to see. I made sure to angle my body so Ward wouldn't be able to look down from the crow's nest and get a look at them. "We have to be careful. I have a feeling these cores are worth more than this schooner." There was power that seemed to ooze from the cores, as if they were emitting darkness that was cold enough to burn. They weren't actually burning me, thank the gods. But I wasn't sure if anyone not used to manipulating and strengthening themselves with light and dark qi should touch them.

"I can tell they are powerful, but I can't really sense anything specific from them. It feels… familiar." Everyone nodded at Jamila's statement. "What are they?" Jamila reached out to touch them, but I pulled them away before she could.

"They came from the *nox*, so it is best not to touch them if you can avoid it." I popped them back in my belt. "I know I have been handling them, but you all know I am a little different." And they might be different now as well. If they were sensing a hint of the dark qi, that meant the pills I gave them had already made them sensitive to the two hidden forms of qi. I still wasn't sure if I should introduce them to light and dark qi yet, but I might not have a choice in the matter anymore.

"What I really want to know is, why are entire villages being wiped out?" Valerie was the one to speak up next, her anger at the deaths of all the innocent people we had seen earlier still very prevalent. Probably due to her new motivation to help others. "And why are we finding a stars-damned *nox* nearby every time?"

"They are clearly connected." Donny was rubbing a fist into the palm of his other hand, as if imagining punching those responsible for all of the murdered people. "I don't know how, but they are."

"I agree." Jamila had stepped back from our little circle and was staring towards the smoldering remains of the small town we were slowly drifting away from. "And I am afraid what we might come across as we get closer to our destination."

"It is certainly a pattern." Chu wrapped an arm around Jamila's shoulders. "And not a good one. We all know there is someone ordering this to happen now. Do you think there is another possessed person in the government ordering this? A *nox* hiding in plain sight, like the Chancellor?"

"We need to get to the capital as quickly as possible." While

I talked, I mentally rummaged through my belt to try to find a change of clothes. "If that's the case, this is only the beginning of this destruction." Everyone gave a sharp nod of agreement. "And we might be the only people capable of stopping it." It was a sobering thought. But none of us were willing to stand aside and let it continue.

CHAPTER TWENTY-THREE

Arrival

It took us another month before the cloudy night sky revealed the glow of a city in the distance. Captain Hail had managed to time our arrival with the sunrise, so we were still several miles from the Western Provincial Capital.

We had passed by seven more burned villages, and one fairly large town. The decision to pass them by without checking for survivors—or more *nox*—was a difficult one, but none of the crew wanted to risk losing another person. My friends and I didn't argue. We were convinced we would save more lives if we could get to the capital faster anyway, so the long delays it would have taken to check the burnt remains of buildings along the coast were cast aside.

The trail of destruction across the coast wasn't constant. All told, from what we had passed by, it had been something like one in four seaside communities selected for extermination. There was no obvious pattern in the wreckage, at least not that we could discern. Whatever it was that seemed to be sentencing these people to death, its reasoning was beyond us.

"Jim!" I looked down from my position in the crow's nest. Sergeant Ward and Captain Hail were looking up at me. As they saw me peek over, they motioned for me to come down. "Come! We need to talk!" The captain pointed towards the rear of the ship, and they both started walking towards the wheel. I jumped down, swinging back and forth from the spar to the stay ropes to the mast, and finally dropping to the deck with a flourish. My time aboard ship had given me a new level of confidence in the rigging, and sometimes showing off was just plain fun.

"What did you want to talk about?" Captain Hail had sent the sailor that was steering the schooner below, so it was currently just the three of us on deck.

"We… we wanted to talk to you about what is going to happen when we arrive." Hail seemed nervous. It was definitely out of character for her to not act completely self-assured. Unless there were mantis-sharks eating her sailors, of course. But that was understandable.

"I already know what is going to happen. My friends and I disembark, take Every to the nearest Auction House, and then continue our business to see the king as planned." I had told them during our journey that we were going to seek an audience with him, but not the specific reason why.

"And that is the problem." Sergeant Ward was standing with his spear-hand a few inches away from his body. Which was exactly how you stood if you wanted your spear to appear out of your storage ring right before a fight. "It can't work that way."

"Why, exactly? Is there a problem?" I already had the qi in my cores spinning, and the shield function of my spirit wood ring was at the forefront of my mind. Was I wrong about these two? Were they planning on attacking us, despite everything we had been through together?

"It is the message we are carrying." Captain Hail seemed to have noticed our tension, and patted at the air to calm us down. "Don't worry, Jim. This is normal procedure in the event of a high-priority message. All that will happen is a slight adjustment to your current plans."

"What adjustments?" I relaxed a little, letting the tension in my body fade a bit. "What is this 'procedure' that you're talking about?" It was a legitimate question, but I thought I knew what they were about to say.

Sometimes, the personnel on a messenger ship were held either onboard their vessel, or in some servants' quarters at the palace, until the recipient had a chance to hear the message themself. That only happened if the message was of the highest importance, and they wanted to ensure no one from the ship that might have overheard something spread the news before the leadership even had a chance to respond.

"Simple." Ward had also relaxed, apparently realizing he had instigated the tense situation. "We need to all go and see the Western Provincial King together, the moment we first reach the dock. That way everyone can part ways as soon as I deliver the message case to him."

"Okay, not a problem." I nodded in agreement, actually happy that I might have a chance to speak to the king right away. "We would be more than happy to do so."

"Well, there is one problem." Captain Hail was nervous again. "We need you all to go without armor, weapons, or storage devices." I opened my mouth to argue, but she talked right over me. "And shackles. You will need to wear shackles."

"Why, in the name of the gods, would anyone under the level of a *Sage* need to wear *shackles*, to see a *King-ranked* cultivator?" I was having trouble not shouting. It was absolutely ridiculous. So much for simple.

"We don't know." Ward was tense again, as if waiting for me to go crazy and kill him. I had no idea why. "It is a relatively new rule that just came out right before we left on this mission. Someone mentioned it might have been because of that storm of dark shooting stars a few years ago. It was a bad omen, and all security measures were increased after someone attacked the Southern Provincial King in his bedchamber not long afterwards."

Whoops. Both those were actually my fault. The law of

unintended consequences wasn't a fun one. Still, it was a stupid rule, and I didn't like it.

"Okay." My agreement made them both calm back down. "No sense fighting something I can't change. I will tell my friends, and we will prepare." They both nodded and moved to walk past me. "One quick question. Should we prepare some smaller shackles? You know, for the baby?" I could tell it stung them for me to say it, but I was mad. And semi-serious. There were plenty of old and powerful cultivators that were more than a little crazy, and provoking him if I didn't need to, didn't seem like a good idea.

They didn't answer my question. Both of them seemed ashamed as they headed below, leaving me on deck with only the horses for company. I knew I wasn't being fair to them, but they had handled the situation poorly. Waiting until the last minute was a bad idea, and I couldn't help but wonder why they had waited so long. Was there some plan to bring us in without a fight, since I had killed Smythe?

A few minutes later, my friends came up from below and walked over to where I was now steering the ship. Chu was in the lead, and stopped short when he saw the look on my face. Apparently, I didn't look happy.

"What happened?" He looked around quickly, as if expecting an ambush. "Do we need to fight someone? You only have that look on your face when you are about to kill someone."

I shook my head in resignation. There was just no staying in a bad mood with these kinds of people in my life.

"No, Chu. We don't need to kill anyone. Not right now, anyway." It took a few minutes, but I explained the situation to everyone. They weren't exactly happy about it either. After a few minutes of discussion, we came up with a plan.

Everyone would wear their brigandine armor, so they could hide the fact that we were protected. Anything we didn't want another person to see or take would be hidden in my belt or the rings hidden inside the belts of everyone else. The only thing the government-people would find when they searched our items at the palace would be exactly what we wanted them to see.

Of course, there wasn't much we could do about being shackled. Donny actually came up with an interesting idea, but we decided against it.

"I still think putting a popper under your tongue would definitely work. All we would need to do is spit them at an attacker, and take their weapons from them! Foolproof!"

He was still arguing his point, but Valerie wasn't having it. "Yeah, and what happens when you accidentally bite down on it while the stupid thing is still inside your mouth?" She was wagging her finger under his nose as she lectured him. "And blow all your teeth through your dumb lips? What then?"

Donny looked sheepishly down at his booted feet. "I guess I didn't think of that…"

"You don't say?!"

"But, I just wanted to—"

"No! No more talking for you. Not until we are finished making plans."

He stopped talking, and only mumbled something about how she was being unfair. Jamila leaned over and smacked him in the back of the head. Chu patted him on the shoulder in understanding.

Yep. Impossible to stay in a bad mood with these four around.

"How about we use the idea of the poppers, but something different carved on them? That way we don't risk hurting ourselves?" Jamila was holding up a blank pebble as she asked the question. Honestly, it was a good idea.

"What?! I just said—"

Smack!

"No! I told you to stop talking! That means no talking until we are done!" Valerie had smacked him in the back of the head again. Poor Donny. Those two were definitely going to get married.

"It is a good idea, Jamila." Donny looked at me like I had betrayed him. "Let me try to come up with something. You guys go on and sort everything the way we talked about, and be sure to get Every and the horses ready to go." As they turned to leave, I redeemed myself in Donny's eyes. "Oh, and Donny should stay with me. He *is* the next best person at carving runes."

There was a bit of a debate about the quality of Donny's carving, but in short order it was just him and I at the rear of the ship. He was grinning from ear to ear. Of course, Valerie had given me a wink where Donny couldn't see as she went below for Every. She knew exactly what I had done, and approved.

He and I brainstormed until the horizon started lightening with the coming sunrise. We both took a break to put on our brigandine armor as we had planned, which was when we were struck by the realization that we didn't actually *need* to put something in our mouths. We could put it on our clothes.

"There aren't any buttons on the front of this vest, just buckles and ties." Donny was quickly taking his back off as he talked. "We could carve some formation on a row of false buttons." He finally had it off, and was looking at the vest as he laid it on the ground and smoothed out the front. "Even better, we could carve them on the *back* of the buttons, and no one would be the wiser!" It was a great idea, and we got started immediately.

We ended up making a small decorative silver button for the top of each shoulder, and a row of four buttons along each side. I had to destroy several silver coins in the process, but it would be worth it if we needed them.

The buttons on the shoulders each formed a thin shield, one to stop qi attacks and one to protect from physical attacks. The small size of the buttons meant we had to keep the functions simple, but the pure silver meant they could store enough qi without us needing to provide the energy to power them. For a little while, at least.

The eight buttons on the sides were offensive in nature. The upper two would send out a sharp ring of ice, ensuring someone attacking from any direction would get a nasty surprise. They were designed to stay on the vest, and could only be activated once.

The lower six—which weren't so high up near the armpits that they would be difficult to reach—were all spike traps. They would need to be pulled off of the vest and thrown, but the handful of thin, waist-height spears of earth and metal qi they each created would be devastating against anyone trying to hurt us. It was the least qi-intensive trap formation I could think of at the moment, so it was what we went with.

I even made two extra shield buttons for Every. When Jamila brought him over, I sewed them onto the sides of his little pants. He immediately tried to pull them off and eat one, so I had to play the 'what-do-you-have-in-your-mouth-don't-eat-that-get-back-here-how-are-you-so-fast-all-of-a-sudden' game with him. Anyone with a child knows *exactly* the game I am talking about.

After catching him, I made sure to sew them in place really, *really* well. It would take one of us to will the shields into place, but once they formed, he would be protected from head to toe. His shields would also last much longer and be far more robust, considering his smaller size required less surface area to protect.

We all looked sharp, dressed in white linen shirts, matching dark blue vests and pants, with our silver buttons gleaming. We looked like a team again. Even Every. It felt good, and I could tell everyone else felt the same.

By the time we were done, the sun had fully cleared the horizon. I even tested them to make sure they could be used while touching orichalcum, and though it was difficult, my willpower was stronger than its dampening effects. The internal stores of qi were enough. We were good to go.

The stiff morning breeze was forcing us closer to the city that was rapidly growing in size. We made our final preparations, and all of us lined the railing to look at the city as the regular crew came up to take over operations. Both Hail and Ward kept their distance, and my concern grew.

So did my worry. I genuinely thought we had become friends, but their recent actions had me doubting them. Ward was even wearing his full suit of armor again, and he hadn't worn that in weeks. We would see what transpired when we got to the palace and spoke to the king.

The city looked to be larger than the Southern Provincial Capital by almost double, and filled with buildings at least six stories tall. Most seemed to be constructed of wood, with only the wealthiest being able to afford stone in such a location. It was surrounded on all sides by a thick forest of incredibly tall trees, making stone a rare commodity. The trees were big enough that the thousand yards of separation between the woods and city wall appeared to be almost nonexistent. Their scale was incredible to witness, and I couldn't help but think about what would happen four hundred years from now. Legend claimed they had grown so tall because of a battle between two clans of wood cultivators that had taken place there over a thousand years ago, resulting in the nearby forest growing to almost impossible proportions. It was an awe-inspiring sight that should have filled my heart with wonder. Instead, all I felt was sadness.

I had been serving in the North when word had come of an organized attack against the city from the neighboring empire. They had sailed to the edges of the city and used a team of powerful cultivators to drop the surrounding trees on the walls, destroying most of the city in the process. The invaders hadn't considered the consequences of dropping that much weight at the same time in a relatively small surface area. It was the ensuing earthquake that had killed most people, buried in the rubble of their homes and businesses.

A team of Enforcers from Ming had retaliated against our neighbors the following year, but the end result had only been more death and destruction. Ming had loved it. I had argued against it, but I was ignored. A team of assassins sent to kill some of the leadership responsible for the attack would have been much more effective, but he wanted their people and economy to suffer as ours had.

When rulers made war, only the people were made to weep.

I was broken out of my thoughts when another schooner similar to ours adjusted course to intercept our path. The harbor patrol must have been warned to keep an eye out for us, meaning either Ward or Hail had sent another message to their leaders without me noticing. Considering their actions recently, they must have also received a reply that involved my friends and I. Stars damn it. Why couldn't anything ever be easy? And to think that I had trusted them at one point.

"Ho the ship!" A man with the aura of a Low Sage cultivator and markings of an Imperial Army Major was standing at the railing of the harbor patrol schooner. He was also in full plate armor. Like an idiot. Where did they get these people? "Permission to come aboard?!"

"Permission granted!" Captain Hail had already positioned a plank of wood that could be dropped in place for a crossing. The Sage let loose his aura, allowing the weight of it to steady the waves in the immediate area so he could cross without issue. Ward was waiting for the arrival of the officer, and saluted him as soon as he stepped on deck.

"Where are they, Sergeant?" The major didn't even bother with niceties. Straight to business with this one.

"There, sir. By the railing." Ward nodded his head in our direction. "The ones in the matching clothing."

"And why are they not in shackles, Sergeant?" He was looking at us like we were unsightly stains. Or maybe bugs he was ready to squash. We would see about that.

"Sir, we only have the arm shackles in inventory. Your orders were to include leg shackles as well, but we don't have any." Ward was refusing to look in our direction.

The motherless dog *knew* about this, and didn't bother to warn me? That was okay. I knew how to deal with traitors.

"I don't have time to deal with this." The major let out a

sigh of frustration. "Fine. Just use what you have, and get them onto the other ship. I am to take you straight to the king, where he will question them personally." He spun on his heel and marched directly back to his ship. The urge to just kill him was incredibly strong. I hated people like him. Then Ward approached us, and I was reminded of the greater evil. The traitor.

"Citizens, I am placing you under arrest for—"

"Ward, if you finish that sentence, I will cut your lips off and rip your tongue out by the root, just so your lying mouth can't speak another word." His eyes were smoldering, as if he was the one offended. "Keep looking at me like that, and I will pluck out your eyes while I'm at it. And don't forget, Ward. You may be nominally stronger than me, but I have already beaten you once. I *will* do it again. It's what you deserve, after all." I pointedly looked down at his hands, where five chains with orichalcum cuffs at the ends dangled from his grip to prove my point.

"Jim, stop. Please." Captain Hail had moved to stand next to Ward. "He didn't have a choice. We don't even know what this is about."

"I don't care. You lied to us, both of you. Feel grateful that I don't kill you both and send this ship to the bottom, like I did the stars-damned pirate." My face must have shown how much I meant every word, because she took a step back when she finally had the gall to look me in the face. "We saved your lives, more than once. And this is the thanks we get."

"It isn't like that. None of this is." She looked over at the horses, and the small pile of our gear we hadn't put in our hidden storage. "Look, whatever is going on, we can talk about it after you talk to the king. To prove it, we will hold onto your horses and items for you, until you come for them. Just ask for an inn called *The Crater*. It's not far from the docks. You can't miss it."

"Hurry up over there! I don't have all day!" The major was

yelling at us from the deck of the other ship, his arms crossed in annoyance. Man, I really wanted to kill something right now.

"Let's just get this over with." Chu's voice broke the tension. "We need to see the king anyway. Who cares if it is while we are wearing those? As long as we get it done, it doesn't matter."

Silently, we all agreed. I held up my hands, waiting for my turn to be imprisoned once again. What a welcome this was turning out to be.

CHAPTER TWENTY-FOUR

Every Problem has a Solution

The trip to the palace was uneventful. We didn't even get to see the city, because the wagon we were forced to ride in was basically just a giant wooden box with air holes cut into the floor and roof. We had all been connected to one another by a long chain before being shoved inside. It was hard to see the positive side of things at the moment. At least it wasn't raining.

We finally got to the palace after several hours of rumbling down dirt roads and wooden streets. Since this city didn't have a lot of stone, they used thick wooden planks instead of cobblestones. I bet it was a constant nightmare for the locals to continually replace them as they rotted or cracked. On the upside, it did make for a smooth ride. Maybe I could see a few positives.

Once the back of the wagon dropped open, we were yanked out by our chains. Valerie, who was holding Every, almost fell down. The guard who was responsible for the jerk on the chain got an earful from Jamila.

"Watch it, you idiot!" She got as up in his face as the chain connecting us allowed. "Are you trying to hurt a baby?!" He took a step back in surprise. Apparently, they weren't used to their prisoners fighting back. After that, they were much gentler in their handling of us.

Our wagon had been wheeled around to the back of the palace, which was impressive-looking. It was more of a series of buildings connected by covered walkways, with most being only one or two stories tall. Since they were mostly made of stone, their shorter height must have been done to reduce costs. Whoever the king was when this was built must have been an economically conscientious ruler. Or just cheap.

We were led to the back door of the main building, and shuffled inside. I wasn't surprised to see Ward already there with the major, both of them standing at attention next to a woman dressed in the clothes of a servant. Since they were at attention, it must have been a very important servant. Possibly the king's personal secretary, or maybe the palace majordomo.

The bronze doors they were waiting in front of were an impressive ten feet tall, with intricate carvings of ships sailing the oceans, and mighty cultivators fighting the monsters hidden within the waves. The rest of the palace we had seen was plain stone with only minimal accents. The doors must have been a newer addition, or the only concession to vanity the original king had allowed.

As we lined up behind the two army personnel, the tall doors were slowly opened from the inside. We marched forward into the throne room without prompting, all of us just wanting to get this done and over with.

"His Majesty, King of the Western Province. Bow to your ruler, supplicants." The woman spoke in a regal tone, waving an arm with a flourish. The man that sat on the oversized chair at the other end of the room was smaller than I expected. He was completely bald, with a clean-shaven face that was wrinkled with age. The man seemed almost shrunken, bent-backed and squinting to see who had walked into the room. The dark purple robes he wore reminded me of the ceremonial outfits worn by the Imperial family during public outings, with heavy thread-of-gold creating swirling designs along the hems.

Despite his advanced age, power drifted off of him in waves. He was certainly a King-ranked cultivator. He must have been on the edge of losing his power to the progression of time, meaning he had less than a decade of strength remaining to him before he began his inevitable decline. It happened to everyone that advanced too slow. Old age claimed us all, only held at bay for as long as we continued to move forward on the path of cultivation.

The throne room was more reminiscent of a long hallway than a grand hall. It was well over two hundred feet long, but only twenty or thirty feet wide. The five of us lined up across the room almost filled it from one side to the other, forcing the guards along the walls to stand with their backs against the hanging tapestries that decorated the room.

The major and Sergeant Ward both bowed at the waist. None of us did at all. It had been a unanimous decision to not do so, even though we hadn't planned it. Being dragged in front of someone while in chains for no specifically-named reason tended to put a dampener on the whole 'respect' idea. The woman doing the announcing wasn't happy with our lack of proper decorum. She waved a hand for the guards, and they stepped forward to try to force us to bow. Thankfully, the king stepped in before it came to blows. Because believe me, there would have been somebody bowing, and it wouldn't have been us.

"I see they have some spine. Good. Hopefully, they have brains to match." He had a deeper voice than I was expecting, but it was already raspy with age. "Bring me the message. Then we can deal with why they are here."

Ward passed a scroll case to the woman, who brought it up to the king. He used a key from a chain around his neck to open the case, and dumped a thick roll of parchment into his hand. Just our luck. It was a long message that took him over an hour to read. The whole time we were forced to stand and wait. Every was surprisingly quiet, as if he was somehow aware of our current situation. We passed him back and forth between us to keep our arms from getting tired. The kid had put on some weight, and even our advanced strength could be tested if we were forced to hold him for long periods of time. He had just been passed to me when the king finally finished the document. He held it up so a waiting scribe standing against the wall could run forward and grab it from him.

"Major, you and I have much to talk about. The plans proposed by my fellow kings and the emperor will take months of preparations to implement." The major nodded at his words. "Now, for the rest of you. I have some questions." His aura flared, causing all of us to grunt with the surprising change in pressure. Every let out a cry of pain, so I held him closer to me in an attempt to shield him as best as I could.

"What would you like to know, Western King?" Despite the pressure, Donny's voice didn't show he was in any discomfort. If anything, he seemed upset at the unnecessary display of power.

"One of your group was named as the last person to ever see a cartographer named Taft. I wish to know where he went, and what he had in his possession at the time." The king's dark eyes seemed to glow with anger, and another flare of power led to another increase of pressure in the room. "He has something of mine, and I wish for it to be returned."

The surprise and confusion on our faces was obvious. That was what this was about? Taft? I didn't even know what to say. Well, I guess I could tell him what had transpired.

"Western King, the last we heard of Taft, he was headed to the Northern Province. He was just a shopkeeper I met briefly, so I could purchase some maps before we sailed west. We haven't had any contact with him since we were kidnapped by slavers." I tried to sound as sincere as possible. I genuinely wasn't trying to hide anything, and Taft should have long since had the time to find the Inheritance he was looking for and moved on.

"Hmm, kidnapped by slavers, you say? I am having trouble believing you, considering there are no slaves in the empire!" He thumped a fist on the arm of his throne, but this time there wasn't another surge of power to match his outburst. It was a telling reaction. If he truly believed what he had said, there would have been power behind his words. At the very least, he knew of the slave rings and was not willing to do anything to stop them. At worst, he was helping them. Even if he was a bad person, I still needed to warn him of the darkness infecting his land.

"That isn't all, Majesty." I was speaking quickly, trying to get out the information I needed to pass on so we could complete this portion of our mission. "On our travels here, we came across at least two cases of dark mana demons called *nox*. They were both next to destroyed villages along the coast that were clearly victims of extermination squads. It is imperative that you mobilize your forces as the Southern King has done, and stop these *nox* before their influence can spread farther throughout your lands." I was out of breath by the time I finished, everything coming out in a rush.

It did not result in the reaction I had expected. The major was suddenly very pale, and the woman still standing in front of us looked like she was going to faint. Even the stoic guards that lined the walls shifted their feet, as if suddenly nervous. The king had become very still, as if the information I had blurted out had frozen him solid.

"Well, I suppose it is good to learn the proper name of the creatures you have been fighting, right Major?" The king's eyes flashed. "Although it is interesting to hear your efforts have missed the mark, at least on two occasions." The major visibly shivered in fear. "And I am disappointed to hear how obvious it was for these *young* and *inexperienced* cultivators to see right through your attempts at hiding the actions of your people, Major. We will talk about this, *in depth*, after you ensure these witnesses are taken out back and executed. We can't have them spreading rumors of our actions, now can we?" He waved his hand, signaling for his men.

We all stiffened, and I saw everyone start reaching for the buttons on their sides. I frantically shook my head, telling them to wait. There was no way our little buttons would do anything to slow down a King-ranked cultivator. We needed to wait until the guards had us outside. They all relaxed somewhat, and their brief nods showed they understood.

As the guards surrounded us, my eyes met with Ward's. He was trying to mouth something to me, but I wasn't able to figure it out. Instead, all I did was mouth the word 'soon.' He blanched, obviously understanding what I meant. Even though we were being led to our execution, I was still promising him that he would pay for his betrayal. And he would pay, as soon as I could track him down. I lost sight of him as soon as we were led back out into the hallway leading towards the back of the palace.

One of the guards was leading as we were dragged down the hallway, while the major led four more guards behind us. Only six men total. Too easy.

I was still holding onto Every, so I turned to look at the guard nearest me as we shuffled past the wagon they had used to bring us here.

"What are you going to do with the baby? Or are you going to kill him for being a witness as well?" The guard ignored me, so I stopped walking. My friends had only been waiting for me to do something, so they stopped at almost the same moment. We were mostly hidden from view of the back door now, thanks to the way the large wagon was angled. Perfect. "Hey, Major Butt-Nugget!" Yep, still remembered to use that one. "You bunch of cowards planning on killing the baby as well?" He opened his mouth to say something, which was when I acted.

First, I activated the buttons on Every's pants. The shield started to form, pushing against my arms. I grabbed him by the arms and swung him straight at the major, letting go just as the shield popped into place. Every, being an insane toddler that had spent the last several weeks climbing all over a ship rocking around in the rough waters of the infamous Ocean of Tears, let loose a squeal of excitement.

"*Weeeee!*"

"What the—"

Crunch!

The hard shell of the shield smashed into the major's face, letting out the distinct sound of his nose breaking. I was honestly a little surprised that a Sage cultivator could be hurt by such a weak impact, but then I remembered that the shields were powered with all forms of qi, including light and dark. Which, of course, he didn't have any defenses against. He tried to catch Every, but the egg-shaped shield was perfectly smooth, and he slipped free onto the ground, laughing the entire time. I didn't blame the kid. It was pretty funny.

"*Enough*! Thab's ib! Jus kill themb now!" The major's broken nose made him sound ridiculous, and it made the guards hesitate for just a second. Which was all we needed.

All of us activated our shields, and started ripping off buttons. The first one to throw down a miniature device was Valerie, and she used it to take out the lone guard that had been leading the group. The spears activated flawlessly, shooting up from the ground and cutting through the cheap, mass-produced armor of the guard with no problem. He was lifted off the ground several inches, and slowly slid onto the cluster of thin spears as they pushed through his body. One down.

I was next, managing to land a button right in front of the major. Since these just used metal and earth qi, they didn't damage him like Every had. It still managed to barely pierce the skin of his thigh, but mostly the spears just pinned him against the wagon. It would take a little more work to kill him. Fortunately, I had a strong work ethic.

Chu threw all of his buttons at once, which accidentally created a much larger cluster of spears than we had intended when making them. They amplified each other, creating a veritable forest of stone and steel spears that ripped two guards to pieces, and formed a nice wall to keep the remaining guards from running away. Three down, three to go.

Donny had thrown just one button at the guard standing closest to him, but it had landed at an angle somehow. The spear cluster that shot out from the ground just managed to make it through his leg armor at knee height, causing the guard to fall forward and break his legs at the knees by bending them in the complete wrong direction. He barely had a chance to scream, because Donny stomped on the back of his neck hard enough to snap it in one blow. Four down.

Jamila ended up not using a button. I missed how she did it, but the woman had managed to jump on the back of the guard nearest her and wrap the chain that had connected her wrists together around the man's throat. The orichalcum in the shackles and chains removed any chance of the guard overpowering her, and she levered her body weight back and choked the life out of him. Five down. Just one to go.

As I approached the wagon where the disgusting excuse of an Imperial Army Major was pinned, I reached over and snapped off the top foot or so of a stone spike left by Chu's overzealous use of the buttons. He was struggling to free himself, but the angle of the spikes was making it difficult. I could tell he wasn't used to combat, because any warrior worth his salt would have just forced his way through the pain and busted loose, or simply used a qi construct to move or destroy the wagon he was pinned against.

"Wait!" His nose had already cleared, meaning he had a good command of the wood qi element and could heal himself quickly. "Stop! We can talk about this!" I stopped, standing right in front of him. He calmed down, seeing that I was listening. "I think all of this just got a bit out of hand, and we can come to some agreement."

"Agreement?" I put my hand on the back of his helmeted head, making sure to touch my orichalcum shackle on the bare skin of his neck. The chain was just long enough to allow me to point the stone spike at his face with an inch to spare. "Tell me, Major. Did any of the people your extermination squads needlessly killed ask you to stop?" He opened his mouth to answer, so I shoved the spike up through the roof of his mouth and into his brain. Six down. Good to go.

It was too fast a death for what he deserved, but we needed to leave before anyone thought the sounds of our fight were something other than the guards killing us. I turned around just in time to see Sergeant Ward round the corner of the wagon, his spear already in hand. His eyes widened in surprise at the scene in front of him, and I pulled free another button, ready to kill him.

Which was when he straightened up and his spear disappeared inside his storage ring.

"Thank the gods you killed him!" He seemed to actually mean it.

I held up my hand to stop Jamila, who had already snuck up behind him and was ready to throw down a handful of buttons right between his feet. That would have *really* hurt. "Give me one reason why we shouldn't kill you right now, traitor."

He jumped and half spun at her speaking right behind him. Ward held up his hands and took a step back, moving farther away from the back door of the palace. "I know this all looks really bad—" Donny snorted, interrupting him, but he continued. "—but it was all against my will. I swear on my cores." A subtle pulse of power came from his chest, confirming he was telling the truth. We all relaxed a bit, except for Every. He was rolling around in his egg-shaped shield still, having a blast as he bounced off of the myriad of spikes and dead bodies lying around. That kid was going to have some pretty serious issues later in life.

"Okay then. Tell us what happened." Chu had crossed his arms as he talked, not quite convinced yet. I wasn't either.

"First, you guys need this." Ward pulled out a key and tossed it to Jamila, who was still standing closest to him. She immediately unlocked her shackles, then popped them into the ring hidden in her belt before handing the key over to Valerie. Ward continued. "So, what had happened was, as soon as we were in range of Captain Hail's communication tablet, we sent in a report of our location. Within minutes, they requested the names of everyone on the ship. We sent them, and then got orders to arrest all of you when we reached the city. They also said not to warn you, and to make all haste. Our oaths didn't allow us to break those orders. That is, until you killed the one that gave them." He nodded towards the slumped form of the major. "Once that happened, I would be able to help. I only came out here to try to do what I could to help you get away." He looked at me. "Hail and I tried to warn you, by telling you about the isolation techniques required by some messenger ships." He motioned around at the dead guards and officer. "It seems to have worked. Either that, or you are just very good at killing Imperial Army officers."

"Maybe a little of both." Chu tossed me the key, and I took off my shackles. Everyone else had already taken their chains off while Ward was talking. "Okay, everyone. We need to move. First stop is getting the horses and the rest of our gear from Captain Hail, since that is where they will check, as soon as they figure out we are gone. Then we get Every to the nearest Auction House, and find a way out of the city."

"What about the king?" Valerie was mad, and I knew why. The king deserved to pay for what he had done to those innocent people in the destroyed villages. "Not only did he order our deaths, but he is killing thousands of his own people for no reason."

"It isn't for no reason." Ward cut in, looking sheepish as we all looked at him. "The king believes the demons you spoke of are brought about by a group of evil cultists that has recently been plaguing the area. Any time there is a report of a demon near a town or village, he has been ordering the execution of anyone nearby, since they are the most likely source of the dark rituals that brought forth the demon. He believes if he can kill all the cultists, he can cut off the flow of demons before they engulf the entire province."

Ah, stars. That wasn't good. In my experience, consistent reports of cultists usually ended up as unfounded rumors. Since the invasion of the *nox*, I tended to lean more towards the idea that if it was something bad, believe it until it was disproven. At least, it seemed to work out that way recently. Meaning there probably were some dark cultists running around somewhere. Possibly already possessed by *nox*.

"Don't worry, Valerie." I reached down to pick up Every. His shield had finally run out of power, and he was headed straight for a puddle of blood. This kid was eight different kinds of nuts. I definitely liked him. "The king will have his turn. But we will need to wait until things calm down in the city before we can take a shot at him. Right now, he is literally sitting on his seat of power, and we have a baby to deal with. It isn't the best time to go after him." She gave me a sharp nod, and held out her arms for Every. I passed him over, and then she smacked me hard enough across the face that stars blasted across my vision. "What was that for?!"

"Jim, I can't believe I need to say this, but you need to hear it." I was rubbing my cheek, and she was glaring at me with a not-so-happy look on her face. "You. Don't. *Ever.* Throw. Babies."

Huh. Yeah, I guess I deserved that one.

CHAPTER TWENTY-FIVE

Everyone at the Auction

We quickly made our escape from the palace grounds with the help of Ward. A few quick passes with earth qi fixed the ground where we had killed the major and the guards, then we tossed the bodies in the back of the wagon to hide them. Ward drove the wagon right out the front gate, while the rest of us walked right behind him. I just hoped our escape went unnoticed long enough that we could leave the city with no issues.

Ward parked the wagon at the first empty alleyway that was wide enough to fit it. Once the people following us found it, they would be forced to widen their search area, hopefully slowing them down even more.

Since none of us had been in the city, we just walked the main road that led back to the docks. To be less obvious, we split up the group, but still stayed within sight of one another. Ward was by himself at the front, and I took up the rear. Chu and Jamila moved to the left side of the road, while Donny and Valerie stayed to the right. Valerie was still holding on to Every, his little hands working to pull off the silver button on her left shoulder. Little bugger would probably try to eat it, too.

It was getting close to dark by the time we found the inn

Captain Hail had named. *The Crater* was the best name—and the worst pun—I had ever come across. The stupid thing had been built from shipping crates. I had never seen such a building in all my days. The walls, the stable around back, the roof, the bar, the chairs, absolutely *everything* was just standard crates that had been nailed together to form whatever was needed. I was simultaneously impressed and disgusted. The level of ingenuity was only matched by the level of laziness this had taken. Chu loved it so much he offered to buy it. Thankfully, the bartender, who might or might not have been the owner, turned him down.

We had only been standing in the common room for a few minutes when Hail came out from a door leading to the rooms people could rent for the night. I couldn't help but wonder if even the beds were made out of crates.

Who was I kidding? There was no chance they were anything other than more shipping crates.

"I see you made it. And since Ward isn't dead, you decided to believe me." She was still a little leery of me, and didn't get too close.

"More than that." I leaned up against the bar, doing my best to convey a non-threatening aura. "Let's just say he was released from his orders, and was able to explain everything. Now, how about our things? We need to hurry up and get Every back to his clan."

She seemed to relax, realizing that she wasn't in any danger. They had certainly lost our trust, but at least they no longer had our animosity. An oath was an oath, and they had no choice. But continuing with them was no longer an option, if all it took was one order from a superior for them to be a knife in our back.

Hail led us out back, where Scout and Cloud were waiting for us. They seemed happy to see us return, and somehow Scout managed to simultaneously nuzzle Valerie and stomp on Donny's foot. No matter how many times he did it, I was still shocked at how clever that horse could be.

We said our goodbyes, and Ward returned with Hail to the inn while my friends and I went back out onto the street. We were forced to lead the horses instead of riding, since silhouetting ourselves above the thinning crowds seemed like a bad idea. Valerie passed Every to Chu so she could lead Scout, and Jamila took Cloud. Donny took the lead, leading us to the eastern edge of the city where the bartender had told us the main Auction House was located. I brought up the rear, with the horses, girls, Every, and Chu all in the middle.

Moving through the city got easier as time went by. The later it got into the night, the fewer people there seemed to be running around. There was a marked difference in the appearance of those that stayed up during the night hours. Most seemed a bit rougher around the edges, with many more hiding in the shadows than most cities would tolerate. I noticed a distinct lack of guards throughout the neighborhoods as we walked. Either the king didn't bother with regular patrols, or he had most of his men and women elsewhere. Probably killing innocent civilians in some coastal village.

The Auction House was visible in the distance, its seven-story building rising above its neighbors. We were working our way through a rougher area, the thick wooden planks on the roads more pitted and broken here than any we had seen thus far. The buildings were closer together, and more than one seemed to be leaning against the one next to it. A distinct lack of light poles or glow stones, even on the main streets, made it impossible to see beyond a few yards.

Donny had stopped at an intersection to try to figure out which road to take. He was attempting to read a faded street sign, but having problems seeing it in the dark. I was trying to catch up to him to help out since I could see in the dark, at least far easier than he could. Suddenly an arrow flashed out of the darkness and pinged off of the hidden brigandine armor on his back before I could get there. Valerie had her own bow up in almost the same second, her responding shot bringing a yell of pain from the darkness.

"Go!" Donny yelled, deciding to run down the left-hand road that more-or-less went in the direction we wanted to go.

We sprinted as fast as we could go. It was even darker down this path, the buildings casting their shadows over the street. As we ran, I could hear the shouts of our pursuers falling behind. Whatever ambush they had set for passing travelers was run by amateurs. But the next one wasn't.

Donny sprinted full-speed into a thin rope stretched across the road, the darkness making it invisible while we were moving so quickly. He was flipped onto his back, and he hit hard enough I could hear his breath leave him with a gasp of pain. The rest of us slowed to a stop, not knowing where the next attack would come from.

"Well, what a nice surprise! Visitors!" Over a dozen men and women came out of the buildings around us. The leader was a Peak Brain cultivator, putting him at the same strength as Donny and I. He was very plain-looking, with brown hair and eyes, wearing simple and well-worn clothes. The kind of person you walked past every day on the street without a second thought. The rest of his people were weaker than him.

"It looks like they were trying to pass through our neighborhood without saying hi. We can't have that, can we?" The second voice came from the rooftop to our right, as a not-so-subtle way of telling us they had more archers ready to fire.

"No, we can't be having that. What do you say, friends? Would you like to stay for a while?" The plain-looking man took a few steps forward, grabbing onto the reins of Valerie's horse. Yes, that horse. Scout, the holy terror of anyone that spent extra time around Valerie. And had a penchant for killing anyone that threatened her. Like this idiot.

"Guys, don't kill them all." I activated the shield function on my spirit wood ring, and spun out a thread of metal qi from my right hand into a whip. "We don't have time to spare right now."

My words had their desired effect. The ambushing street thugs must not have come across many smaller groups that didn't immediately give up, because they all took a step or two back. Except for the leader, who still hadn't let go of Scout's reins.

Scout started us off. He used a short forward hop to destabilize the man, and then stomped down so hard on his foot that I could hear the crunch of bone through his boots. So much for fortifying his body. Some just never learned.

His shout of pain was the signal for Chu to throw down a shield plate that sprung up around us in a dome of opaque fog. It wasn't strong enough to keep out people, but it certainly kept the archers from getting an arrow through. The fog also kept anyone not inside the dome from seeing exactly what was going on. That was probably why they continued to rush to the aid of their comrades, like lambs to the slaughter.

Jamila did the majority of the work. Her shuriken were flying stars of instant death, coated in a thin layer of fire qi that set her targets alight, providing us plenty of impromptu torches. It gave Donny some time to get back on his feet. The first thing he did was cut through the cord blocking the road, and then he quickly finished off the few attackers that came in from the front.

Once the route was clear in front of us, we took off at a dead sprint. I trailed behind, using my whip and shield to deflect the few arrows that came our way. The shield dissipated shortly after we cleared it, and the pile of bodies we left behind was exposed to the rest of the ambushers. None of those remaining decided to follow us.

After a quick run through the streets, Donny eventually led us into a city square. We stopped to regroup near a fountain, where Chu gave Donny a quick once-over to make sure he was okay. While he did that, the horses got a drink and the rest of us took a breather. All this running was making me tired. I overheard Jamila talking to Chu.

"How bad is the situation in the city, if citizens are ambushing people out in the open like that?" She had moved beside Cloud, and was watching the rooftops.

"I don't know, but it speaks to larger issues in this province than just the *nox* and execution squads." Chu was trying to get Every to take a sip of water, but the kid was more interested in splashing around at the edge of the fountain. "If they are desperate enough to turn to banditry in the night, what does that say about their lives during the day?"

I cleared my throat to interrupt. "Yes, the problems speak to a wider range of issues. But we need to know more before we try to take down the most powerful cultivator in the province." I looked to the part of the city where the palace was located. "Answers to questions like, who will be his replacement? Will they be any better? Should we kill everyone in the line of succession first, and then the king? Is the successor in a position to actually take power upon the king's death?" Everyone just stared at me. "What? Those are all very important questions to know the answers to."

"Yeah, Jim, we get that." Chu was slightly shaking his head in disbelief. "Sometimes we just forget that you know about more things than fighting, cultivating, and crafting." Whew. If he only knew!

We were interrupted by shouting in the distance, along with the screaming sounds of steel on steel echoing off of the tall buildings lining the streets. It was time to go.

Donny took the lead again, taking us down the widest street he could find. Whether it was the stench of fresh blood on us, or the speed we confidently moved, no one else tried to challenge us. It was deep in the night, closer to sunrise than sunset, before we finally found the front gates of the Auction House.

"No admittance to the Auction House outside our normal hours." The guards at the front gate didn't even give us a chance to talk as we approached.

The tall building that housed the auction facilities, and housing for the branch employees, was surrounded by a high stone wall lined with protective runes and topped with iron and glass spikes. While the wall would only provide a token defense against most powerful cultivators, the runes might give a whole team of Duke-level cultivators some issues. I might have seen it as overkill before now, but after experiencing the night-life of the capital, I completely understood.

"Gentlemen, I apologize, but we can't take no for an answer." The guards stiffened at my words, and I could feel more than one person hiding out of sight spin up their cores. "The baby we brought with us was kidnapped from the Feng clan, and we wish to return him safely." Now *that* changed their attitudes rather quickly.

We were ushered inside, the wrought-iron gates slamming closed behind us. The apparent leader of the gate guards silently led our group around back, to a secluded courtyard next to a set of stables.

"Please allow us to stable your horses for you." He said it loud enough to alert the stable hands inside that they needed to come outside. "One of our representatives will be here shortly to escort you inside." Seeming to have run out of his daily allotment of words, the man stood silently to the side while Scout and Cloud were led into individual stalls.

The horses seemed anxious, but a few apples from the experienced stable hands fixed that issue quickly. I could feel eyes on my back, meaning we were being watched by more than just the single gate guard we could see. The atmosphere was tense, and Every started to pick up on it. He was making fussing sounds, right on the edge of crying, when the back door to the building finally opened.

Out walked a man that looked like the king's older brother. He was well past his prime, with age spots on his hands and shiny bald head. I couldn't sense his cultivation level, meaning he must be hiding it with a medallion or formation of some kind. It was common for cultivators to do that in large cities, so I wasn't surprised. His hooked nose looked like the beak of an eagle, and his watery brown eyes were dull from the late hour. Or ridiculously early hour, if you were one of those secretly evil early-risers that actually enjoyed the mornings. Don't get me wrong, I got up with the sun all the time. But that was more out of habit than enjoyment.

"Well, might as well come inside, so we can sort this mess out." We followed behind the man, him mumbling the whole way. "...don't see why they couldn't come at a *decent* hour... Young people today, always in a rush... Only think about themselves... Better be worth it..."

Definitely not an early riser. I understood. At least we finally got everyone safely to the Auction House.

CHAPTER TWENTY-SIX

Markings

We were led through a maze of narrow hallways, an area clearly not intended for most people to see. I had no doubt the public spaces were much more open, with decorations and fine artwork on the walls so as to dazzle the patrons. There was no wasted money on such frivolities in this part of the building.

The office we were taken into was large, but with the five of us, the old man, and the baby, it got cramped pretty quickly. I was forced to stand in the corner, while everyone else got a stuffed leather chair positioned in a semicircle in front of the large desk. The walls were covered in bookshelves, heavy with old tomes and knickknacks from across the empire. A cold fireplace sat along the wall, the fall-year nights still not cold enough to warrant a fire. The well-worn chair behind the desk seemed too large for the old man as he plopped down in his seat, but he seemed to enjoy the extra comfort it gave him.

A few seconds after he sat down, a woman dressed as a servant—but was clearly a guard in disguise, given the callouses on her hands and the way she carried herself—brought everyone a cup of tea and a small bowl of fresh fruit for Every. He was sitting on the floor between Jamila and Chu, getting more of the berries on his clothes than he was in his mouth, but it kept the boy busy.

The old man cleared his throat. "Well, now that we are settled, why don't you explain to me what you said to the guards." He nodded towards Every. "You stated something about getting a reward for returning a child?" Chu leaned forward in his chair, placing a hand on Every's head.

"No, we didn't mention a reward. The five of us just want to get Every back to his parents, where he belongs. When we rescued him—well, technically Jim rescued him, and we helped—the slavers said the boy belonged to someone important in the Feng clan." Every grabbed his hand, smearing it in berry juice. Chu winced and tried to wipe it off on his pants while he talked. "We were out in the middle of the Ocean of Tears, so it took us some time to make it to the nearest Auction House. But, well, we're here! Better late than never, as they say."

The old man squinted his watery eyes at us, like he was trying to see through Chu's words to some hidden secrets we might be hiding. "Okay then, we will have to see how this goes." He turned to look at the guard pretending to be a servant. "Wake Shin and tell him to come here, please. And tell him to bring a truth stone." She turned to leave. "Oh, and the blood testing device." She nodded and moved to the door. "Oh! And see if the cooks are awake, and have them send over some breakfast." She hurried out the door before he could ask for anything else.

As we sat and waited, the old man quietly watched Every munching on berries. And fingerpainting on the fine rug with the juice from the fruit. Whoever cleaned this place was going to be mad.

No one spoke, the tension in the room making it uncomfortable. The old man clearly didn't believe us, and his disdain was clear. Our attitude towards him wasn't much better. We went all this way, took care of Every this entire time, and we get treated with suspicion? Not the reaction we were looking for. After what felt like a ridiculously long time, a bleary-eyed and ruffled-looking man stumbled into the room.

"I'm here, Branch Manager. What is the problem?" Shin was of a similar age to the old man sitting behind the desk—who was apparently the branch manager, not that he ever bothered to introduce himself—but that was where the similarities ended. He had smile lines that practically took over his face, and a thick beard of gray hair that matched the tight topknot of gray hair on his head. He must have been wearing a medallion that hid his cultivation level, like the branch manager, but it was obvious the man was strong. He hadn't let his age prevent him from keeping up with his training.

"We have another group trying to collect the reward money for the missing kid." The branch manager waved his hand at us. "Let's get this over with. Test his blood, and then we can use the truth stone to find out what they are really up to afterward." My friends and I stiffened in anger. I was about two seconds away from showing this old guy a thing or two, but Shin interrupted my train of thought.

"Why don't we find out if they are telling the truth, before we condemn them as liars?" He pulled out a small rectangle of iron and crouched in front of Every. "This will give him a little prick on his finger, but it will tell us if he is actually a child of the Feng clan bloodline." He placed Every's little finger in a hole on the side of the box, and I felt a tiny burst of qi come out of him and into the hunk of metal. Every jerked his hand back, staring up at the man with a sense of pure betrayal. Jamila reached down to pick him up as he began to cry.

"Now that we have the formalities over with, let's move on to the next phase." The old man behind the desk in front of us released his aura, showing himself to be a powerful Duke-level cultivator. His advanced age meant he wasn't as powerful as he could have been, but that didn't mean much when you were three full levels higher than the person you were trying to suppress. Well, for most people.

All five of us barely reacted, making the old man stare at us in shock. Jamila hunched around Every to protect him, and all of us spun up our cores in preparation of whomping the living snot out of this guy. Realistically, the five of us didn't have much of a chance unless I used light and dark qi, but if I did, we could rip this guy into pieces without having to destroy much of the building.

Instead, Shin stepped in. "What is wrong with you?!" He slammed the small metal box onto the table. "You didn't even wait for me to finish! And, worst of all, you could have hurt a defenseless child with your stupid posturing!" He pointed at the box. "And guess what? It's *him*. The missing child is *here*, with us, in this room. The great-grandson of the current *Leader* and *Owner* of the Auction House and Feng clan, and you almost hurt him. You could have *killed* him!" You could hear the capital letters in the words 'leader' and 'owner.' Apparently, Every was kind of a big deal. In certain circles, anyway. He still pooped his pants, after all.

"Wh… Wha… What?" The only color on the branch manager's face was his age spots. His aura disappeared in an instant, and he was literally shaking in fear.

"You have gone too far this time, Izeaj. I am enacting the Charter, and you will be placed into custody until such a time as the review board can collect a full accounting of your actions. Those of today, *and* any crimes committed in the past." The old man opened his mouth to argue, but Shin didn't give him a chance. "Guards! Come and take the *former* branch manager to his rooms, until such a time as his actions can be completely reviewed."

They had clearly been waiting outside the door, the six men rushing inside the already full room making it an even tighter fit. For a moment, it looked like he was going to try to fight. I saw his eyes dart to Every, and his shoulders slumped in defeat. Now that he knew how important the child was, he wasn't willing to risk injuring him. I had a feeling if he did, it would be a certain death sentence. And he knew it, too.

"This isn't over, Shin." Izeaj was enraged, his face quickly going from pale to red. "I will have my day before the council, and when I do, you will regret this!" The guards handed him an orichalcum ring, and he put it on without a fight. Shin held out a hand, and after a long hesitation, Izeaj took off two storage rings and two necklaces. Possibly the key tokens to lock or unlock important formations around the building, or maybe just more storage devices. It seemed to cause him actual physical pain to hand them over. He couldn't leave the room without a parting threat. "The king will be asking for me eventually, Shin. And when he finds out about this, he will not be happy that his *friend* was locked away by an underling."

"The king won't do anything to anger the Auction House, Izeaj. Not to help out a lackey like you." As they led him away, Shin had already stopped paying attention to the old man and was looking at the rings and necklaces in his hands. He was emitting more qi, forcibly breaking the blood links on the items he had taken from the old man, and putting his own in their place. It was normally a difficult process to break a blood bond against a living owner's will, but he must have had some practice. They survived the process, and he put them on before sitting in the recently-vacated chair.

"Well, that was exciting." Jamila sat Every down on the floor again, now that things seemed to have calmed down once again. She was paying close attention to the man's actions, obviously noticing the casual and quiet display of skill and power. "What now, new Branch Manager? Can we finally find out what is going on?"

"I must apologize to you all." He waved a hand at the closed door. "That man has been a menace to this organization for years. He was a symptom of the sickness wrought upon the province by a faulty system of leadership. One that prides itself only on its own laurels, and not on the things it can provide its people." We all nodded. It was pretty obvious that if the capital was having problems, the province would as well. "But that isn't why you are here. You have brought us a new issue to deal with. A good issue, true, but an issue nonetheless." He looked down at Every, who had now found a loose thread in the carpet and was busy unravelling as much of it as he could. The kid had a penchant for destruction. "This little one has been missing for nearly a year. He was taken from his nursery only a few months after his birth by a traitorous nursemaid, who was working for a notorious pirate. We lost all trace of him after they passed over the border. His parents were visiting an important Auction House location near the border between the Western and Southern Provinces. It is located on the Great River, where ships come and go, as numerous as the stars in the sky."

"That would make it hard to track down any ship suspected in the kidnapping." Donny had pulled out a shiny beast core and rolled it over to Every. He gave up trying to wreck the carpet and instead concentrated his extreme talent on eating the fist-sized crystal. It shouldn't be possible for him to manage it, but the kid had determination and time. I would put my money on him pulling it off.

"We got word of his abduction here in the capital almost instantly, thanks to our communication networks." Shin waved his hands in the universal motion of 'gestures at everything.' "Teams were sent from every part of the empire, and we shortly had a full report on where he *wasn't* located. As you said, young man, the amount of shipping traffic made it quite the chore to figure out where he could have gone." He leaned back in the chair, shuffling through some documents. After finding what he was looking for, he pulled out a piece of parchment with the word 'reward' written large across the top. "So, we did the only thing we could think of, and posted reward notices for his return."

"I can see how that might cause some problems." Chu shook his head. "There are plenty of people out there that would try to pass off their *own* child, if the rewards were big enough."

Shin nodded in agreement. "That is true, but it still doesn't excuse Izeaj's actions." He looked down at his hands that were resting on top of the desk. "And you only experienced the tiniest portion of that man's venom. He has done far worse than threaten children in his time here." I stepped forward and took the beast core from Every. He had started banging it on the ground, scarring the wooden floor through the shredded carpet. Seriously, this boy was a one-kid wrecking crew.

"We rescued him when we broke free of a group of pirate slavers a number of months back." I handed Every a piece of bread before he could cry about me taking the beast core. He then commenced with spreading a fine layer of crumbs as far as his little arms could manage. I was beginning to wonder if the cleaning crew would actually try to hunt us down and murder everyone. "We have been taking care of him ever since."

Shin looked at Every thoughtfully. "You brought him back safely, and we can't ask for more than that. Not just that, but he appears to be happy and healthy. Once I get the message to his family, I am sure they will want to meet you. To thank you in person, and add to the simple rewards that were listed on the 'missing' notices." It was tempting to look at the list on the paper he had placed on the desk, but that wasn't why we were here.

"No." He seemed surprised by my rejection. "We didn't do this for a reward. And we don't have time to sit around for Every's family to make it here, anyway." My friends nodded in agreement. Chu was maybe a tiny bit slower to agree compared to everyone else, but that wasn't much of a surprise. He was Chu, after all. "Since you have Every now, we will be leaving."

Now Shin seemed confused. "I don't understand. You don't want *anything* for saving the boy? What is more important than meeting with some of the highest members of the Feng clan? And who in the stars is Every?"

We all laughed. I couldn't hold back the smile as I answered him. "Every is the name we gave him. We didn't know his name, and he has a habit of getting into *everything*, so we just called him Every."

Now it was Shin's turn to laugh. "I see. I suppose it's as good a temporary name as any. His real name is Jang. Jang

Feng." It was sobering to hear his real name. I guess it made it real that we were leaving him behind. "But you didn't answer my other questions. Why such a rush? And why wouldn't you want the favor of the Feng clan?"

"On our way here, we saw several villages that had been wiped out by violence. The king was behind it, but we just found out it was motivated by reports of a cult in the region." Shin didn't seem surprised. He had mentioned the Auction House had an information network, meaning this must have been old news to him. "We are going to track down the cult, stop it, and then do our best to kill the king. Not necessarily in that order."

He seemed surprised again. "That is quite the ambition. Dealing with a dark cult is hard enough with just five people, but killing a King-ranked cultivator is downright crazy." He looked us over, gauging our confidence. "I even believe you think you can manage it. And maybe you can. Stranger things have happened. Normally, I would be honor-bound to report such plans to the authorities. Considering the situation though, I think I can let this one slide." The corners of his mouth turned up in a sly smile. Then he looked around at all of us, the smile quickly disappearing. "I still don't understand why you wouldn't want the favor of the Feng clan. The benefits are nearly uncountable!"

It was my turn to smile. "Simple. We already have it." I held up my hand, showing the markings left behind by the witch Ling Feng. I had survived a run-in with her back in Roh City, where she had burned my hand with some unknown power. I still hadn't been able to figure that one out.

As soon as Shin saw the markings, his jaw nearly hit the ground in shock. He was around the desk in a flash, his quick movements showing his age hadn't slowed him down in the least. My instincts cried out for me to strike out at the man, but I held back at the last second. Shin was only studying my hand, not quite close enough to reach out and touch me though.

"May I see it?" I shrugged, holding out my hand. He took

another step closer and took my hand. "This mark isn't one I am familiar with, but I do recognize the unique scars the Feng clan members leave behind. May I ask who gave you this?"

"It was a woman named Ling Feng. She was at an Auction House branch location in Roh City, one of the smaller clan hubs in the center of the Southern Province." I winced from the memory of the burning pain she had put me through. "It was a rather unpleasant experience." Shin grimaced, holding up a hand that had three small lines that traveled the length of his palm. From experience, I knew he would have an identical scar on the back of his hand.

"Believe me, I understand. It isn't something I would want to go through twice." He released me, and moved back to the desk so he could sit down again. This time, at normal speed. "If you had shown that when you first approached the gate, you would have received an entirely different reception. Technically, you hold the same rank inside the Auction House as I do. Or, as Izeaj had, before he showed his true colors." He gave us a genuine grin of joy. "Although, this does compound his crimes. Attempting to intimidate or harm another high-ranking member of the Auction House without provocation is a serious offense. And ignorance is no excuse."

"Well, I guess I am happy to have helped. Even if it was an accident." I looked around, ready to leave. "Is there anything else you need from us? Or are we done here?"

Shin glanced down at the baby. "I don't need anything else from you. But you might need something else from me." He looked at each of us, as if measuring the five people before him on some imaginary set of scales. "How about this? Give me some time to put together the information I have on this dark cult everyone is worried about, along with some things you might need. You can rest here for a bit, get cleaned up, say your goodbyes to Jang, and then be on your way. I can even show you some things for sale in the display room. I'm sure you could find an item or two that could be useful." We all looked at one another, noticing the glaring necessity for a bath. And laundry.

I hated not having self-cleaning clothing for everything we wore.

"We can certainly agree to that." Nods of agreement from everyone confirmed I had made the right call. "You could save us a lot of time by pointing us in the right direction." He got up to lead us out of the room, when I remembered something important. "Oh, and we all should make some deposits into our accounts. And I would like to check for some messages from a man named 'Wisp,' or maybe Kory. There should be at least a few notes from them by now." He made a quick note on a scrap of parchment.

"No problem. I should have everything arranged by the time you wake up." He motioned for us to follow him out of the door, Jamila scooping up the baby by force of habit. "Now come along. You just gave me a lot of work to do, and I'm sure all of you would appreciate some sleep."

The sounds of agreement from all of us were unanimous. Sleep did sound good right now.

CHAPTER TWENTY-SEVEN

Long Time, No Dream

————

It had been so long since I had entered the dream world, it took me a minute to figure out what was going on. I knew that either Wrath or Pride, the gods that had sent me back into my younger self, were responsible for showing me glimpses of the things they thought I needed to see. They hadn't shown me anything since I had dealt with the Chancellor and the *nox* that had been inside him. I guess they thought kidnapping slaver pirates and roaming leviathan weren't worth their time and energy to show to me, even if a heads-up would have been nice.

Time was usually limited in the dream world, so I needed to hurry to find what it was the gods wanted to show me. I was near a building I vaguely recognized, but the large palace in the distance was what really helped me identify my location.

I was standing outside one of the nicer outbuildings that surrounded the main palace structure. Seeing a side door that wasn't closed all the way, I went inside to try to see what I could find. After only a few steps into the building, I could hear shouting in the distance. I moved that direction, remembering it wasn't necessary to try to sneak after already walking halfway across the room. Like I said, it had been a while since I had last dream walked.

The room where all the voices were coming from ended up being a kitchen. I stood in the doorway, looking at who I hoped the gods had wanted me to see. Inside, the king was sitting on a stool at the food preparation table. He was nibbling on a hunk of meat cut from a freshly-baked ham. In front of him, three large and muscular men in dark green cloaks and leather armor knelt down on one knee on the slate floor. I came in partway through the conversation, but it was easy to figure out what was going on.

"You are *sure* you can track them down? For a price like that, failure wouldn't be an acceptable outcome." The king was clearly upset, his mouth twisted in a frown.

"Yes, my king." The speaker had a surprisingly high voice for being such a large man. "We know they are still within the city walls. They will not be able to leave without us knowing about it. If they choose to stay in the city, it is only a matter of time until we find them. When we do, killing them won't be a problem."

"Good." The king took another bite of food, making them wait on their knees while he finished swallowing. "I will inform my treasury of your impending arrival. Take your rewards, and don't come back without their heads. I will not suffer being made a fool in my own court." The three men stood up to leave, but the king gave them one final order. "Make sure it hurts. I want them to die regretting ever entering my city."

The leader of the three men gave a sharp nod of agreement. "Yes, my king. They will most definitely know it was your order that brought about their long and painful ends." As they left, I noticed they each had the tattoo of a dagger behind their left ear. The symbol was familiar, but I couldn't quite place it. It was certainly some kind of guild or sect marking. The choice of a short blade design meant they were probably assassins of some variety. Ugh. I was getting tired of dealing with these kinds of people.

After they left, the king motioned to the wall. A hidden panel lifted, and the woman from the throne room walked out. She was holding several sheets of parchment, and quickly handed them over to the king. It must have been his nightly intelligence briefing. Odd to have it in a kitchen, but once your age reached a certain point, people could begin to get a little weird. He looked over the documents quickly, pulling out a single sheet and setting it off to the side.

"Explain to me, please, how an entire section of the city can suddenly stop paying taxes?" He was stabbing a greasy finger onto the parchment, smearing the numbers written on it as he talked. "This isn't some section of the slums. It has three shops, a horse stable, and two inns in this neighborhood. That means we should have at least half a dozen gold from the area!"

The woman didn't react to him raising his voice. She was probably used to it. "Majesty, there were four tax collectors sent to the area over the past month. None returned." She shrugged, clearly not concerned with some low-level employees going missing. "The last two even went with a small contingent of guards. None of them reported for duty the next day, either."

The king frowned. "Ensure a meeting with the guard captains is on the schedule in the next few days. I want to hear what they have to say about this. If one of the street gangs thinks they can get away with taking from us, they will have to be shown the error of their ways." He threw the half-eaten hunk of pork at the fireplace, causing sparks to shoot up into the ventilation shaft. "And if it is the business owners doing it, make sure the guards burn down their homes with the families still inside. It is best to remind the people of what happens when they defy my orders."

"As you command, Majesty. I will see to it right away." The woman gathered the papers up and left the room. Both her and the king then headed out the door.

I moved to follow them to see what else I might find out, but instead I walked into a wall of white light.

CHAPTER TWENTY-EIGHT

Too Quiet

I jerked awake, the momentary confusion of a dream walking experience making my head spin. Every time I had one of these, it made me tired. And it usually meant I was about to have some pretty nasty fights.

Looking around the room, I saw that I was alone. The dream had given me a warning about the assassins, but it felt like the second part was more important. The gods wouldn't have shown me that without it having some form of relevance to my mission, meaning I needed to figure out what was going on.

After talking with Shin, we had been led through a series of hallways and stairs to a suite of guest rooms. It was a small apartment with two bedrooms, one bathing chamber, and a sitting room that doubled as a cultivation chamber. The girls had taken one room, and the guys had been put in another. Rotating through the bath had taken a long time, and I hadn't managed to stay awake long enough to do any cultivation exercises before bed. Since everyone seemed to be off doing their own thing, I might as well take the time now to get back on schedule.

Cultivating every day was important if you didn't want to lose any progress. When you were at the Peak stage of a certain level, it was especially important. Cultivation systems didn't like being at the edge of advancing for very long. It was uncomfortable to have a lump of solid crystal qi in your cores, but it was the only way to force your walls and meridians to expand into the next level. Since I was at the Peak of Brain, I needed to make sure my own body didn't betray me and slide backwards into the High stage.

I sat down on a pile of pillows, crossing my legs and mentally preparing myself for circulating qi through every meridian and core. I was always doing this subconsciously thanks to my training, but it didn't have nearly the same level of effectiveness as when I concentrated on the process.

Turning my focus inward, I started to pull in as much ambient qi as possible. I pulled it into my lower core, then spun it upwards into my heart core for purification. Packing the purified qi into another layer of hardened qi inside all three cores was the hardest part of the process, but I was used to it.

I lost track of time, losing myself to the process. I was incredibly close to breaking through to Saint, and every little bit of extra qi brought me closer to my goal. All it would take was just a little more. The impending fight with the assassins might be just the thing I needed to advance. The strain from a battle was often a good way to provide the necessary impetus for a cultivator to reach the next level. When I did, I was certainly looking forward to getting a chance to speak to Wrath and Pride again. I hadn't spoken to them in a few years, and I was sure they had some helpful information for me. At least, I *hoped* they had some helpful information for me.

Thinking about the gods put me out of rhythm, and I decided that was enough cultivation for the time being. I didn't want to get bogged down in a trance that made the whole day pass by. Some cultivators lost entire weeks of their life when focusing too deeply on cycling qi. It might help their advancement, but their bodies usually suffered from neglect. No thanks.

There was an entire sect dedicated to helping cultivators reach that level of concentration. They liked using daises in a ring around a single larger dais, carved with more dais-shaped symbols. I wasn't sure how they thought a bunch of daises were supposed to help them cultivate, but the Dais Sect always stayed true to their name. I think they just liked to say dais a bunch. Weirdos, all of them. The founder of their clan, a man named Travis, had convinced thousands to join him, so maybe they were onto something. Either way, I didn't have time to lose a few weeks cultivating on top of a silly dais. Or daises, for that matter.

Just as I got up from my pile of pillows, I heard a knock at the door. I walked over and opened it, finding a servant with the Auction House symbol of a gavel hammering on a pile of coins on their shirt.

"Spirit Knight Jim?" I nodded my head. The servant was using the old-fashioned form of formal address for anyone that could use all elements of qi. Modern times had made it more common to use it just for Brain-level cultivators. I guess it made a certain level of sense. Using 'Brain' in front of someone's name just sounded weird.

"That's me. How can I help you?" The servant just held out a slip of parchment and walked away. I guess they weren't much of a talker.

The note was from Shin, and he was asking me to join him in the basement. Odd. Why wouldn't he just have a servant tell me that instead of writing it in a note? Or lead me to him? Oh well. I needed to get moving. Every delay was more time the king had to authorize another extermination of an innocent village.

I took a minute to finish getting dressed, happy to see my brigandine armor had been freshly laundered while I slept. I had no idea how they had done it so fast, but I wasn't going to complain. I smelled completely clean for the first time in far too long, and decided to just enjoy it while it lasted. After getting my belt on, I made sure to clip the green sword held in the wind blade sheath on my left side. I had learned that a cross-draw would best suit the use of the wind blade that came out upon unsheathing it.

After leaving the guest apartments, I started working my way downstairs. The basement had to be around here somewhere. The entire building seemed emptier than it should have been. Such a large building should have had all kinds of servants and workers shuffling about, especially this close to the midday meal. Instead, I was all alone. It set my teeth on edge.

Finally reaching a darkened stairwell that went down, I stopped at the top to see if I could hear anything. That was when I finally figured out why something felt so wrong. It was completely silent. I tried to review in my mind when it had gone totally silent, but I couldn't remember hearing anyone moving around since the servant had handed me the note. What was going on?

Slowly walking down the steps, I found a bloodstain on the landing. Oh boy. Here we go. I activated my spirit wood shield and placed my hand on the grip of my sheathed sword. Had the assassins from the king found us already, or had we been betrayed by the Auction House? Maybe I was just being overly paranoid, and nothing untoward was going on at all.

Yeah, and gold coins rain from the sky.

I shuffled down the stairs slowly, doing my best to stay quiet. My main priority was finding my friends and getting out of here. I should also check on Every, and make sure he was okay. Er, Jang. Make sure Jang was okay.

The stairs ended at an arched opening that led into a room filled with racks of storage shelves. All kinds of items lined them, from rare preserved herbs and alchemy pills, to dusty arms and armor that practically glowed with power in the dim light. The glow stones illuminating the room were set on dim, making it difficult to see past a few dozen feet, even with my enhanced vision. The not-quite dark, not-quite light, made my usual advantages useless. I couldn't actually see far enough to know how large the room was, but I had a feeling it was big. It probably ran the length of the entire building, which would make it quite the impressive storage space. Especially if all the shelves were as packed as they were near the entrance. The walkways between areas were narrow, with just enough space for a single person to walk up and down the aisles. The perfect place to ambush a single person as they rounded a blind corner.

I stopped to listen, trying to once again figure out if I was being set up for an ambush. Let's be real. There *had* to be an ambush around here somewhere. It was just how my life seemed to always turn out since I had been reincarnated. Still not hearing anything, I moved deeper into the room.

Keeping a close eye on my surroundings, I couldn't help but notice how odd the stored items seemed to be. The shelves were either completely unorganized, or their system was just beyond my understanding. I saw a broken and practically worthless fire whip resting on top of a glass box that contained priceless clippings from a Golden Ring Tree. A rack of vials that must have held the blood of a Silver Phoenix—one ounce of which was worth a Celestial core—leaned precariously against a dusty tome titled 'Flora and Fauna of the Godless Age.' I had actually read excerpts from that one. It had been out of date over two thousand years ago, making it absolutely useless to anyone but a historian. The whole place was a dichotomy of incredible value and total garbage.

There were a few items I really wanted for myself, but I left everything alone. Faint lines of power ran through the shelves, meaning there had to be some form of trap or alarm formation that would go off if I touched anything. If I had more time it might be worth it to figure it out, but right now I needed to walk into this ambush and see what popped out.

I finally made it to an area that was probably intended for storage of rare beasts and exotic animals long ago, but had fallen out of use in more recent times. Right before I was about to step out of the shelves and into the wider space, I heard a cough. I crouched down and moved to the end of the row of shelves to get a better look into the area. Of course, it was occupied.

The first person I recognized was Shin, chained to the wall with his hands held over his head. There were over thirty people lined up with him, all of them wearing Auction House livery. It didn't look like they had been harmed, beyond a few bumps and bruises. In the corner, near another door leading down into the basement, I saw my four friends in a cage. I was worried at first that they were dead, but the rise and fall of their chests made the tight feeling in my own chest go away. They must have been sleeping. And for some strange reason, Chu wasn't wearing any pants. Before I could figure out what else might have been going on, two men walked into the room from the entrance.

"Are you sure this will work?" The speaker was the guard that had been at the gate when we first arrived. "He still hasn't come down here yet, and the guys on the landing are getting anxious." The man he was speaking to was Izeaj.

"I'm sure. The message was delivered, and it is only a matter of time until the last one walks into the trap." Izeaj was rubbing his hands together, his diabolical mind already picturing his total victory. "Once the youngest one is subdued, we can force them all to swear oaths of silence, and then claim that it was *us* that rescued the child. To think, those fools walked right up to the gate with such a prize! The rewards from that kid's family will push us straight to the top!"

The guard looked back at the row of prisoners. "But sir, what if they don't agree to swear the oath?" He was specifically looking at Shin. "This whole plan would fall apart in an instant!"

Izeaj gave the guard a lopsided grin. "Then we just kill them. If it weren't for so many people already knowing the truth, I would have just ended the few that had actually seen the child." He followed the guard's gaze to Shin. "It would make things *infinitely* better if they turned us down anyway. But too many people disappearing at once might raise some questions. Questions we *don't* want to answer."

"Would you rather my men and I just go track the last one down, and bring him here? Or I could have another servant deliver the same drugged breakfast everyone else ate." The guard shifted his weight back and forth from foot to foot, giving away his nervousness. "He is taking a long time to get here."

Izeaj thought about it for a moment. "That might be best. Maybe the boy got lost. I don't know how he could be stupid enough to miss the main entrance to the basement, but we could get this over with if you tracked him down." The guard nodded in agreement, and they both started up the stairwell.

So, Izeaj had people loyal to him, and not to the Auction House. Drugging everyone's breakfast would only take a single kitchen worker to accomplish, and after that, a few people could chain everyone up and lock them away. Impressive, if they hadn't been so stupid. Just because *they* knew where the main entrance to the basement was, didn't mean *I* knew. It was a very fortuitous case of tunnel vision. Little details like that could really mess up a plan. So, it was time for me to go and do my part to wreck it. After all, that was one of my specialties.

I waited until the sounds of their clomping footfalls had faded, then moved to check on my friends first. Most of the Auction House people were awake, but they thankfully stayed silent as I walked across the open area to the large cage holding everyone, their eyes tracking me as I moved.

A few threads of wood qi threaded through the orichalcum-infused bars confirmed for me that everyone was just sleeping. I tried to heal them so they could wake up, but there was no effect. That meant it wasn't a poison, just some mixture of medicinal herbs. They would have to wake up on their own.

"You might want to hurry, young man. They could come back at any moment." Shin had finally broken the silence, his quiet whisper sounding loud to my heightened senses.

"Fair enough. Once I get you free, I will need you to handle Izeaj. Do you think you are up for it?" I pulled my malachite sword free from its sheath slowly, so as not to set off the wind blade function. "I might be able to handle him myself, but I wouldn't come through unscathed. And I have too many things to do to spend a week or two recovering."

Shin gave me a wolfish smile. "Oh, don't you worry about Izeaj. I will be solving that problem immediately, and permanently." He looked around at the people chained up alongside him. "With all of us working together, it should be over quickly."

"Sounds good. Now, everyone hold out your hands and feet so I can get those chains off of you." They complied, and I went down the line, slicing through the bolts keeping the shackles closed. Shin got everyone organized, and they spread out into the shelves around the basement to arm and armor themselves. I guess everyone here knew the trick to grab the items without setting off the traps and alarms. While they did that, Shin walked over to talk to me.

"I must apologize. I underestimated Izeaj, and as a result the Auction House is even more in debt to you." He glanced over to my friends. "I have someone grabbing some things from storage that will wake them up."

"This wasn't your fault, Shin. Sometimes, the ones we trust the most become the knife in the back we don't see coming." Visions of Ming flashed through my mind. I definitely knew what it was like to be betrayed by the people you were supposed to be able to count on.

Shin shook his head. "That doesn't release us from our debts." He looked back at the stairs, where a lookout was keeping an eye out for anyone trying to return. "But I did manage to find out something important, before being imprisoned."

I raised an eyebrow in surprise. "Your intelligence network must be very impressive, for it to work this fast." Which was true. If he had found out anything about the cult this fast, it must be a very robust system of spies and informants.

"Actually, it was something we were already aware of. I just hadn't put the facts together yet." He made a motion with his hands, as if trying to draw out something from a storage device.

Nothing happened. "Stars damn it. I forgot he took my rings. Anyway, a few days ago there were reports of small groups of hooded figures sneaking into the city. They all headed in the same direction, to the western edge of the city. Exactly opposite from our current location, but closer to the outer city wall than our building." He pointed in the direction he was talking about. "Ever since they showed up, things in the area have gotten… strange. Too quiet, if that could be described as a bad thing."

I nodded in agreement. After the last hour, I knew exactly what too quiet sounded like. "So, you think the cultists have moved to the capital, and taken over an entire neighborhood?" After hearing what the king and his advisor had talked about, I thought that might actually be the case.

"Exactly." Shin shrugged his shoulders. "Either that, or a new group has moved in, and managed to quell all opposition without making any waves." His tone told me how unlikely that would have been. Having experienced how brazen the street gangs in the city were, it did seem unlikely that a normal group would have been able to take over a portion of the city without violence.

Before I could reply, one of the Auction House people returned with a handful of vials. The woman passed them over to me and moved to the few members of her own people that hadn't fully woken up yet.

I used my sword to slice through the lock keeping my friends in their cage, and poured a healthy portion of the potions into their mouths. There was some coughing and spluttering, but everyone got a good amount. Before they could get back on their feet, I heard shouting coming from the direction of the stairs. I needed to give my friends time to wake up, and then we had to see what was going on in the quiet part of the city.

It was time to get loud.

────────────────

CHAPTER TWENTY-NINE

But Not Too Loud

There was a blast of fire qi that came rushing out of the doorway, washing a wave of flames across the Auction House servants that were running toward the stairs. They handled the situation well, all of them positioning themselves behind the people that had grabbed shields off the shelves. The few screams of pain out of sight meant that not all of them had come through the attack unscathed.

Shin was at the entrance in a flash, his own power rolling off him in waves. Both Shin and Izeaj were Duke-level cultivators, meaning this battle was going to be something fierce. Behind him, the rest of his people were trying to get into the semblance of an organized formation.

I stepped out of the cage and got ready, positioning myself to protect my sleeping friends. They were already beginning to stir, except for Chu. He was snoring loud enough to shake the cage.

Just as the Auction House people got in position, Izeaj walked into the room. He was flanked by a small contingent of guards, four to his right and five to his left. They seemed nervous, facing off against a group over three times their number. The only one that seemed to be unconcerned was Izeaj, his focus entirely on Shin.

"I have been waiting for this moment for a long time, *friend.*" His face was twisted in a sneer, and his aura buffeted off the waves of power coming from Shin.

"I bet you have, Izeaj. You have hated me for a long time. Don't worry though, the feeling is mutual." He leaned forward into a ready stance, his hands swirling with pent-up energy. Both sides copied him, preparing themselves to fight.

At some silent signal, the two groups collided with one another. Qi flashed outward in shooting sparks, their rough tangling with one another making the dust fly off the shelves along the edges of the room.

It was quickly apparent that the two clashing sides were more evenly balanced than they should have been, given the disparity in numbers. The nine guards fighting alongside Izeaj might have been less than a third of the people, but they were still trained to work as a team. The servants and clerks that fought with Shin were untrained, and had no idea how to attack as a group. It gave the guards a chance, and they were taking advantage of every mistake their opponents made.

I watched as a man in servant livery with a two-handed axe got in the way of a woman holding a shield and spear next to him. The guard they were facing used the gap it created in her defenses to whip his sword across the inside of the woman's arm, forcing her to drop back with a shout as her spear clattered to the ground.

Shin and Izeaj were moving at such high speed it was hard for me to follow. Both of them were fighting bare-handed, choosing to forsake the use of massive qi constructs or weapons. Either they wanted to avoid any structural damage to the building, or they were waiting for the other to up the stakes. They had created an area clear of anyone else, effectively splitting their groups in two. Anyone stupid enough to walk into range would certainly regret it. Not for long, considering how short their lifespan would be afterwards, but they would certainly regret it for the few seconds remaining to them.

The group of servants, cooks, and groomsmen on the side facing the guard captain were beginning to struggle. He was much better at wielding his weapon, a halberd, than anyone he was facing. An older woman, wearing the brown robes of an Auction House accountant, was attempting to match him with a jian—a double-edged straight sword—but was quickly being driven back into the fight between the two Duke cultivators. Her death would free the man to attack the rear of the others. They wouldn't last long after that. It looked like it was time for me to help.

I spun up the qi in my brain core, slowing time for me. I then doubled the rate of the spinning qi in my heart core, giving me a boost in speed. To my perceptions, everyone else seemed practically frozen in time. Well, not the two Duke cultivators battling it out. They were just moving at a normal pace now. Both men seemed equally matched, with Shin having a slight edge in skill, and Izeaj making up for it in strength.

Not wanting to risk my muscles tearing at such extreme speeds, I took what felt like a slow and deliberate step toward the guard wielding the halberd. I felt a strain in the muscles of my calf, forcing me to shift my balance slightly and perform more of a hop than a dash. As a result, I flew past the man, basically gliding just a few inches over the stone floor of the basement. I had wanted to stop right in front of him and use my sword to remove his head. Instead, I could only use the edge of my spirit wood shield to chop at the side of his neck as I sailed past.

I relaxed my brain core, returning time to normal. The guard captain was blown sideways off his feet from my strike, plowing over the man standing next to him. The servants used the opportunity to pounce, and neither man got up again.

The sudden change in the battle dynamic gave an instant boost of morale to the people fighting with Shin. The three remaining guards on this side were quickly overwhelmed, and the four guards on the opposite side of the dueling Dukes started to slowly back towards the stairs.

I reduced the spin of qi in my heart core, but left enough extra spin to give me a boost to beat them there. No seditious members of the Auction House would be escaping today.

They didn't notice I was there until I unsheathed my sword, sending the wind blade at the backs of their unprotected knees. All four were of a high enough level that it didn't do a lot of damage, but the distraction it caused was damage enough. Just like their compatriots on the other side of the battle, those fighting with Shin were quick to take advantage of the opening I provided.

And just like that, Izeaj was all alone. Those uninjured from the fighting so far headed up the stairs to see if there were any stragglers they had missed, and probably to spread word of the betrayal by their former Branch Manager. Those that had been hurt moved back into the dusty shelves to find some healing device or herb to take care of their wounds. Two of them would never have the chance, their wounds claiming their lives before the battle had ended. None had even thought for a moment about interrupting the fight still going on in the middle of the room. Given my penchant for fighting those stronger than me, I decided it was time for me to meddle.

I decided that it might be best to try to distract Izeaj, instead of just jumping in like I normally did. Especially since that same idea had not worked as intended against the guard captain. I sheathed my sword and pulled out my silver bow, selecting an arrow with faint carvings running up and down the shaft. It was a leftover from an attempted project I had made since starting on this journey against the *nox*. The experiment had failed, but the arrow did allow for me to store an extra bit of qi in the shaft, compared to just a normal plain wooden arrow.

I dumped in as much earth qi as it could hold, and pulled back the string. I had to slow time again to manage a shot, this time paying closer attention to the movements and patterns of the two fighters. Both of them had clearly gone through similar training, making their fight more of a dance than a normal battle between two cultivators would have been. After watching them move through three full sets of katas, I felt sure enough about taking a shot that at least wouldn't hit Shin.

The first move in the series that Izeaj favored was a low kick aimed at the knees, followed by a hammer fist swung sideways at the head. I waited for the low kick, and then released the string of my bow. My shot flew true, striking the back of the leg Izeaj was pivoting on for the kick. His arm was already cocked back for his hammer fist, but this time it landed with only a fraction of the normal power behind the blow. My arrow wasn't able to puncture his skin, but the weight of the earth qi-infused shaft pushed him off balance just enough to make the difference.

Shin was quick on the uptake, using the opportunity I gave him to the fullest. He ignored the weak punch, allowing it to land on his shrugged shoulder. It gave him just a little more momentum in his own hooking punch, the blow to the gut he delivered blasting the air out of Izeaj's lungs. He followed up with a sweeping kick that connected solidly on his hip, sending the gasping man stumbling.

It was over soon afterwards. Izeaj never even had a chance to recover, the edge in speed Shin had over him being just enough to keep him off-balance. I fired two more arrows at his legs, never giving him the chance to get in a steady stance. The third arrow earned me a murderous glare, so I returned it with a small smile. When the sound of snapping bone echoed through the chamber, it was Izeaj who ended up stumbling back against the shelves with an arm bent the wrong direction.

Shin paused, taking a moment to gauge the other man's injuries. "This fight is over, Izeaj. You have no chance to beat me now. If you surrender, I promise that you will live long enough to see trial." I was a little shocked to hear him say that. I could have sworn this was supposed to be a battle to the death. A quick look at their energy levels explained why.

Both men were nearing qi exhaustion, their advanced age making such a protracted fight more than they could easily handle.

"If you think a broken arm is enough to defeat me, you have another thing coming! Why, if it weren't for your little helper over there, your dead body would already be leaking blood all over the floor!" He took two steps forward, a burst of wood qi from his body setting the bone straight and allowing him to lift his arm again. "You and I are both goin—*urk!*"

The familiar sound of Jamila's garrote drawing tight over a windpipe was music to my ears. I wondered when they were going to wake up.

He tried to slam his body backwards into the shelves, but Jamila just shifted to the side, pulling the incredibly thin wire even tighter. It wasn't able to cut into the skin of a Duke-level cultivator, but it was certainly enough to cut off his air flow.

Under normal circumstances, a Duke cultivator would be able to go without fresh air for a good amount of time. The long fight, coupled with a slight sense of panic, meant the man's cultivation base wouldn't be enough to help him this time.

After a minute or two, Izeaj dropped to his knees. The man was clawing at his neck, while trying to occasionally punch behind himself to hit Jamila. She had trained too much in the use of the garrote to be caught by such mundane tactics, and finally he went limp. Just to be sure, Jamila wrenched down even tighter. Five full minutes from when she wrapped the wire around his throat, she was convinced he was dead.

Shin walked over to inspect the body as Jamila took a step back. She was massaging her hands, the strain of holding the wire tight for so long clearly having been an issue. He fumbled around in the pockets of the dead man's robes, pulling out several familiar-looking rings and medallions. He held them up to look at them in the light before turning to speak to me.

"We are all lucky he wasn't skilled at severing the blood bonds between items and their owners. If he had been, it wouldn't have been such an easy victory. The tools and weapons in here could have ended this fight before it even began." He slipped them on, tucking the medallions away in his shirt.

I walked over, looking down at the body. "That explains why he was fighting bare-handed like you were. He couldn't access his weapons stored inside the devices." Just to be sure, I pulled out my favorite plain stiletto blade and stabbed it through his eye, straight into his brain. There was no reaction, meaning he really had been dead. I wiped the blade off on the collar of his robes and put it away. "So, Shin, what's next?"

He shook his head at me, apparently surprised at what I had done.

Hey, I was just being thorough!

"I need to check on Jang, and then I must report this to my superiors in the Feng clan. Afterward, I need to see what else Izeaj has been up to while running this branch. If he was willing to do this, I can't help but think he was doing plenty of other dark dealings in the shadows." He pulled out a few sheets of parchment. "These are the notes we gathered on the king, as well as what we know about the cult. Before all of this happened, I had arranged for you five to pose as the delivery crew for a weekly shipment of hay that gets dropped off at the stables in the suspect area. If you hurry, you might still be able to make it."

Jamila and I traded glances before I nodded in agreement. "That sounds good, Shin. Thanks again. Once we go with you to confirm that Jang is safe, we can sneak into the area without raising any alarms, and try to find out what is really going on in that neighborhood. I think—"

"Whashamata! Whereweat! Whotookoffmypants!" The shouting voice of Chu interrupted me. I guess he was the next person to wake up. Now to get the rest of them conscious, and move on to the important parts of our mission.

But not until Chu found his pants.

CHAPTER THIRTY

Dark Tidings

We made it just in time. After getting everyone awake, making sure baby Jang was okay, and preparing for a fight with dark cultists, the five of us practically ran to the road where the wagon was waiting. It was a large freight wagon, pulled by eight horses. The wagon driver was an old man, and the six men walking alongside the oversized buckboard were similar enough in appearance that they were probably his sons and grandsons. They were the unloading team, and all of them were stout and strong-looking men wearing rough-spun clothing. We wouldn't be a great match in switching off with them, but hopefully no one would pay close enough attention that it would matter.

As we approached, five of the six men wordlessly broke off and headed for the nearest tavern. By now, it was well past midday, and they blended into the crowd seamlessly. We fell into place, walking next to the wagon as it trundled down the road. None of us were displaying weapons, so we could better blend in with our fake positions as members of the work crew. I was closest to the driver, and he leaned over slightly to talk to me.

"We was wondrin' ifn' y'all was gonna make it." He gave me a wink, his crystal blue eyes sparking in the afternoon sun. "I made sure ta take it real slow, ta give y'all more time ta catch up." He was weathered, like an old oak tree. I instantly liked him.

"I appreciate your help. Once we get there, it might be best for you and your son to get out of the area for a little while." I looked back at the full load of hay. "It might take us a while, but we can get the hay unloaded for you. After a couple hours, you can come back and pick up the wagon. Don't wait for us if we aren't there when you return."

The old farmer silently nodded in agreement and turned to relay the information to his son on the other side. As he shifted, I thought I saw a flutter of movement on the opposite roadside rooftop . I looked closer, but didn't see anything else. Probably a bird or something.

The trip through town was uneventful, and we finally turned onto the street leading into the heart of the neighborhood the dark cult was suspected of having selected for its base of operations. The ambient noises of the city were nearly cut off, putting us all on alert. There were no barking dogs, ambling stray cats, or citizens walking the sides of the road. A few houses had smoke coming from their chimneys, but that was the only visible evidence of life.

Our wagon finally made it to the stables we were scheduled to deliver at, pulling around back into a narrow alley that ran behind the long two-story building. It felt wrong. Something was off. I was spinning the qi in my cores, ready for an ambush at any moment. The farmer parked the wagon underneath a second-floor door that was intended for easier loading of hay into the hayloft. The old farmer hopped down and joined his son, both of them headed towards a back entrance to the stables.

"We'll make sure they're ready for y'all, an' open the haylof' so ya can load er up!" I held up my hand to tell him to wait, but they had already reached the doorway. As the son reached out for the handle, it was jerked open from the opposite side. I saw a cloaked figure reach out and grab him, pulling the son into the darkened interior. The old farmer gave a shout, but another figure reached out and yanked him into the stables as well.

The five of us reacted quickly, Chu being the first one through the door after them. As we rushed into the room, I could hear the pounding of feet in the hayloft above us. The only light source in the stables came from the open doors on the opposite side of the building. I pulled out a handful of green glow stones from my belt and tossed them into the middle of the room.

It illuminated the space, showing two long rows of empty stalls along the walls. The center was an open space lined with posts that supported the story above. It also illuminated the six men wearing cloaks arrayed in an arc in front of us. Two more men were dragging the unconscious forms of the farmer and his son into a stall off to the side. At least, I hoped they were unconscious.

Jamila stepped in their direction, her katanas already in her hands. "If you hurt those two, I will personally peel the skin off your face and make you eat it." Apparently, I wasn't the only person the old farmer had made an impression on. Jamila gave her weapons a spin, flames leaping along the blades.

"Ha! You are a funny one, aren't you?" The man standing in the middle of their little group dropped his hood, and I recognized him from my dream. He was one of the assassins hired by the king, meaning this wasn't the group of cultists we were searching for. "Don't worry. We didn't kill them. Our group tries to avoid collateral damage when we can."

I activated my spirit wood ring, this time selecting the spear function. I took a step forward so their focus would be on me. "Can you guys come back later? We aren't here for you. You see, there is a dark cult around here somewhere, that we believe is responsible for a lot of senseless death all over the province. I would appreciate it if you waited your turn." I pointed the tip of the wooden spear at them. "You can come back later, when we have an opening in our schedule."

The leader gave me a genuine smile. "I do love it when our

targets don't show fear. Too often, all they do is cry, and beg for their lives. You will probably do the same, in the end." With a flick of his wrist, he snapped a throwing dart at my face. The quick attack was the signal the rest of them had been waiting for. Two more assassins I hadn't noticed dropped from above, landing behind us. I was ready for him to do something, so I managed to deflect the dart to the side with my spear shaft. It left a sizzling blotch of green on the spirit wood, meaning they were using weapons coated in some type of poison.

"Poison! Don't let their weapons touch you!" I didn't receive a reply, but I did notice Chu coat his arms in metal qi to give him an extra layer of protection.

The two assassins that had dropped behind us were both facing off against Valerie. She had been forced to drop her bow, and had her cleaver-like sword and skinning knife in hand. The two facing her were certainly unprepared for her ferocity, their twin daggers having a hard time keeping up with the chopping strikes and quick slices. She had spent plenty of time practicing against Jamila, who was far more skilled at pure combat than either of the cloaked figures facing off against her. Their normal tactics of ambushing the unprepared worked against them now, as the element of surprise had been lost the moment they grabbed the farmer and his son.

That seemed to be the situation for all of us. We were each facing two attackers, and our individual skill seemed to be the equal of our paired opponents. We could beat any opponent individually, but paired up it was nearly balanced. The leader was the only opponent that was close to our own level of training.

I was paired against him, and he favored a thin rapier combined with a long punching dagger. His partner was using twin daggers like the rest of them, giving me the advantage with the longer reach of my spear. I used it like a fighting staff, cracking knuckles with the haft and stabbing out with both the sharp and dull ends.

Our fighting had fallen into a pattern of attack-defend-attack, turning it into a battle of stamina. Everyone seemed to be using their qi for defense and increased reflexes, instead of more offensive constructs. Whoever could sustain the pace of battle the longest would win, making everyone conservative with their qi usage.

I had just settled into a comfortable rhythm when an entire wall of the stable was ripped off and thrown to the side. We all froze, the massive wave of power that shattered the wall unleashing an oppressive aura of malevolent energy.

The cultists had found us.

CHAPTER THIRTY-ONE

Putting the Cult in Cultist

"Well, well, well. What do we have here?" The woman standing at the brand-new entrance to the stables wasn't actually a person. Or, to be more accurate, it wasn't *just* a person. It was a *nox*. "It looks like we have some extra sacrifices to power the gate, doesn't it, boys?" Her features were twisted up into a semblance of a smile, but she didn't have much of what most would consider to be a mouth anymore.

Standing outside, in what must have been the main yard of the stables, there was a collection of what I could only describe as ant people. They were darting about, making it hard to get a solid count, but I was pretty sure there were at least twenty of them present. Maybe more. It was the largest collection of *nox* I had ever come across, and all of them were completely malformed.

They had antennas coming out of their foreheads, and their multifaceted compound eyes gleamed like hard brown gemstones in the late evening light. I winced at the mandibles that pierced their cheeks, the bases of which must have been somewhere deeper in their throats. Their heads were oversized, and their chests—or thoraxes, I supposed—had been elongated so they could fit an extra set of limbs at the base of their rib cages. Instead of hands or feet, they ended in bladed tips reminiscent of the same limbs I had seen on the shark-mantis hybrid I had killed. Great. The creepy bastards had built-in daggers.

Their abdomens had been elongated as well, becoming swollen and distended. Their legs were twice the length they should have been, and they bent sideways at their stretched knee joints. Instead of looking unstable, their skittering movements as they swarmed behind the woman seemed completely sure-footed and balanced.

The only one not completely deformed was the woman, who must have been filling in for the position of queen. She seemed completely normal from the neck down, only sharing in the antenna, strange eyes, and sharp mandibles.

"What in the…?" The leader I was facing seemed to be dumbfounded, and his fellow assassins didn't fare much better.

"It's the dark cult I tried to tell you about." I used my spear to point at the group of *nox*. "They must have heard us fighting, and came to say hi." I took a step back from the two people I had been fighting, and angled myself so I could see both the assassins, and the dark mana demons wearing skin suits.

"Boys, you know what to do. Collect our guests, and bring them to our little party next door. The more, the merrier, after all." She waved her hand, and the mass of *nox*-ant-people rushed into the room.

In an instant, the fight between us and the assassins was forgotten. Instead, we fought as one group, doing our best to hold them back. They were incredibly difficult opponents to handle in such tight quarters, given their superior size and numbers. Donny was the first to start throwing out poppers and trap plates, but the rest of us soon followed. Jamila and Chu tried to circle around to grab the unconscious farmer and his son, but they were snatched up before they even got close.

We were forced back towards the rear entrance, our battle-line curling inwards on the sides. Every time a particularly effective trap plate gave us a moment's reprieve, we were able to back up another step. The first to fall from the bladed limbs of a *nox* was one of the assassins standing next to me. One second they were there, and the next they were gone. One of the smaller *nox* had darted in from the side, taking them off their feet. It was pulled backwards into their lines, with the man still buried under its mass. I could hear him screaming as he was dragged away.

By the time we were backed up against the wall, we were down another four assassins. I wasn't sure if I should be relieved, or terrified, but the *nox* had captured everyone instead of outright killing them.

I pulled out my only remaining gravity plate and threw it in front of the *nox*, loading up over half of the qi from one of my qi batteries into the runes. It was as much as it could handle, pushing the plate to the brink of its capacity. I tossed it at the largest cluster of *nox*, a group of four that was charging at Donny and Chu. They were slammed into the ground the moment it activated, and I had to grab my friends to keep them from being pulled in as well.

The assassins used the timing to escape, and we weren't far behind. We barely had time to clear the entrance before the freight wagon was slammed against the doorway, the five remaining assassins shoving it in place. The *nox* must have circled around while we were busy fighting, because they had snacked on the poor horses. There wasn't much left of them, besides the bloody scraps strewn about the alley. It didn't bode well for the future of the people that had been captured.

Besides the 'queen,' these *nox*-possessed people were by far the most bestial we had come across. Or is it insectual? Same difference. Either way, they were barely people anymore, making me wonder about the hierarchy of the *nox* again. Was I dealing with another Knight of the Dark, leading a bunch of foot-soldiers? Or was this something else? I was jolted out of my thoughts when one of the *nox* on the other side of the wall slammed against the wagon. We joined the assassins, shoving it back in place before they could get through. Valerie quickly used her qi to form a low wall of stone at the rear of the wagon to hold it in place, and we all turned to run. The assassins chose to run left, so we went right. Just because we had fought together for a few minutes didn't mean I trusted them at my back. I mean, really.

As we were about to clear the alley, the long shadows of the ant people appeared in front of us. Jamila, who had been in front, skidded to a stop. She pulled out a formation plate and threw it at the entrance, a wall of stone spikes quickly popping up from the ground. The *nox* rounded the corner, piling up in front of the obstacle. Now that we were out in the open, we could finally move about more freely. The *nox* were larger and stronger than us, but I had a feeling their large mass meant they weren't very good at jumping.

I was gauging the energy it would require to jump onto the roof of the building beside me, when a barely audible whistle pierced the air. The *nox* stopped trying to find a way across the spikes, and instead turned to run back the direction from which they came. I made the leap onto the rooftop, tracking their movement. They ran a few buildings farther down the street, before turning out of sight. It looked like they were headed towards a large building near a market square, but I wasn't high enough off the ground to be sure. Stars damn it. I was going to have to play the fool, and chase down the overwhelming number of dark mana demons. Most likely, straight into their home base.

"Jim!" Donny shouted up at me from the ground, his body turned back around to face back down the alley. "We need you back down here!" I walked over to the edge of the roof to see what had him worried. The assassins were headed right for them, their daggers in hand. There were only four of them left, meaning they had most likely run into the *nox* at the other end of the alley. I jumped back down, using a strand of air qi from the meridian at the base of my spine to slow my drop. I landed without straining my knees, and I used the strand of qi to clear the immediate area around me of the remains of the horses. I felt a momentary pang of sympathy for the poor animals. They had been locked in place, not even given the chance to run.

I would be avenging them soon enough.

As the four dark-cloaked assassins approached, I once again leveled my spear in their direction. If they wanted to finish this now, I would do my best to make it fast. No more playing fair. I had already used the invisible thread of air qi to pick up a thick shard of bone, and I was only waiting for the right moment before returning the lead assassin's earlier trick with the dart. Flicking it in his direction would hopefully cause enough of a distraction that I could take at least one or two of them down, before they even knew what happened. Instead, the man sheathed his weapons and held up his hands.

"Look, I think you and I might have got off on the wrong foot. You see, my name is—"

"I don't care what your name is." I cut him off, pointing my spear directly at his unprotected face. "You and your people were hired to kill us. There isn't anything else to say to one another."

"Wait!" He waved both hands in surrender. "We were wrong! I didn't believe you when you tried to warn us. But you looked just as surprised as we were when those creatures showed up!"

I didn't let down my guard, but I did change my point of aim to his chest instead of his face. "I wasn't expecting to be attacked by a bunch of assassins just because I refused to roll over and die for a man that sees his people as nothing but a revenue stream." I shrugged. "But here we are."

"That's a fair point, but—"

"No buts, asshat. You assaulted two innocent men, then tried your best to kill us. We should just kill you where you stand."

"I can't disagree with your opinion, but I feel like we have been misled by our employer. Wait. How did you know the king—"

"Enough. I already know what you want." I needed to cut

him off before he could finish that thought. "Your people were taken, and you need our help to get them back. If they are even still alive."

"Exactly!" He jumped on the idea, thankfully glossing over my earlier slip of the tongue. "If we work together, we have a chance to save my men. And the two people that were with you."

"Fine. I can agree to that, but only if you agree to follow our plan exactly. And before we go any farther, you swear on your cores that you won't pursue us any longer."

"That all sounds fair." He lowered his hands, and the three men behind him finally relaxed their tense posture, sheathing their own weapons. "But first, I need you to do something for me."

I shook my head. "No, I am not giving you any of our weapons or formation plates." I shifted my spirit wood spear into a shield, not willing to let down my guard any further than that.

"It isn't that, although it would have been nice. What I need is an explanation." He waved his hands around, as if swatting at flies. "Starting with what in the stars those creatures are!"

Oh, yeah. I sighed. This was going to take a minute.

CHAPTER THIRTY-TWO

Dark Gate

It actually took a little over five minutes, but I gave the four assassins the quick rundown of the *nox,* as well as some information on what the king had been up to recently. I don't think they would have believed me if they hadn't just been fighting for their lives against the dark mana demons just a few minutes ago.

Making a plan to rescue the captured people took even less time. Since we had no idea what we were walking into, it was pretty basic. The four assassins would take the high ground and approach from the rooftops. The five of us would move in on the ground. We would attempt to serve as a distraction, while they worked to free anyone still alive when we got there. Like I said, it was pretty basic.

We finally split up, and started down the same street we had seen the *nox* take. It was only a few blocks before we had to turn down the side path they had traveled. Our quick walk was enlightening. Now that we knew what we were facing, the reasons for everyone being missing had become pretty apparent.

Almost every dwelling and business we passed by had been ransacked, their doors forced open and the occupants taken. The ant people had done their best to close the doors behind them when they left, but several seemed to only be held in place by leaning them against the shattered wood of the door frames.

I blamed not noticing the first time on simply being blind to the scale of the destruction that had been wrought on these people. While I knew it wasn't likely, I couldn't help but wish that they were simply being held captive by the *nox*. The queen ant had mentioned needing sacrifices for some kind of gate, and I could only hope they needed them all at once instead of broken up over time. If that was the case, we had a chance to hopefully save most of them.

Piles of what I had believed to be rubbish along the edges of the road were actually the last signs of a struggle. A broken kitchen knife, a shattered chair, the occasional pot or pan told a sad tale of people that tried to fight back. A small tattered blanket next to a tiny stuffed doll told an even sadder tale. One that made me angry enough that I was having trouble focusing on my surroundings. A few deep breaths centered me, and I focused on drawing in as much power as I could hold.

Following the trail of discarded items, we finally made it to the back of the large building I had seen in the distance. From the outside, it looked like either a high-end inn, or a major business of some kind. Considering my history with inns, I couldn't help but think that was what I was about to enter. I had bad luck with them, and it would certainly fit the theme my life was shaping up to be, this time around.

The door to the rear of the building had been smashed flat onto the floor of the interior, but it was too dark to see inside. I caught a whiff of old blood and rotting meat. Yep, this was definitely the right place.

The sun was just starting to dip below the cityline, and I could just make out a red-tinted moon beginning to rise. A harvest moon, and at the wrong time of year. I felt a chill run down my spine. Pushing it to the side, I went in first, my eyes quickly adjusting to the absence of light. This time, my improved vision didn't fail me. The first thing I noticed was the carpet of bones. Everywhere I looked, all I could see were gnawed-on bones, most of them cracked and sucked dry of their marrow. A closer inspection showed the majority of them to be from animals, the skulls and jawbones clearly not from humans. At least now the lack of dogs, cats, chickens, and other animals had an explanation.

The room still made my blood boil. As I said, the *majority* of the bones were from animals. There were still a few that were unmistakably from the former residents of the neighborhood.

As I had suspected, the door I entered from had been the back entrance to an inn. I was standing in what had once been a well-appointed kitchen, making the scene even more grisly. The people that were possessed by the *nox* still retained enough memory to know that the kitchen was where you prepared your food. Not a keep-your-food-down kind of scene, but I wasn't a dark mana demon grabbing a midnight snack.

I paused to listen for any sounds that might give away the position of the enemy, but I only heard muffled chanting coming from far away. Not finding any immediate threats, I moved out of the way to allow my friends to enter the room. Donny led the way, holding a glowing formation plate in his fist. It cast just enough light to send long shadows jumping around the already disturbing room.

We silently moved into the common room, finding more of the same. The remains of their meals were fresher in this room, and I was pretty sure a large portion of one of the old farmer's horses had been brought back here for a snack.

Once we made sure there was no one in the common room, Donny and Valerie broke off to silently check the upper floors while Chu and Jamila headed off to inspect a side door that probably led towards some private dining rooms. I went to check the stairs leading down. Since I didn't need a light source, it only made sense for me to check the basement.

While I had been expecting a den of horrors, all I found were signs of recent habitation. It looked like either the *nox*, or their prisoners, had been using the space as a place to sleep. Discarded heaps of clothing were layered into makeshift beds, and the far corner had an old ale barrel that smelled as if it had been used for a latrine. By several people. *Very* recently.

After clearing the space, I headed back upstairs to join my friends. They signaled that they hadn't seen anything either. We didn't speak, none of us willing to alert whoever was chanting outside that we were close. I knew that out the front door, we would find a large, open square. The perfect place for ceremonies that required chanting.

As we approached the surprisingly intact front door, the red moonlight tinted the scene on the other side. There was only a small square of dirty glass centered high over the entryway, making it hard to see anything besides some indistinct figures moving around, and the top of some kind of archway that had been built in the center of the square. The chanting sounded like it was building into a crescendo, telling us all that we were running out of time.

Donny led the way again, this time stopping to pull out a thick tower shield that covered him from neck to knees. We lined up behind him, preparing to rush out into the middle of a group of very strong and violent monsters. Not one of my friends even paused for a moment to reflect on their decision to run straight into danger. These people were by far the best I had ever known. In both lifetimes.

We hit the entrance hard, knocking the door open and running out the front of the building. The chanting that had been getting louder stuttered to a halt. It looked like we had made it just in time. Well, kind of, depending on your definition.

The indistinct figures we had seen moving around were the *nox*, and there were a lot of them. A rough estimate put them at about forty, standing in a ring around the center of the square. The queen, standing on a raised stage in the middle of their circle, had been leading the chanting with her arms raised over her head. It was hard to read her features, considering their twisted shape, but I was pretty sure she wasn't happy to be interrupted. Between the queen and the ring of *nox*, there were rows of dirty and emaciated people on their knees. It wasn't nearly enough to account for all the missing people that must have filled this neighborhood before the arrival of the *nox*. And the arch explained why.

It was formed from the remains of the dead. The grisly artifact was crafted from meat and bones, held together by glistening sinew and braided intestines. The whole structure, an arch that was over ten feet tall, seemed to be continuously weeping blood. A closer inspection revealed that the blood was moving *up* the arch, pooling at the top, where a pelvis bone served as a keystone. The swirling pool of blood seemed to drain back inside the arch, maintaining a consistent size. It was a horrifying sight, only made worse by the waves of dark energy wafting off it. This must be the dark gate the queen had mentioned. Speaking of the queen, she finally got over the disbelief of being interrupted.

"You *dare* to interrupt the opening of the Dark Gate?!" She clacked her mandibles together hard, making a sound reminiscent of snapping bone. "No matter. Your deaths will help usher in the arrival of our brethren! Rip them apart, and bring their bloody corpses to me!"

She restarted her chanting, this time picking up the pace. She somehow managed to be just as loud by herself as they had been earlier when all of the *nox* had been chanting along with her.

The majority of the ant people rose from their positions and rushed towards us. Only eight stayed in place to keep their prisoners from escaping. I tossed out two of the spike plates, creating a funnel the *nox* were forced to follow. A couple started using their bladed limbs to start hacking their way through the narrow field of stone spears so they could flank us, but it would take them a minute or two to get through. That was all I would need.

I stood at the end of the funnel, Chu to my left and Donny to my right. As they approached, Chu pulled out a tower shield to mirror Donny. Valerie stood a little farther back, her bow already singing as she fired arrows into the cluster of approaching enemies. Jamila stood next to her, ready to rush forward and assist anywhere we might need an extra blade.

There were only a few seconds before the *nox* slammed into us, but with my brain core ramped up to maximum, it was more than enough time. I wasn't going to hold back any longer, so I spun out over a hundred razor-thin threads of qi, my meridians pushed to the brink of rupturing. I made sure to have an equal number of all elements, that way I could capitalize on any weaknesses the *nox* charging us might have. I layered earth, wood, water, and metal threads just under the surface. Wind, fire, light, and dark threads formed strips of deadly energy that floated above the approaching masses. Just one agonizingly slow heartbeat after positioning everything, the *nox* came into range. It was time to make them pay.

CHAPTER THIRTY-THREE

Bills

The misshapen and malformed cultists stepped into range, funneled into a tight cluster by the angled walls of stone spikes. I held on tight to the control of my perception of time, willing to accept the strain of using so much qi in order to track every movement the *nox* made. As soon as the majority of the monsters were within my 'net,' I started.

I lashed every single one I could reach dozens of times, the sharp threads of qi whipping into their malformed bodies. Just like with the shark *nox*, some elements were more effective than others for each of them. The threads that rose up from the ground lashed at their legs and abdomens, while the ones that fell from above ripped off antennas and tore through bulbous eye clusters. I wrapped the joints of their limbs in the elements they were sensitive to, the slowed time giving me the needed moments to test which would work best on each individual demon. A flex of my will, and the strands sliced through them with little resistance. The spray of blood and tumble of limbs and bodies slid across the ground, their forward momentum enough to carry them the last few feet to our position. I hadn't killed all of them outright, but they were certainly no longer a threat. A lack of arms and legs could do that.

Having taken down all but the few remaining *nox* that had been trying to flank us, I relaxed my hold on time. The strain of the last few moments had taken its toll, leaving my meridians throbbing and cores aching. I was nearly drained of energy, and I could feel a headache start to pound behind my eyes from the lack of qi. I pushed through my discomfort and began pulling in qi as fast as I could manage.

Suddenly, there was a tremble throughout my cultivation system. Oh no. I had known it was close, but this wasn't the time to advance to Saint. I would be forced out of the fight, and we still had the queen to deal with. I forced my body's urge to advance to stop, and finally got myself back under control. Whew, that was close!

"Jim!" Donny shouted at me, his shield still held at the ready. "That was great and all, but now isn't the time to relax!" He stepped towards the *nox* that were about to break through the stone spike defenses I had hastily emplaced. There were only three on his side, and two on Chu's, but the flankers were in a frenzy. Seeing their brethren killed had certainly riled them up.

Valerie managed to land an arrow directly in the open mouth of a screaming *nox* on Donny's side. It reared back in pain, stumbling away from its fellows. Jamila, seeing that Chu was by himself, went to back him up. I had no doubt they could each handle one of the demons one-on-one. The *nox* that had taken an arrow to the face had recovered, and the group of three finally managed to work their way through the narrow row of spikes. I started to head that way to help kill them, pulling out a formation plate that would cast a staggered series of wind blades. I managed to land it at the feet of the lead *nox*, just as the queen let out a triumphant roar.

"*Yes*! It is time! The gate *opens*!" There was a wave of power that washed over us, and the arch let out an ominous groan that shook the ground. "Kill the sacrifices! The darkness *demands* it!"

The remaining *nox* that had stayed to guard the captives reared back, their bladed limbs flashing in the red light of the moon. At least there was enough light to see by. I saw a mother wrap a small child in her arms, trying to shield her baby with her body. I was too far away to do anything, even if I ripped myself to pieces using my adjusted perception of time and speed. We were too late. Which was when a dart flashed out of the darkness, plunging into the throat of the unsuspecting queen.

Her scream of pain froze the *nox*, their leader's agony making them unsure of what to do. Four shadows detached themselves from the dark corners of the square, their poisoned blades gleaming red in the blood-tinted moonlight.

"Sorry it took us so long, but they had one on lookout!" The leader of the assassins was on the opposite side of the square, but I could still hear him over the screeching queen and whimpering prisoners. "But better late than never, right?!" The four *nox* nearest the assassins turned to face them, leaving only four more to keep the frightened prisoners from escaping. Only the leader might be able to face a malformed ant person *nox* and live, but the other three could at least run around and cause a distraction.

The queen finally got the poisoned dart out of her neck, the wound closing up almost instantly. Instead of organizing her troops, she let loose another shriek of rage and charged at the assassin leader. Now was our chance.

My well-placed wind blade formation plate had sliced deep into the *nox* I had thrown it at earlier, and it laid on its side as it bled out. It was pure luck, but that one must have had a weakness to wind qi. It was about time something went right.

Everyone else was fighting the last of the *nox* that had attacked us. Chu had already smashed in the side of the one he was up against, and Jamila was whittling her opponent down. Literally.

Donny was being purely defensive, using his shield to keep the two he was facing from getting close to Valerie. She was turning them into a bloody version of a pincushion, their movements slowing as her arrows found homes in their vitals. It was amazing to see how efficient she could be with a bow, even in close quarters.

I was still far from fully recharging my cores, but I still had my qi batteries that I could use. And it was definitely time to use them. The four remaining *nox* that were guarding the prisoners were still waiting for the queen to return to her macabre archway, but it was only a matter of time until they remembered they were supposed to be killing everyone.

The queen was still fighting the assassin leader, but I knew he wasn't going to last much longer. He could barely stand up to one *nox*, and the queen seemed tougher than her subordinates. No real surprise there.

I used the qi battery that still had half its power to spin out a pair of air qi whips. Snapping them around two of the tallest stone spears to either side of me, I worked them like a slingshot to launch myself towards the nearest *nox* standing guard. I still had the shield form of my spirit wood ring in place, so I brought it around to use like a battering ram as I flew through the air.

The creature must have sensed my approach, because it started to turn toward me. I had overshot my approach a bit. Instead of slamming into the ant monster center mass, I ended up clipping the *nox* on the top of its head with the rim of my shield. I ricocheted off, the angle of impact flipping me around onto my back and slamming me onto the ground. Then the *nox* —skull shattered and brain matter leaking from its ears—fell on top of me. Ouch.

My somewhat showy arrival drew the last three *nox* straight to me. Given the seven hundred pounds of deformed creature on my chest, I wasn't exactly in the best position to do anything about it. Which was when the arch finally did something again.

When the queen had said the dark gate demanded sacrifices, I guess it wasn't exactly picky. The earlier fighting must have been out of whatever range the arch had, but the *nox* I had just killed was certainly close enough.

The body lying on top of me just… *melted*. Which was *exactly* as disgusting as it sounds. The liquid goo flowed across the ground, and was sucked into the arch with a wet slurping sound. All of the bones clattered across the ground, piling up along the sides into some form of deranged structural support. As soon as everything settled into place, the earth began to shake again.

I jumped to my feet, using the last of the qi in the partially used battery to heal myself. The grinding of broken ribs shifting back into place made me clench my teeth hard enough that I felt a molar crack. Which was then healed in turn, causing me more discomfort. It wasn't the pain, so much as the itching that I had problems dealing with. At least it distracted me from the greasy film that coated me, left behind when the ant creature's flesh dissolved. Ugh. Just… gross.

The quivering earth under my feet made it difficult to stand, so I tapped my remaining qi battery to make two strands of metal qi that I used to steady myself. The three *nox* running towards me were struggling as well, giving me the time I needed to pull three steel-tipped spears from my storage belt. I used three more strands of metal qi to lift them off the ground, and then whipped them as hard as I could straight at their heads.

Their concentration had been on their footing, meaning none of them even tried to deflect the attack. None of them even hit the ground, the gate liquefying them and pulling their remains into its structure even faster than the first one. The shaking increased as well, and all four buildings surrounding the square collapsed. It sent up a massive dust cloud, which cut visibility down to almost nothing. Now was our chance.

"*Hey*! All you people!" I couldn't actually see any of the prisoners, but I knew they could hear me. "You need to get out of here!" There were a few questioning shouts, but I didn't hear or sense any of them get up from the ground. This had backfired the last time I had tried it, but I pulled out a few poppers. Throwing them towards the arch, I shouted at the top of my lungs. "*Run!*"

That did it.

The captives scattered, all of them running everywhere. It was chaos, and I couldn't help but chuckle when I heard the queen roar in outrage. The dust did a fine job of making sure she couldn't stop them. Instead of even trying, she blurred past me, back to where I had massacred the *nox* she had sent after us. Stars damn it. She was just going to use the dead bodies of the *nox* to complete her ritual!

I didn't have any stone spikes nearby to slingshot myself, so I was forced to use more energy from the qi battery in my belt to boost my speed. By the time I reached the queen, she had already started throwing limbs and torsos into range of the arch. Apparently, she was incredibly strong, despite her smaller size. In fact, now that I was close enough to sense it, I would put her power levels at or above a High Duke. Definitely a real threat.

Using the qi battery still, I created eight simple arrow constructs, one from each element. I fired them at her all at once, spacing out their impact points so I could better gauge which one did the most damage. They were small enough that she ignored them, trusting in her healing and strength to handle such a minor nuisance. She was too busy to deal with something non-lethal anyway, all of her focus on tossing enough flesh and bone at the archway that it could finally complete her dark ritual.

The water arrow seemed to do the most damage to her, with the light qi a close second. Now that I knew what element to use, I dumped all of the remaining qi in the battery into a tightly-condensed spear of water qi. This was it. The final shot to bring her down.

I better not miss.

CHAPTER THIRTY-FOUR

Fissure

The queen had just lifted the torso of an ant person over her head—dripping a disgusting mix of viscera and blood all over herself—when I launched the spear at the middle of her chest. Time seemed to slow on its own, in one of those fated moments where the world decided you need to see every detail of the events unfolding right in front of your eyes, because it just knew you were going to think it was horrible.

A massive flare of power erupted behind her, forcing her to spin around and drop the hunk of meat behind her. Of course, this put it directly in front of the path my spear was taking on its trajectory to her heart. The dust still floating in the air was blasted away, flowing past me in a wave that blocked my vision just as the spear made contact with the torso dropped by my target. As the air cleared, I could see the queen facing off against the person that had cleared away all of the fine powder that had been providing us with cover. She was in the way, so I couldn't see who it was yet. My water qi spear construct had been lodged in the ribcage of the torso the queen had dropped. The sheer density of qi I had used to form the spear meant it hadn't dissipated yet, but it would be gone in a few minutes. If I could retrieve it while she was still distracted—by whoever the cultivator was that came at the worst possible time and messed everything up—I still had a chance to take her down.

"*You!*" Well, surprise, surprise. Either the gods were pulling some strings, or fate was finally on my side for once. The King of the Western Province had shown up to fight the queen *nox* for me. Maybe I could just take a step back and let him handle it. "First you defy me in my own palace, and now I find you here?!" Nope. Fate still hated me, and wanted me to have to work for it.

Instead of targeting the obvious threat—the actual, real-life *monster* standing right in front of him—the king was focused on *me*. This made absolutely no sense. Unless…

"Why are you here?" The queen walked right up to the king, as if she knew him. "Your place is behind the walls of your little buildings, not where someone might see the two of us together. If you want to rise in power, we require your absolute obedience." The king puffed up his chest, as if about to argue. She just kept talking, not giving him the chance. "Failure to follow instructions will delay our plans. Any delays caused by you, will result in slower progression. And we both know you don't have much time left, *King*."

I was confused. The king was assuredly not possessed by a dark mana demon. I didn't feel a bit of darkness coming from him—besides his generally evil disposition, of course. Why would any sane person side with a creature determined to destroy everything? Did he fear dying of old age so much that he would willingly allow the destruction of the world to extend his own life only a few decades? And why all the theatrics in the throne room? None of this made sense.

"This is not what we agreed to, *nox*." He seemed proud at that statement. "Yes, I have learned what you are, creature. Now that I know the truth, we will be renegotiating our deal." He looked around the destroyed section of his city. "And we will also discuss your presence *inside* the walls of my capital. None of this was part of our agreement." Ah, so he was just stupid. He had entered into a deal with the *nox* without understanding what he was dealing with. Just another poor decision maker in power. "But we can talk about that later, *after* I have dealt with this annoying pest that continues to live, despite my orders to the contrary."

"There will be no further discussions, *King*." The queen smirked as she reached down and grabbed a severed arm from the ground, tossing it toward the arch. "We have your oath, and there is no going back for you. Besides, once I am finished here, there will no longer be a need for you to cover up our movements elsewhere. Someone… *outside*… wishes to speak with you about your next position, *hosting* a visitor, you might say. If you want to wait, I can arrange the meeting shortly." That didn't sound good for the king, in my opinion. Or us for that matter. With a sharp kick, she sent another torso towards the arch. It was liquefied and absorbed almost instantly. "You can certainly entertain yourself with the boy while you wait. I, too, find him to be an annoying pest."

What could I say? You had to be good at something, I supposed.

Instead of being worried over what the queen was talking about, the king just seemed to focus on the part where she was okay with him killing me. Did my refusal to be executed really bother this guy that much? Had it been so long since someone stood up to him, that he couldn't stand for one of his orders to be disobeyed? More likely, it had been the loss of 'face' that he couldn't deal with. He was very old, after all, and the ancient idea of losing face must still be important to him. Complete stupidity, if you asked me. Then again, no one did.

Compounding his crimes, I also just heard confirmation that he was sending out extermination squads to *cover up* any sightings of *nox*, *not* trying to kill them. What an absolute *bastard*. You couldn't trust anyone these days.

"Looks like it's time for you to die!" He snapped out a low kick from over a dozen yards away, launching a hooking wind blade at shin height that moved so fast I could barely see it. I had no chance of dodging, so my armor took the full force of the blow. It held, keeping my legs attached, but the hit knocked my legs out from under me, slamming my face into the ground at a very high rate of speed. First of all, *ouch*. Second, I think I was in trouble.

I was barely back up to a third of my own capacity, and my belt batteries were almost empty. I had to constantly concentrate a small portion of my focus on keeping myself from breaking through to Saint. This was a King-ranked cultivator with somewhere close to seven centuries of experience. One third of the power a Brain cultivator could bring to bear wouldn't be enough to bring him down, not to mention the queen standing only a few dozen feet away. She was still busy feeding her ritual all the blood and bones she could get her hands on, but I was sure that wouldn't last forever. Not to mention whatever bad thing happened when she finished. It really wasn't looking good for me.

"That was easier than I thought it was going to be." The king let loose a dry chuckle. "Now, do I kill you fast, or take my time?"

Oh, buddy. This was just starting.

Given the lower amount of qi than I would like, I couldn't afford to make any mistakes. I jumped to my feet and spun out a thread of dark qi from my left hand, and a thread of light qi from my right. Using the two hidden forms of qi was my trump card, and I hated having to use it right away. It was now or never, and never wasn't an option.

"Interesting trick you have there." He formed two massive hammers of extremely dense fire qi, both bigger than my whole body. Since they were constructs of his own energy, they would be practically weightless for him to wield. If they hit me, I wouldn't find them to be nearly as light. And that was ignoring the whole 'lighting' me on fire part. Sorry, bad joke. "Whatever strange energy that is, it won't matter. There is no way it can stand up to my power!"

The queen looked over at his words, her eyes narrowing

when she finally noticed that I was using dark and light qi. I supposed she was too preoccupied to notice it the first time. She turned back to hurriedly continue chucking body parts at the arch, and I almost got smashed because I wasn't paying attention. I *just* told myself not to make mistakes, and what was the first thing I did? Ugh.

The king had swung straight down toward the top of my head, forcing me to spin to the side. The problem was, the stars-damned bastard was right. One qi strand—no matter the element—against such a massive construct had no chance. My only hope was to get close enough to touch him with my qi strands. His body would have no natural resistance to the secret forms of qi, meaning I could take him down easily. Getting close enough, however, was the problem.

He had followed up his double smash with a sideways swing, the massive hammer coming at me like a wall of flames. Well, more of a large door than a wall, but you get it. I had to burn some more power to jump high enough to clear it, but then he just lifted the hammer straight into my feet. Which was not fun for me.

On a positive note, the construct was solid enough that I was able to use it like a springboard and jump off of it. Which was only positive for as long as it took the other hammer to come around, and blast me into a pile of rubble over fifty feet away. I've said this before, and I will say it again. *Ouch.*

The portions of skin that weren't covered in my brigandine armor were reddened and blistered, and the cloth covering the metal plates was burned away in several places. It felt like the impact with the rubble had broken a rib or three again, so breathing was the opposite of fun right now. I also had a wooden splinter of impressive size that somehow stabbed me in the exact same place on my foot shortly after being reincarnated back into my younger self. That, coupled with the burnt soles of my feet, made standing up a future prospect I didn't want to face.

I hadn't been the only one hurt, though. As I was flailing

through the air in my best impression of a punted thunder chicken, my dark qi whip had managed to snap across the back of the king's left hand. He was currently nursing the wound, trying to heal it with a large influx of wood qi to the injury. I had no idea why, but it seemed like he was having some trouble with it. The most important thing was that he had lost concentration on his hammers, and they were already half the size they used to be. If I could get back into the fight, I still had a chance.

Grunting, I levered myself back onto my feet. Just in time for the ground to suffer from a massive earthquake, causing me to stumble and tear some of the burned flesh off the bottoms of my toes. How can toes hurt so bad? Stubbing your toe in the middle of the night was bad enough to make a Saint curse, but this felt even worse.

The cause of the earthquake was quickly apparent. The queen had finally gotten the arch to what must have been a suitable size, because the air inside the archway became hazy. Not like 'fog' hazy, but the wavy kind of hazy that happened when the sun shimmered on desert sands in the distance. Almost watery-looking, with enough distortion that you can't see the other side. Except, after the arch made a sharp cracking sound, I could suddenly see through it just fine.

Straight into a world swarming with nightmares.

CHAPTER THIRTY-FIVE

Gateways and Guillotines

"Yes!" The queen was dancing around, her mandibles clacking with glee. "The fissure is finally open! Welcome, my brethren! Come, let us *feast*!" There was a bulge inside the arch, which was definitely really a gate, and I thought I saw a clawed hand push against some kind of film over the entrance. With a rumbling groan, the soap-bubble-like haze stretched, but didn't break, which looked especially eerie in the moon's blood-red light. The sharply-tipped appendage pulled back, giving me a better look at what was on the other side.

The gate was like a window, looking out over a dark hellscape of twisted creatures that nearly covered the cratered surface with their various tentacles and clawed, spindly limbs. An involuntary shiver ran through me, as far in the distance I saw what I first thought was a mountain begin to move. It was still hazy, but I was pretty certain the mountain was a swarming pile of tentacles larger than the city where I currently stood. A row of massive eyestalks running along a ridge turned and *looked* at me, and I felt a physical blow strike me across the miles of distance between us. Just a glance from that thing knocked the breath out of me. It was eventually blocked from view by the piling swarm of man-sized creatures trying to shove through the gate, and I was finally able to suck in some air.

"What *was* that thing?!" The king must have seen it as well. "What have you done?!" He looked as horrified as I felt.

The queen clacked her mandibles in joy. "I have opened a way for more of my kind to enter this world! Now, with their arrival, we will turn this world to the dark, just as we have the countless ones before it!" She waved her hand, as if presenting a prize. "Welcome your new rulers, fools!" I held my breath in anticipation of a flood of *nox* pushing through the gate. Nothing happened. The thin film still held, keeping the *nox* to their side of the gateway.

"I will not stand for a new ruler to usurp *my* throne!" The king picked up his diminished hammers, twirling them in his grip. "You have forsaken your oath, creature, freeing me from my own! Now, *die*!" The old man moved with blurring speed, flashing across the open space and slamming into the queen. Finally. The threat to his throne ultimately made the idiot realize he had picked the wrong side. Or he had snapped after seeing the things on the other side. Either option worked for me. Now that those two were keeping each other busy, I could concentrate on destroying the arch.

As I limped closer to the gate, I tried to absorb as much ambient qi through my meridians as quickly as I could. Bending over, I pulled out the wooden splinter still in my foot. Ouch again. Refocusing, I flexed my will, coiling up my qi strands in preparation. As soon as I was in range, I lashed out at the gate, striking it with as much force as I could bring to bear. There was a faint ripple in the film blocking the *nox* that were trying to force their way inside, and the arch of flesh, blood, and bone, lost a chunk from its base. Since nothing was ever easy, my actions caused a reaction from the queen. She let out a screech of anger, and four *nox* came sprinting for me out of nowhere. Figured.

I had forgotten all about the *nox* that had been chasing the four assassins. I guess it was too much to hope that they had managed to kill them, leaving me to deal with them. A quick glance showed that the king was keeping the queen on her back foot, but he wasn't able to actually hurt her. He was fast, but she could move at ludicrous speeds.

The four *nox* came within my range, so I used my qi whips to slash at their outstretched arms. It didn't do much damage, but it paused their forward progress. I also noticed that the blood leaking from their slashes never hit the ground. Instead, the arch was sucking the blood straight off their wounds, using it as more fuel to power its existence. Looking down, I noticed the blood leaking from my foot was doing the same. Oh, so gross.

Instead of continuing to deal with these four all at once, I pulled out a bag of poppers and threw it at the monster closest to me. The sack hit it in the chest, blowing it off its feet and straight into a pile of rubble I had recently made an acquaintance with. Now that I was down to three, it made it easier to concentrate on tearing them apart. Which I did. Violently.

I wasn't very mobile, given the problems with my feet, but I had no problem swinging a whip. I had to spin out a thread of air qi from the meridian in the small of my back to help keep my balance, but that was the only extra expenditure of qi I needed to make. The other three tried to rush me again after seeing their friend get taken down, which only brought them into range of my qi strand whips.

The one trying to be sneaky by coming at me from behind caught a whip to the neck. I tore out his throat, and he dropped to the ground clutching at his gaping wound. The arch seemed to kill him even faster, sucking the blood from his body at a much faster pace than normal. Seeing the advantage the gate was giving me, I started lashing the two in front of me as quickly as I could. The open wounds my whips were causing only provided the arch with more ways to suck out their blood, turning the two *nox* sluggish and pale. I eventually found an opening, and tore out their throats as well. Their bodies quickly joined with the arch, causing it to thicken further up from the base.

I spun to face the final *nox*, but it was having some problems of its own. The impact with the rubble had opened a long gash on its back, and coming into the range of the gate turned out to be a fatal mistake. It fell on its face, quickly liquefying and being sucked into the structure as well. It appeared to me like the gate was still incomplete, the pelvis section of the keystone still thinner than the rest of the arch. A little more mass, and the thin film holding back the dark mana demons would fail.

I tried to take a step forward toward the arch, but I stumbled to my knees instead. What was going on? A thin stream of blood floated past me, straight towards the keystone. My foot! I had been slowly drained, just like the ant people. A quick flex of will closed the puncture wound, but the damage was already done. I felt weak and light-headed, and it took far more effort than it should have just to get back to my feet. The motion also revealed to me that my broken ribs were not happy with me, and a weak cough showed I was bleeding internally. The arch carried it away. More blood for the blood god, I supposed.

Lifting an arm, I lashed out at the base of the arch once again. The extra thickness added by the *nox* I had just killed made it more resilient, instantly healing the damage I had done. Crap.

To make matters worse, the queen let out a roar of victory. A blurring form slammed into me, and we both were knocked back into the stone spikes we had used to funnel the *nox* towards us earlier. That didn't feel good either.

I came to a stop leaning against one of the thicker spikes, thankfully avoiding being run through by anything this time. The impact had made me lose focus, my qi whips and balancing strand dissipating into the air. The king, who had been thrown into me, wasn't as lucky. A thin spear of stone jutted from his shoulder, the angle keeping him sitting upright. I noticed his blood wasn't being sucked out of him, but the pool of blood that formed beneath him was gradually being pulled toward the arch. As soon as it hit a point a few inches past his outstretched feet, it was sucked through the air and into the gateway. Its range was growing. I was brought out of my distraction from the streaming trickle of red by the queen. She sauntered up to us, one arm scorched and hanging limply at her side. At least the king had gotten a few hits in.

"It took more sacrifices than it should have, but the gateway is almost complete. The fissure into this dimension will open, and let in a flood of my kind. And there is nothing you can do about it." She let out an evil cackle, before turning to look at me. "I think you will serve nicely as the final piece to the arch. The king is too powerful of a vessel to waste." What was it with people and wanting to make stupid speeches right before they tried to finish things? She snapped loose the chunk of stone holding the king in place, spinning the pointed end around to me. "I am going to enjoy this!" I was trying to pull out a shield plate to activate it in time, but an arrow slammed into the queen's chest, knocking her back a step. It was quickly followed up by a blowgun dart, crossbow bolt, and flame-coated shuriken. My friends had arrived.

"Get away from him, you freak!" Donny's voice was music to my ears. I hadn't seen them since the collapse of the buildings around the square, and the escape of the prisoners. They must have been helping them to get away. Better late than never, I guessed.

Instead of saying anything, the queen just snatched the leg of the king and dragged him into range of the arch. He screamed in pain, but quickly passed out from the blood loss. If he died, and that gate finished, we were all done for.

The queen was driven further back by another round of projectiles, taking the king even further away from me. I tried to think of something I could use inside my ring, simultaneously looking around for something that could help. That was when I noticed the torso of the *nox* that held the spear construct I had tried to use to kill the queen. The spear had dissipated down to something that looked like an extremely long needle, its thin point sticking out dangerously from the end. It just might do the trick.

I spun out a qi strand of air, trying to grab on to the spear. Which was precisely when the earth let out another shudder, throwing off my aim. Instead of pulling free the weapon, I accidentally nudged the torso it was lodged inside. That, coupled with the shaking ground, put it within range of the power of the gate. It sucked the torso, spear and all, straight towards the keystone so it could finish the construction. Butt-nuggets.

The flesh holding the needle of power liquefied, causing the needle to come free. The momentum and direction imparted to it by the suction force was enough to drive the construct directly into the pelvis holding the arch upright. A loud crack echoed through the square, and a flash of light momentarily blinded me. Out of reflex, I activated the shield plate I had pulled out when trying to save myself from the queen. It was the only thing that saved me from the explosion that followed.

It turned out, gateways to other dimensions didn't like to be broken. They got pretty mad about it. The explosion leveled everything still standing in the square, obliterating all in its path. More of a disintegration, really. The queen opened her mouth in a silent scream as she was turned into dust. Well, she could have been actually screaming, but the explosion had blown out my eardrums already. So, from my perspective, she was silently screaming. It really couldn't have happened to a better person.

The king, being a King-ranked cultivator, lasted a little bit longer. He might have even survived if he was awake, but the blood loss rendering him unconscious didn't allow it. The first things to go were his limbs, the joints not being strong enough to handle the forces they were subjected to. Then his head came off, the explosion serving just as well as any guillotine he would have faced when the truth of his actions came to light. The rest of him turned to ash, only leaving an etched shadow on the surviving cobblestones.

I scrambled to see if my friends were okay, but I needn't have worried. They were crouched inside their own shield, riding out the wave of destruction the same way I currently was. All of them were also silently screaming in fear. Or, really screaming. I still couldn't tell.

Turning around and squinting, I could see the film of the gateway to the dark mana dimension. It was still in the shape of the arch, but none of the meat and bones were holding it up. The edges were frayed, as if it were a piece of cloth coming unraveled. Through the film, I could see the other side had faced the same devastation we had experienced. A cone of destruction had blasted through the gateway, turning the *nox* on the other side into a thick carpet of ash. I thought it added to the ambiance they were going for.

In the distance, the mountain of tentacles and eyestalks looked at me again. I could feel its rage, and a crushing force seemed to squeeze my brain inside my skull. The walls of my brain core flexed in response, protecting me from instant death. A spurt of blood came from my nose, letting me know I still hadn't escaped its gaze unscathed.

Just before the doorway completely frayed apart, I heard the mountain speak. It was gravelly, as if two stones rubbing against one another were imitating the sounds of speech.

"Soon. We come for you, insignificant meat sack. Soon."

Well, that wasn't ominous or anything. Now was a good time to pass out.

CHAPTER THIRTY-SIX

Tough Times

———

I woke up in a chair, facing a fireplace with green flames. To my left, Pride was sipping on something bubbly. Wrath was to my right, and she didn't look happy. Which wasn't a surprise. Her name *was* Wrath, after all. She was usually pretty angry.

"It *took* you long enough. I was wondering if you were ever going to reach the next level." Wrath didn't call me her usual name, King of Fools, so maybe this was going to be a good visit for once. And finding out I was leveling to Saint after I passed out from blood loss was also good to hear. "Oh, you are still a fool, Jim Roh, just not as big of one as I first thought."

Stars damn it, I forgot they could hear my thoughts. Thankfully, Pride cut in before she could call me some new derogatory name I wouldn't appreciate.

"I have to admit, the destruction you caused to the *nox* home plane was truly magnificent." He waved his glass towards me in congratulations. "I don't think I have seen Hastur that upset since that time Lust poked him in the eyestalk with—"

"That isn't important right now." Wrath cut him off before

he could finish the sentence. I felt like it was a good thing. I was pretty sure I didn't want to hear what the personification of lust had done to an eyestalk of a dark tentacle god-monster-thing. "What is important is that you were able to stop the gateway from opening. If it weren't for the imbalance of dark mana already present in your world, they would have been able to break through much faster. Their own success worked against them this time."

Pride nodded in agreement. "Yes, but be warned. The more *nox* you kill, the closer the scales return to balance. That is why leaving even one of them on your planet can lead to disaster." He waved at the fireplace, where an image of the queen I had just seen destroyed appeared from the green light. "This was a high priestess in their world, but she wasn't the only one with the knowledge of gateways to slip through the cracks. We will try to guide you toward any others we come across, but keep your eyes open. There is no telling when another might appear."

"Just so I know, how many *nox* are left on my world? Am I making progress?" I felt like it was a good thing to know just how much further I had to go. Wrath answered me before Pride could respond.

"We believe there are close to one hundred and fifty remaining, give or take a handful. Once you have killed all of them, we will be able to sense if your world is clean of their dark taint." It was her turn to manipulate the fire, this time showing me a map of the entire empire. "As soon as you awaken, there are two places you must investigate." A spot in the western part of the Northern Mountain Range, that marked the border between empires, began to glow a little brighter. "There has been an influx of dark energy here. It is causing a stir amongst the more powerful beasts that reside in the region. We fear the darkness will push them east, and then the winter-year will force them south. Straight into the unsuspecting border forts your current emperor has left undermanned and underfunded." The glow on the map changed to reflect her words, turning the mountains